Totally Bound Publishing books by Pamela L. Todd:

Escaping Normal
When You're Gone

Beautiful Sinners
Secrets, Lies and Vegas
Secrets, Lies and Imperfections

What's her Secret?
Now You See Me

I0563702

WHEN YOU'RE GONE

PAMELA L. TODD

WHEN YOU'RE GONE

Dedication

For Nana and Papa.
I wish you both could have seen this.

Prologue

April 25th, 1939

I saw a girl today.

The best damn looking girl I've ever seen in my life.

I was waiting outside a department store while Paul flirted with a counter girl when I spotted her walking down the street toward me. Paul told me there were plenty of dames in his hometown, but Jesus... He didn't tell me they looked like that! Long, dark hair that hung in loose waves, curves to bring a man to his knees and legs for days. She quite literally stopped me in my tracks.

She paused to look in a store window and I stood in the middle of the street, gaping like a buffoon at the poor female. She bewitched me... Turned my brain to mush. A thousand thoughts raced through my mind and I couldn't think of a single thing to actually say to her.

She moved on, walking past me so close I could have reached out and touched her. I even opened my mouth to speak, but nothing came out. I turned around, watching her get farther and farther away from me. Short of chasing her down the street, I'd missed whatever fleeting opportunity I'd had. Even still, I almost took off after her, feigning some reason to excuse my behavior.

She dropped something.

Didn't I know her?

Was this her...gum?

For every second I lingered, she was another step away.

And then it was too late – she turned a corner and disappeared from sight.

What an idiot... How hard would it have been to introduce myself? Ask her name? Offer to walk her someplace?

It's not uncommon for men to drop at the feet of beautiful women – to make outlandish gestures and be all romantic without even knowing their name. But she didn't know me from Adam, and I couldn't throw myself at her like that.

Standing on that street, it felt like I was changing. That I have changed. That this girl who I saw for maybe thirty seconds has changed me. No, the sky wasn't bluer and the birds didn't sing sweeter... But this feeling is new and so, so foreign. I've enjoyed the company of women before, approached them just fine and charmed my way into their lives.

But I've never felt like I've been struck by lightning with a single glance at one.

I stood on that goddamn street, staring in the direction she'd disappeared, for far longer than I'd admit. It felt like years. It felt like a heartbeat. I took a deep breath to try to clear my mind and turned back around, fully intent on marching into the store and dragging Paul out by his collar. I needed to know all the local spots a dime like her might go.

But before I'd had the chance to take a single step, my mind rushed back to her. Even though it felt like I'd stared at her for hours, I couldn't remember what color her dress was. Or was it a skirt and blouse? I hadn't even been sure if I could describe her to Paul. How do you properly express the way the sun made her hair shine like it was woven silk? How do you describe skin so flawless it was like cream? How do you make someone else believe a body like that surely belonged to a goddess?

I want to know everything about the girl. But there's no way to get the answers. In the end I didn't tell Paul about her when he finally left the store with a date for the weekend with his counter girl. I had no doubt he'd help me try to find her – he chased skirts like it was his mission in life. For the first time in my life, I'll have to take something on faith. I have to believe I was meant to be on that street at that time on that day. I was meant to see her... You couldn't have a reaction like mine and not have it mean something.

I'll see her again... I have to.

Chapter One

"Barb, are you about ready?"

I jumped about a foot in the air at the sudden appearance of my father in my bedroom doorway. "Yeah, I'll just be a second."

"Make sure that's all it is." Dad glanced over his shoulder before lowering his voice. "Your mother is ready to pitch a fit if we don't hurry up."

"For someone so against me leaving, she sure can't wait to get out of here this morning," I mumbled.

Dad's face softened and he stepped inside the room. He squeezed my shoulder. "She just hates to be late. Rushing stresses her — you know that."

I nodded and swallowed the sudden lump in my throat. The truth of it was, it stung more than I let on. Mom had woken me close to six a.m. that morning to make sure we were on schedule for the train.

Which left at ten.

And we lived fifteen minutes from the station.

Mustering a convincing smile, I nodded toward the door. "You go ahead, I'm going to do one last check to make sure I have everything."

Dad nodded but lingered a moment before leaving.

I turned back to face my bedroom, sparse of my favorite things. My desk was tidy for once, all papers and paraphernalia either tossed or stored somewhere out of sight. My dresser was near-bare and my vanity table empty.

All essential items were packed away in two large suitcases, waiting to travel with me to Wellesley.

I crossed the room to my narrow childhood bed and straightened one corner until the quilt could have passed military inspection. Which, where my mother was concerned, was about right.

"Barbara!" my mother called in her sharp voice from downstairs.

Rolling my eyes skyward, I mouthed something I would never have dared say in her presence. "Coming!"

She voiced her displeasure to someone—my sister, probably.

I let out a huff and turned back to my room, giving the place one last cursory glance before admitting it was time to leave.

It was a bittersweet moment to close the door to my room, knowing it would be a few months before I would open it again.

Anna, my older sister, met me at the bottom of the stairs. "All set?"

Dad passed us both then lifted my two cases to take out to the car. "In the car please, before—"

"You haven't even packed the car yet?" Mom demanded as she rounded the corner, staring at us all as if we had done it to antagonize her intentionally.

"Mom, we have almost an hour before my train leaves. I'm sure we'll make it," I said, doing my level best not to let annoyance seep into my tone. "You don't have to be worried about being stuck with me."

Mom turned a cold look my way. "I don't think I need to remind you that it wasn't me who put this ridiculous notion in your head."

Oh, God, not this argument again. "You can't deny that it comes with perks, though, right? Well, just the one." *Me, out of your house. Out of your sight, where I can't disappoint you anymore.*

Anna slipped her hand in my mine and tugged me toward the front door. "Come on, Barb, let's get going. Do you have everything?"

I picked up my purse and double-checked its contents. "I think so."

"Well, what are we all waiting for? We're gathering dust." Dad bustled out of the door, clattering my suitcases off the doorframe.

Mom took off after him, muttering something about him being obtuse and careless.

Anna rolled her eyes at me and we followed our parents outside to the car.

* * * *

The train station bustled with activity when we got there — people arriving and departing, people crying over departures, laughing at reunions.

Because we were devilishly early, we stopped for a coffee at the little café inside the station. I chose the seat by the window, better to see the comings and goings. It took every ounce of self-control I possessed not to squirm with anticipation in my chair. Patience wasn't exactly my forte, and I had been looking forward to this day for months.

Years, really.

"Have we lost you already, Barb?" Anna asked, nudging me with her elbow.

I turned to my sister with a smile. "Almost. I'm just... I'm very excited. I can't wait to see—"

Mom sighed quietly and replaced her teacup in its saucer. "Are you seeing Kenneth tonight, Anna dear?"

"No, not tonight, Mom," Anna replied before facing me again. "You must be so keen to meet your roommate. What do you think she'll be like?"

"Here's hoping she has a better understanding of female obligation," Mom said with a stiff smile.

Here we go...again.

"There are plenty of other colleges in the area. Maybe this new roommate of yours will help you meet a nice young man."

"I'll have a full plate with my classes, Mom." I dropped my eyes to my teacup, willing my irritation to diminish.

"Well, perhaps if you had listened to my wishes and taken your courses in women's studies, then you would have the time to pursue some prospective husbands." Mom smiled over the rim of her cup. The smile was cold, as it had been since I'd told her I was not going all the way to Wellesley to attend a finishing school.

"And if I wanted to study how to arrange the seating plan for a dinner with my husband's boss, I have no doubt that I would have plenty of spare time on my hands." I couldn't hide the bite in my tone and I placed my cup down a smidge harder than I intended. Coffee sloshed over the side, staining the tablecloth.

Mom glared at me—a hard and wrathful look.

It was one I'd seen countless times, not just recently, but throughout my entire life. I turned my head so I faced away from my family. My family who just didn't understand why today was so important to me.

13

Wellesley College.

At a college fair way back in my junior year, a rep had handed me a brochure for the college and I'd known that was the place for me. The pictures of smiling women riding bicycles and attending classes in the old brownstone buildings had me hooked.

Mom had pitched a fit when I had said I wanted to go.

Hardly any of my female peers were leaving home to go to college, and even fewer to go to an all-girls one. For most of those who *were* leaving, it was to widen the pool of potential husbands.

I, clearly, was not.

Even once she had admitted defeat and allowed me to enroll at Wellesley, my mother couldn't help but pray that some fraternity boy would steal my heart and turn me into the daughter they made no secret of wanting me to be.

A husband was the last thing on my mind. I was going to Wellesley to become brilliant — to be a modern woman, independent, with a ferocious mental appetite. Successful. Bold. Smart. Many girls attended the prestigious college for the finishing school curriculum, to better prepare themselves for their futures as wives and mothers.

Those girls would truly make my mother proud.

I, however, was going to study art history, mathematics, ancient history, Latin and English literature. Even as a child, I was scolded for having a curious mind, and the inquisitive little girl had grown into a young woman hungry for knowledge.

Ever since that college fair, I'd known Wellesley was where I belonged. And so I had been counting down the days until *this* day arrived, and it was finally time for me to leave.

The fluttering of excitement that had kept me awake since dawn was stamped down by thick, omnipresent irritation at my mother, who just couldn't let me be happy.

"Maybe we should make our way to the platform. There's only half an hour until it leaves." Dad rose from his chair, knocking his knees against the underside of the table and making the cups chink and wobble.

"Great idea," Anna agreed.

I left Mom and Anna to follow Dad back out to the parking lot. He hauled my cases out of the trunk and found a luggage cart to make it easier to get onto the platform with them.

"You know," Dad said as he wheeled the cart in front of him—studiously watching the suitcases and *not* me. "It's not too late to change your mind. You know, if you had. Not that you *have*, but…"

Releasing a quiet sigh, I said, "I haven't changed my mind, Dad. I haven't even had a single doubt."

Dad pushed the cart with one hand so he could loop his free arm around my shoulders. "Call me selfish, but I don't want my daughter thousands of miles away from home. I'll miss you, kid."

"I'll miss you too, Dad." *Just not enough to stay.* "And it isn't *thousands*, you silly old man."

His lips twitched into an amused smile before he turned serious once again. "And… Give your mother a break. Today is hard for her. Despite how she may act."

What was harder for her—having to finally accept that I wouldn't be bullied into staying at home and marrying myself off to whoever asked first, or realizing that I had no intention of using my college career to find a match.

We joined Mom and Anna and the four of stood in an awkward, uncertain group.

"Come to the ladies' room with me, Barb," Anna said after a few minutes of stilted conversation.

"You had better not be long—the train will arrive at any moment," Mom called to our backs as we headed away from her and Dad.

"How are you feeling?" Anna asked as she hopped up to sit on the edge of a sink. "Are you nervous?"

I laughed. "I'm impatient."

Anna wrinkled her nose. "Should I take it personally that you're in such a rush to run away?"

"*You* shouldn't." I peered into the mirror and dabbed a spot more powder on my nose. The pin curls I'd spent more than hour perfecting that morning were still in place, not a flyaway hair in sight. There were perks to getting up excruciatingly early, it seemed.

"She's trying, Barb. She just...doesn't understand."

"Do you?" I asked, turning to look at my sister—the one who had come before me and done everything right. The one I was measured against...the one who was perfect. In our house, Anna didn't get the best grades, but she always had a boyfriend. Anna didn't get a job when she left high school, but helped Mom around the house. Anna broke curfew, but it was okay because she was with Kenneth, the dreamboat whose proposal was imminent.

Then there was me.

The outspoken one. The rude one. The one who butted heads with her mother. The one with absolutely no interest in marriage. The one who dared want more out of life than an apron.

"I try to," Anna said after a while. "I really do. But you want such different things than me. It's hard to understand the reasons behind your choices."

I let out a breath. "It shouldn't be hard, Anna. I want...I want *more* than being someone's wife or mother. I want my world to be bigger than a kitchen. I have brains in my head, and I don't want to waste them creating the perfect roast chicken. And boys are… Boys are… Boys are so stupid."

Anna snorted a laugh. "Is that what those big brains of yours could come up with, is it?"

"Shut up," I mumbled, flicking water from the faucet at her.

Anna shrieked and leaped off the sink. "You cretin!"

"See? You should be glad I'm leaving — your annoying little sister can't bug you anymore."

She softened, her eyes showing just how wrong I was. "Barb, don't be an idiot. I'm going to miss you like crazy."

"Me too." For all we were polar opposites, I doubted any two sisters were as close as Anna and I were.

Anna sighed and pulled me into a tight embrace. I sank into her arms, breathing in the familiar honey scent of my sister. "Come on, we really will be late." Anna led me out of the bathroom, threading her arm with mine.

The butterflies started again in my belly, the excitement back and then some.

"And who knows — you may surprise us all. You keep saying you have no interest in boys, but what if, when you get there, a handsome, intelligent and forward-thinking one appears and you fall head first in love with him?"

I snorted a laugh. "I doubt it. What experience I've had has been enough to put me off the male race for life."

"Barb, you've had a couple of dates that Mom bullied you into going on. You probably had more in common with a sponge." Anna squeezed my arm. "I'm just saying, you could meet someone with similar interests to you."

"Please, please don't start this, Anna," I said quietly. I needed someone on my side. Someone who understood the fact that college—Wellesley—was for me, and me alone. No finishing school. No boys. Just...knowledge. And, hopefully, a lot of fun.

The train was waiting at the platform when we rejoined our parents. Anna threw her arms around me and hugged so hard I feared for my ribs. She whispered for me to write often and to call when I could.

I turned to face my mother. She wore her usual tight-lipped smile that was barely even there. Her face was stern, unflinching as she took in her outspoken daughter she had always resented. "Mom."

"Barbara. Let us know when you get there."

With a nod, I turned to follow Dad onto the train. He found me an empty seat and stored my luggage.

"Will there be someone to help you get your things off? What if you miss your connecting train in New York?" he asked, his forehead puckered in worry.

I kissed his cheek and ushered him back to the door. "I'll be fine, Dad. I promise."

Dad nodded and turned to give me a stiff, awkward hug. "So... I'll see you?"

"I'll see you," I agreed.

He studied me for a long moment, maybe trying, even at this last minute, to find some kind of reason on my face as to why I was doing this. I was the first person in our family to go to college, and even my father, who supported me as much as my mother allowed, struggled to understand my desire to go.

Finally, he nodded once, and turned to make his way off the train.

I went back to my seat and slid the window down. Anna rushed to the side of the train and reached up. I leaned out of the window as far as I dared and grasped her outstretched hand.

"Be amazing, Barb!" she cried.

My eyes stung and a thick lump formed in my throat. "You too. I'll see you at Christmas."

Tears welled in Anna's eyes, and at last she had no option but to let go of my hand…and let her little sister go.

I sank back into my seat and waved as hard as I could, grinning like a maniac. For all their faults, it was hard saying goodbye to my family. After all, they were the only one I had.

* * * *

The train slowed on its approach into the station, and my heart galloped faster in response. This was it—the last stop on my journey.

At last the train lurched and shuddered to a stop and the aisle flooded with bodies. With a deep breath, I rose from my seat and was pushed forward by the sea of people departing.

I struggled with my two heavy suitcases and, apart from bruising my shins a charming shade of blue, I made it off just fine. *Someone to help me, my behind…* Finding a little out-of-the-way spot, I pulled the small scrap of paper out of my pocket. It bore a hastily scribbled address. A foreign street in a foreign town, and I had no idea how to find it—but it was my home now.

My belly bubbled with excitement again and I had to bite my lip to keep from grinning. I sucked in a deep breath and marched outside to the line of waiting yellow cabs. My cases were taken from me and placed in the trunk on one. The cabbie was an older gentleman who tipped his hat and held open my door. I gave him a broad smile in return and rattled off the address.

"Are you going to be starting at the college?" the cabbie asked in a thick Boston accent.

"Yes," I said, shifting in my seat. It wouldn't be proper to hop around like a child.

"Nervous?"

I opened my mouth to laugh the question off, but something made pause. Over the summer, when people had learned of my plans, they'd asked if I was excited, scared to leave my family, if I hoped to meet a boy... But no one had asked if I was nervous.

And now that the day I had looked forward to with as much impatience as a kid waiting for Christmas was finally here, I had to wonder if maybe I should have prepared to feel a smidgen nervous. I was still happy, still over the moon to be here... But there was more to leaving home than being away from my mother.

My classes would be harder than high school.

I had to start all over again when it came to friends.

What if I had no friends?

What if my roommate was a horror and I was stuck with her for the next year?

I swallowed my sudden unease. "No."

"Not even a little?" he asked, meeting my eyes in his rear-view mirror.

"No...?"

"You sure will miss your family."

At this I turned my head to stare out of the window as the unfamiliar scenery flashed by. It wasn't that I wouldn't miss my family, because I would. I'd miss my sister like crazy, and my dad. But my mother... Our distance and separation could only be a good thing — for both of us.

The cabbie glanced at me but didn't try any further conversation, instead leaving me alone to my thoughts, which had taken a sudden nosedive.

The trip took only twenty minutes, a relief after such a long day on the stuffy train. Wellesley College loomed in the distance, growing larger with each passing second, and something not unlike nerves rattled in my belly.

He slowed the cab to a stop outside a tall building. Ivy snaked its way up the side of the large, brown-bricked edifice and I was sure, if climbed, it would remain intact. My heartbeat skittered as I took in its vastness. *So much for not being nervous...* "Is this the dormitory?" I asked the driver, trying to ignore the quaver in my voice.

"Sure is," he said before he jumped out and opened my door. He whistled as he walked to the trunk and pulled out my suitcases. "Would you like me to carry these to your room for you?"

"No thank you. I can manage from here." I gave him a smile that I knew didn't look the slightest bit convincing.

The cabbie paused as he passed me my suitcases.

"Is there something wrong?" Had I not tipped enough?

He jerked his head in the direction of the dorm. "Don't let them intimidate you in there. I see plenty of girls coming this time of year, all smiles and big dreams. A lot of them end up going back home, crying after a few months. You seem to have a good head on them shoulders — don't let 'em get you down."

A ball of gratitude unfurled in my stomach for this kind man. I smiled, wide and confident. "I won't."

Turning around, I braced my shoulders and marched through the large double doors that led to the next chapter of my life.

A flood of chattering girls stood inside the foyer of the dorm. Their excited voices reached impossible levels as they stood in their perfectly pressed dresses with flawless hair and makeup like a flock of beautiful, exotic birds. I couldn't help but feel intimidated…especially given that my hair had come undone and I was sure my makeup had smudged. All I wanted was a shower.

I made my way through the crowd until I finally emerged at the reception desk. A stern-faced older woman peered at me above her glasses.

"Freshman?" she asked.

"Yes, I'm Barbara Howell—"

"The next tour begins in a few moments. I'll add you to the next group and the guide will see to it that you make it to your room." The woman lifted a clipboard from its hook beside her and scribbled what looked like my name under a long, long list of other names.

My palms throbbed from carrying the weight of my suitcases and I hoped I would be one of the first to be deposited at my room. I murmured my thanks to the woman and turned to find an out-of-the-way place to stand while waiting for the start of the tour.

Mere moments later we were ushered up a wide staircase and were shown through a maze of corridors, which I instantly forgot. It was another three floors before my name was called and all I could think about was soaking my wrists under a cool faucet.

I stepped forward and the tour guide crossed me off her list. The group moved on, leaving me outside a plain, dark wooden door with brass numbers. So this was it. My new room… New home. Squaring my shoulders, I took a breath and opened the door.

And was greeted by a blonde tornado. "Hi there, I'm Lois. Who are you?"

I blinked as the blonde rushed across the room to shake my hand so hard she almost pulled my shoulder from its socket. "Barbara Howell. Pleased to meet you."

Lois laughed and placed her hands on her hips. "Well, look at you! You look scared, kitten. Don't be afraid." Without waiting for a response, Lois turned and pointed to a bed with an open suitcase, clothes strewn across the quilt as though the case had vomited. "I took this bed, I hope you don't mind."

"No, of course not," I said, letting out a breathy laugh. Well, at least my roommate was friendly. That was one worry crossed off the list I'd been making since the darn cabbie put the idea of nervousness in my head. Crossing the room, I placed my suitcases on the floor beside the empty bed.

"Not too bad, is it?" Lois asked. "I mean, it's a little small for the money my folks paid for it, but who can put a price on freedom? I got here hours ago. Eager, huh? I was just *dying* to get away from my parents!"

I spun around to look at her. Was I lucky enough to have been paired with a kindred spirit? "Really?"

Lois laughed. "Oh, you have no idea, baby-doll. Why? Do you have problems with your folks?"

"Yes," I said. "Well, yes and no. My mother and I clash, mostly."

"All my parents do is nag all the time, husband this and husband that." She rolled her eyes and put on a scolding tone. "I just want to have fun! I have no interest at all in becoming a wife or mother."

I laughed. This girl was growing on me more and more with each passing second. "Me too. They never listen though, do they?"

"Never. They keep asking when I'm going to settle down, and I keep telling them I'm not ready to limit myself to just one boy. They get real sick of me sometimes. I love courting and have a different partner every night. Life is about variety, right?"

Oh. That I hadn't expected. Maybe we weren't so similar after all. It wasn't that I was naïve. I had plenty of friends back home who enjoyed a full dance card. But it wasn't for me.

Shock and surprise must have shown on my face as Lois' smile softened. "What's the matter, sugar? You're not so into dating?"

"No," I admitted with a frown. Was this when Lois realized I was a boring dud and whatever friendly connection we'd had was now doomed? "I don't like boys."

Her smile widened again. "Well, there's your problem. Who wants a boy when you can have a man?"

A blush scorched my cheeks as I let out a startled laugh. "I don't really have any interest in them — men or boys. They come on too strong and act so stupid, and all they want is a nice wife. At least the ones back home do."

"Have you ever been on a date?" Lois asked, sitting on the edge of her clothes-covered bed.

"Of course."

"That you didn't do just to please your parents?" She smiled at my silence. "Well, I can see what my aim will be this year. Dating can be fun, why haven't you given it a chance?"

I shrugged and picked up one of my suitcases. Placing it on the bed, I took a breath before throwing the lid open and pulling out clothes to give myself something to do. "I guess I try so hard to avoid what my parents want for me, I miss out on other things too.

But I haven't met anyone I'd like to get to know better. Most boys back home don't really try anymore, they know I don't date."

"The *men* here don't know that," Lois said with a glint in her eye. She stood and gave me a warm smile as she headed for the door. "I'm going for a walk. It'll give you a time to settle in."

Maybe she knew I was feeling vulnerable, but I appreciated the room to breathe. My initial comparison to a blonde tornado was dead on, and I found Lois' bluntness refreshing. She was like a burst of sunshine after a rainstorm and somehow managed to pull more details from me than people I'd known for years.

Sighing, I walked over to the window to look out over the school grounds. My conversation with Lois played hauntingly in my head. The reassuring thing was that even after it was clear we were two very different kinds of girls, she didn't look at me as though I was an alien. She didn't look at me like my friends did, or my family. She seemed to laugh in the face of authority and didn't care if anyone disapproved of her lifestyle. Best of all, Lois seemed to accept me — and my quirks — at face value.

Instead of feeling awkward or out of place with Lois, I would be a grown-up about the situation. She was here and so was I. Nothing was going to change that. Unless of course she turned out to be one of the crying girls the cab driver had told me about, but I very much doubted it. She lived life her way with no apologies, and I did the same. Besides, a girl like Lois seemed like a good ally to have.

It was good to unpack my things — made me a little more grounded, as if I wouldn't blow away if a strong wind happened to get hold of me. I stretched up as tall as I could. My skin was grimy after traveling and unpacking, so braving the washroom facilities was next on my agenda.

* * * *

With a towel wrapped around my torso, I took in the reflection in the mirror. The first thing I noticed was my eyes. Large and hazel with flecks of brilliant green, they sparkled with vitality. Gone were the apprehension and nerves. Only jittery excitement remained. My long, dark brown hair hung down my back in damp waves and even my skin, flushed pink from the warmth of the shower, looked healthier now that the smog of the day had been rinsed away.

I might not appear as confident as Lois, but I wasn't a frightened little girl, either. My name was Barb Howell and I was a brand new, fresh-faced Wellesley girl. I pulled on my robe, tied the knot and tucked my things under my arm then walked back to my room.

Lois lounged on her bed, a cigarette dangling from her fingertips. She looked up when I stepped into the room and gave me a wide smile. "You look better."

"I feel better," I said, returning her smile and sitting at the dressing table. "It's good to be unpacked."

"I just walked around the entire campus twice. I could sleep for two weeks," Lois said, moments before she sprang to life and sat beside me on the narrow bench. "What do you say we do something tonight?"

"Like what?" I asked with a laugh at her contradiction.

"I saw a neat-looking bar off campus — we could go for a cocktail."

"I'm not sure. Don't we have Flower Sunday tomorrow?"

Lois rolled her blue eyes. "That doesn't matter. Come on, it'll be fun!"

Knowing she wouldn't relent, I sighed as if it were the biggest chore in the world. "You'd better let me get ready then."

She squealed and hugged me before darting back to the mound of clothes she still hadn't put away, and started tossing outfits around the room.

* * * *

The bar was called the Green Dragon and it was dark, dirty, dingy and I loved it. Nobody knew who I was so nobody made preconceived judgments based on what they'd heard about me. If I wanted to be left alone, all I had to do was invent a boy back home — easy. Except that I didn't really need to. The locals assumed we were liberal females since we were in a bar unescorted. If we wanted attention, we would go and get it.

A sisterhood bond was forged that night. Lois and I laughed so much it hurt. She understood me, and I her. We were both free spirits who wouldn't let anyone tame us. As we made our way back to our room, arms linked and singing, I knew I had a friend for life in Lois Dubbs.

Chapter Two

My first semester at Wellesley College passed in a blur. I did well in my coursework and exams and received top marks. Lois and I spent a lot of our free time at the Dragon, making new acquaintances. I enjoyed my newfound freedom so much I didn't want to be reminded of my old life. Christmas with my family was a daunting thought after enjoying so many months at Wellesley with my partner in crime. I begged and pleaded with Lois to come with me, but she wouldn't budge.

"You don't realize what I'll have to put up with. Why would you make me do that on my own?" I asked her, not for the first time. "Come on, it would be so much fun if you came."

Lois laughed. "I know it would, but remember why you're going—because it's Christmas and you should be with family. I'd much rather bring in the New Year down at the Dragon with a highball, but as horrid as they are, they *are* still my family."

I pulled a face. "You're really going to make me go alone, aren't you?"

"Yes," Lois said firmly, planting her hands on my shoulders. "I'll see you next year."

She pulled me into a tight hug then pushed me toward my waiting cab.

"Traitor," I mumbled.

She blew me a kiss in return.

* * * *

The train was busier than when I'd traveled to Wellesley in the fall. I found a seat and sank into it, already dreading the journey. It would be cramped, hot and sweaty and completely uncomfortable. Worst of all, each passing second took me closer to the world I longed to forget.

I knew I sounded melodramatic. My family wasn't all bad, not really. It was just that I couldn't help but wish they could, just once, see things the way I did. Accept me the way I was and not try to force me into their idea of who I should be.

The aisle began to clear as people finished stowing their luggage and found their seats. I recognized a few Wellesley girls who were heading to New York City and a few of them waved or said hello. Their excited voices made me miss Lois.

As the train picked up speed, I lost myself in the scenery that flashed past the window. My thoughts began to drift and despite my unwillingness to leave Wellesley, I realized I was actually a little excited to return home. I would see my sister, whom I loved dearly. There were so many stories I could tell her about the adventures Lois and I had gotten up to. And I'd bet Dad was looking forward to having me home again, even if it was only for two weeks. Mother always drove him crazy by fussing over everything.

It was my mother I wasn't looking forward to seeing. She would launch into her tirade the second she saw me, no doubt, and leave the newspaper open on the wedding section—one of her favorite subtle hints. *How did we get this way?* I wondered. Even when I was little, I couldn't remember being close to her. She worshiped Anna, of course, but never me. I was always the disappointment.

We did a good job of avoiding each other most of the time. The rest of the time she jumped down my throat, telling me to get a husband who would provide for me and take me away from her. I vowed to myself at a very early age that I would never do anything just to appease her...and to prove that I didn't need a man to look after me. I was perfectly capable of doing it myself.

The first part of my journey passed quickly, as I had been lost in my thoughts for most of the way. Disembarking, it was as though I was a fish struggling against the confines of the fisherman's net, flapping against all the other fish bodies and fighting for my freedom. The people on the train became crazed once again—everyone trying to push their way out of the steel prison. I would not admit defeat, nor would I look like a helpless female who couldn't handle herself.

There was a short wait at Penn Station before I had to board my connection. Unable to think of anything on the spot for me to do, I realized I was standing beside my luggage, looking every bit the helpless female.

I'd been sure I'd step off the train in my hometown a confident, self-assured young woman. I'd convinced myself that whoever would meet me at the station would be astounded at the change in me. Instead, the second I laid eyes on my beautiful sister, I was straight back to being the girl who'd left four short months ago.

I ran into her waiting arms, hugging her so fiercely she stumbled back a step.

"Wow — pleased to see me?" Anna asked, unable to hide the happiness in her voice. "Come on. Mom and Dad are outside waiting with the car." Anna linked our arms and we pressed our heads together, giggling like schoolgirls as we walked outside to greet my parents.

My father enveloped me in a hug when he saw me, then stood back for a moment to take me in. "You're taller."

I laughed. "I'm not."

My mother stepped closer toward me. "Barbara."

The smile on my face slipped. I couldn't help it — my entire body braced. "Mother."

She scanned me from head to toe, her usual frown deepening. "You look well."

I bit the inside of my cheek. "So do you."

My father, no doubt picking up on the strained atmosphere, hustled us into the car.

Anna held a steady stream of cheerful conversation during the short journey, and for that I was thankful. When we arrived at the house, I stole away upstairs to unpack my things.

My bedroom was exactly the same as I'd left it. My bed, my radio and dressing table, my books, all remained untouched. I ran a finger down a spine of a book on the shelf and examined my gray fingertip. It seemed my mother hadn't felt the need to come in here, now that I was no longer a regular presence in her house.

Dinner was a quiet affair of pot roast and vegetables. I found it strange to eat around a cozy table again, having grown accustomed to the enormous dining hall at school. Most of the students could fit into it at once and at its busiest the noise would reach unbelievable limits. My mother poured us each a cup of coffee once dinner was finished, and we all leaned back in our chairs.

"Tell us a story about college, Barb," Anna said, leaning forward with her elbow on the table. Until Mom coughed, and she removed the offending item from the linen.

"Like what?"

"Anything. I'm sure you have a fair few by now."

I couldn't very well talk about the hijinks Lois and I got up to. Not in front of my parents, at least. "Not really. It's harder than I thought it would be, but in a good way. I find myself challenged in new ways every day. The people are extraordinary."

"What's the dorm like?" Anna asked, not about to be put off by my vagueness.

"Crazy," I said with a laugh. "The hallways in the dorm get overexcited at night, with girls coming and going from one another's rooms. It doesn't last long — the warden comes and quietens everyone soon enough."

Anna smiled. "Sounds fun."

"Sounds like Sodom," Mom muttered under her breath.

My father gave her a look that told her to be quiet.

"What are your plans for tonight?" I asked Anna, keen to change the subject. If I let her, Mom would ruin this entire visit home. I wasn't a petulant, stubborn child anymore — I was a calm, collected and educated woman. Rising above — I was rising above.

"I have a date with Kenneth." Anna had been courting with Kenneth exclusively for what felt like decades and we were all waiting for him to pop the question. It was hard to tell who was most impatient for it — Anna, or our mother. "Why don't you come?"

I panicked. I didn't want to upset my sister, but I'd only been able to stomach Kenneth in small doses. Or after three cocktails. "Oh, no, Anna, that's okay. I'm really tired after traveling all day anyway. You go. Have fun."

"Are you sure? We could all go dancing?"

"I would fall flat on my face if I even attempted it. I'm dead on my feet. You can tell me all about it in the morning."

Anna nodded and I breathed a sigh of relief as she believed me. Soon after, I made my excuses and headed upstairs. I flopped down face first onto the bed and what little energy I had left slipped away.

It did not take long for sleep to take me. I stayed exactly where I was—fully dressed, on top of the blankets, until morning.

* * * *

My father had already left for work when I eventually made it downstairs. The smell of breakfast cooking pulled me from sleep and the responding growl of my stomach had me washed and changed in record speed.

Eggs and bacon were in the pan and toast in the rack on the table. With fresh orange juice in a jug and coffee in a flask, the sight was very homely. "Good morning, Mom," I said as I sat down at the table. "Everything smells fabulous."

My mother nodded as she served me a plate of bacon and eggs.

"What are you doing today?" I asked, picking up my knife and fork. I'd decided before coming down that morning that I should make more of an effort with my mother. No, we didn't have the best relationship, but it wouldn't get any better with my prickly attitude.

"I'm very busy."

She made it hard to keep my smile in place. "You usually are. I was just curious as to what would keep you very busy."

"It's the twenty-third of December, Barbara," my mother answered, not even bothering to keep the ice from her tone. "I have a lot of shopping to do."

I knew I would regret my next question, but I had to ask anyway. "Would you like some help?"

Mom paused, as if trying to figure out what game I was playing. "I'll be fine. But thank you for the offer."

Focusing back on my plate, relief flitted through me along with a sting of rejection. "What time did Anna get home? I didn't hear her come in."

"Eleven-thirty, I think. Kenneth usually gets her home at a decent time. He's a good man," Mother ventured. "A decent man."

This conversation turn couldn't end well. Relationships of any kind were never a safe topic for my mother and me. "I know. Anna is head over heels for him."

Mom tittered as though the idea was ridiculous. "I wouldn't say she was that passionate. She has realistic expectations about what a man can provide for her." She wasn't letting me get out of this one and we'd be lucky to escape unscathed.

"She knows how Kenneth feels for her. And she for him," I said carefully.

"Yes, she is fond of him."

I put down my knife and fork, my patience all used up. I hated that she downplayed my sister's relationship to try to turn it into a lesson for me. "Mother, she loves him."

My mother smiled—a cold smile that was barely a twitch of her lips. "And you know this? You have the life experience to see a look passed between two people and interpret it to be love?"

"Don't start, Mother. I'm not in the mood." All at once I was exhausted and wanted nothing more to do with the conversation. I stood up and carried my plate into the kitchen, almost throwing it in the sink in my frustration.

But Mom wasn't done and she marched after me. "Don't you dare talk down to me, Barbara!" It was as though a volcano had erupted inside her and all the lava was aimed for me. "Anna is realistic. She knows that Kenneth is a good match and he can take care of her. She has no illusions about a great love — she knows when to settle."

I whirled around, my face burning with anger. "You think Anna is settling? She loves him, Mom. How is that settling?"

Mom scoffed. "Love? How would you know the meaning of the word?"

"Of course I do!" I exclaimed, throwing my arms out. "I love Anna — a great deal more than you do if this conversation is anything to go by. She would never lower herself to settle for any man."

Mother nodded and folded her arms across her chest, her face stony. "At least she has a man. What is it you have, Barbara? A sinful roommate at that college of yours, where you delude yourself over your future."

I gasped as though she had struck me. "Is that what you think I am doing at Wellesley? Deluding myself?"

"Well, despite my hopes, it certainly isn't what most respectable girls do, which is to go to college to find a husband."

Holy mackerel, this woman was never going to relent. "I go to an all-girl school!"

Mom lifted her eyes toward the heavens. "That is beside the point. Mrs. Talley's daughter went to Wellesley two years ago. It only took her one term to find her husband."

I sucked in a steadying breath, trying, and failing miserably, to hold on to my temper. "I go to Wellesley because I want to be able to support myself. I've never wanted to rely on anyone else. What does it matter to you if I'm supporting myself or if a man does it? I'll still be away from you and your disappointed looks."

"What's wrong with wanting you to be happy?" Mother demanded, looking at me as if *I* were the unreasonable one.

"Nothing," I said. "What's wrong with accepting what makes me happy?"

She lifted a solitary eyebrow as she tried to stare me down. "And you think you know what makes you happy?"

"Being independent makes me happy. Or it will when I *am* independent."

"And what would it mean, without a husband to share your success?"

"I don't need a man's approval!" I took another breath and smoothed my hands down my dress. "Mother, we've had this argument so many times now. I see your point, truly I do. But being married doesn't go hand in hand with being happy. I've always wanted my freedom, and I have a taste of it now at Wellesley. I know I can take care of myself when the time comes."

Her shoulders sagged with defeat. "I have never doubted your survival skills, Barbara. I just wish you wouldn't embarrass me."

Her words cut me to the core. "I embarrass you?" I asked, quietly.

Mom took a step toward me, her face stern and unflinching. "Every day someone new asks me how you like it at Wellesley. Just fine, I always reply. Rich husband, that's what comes with a Wellesley girl, they say. I always smile back, but they all know about you and your strange ideas of courting, which is no courting at all. So yes, Barbara, you embarrass me. Every single day."

A lump formed in my throat. Mother had never made a secret of her distaste in my dating ideas, but she had never attacked me with so much venom before. "I'm truly sorry I've been such a disappointment to you. And if I'm being truthful, you embarrass me." I squared my shoulders in a vain attempt to deflect whatever hurt she might throw next. "I have walked on eggshells around you my entire life, secretly praying that, just maybe, tomorrow will be different. You'll realize I'm not like the girls who dress up nice just for a man's approval. I do things for my own approval. Who knows, maybe one day the right man will find me, and he'll understand me in a way that you never will."

"One day." Mother smiled, her eyes pinching at the corners. "Well, I won't hold my breath."

I was frozen to the spot with tears stinging my eyes as though she'd slapped me. In that moment I had no idea how we would never recover from this unpleasantness, but I knew we would get past it. Somehow. We always did. My father and Anna would act as buffers between us while I was home for the holidays. Then I would be back where I belonged, and far enough away that her vicious tongue couldn't reach me.

Anna heard us arguing, of course. But being Anna, she had the good sense not to mention it. Instead, she busied us both with preparations for the coming holiday. We went gift shopping, made Christmas cards and signed up to volunteer on Christmas Eve at the church, serving meals to the homeless.

Anna tried her hardest, but I managed to avoid spending time with Kenneth. It would be unavoidable since he and his parents were invited to lunch on Christmas Day. I could comfort myself with the fact that wine would be flowing and merriment would drown out everything else.

Mother and I avoided each other throughout the remainder of my visit. Anna and my father seemed to have perfected a strange routine in the house, neither of them leaving me and Mother on our own for any longer than a few minutes.

But they, too, of course, managed to throw in their two cents. My father cornered me on one occasion and mentioned a few boys he knew who were home from college, and perhaps I would be interested in taking some baked goods round to them. I happily declined.

Anna was a gentler creature. She offhandedly commented on the perks of dating and how nice it was to have someone in your life that was just for you. I never uttered a harsh word to my sister, as I knew she never meant any malice. She just didn't understand me.

Did anyone?

* * * *

Christmas morning was a low-key affair. It no longer held the magic it once had when Anna and I were young. Still, it was fun to sit and have coffee together while passing around the few gifts we'd got one another. Even Mom managed to remain pleasant to me.

The pleasantries didn't last for too long. She reminded us soon enough that there was plenty of

work to be done and set each of us a job to do. I earned
a swat on the buttocks with her rolling pin for asking if
my job could be keeping out of the way.

Anna hummed while she worked. A tune I didn't
recognize. There was a buoyancy in her step, some
deep-set happiness the rest of us were unaware of.

After what seemed like an eternity of being cooped
up in the kitchen, I was finally able to sneak out. Mom
either didn't care or she didn't notice as I crept out of
the back door. I found my father sitting in a lawn chair,
wrapped up in the new sweater Anna had knitted him.
He smiled as I sank into the chair beside him.

"Is everything coming together for dinner?"

"Yes," I said, pinning him with a look. "I noticed you
kept a clear distance."

Dad coughed and reached for his cigarette pack. "I
know how your mother likes everything done her way.
I would have just caused an unnecessary headache."

"Of course," I said with a laugh. Nodding to his pack,
I asked, "Got another?"

Dad nodded and tapped another cigarette out of the
pack.

"Do you know why Anna is so…chirpy today?" I
asked, leaning over so he could light it for me.

He flicked his lighter closed and tucked it in his
pocket. "Give Anna a break today. I want best
behavior."

"I'm always on my best behavior," I said with a huff.

"I mean it, Barb," Dad said, his tone full of warning
and I knew not to push it any further. "This is a big day
for her, having Kenneth and his family here like this."

I sighed and looked over at him. "Why don't you just
say what it is you're trying to, Dad?"

Dad reached over and took my free hand. "I just want
to see you taken care of, Barb."

"I don't need a man to do that. You should know me better than that by now." I glared at the ground. His message was wrapped in a prettier package than Mom's, but it was still the same.

"I know how self-reliant you are and I respect that." Dad squeezed my hand. "These aren't easy times we live in, Barb. My business isn't bringing in money the way it used to. I just wish you would find yourself someone like Kenneth who can provide security for your future, that's all."

"*That's all?*" I repeated, incredulous. "I know you and Mom have your reasons for wanting to see Anna and me settled down and happy, but what is so wrong with the idea that maybe a man isn't going to make me happy? Learning, independence, freedom—those things make me happy. Anna has Kenneth who makes her happy, and that's wonderful. For her. But it's not for me."

Dad's face softened. "Barb, all I want is for you girls to be happy, but can't you see where I'm coming from? Putting financial security aside, for a father, there is no greater fear than the thought of leaving your children alone in the world."

"Dad," I said quietly, my heart pinching at the admission he'd never vocalized before. "You aren't going anywhere. And… I'm not saying no forever, I'm saying no for now. Wouldn't you rather I met someone I truly cared about rather than settle for something mediocre?"

He released a heavy breath and stubbed out his cigarette. "You're really happy at Wellesley? It's not just to upset your mother?"

I smiled and got up to kiss Dad's cheek. "Yeah, Dad. I'm really happy."

* * * *

After dinner, I helped Mom serve brandy to our small group of guests gathered in the lounge. Anna flitted around the room, dishing out cigarettes and clearing away glasses that some of us hadn't even finished yet. I couldn't take eyes off my eager sister, and had to choke back laughter when she sat down only to jump back up a moment later. Since Kenneth and his parents had arrived, Anna seemed as though she were fit to burst and could barely sit still.

Kenneth cleared his throat and moved into the center of the room. "Everyone? Could you all take a seat, please? I have something I would like to say."

I tried to catch Anna's eye, but she seemed to be purposefully ignoring me.

Once we were all seated, Kenneth took a deep breath, and faced us all with a wide smile. "The holidays are very important to me," Kenneth began, dropping his gaze to his drink as though it contained his speech. "They're a time for family — to remember the love we share for one another, the thanks we owe each other. They're a time for celebration."

Anna made a weird, gasping sound in her throat.

On my left, my mother began to whimper softly.

Oh, God.

Kenneth peered at each of us in turn. "I look around here this evening, and I'm proud to be the man standing before you all. Especially now that our two families are going to be forever joined, as Anna has agreed to marry me." Anna rose to stand beside Kenneth, who pulled a ring out of his pocket and slipped it onto her trembling left hand.

Beside me, my mother let out a sob and wasted no time in rushing to Anna's side to pull her into a fierce embrace. My father jumped to his feet, shaking Mr. Dixon's hand and slapping Kenneth on the back.

Excited chatter broke out around the room and it sounded as if Mom and Mrs. Dixon were discussing colors for bridesmaids' dresses.

Anna's eyes locked with mine and I knew she would be desperate for, but also terrified of hearing my opinion. I was torn between feeling elated for her — despite my own personal views, Kenneth really did make Anna happy, and that was all anyone can ask for out of life — and jealous.

My sister was being taken from me.

She would insist that nothing would change, but we both knew it would. She wouldn't be my young, carefree sister anymore. She would be a wife, and, before long, a mother. Anna would have her own little family…and I wasn't sure if I would fit.

Despite my fears and reservations, I didn't want to ruin this night for her. Anna would remember it forever and tell her great-grandchildren about. And I didn't want there to be a story about moody old Barb who threw a tantrum like a baby and made everyone angry, stealing all the attention from the blushing bride-to-be.

So I smiled, deciding to be pleased for Anna, and not worry about being left behind.

* * * *

The house was deathly quiet when Anna crept into my room in her nightgown and rollers in her hair late that night. Despite my heavy mood, I was pleased to see her. Mom and Kenneth's mother had monopolized her for the entire evening, firing dozens of questions at her with barely a breath in between.

"Hi, Mrs. Dixon," I said, sitting up and leaning back against the pillows.

Anna toyed with her fingers as she crossed the room to sit on the edge of my bed. "Are you mad at me?"

"Why would I be mad at you?" I asked softly, reaching for her hand.

"I don't know." Anna shrugged. "You could be disappointed in me. I'm just like all those other girls you hate so much."

Never in a million years could Anna be like the preening, self-centered girls I despised, whose only life goal was to find a rich husband. "Are you happy?"

Anna sighed as if she were caught up in a torrid romance novel. "I'm so happy I feel like I'm floating."

"Then that's all that matters," I said. "And you could never be one of those girls I hate. You love him, Anna. Marriage is the next chapter of your life. Just because it isn't something I want for myself, doesn't mean I'm not so, so pleased for you."

"I kind of love you, Barb." Anna grinned. "We're announcing the engagement tomorrow, but we're telling all our friends before it's in the paper."

"Are you having a party?" I asked, already knowing the answer. My mother would find a dozen excuses to celebrate this engagement before they even got close to walking down the aisle.

"Yes, I'm hoping we can throw something together very soon so you can be there before you go back to school."

"Anna, you don't have to do that. And you know Mom won't let you."

"But I want you there."

"You just want me to see how nice it is to have a lovely fiancé."

Anna laughed. "Maybe."

I sighed. "If you really want me to, I'll come back for the party."

"No, you don't have to do that. It's such a long way for you to travel."

"I wouldn't mind. I would do it for you."

"I know you would, but I'm not going to let you. Showing up for the wedding will be enough."

"Okay." I laughed. "But go to sleep, you'll have a long, long day tomorrow. I imagine Mom will already have made appointments at the florist, bakery and bridal store."

Anna groaned and got up.

"Goodnight, Mrs. Dixon."

She kissed my cheek and snuck from the room.

* * * *

New Year's Eve, 1939

After the excitement of Anna's engagement at Christmas, I got the peace and quiet I'd craved since leaving Wellesley. Mom and Mrs. Dixon had indeed whisked Anna away the next day, and had kept her busy ever since, which left me with plenty of alone time.

So I read. A lot. I'd already finished all my essays and assignments that I needed to do for returning to school, so I could read what I wanted at my leisure. On December 31st I was sitting at my desk, thumbing through an old copy of *Little Women,* which was coming apart at the binding, when Anna burst into my room in an overexcited frenzy.

"What are you doing? Reading again?"

"Yes. Why?" I asked, not looking up from the pages.

Anna's hand curled around the top of the book and she tugged it from my grasp. "Not anymore. We're going out tonight."

I blinked at her. "But tonight's New Year's Eve."

"How very observant you are, Barbara. I can see college is paying off."

I rolled my eyes at her sarcasm.

Anna huffed and caught my hand, pulling me to my feet. "Yes, it's New Year's Eve and I want to spend it with my little sister before she disappears back to college again."

"What does your fiancé say about that?" I asked, lifting my eyebrows. I couldn't imagine Kenneth would be thrilled to lose Anna for the night.

"He doesn't get a say about it. I told him I've barely seen my sister this entire two weeks and tonight is our night. There's a band playing at the club in town. It'll be fun, just us girls."

A bubble of excitement grew in my belly. It had been too long since Anna and I had gone dancing together, and this could be the last time it was just the two of us. Soon she would have a husband escorting her everywhere. She squeezed my hand and pulled me toward her bedroom so we could find the perfect outfits.

Once we were dressed and had our faces made up, it was time to hit the town. We took a cab, giggling like schoolgirls the entire way. The music emanated from the club as we drew up outside. Lights danced in the windows and people rushed inside, holding hands and laughing. We paid our fee and the door was held open for us, louder band music rushing out to greet us.

Anna went to the bar to get our drinks while I found a table. It was some time before she returned with our highballs. "Wow, it's busy up there!"

It was about thirty minutes after we arrived that Anna was stolen from me. People flocked to her as though the diamond Kenneth had put on her finger was a magnet. Congratulations were bellowed from across the room, drinks were thrust into her hand from every angle. It wasn't long before she succumbed to the attention, secretly adoring each second of praise. I didn't resent her for it. She had an inner glow that came from being perfectly happy and contented, and not wishing for anything else in the world.

Leaving her to wedding talk, I wandered around the room a few times, talking to people I recognized from high school. I received a few dance offers, but my heart wasn't in it. The offers tended to come once the band slowed to a more romantic pace. It didn't appeal to me to be pressed up against a balding bachelor or over-eager college boy.

I glanced toward our table and saw Anna still wrapped up in conversation. Releasing a breath, I decided to get some fresh air. The packed room was relentlessly stuffy.

Outside, I fanned myself with my hand and leaned against the wall. I'd left my cigarettes in my jacket pocket and wished I'd had the thought to retrieve them.

"It's cold out here. You should have a jacket."

I snapped my head around to look in the direction of the voice. A few yards away stood a young man, possibly a year or two older than I was. He was tall with a lean build and slicked-back brown hair. His eyebrows were drawn together as though in concern and he jammed his hands into his pants pockets.

I raked my gaze over his thin shirt and braces, but stuttered and locked on the rolled-up shirtsleeves. They revealed tanned, sinewy forearm muscles that made my stomach give an odd little flutter. I didn't recognize him, so he probably wasn't a local. *I'd remember that face...* The thought made my body stiffen and I pushed off the wall. "So should you," I said before hurrying away.

The heat of the room assaulted me the moment I stepped inside. My skin was flushed from the encounter with the man outside, the image of him burned into my mind.

"Barb! Over here!" Anna's voice only barely registered as she attempted to shout over the others.

Spinning around, I spotted her at our table, which had filled with other people.

"Where have you been? I looked for you," Anna asked as I sat down in the empty chair beside her.

"Outside, I was too hot," I replied, fanning myself with a napkin.

"Have a drink." She slid a glass in my direction. "People keep buying them for me, and I can't manage them all myself."

A laugh bubbled in my throat, and I accepted the drink. It was refreshing and I had to stop myself from gulping down the whole glass.

"Barb," Anna said in an innocent voice that I knew not to trust. I glanced at her and frowned at the mischievous twinkle in her eye. She gestured to someone beside me. "This is Paul Charnock. He goes to Harvard."

The gentleman, who previously had his back to me, turned at the sound of his name. He looked from Anna to me, before settling his gaze on mine, a smirk forming on his lips.

Anna touched my arm. "Paul, Barb goes to Wellesley. You two are practically neighbors."

My sister, the matchmaker... I smiled sweetly at her, and she pulled a face at my warning.

"Oh? How are you enjoying it?" Paul flashed me a dazzling smile, revealing a row of perfect white teeth. He was an attractive guy and I'd guess he was used to having a certain effect on most women. His blond hair, made darker from the wax, was styled in place and his suit spoke of good fortune.

"Very much, thank you," I answered, mustering a polite smile. One of the only things my mother had taught me.

Anna turned away, leaving me alone in the conversation with Paul. What a sneak.

"What are you studying?" Paul asked, reaching for his beer glass.

"Art history, mathematics, ancient history, Latin and English literature."

He lifted his eyebrows. "Impressive. How are you finding it?"

"Fine," I answered with a shrug. "I'm only a freshman."

Paul nodded in understanding. "My freshman year was killer. I'm in my third year at Harvard. My dad is pushing me to go in for another four to do law."

"And you don't want to?" I asked, leaning my elbow on the table and resting my chin on my fist.

"No, it's not that." Paul frowned. "I think I'd like to have a break from school for a little while."

I was intrigued. "And do what?"

"I don't know for sure. It's tempting to just jump in my car and disappear. Live life day to day with no responsibilities... No worries." Paul smiled. "What do you say, Barb, want to run away with me?"

For a second or two all I could do was stare at him. That kind of pick-up line would usually have irritated me, but it was delivered with such expectation that I couldn't help but let out a bubble of laughter.

Paul frowned and leaned back in his chair. "Are you all right?"

"I'm fine." I dabbed under my eyes with my napkin as the laughter slowed. "But I have to ask—does that ever work for you?"

He opened his mouth to answer but closed it again. Paul sighed. "Actually, yes. *Often*. Women like a man with a romantic soul. And nothing says romantic like running away together." He glanced at me. "But I can see you aren't like other women. I'm sorry. I shouldn't have jumped straight into flirting with you."

"You're right about that," I mumbled. I lifted my glass and took a sip of my drink. "But I appreciate the joke. I don't think I'll be forgetting it in a while."

"I really am sorry." Paul sounded sincere. "Will you accept my apology and peace offering?" He pulled out a thin silver tin filled with cigarettes.

"Apology accepted." I took one and leaned into the flame of the struck match Paul offered.

He tucked the tin away and grinned. "Good. So now that I'm forgiven, how about a dance?"

My eyebrows shot up. "You're not that forgiven. I bet there are lots of girls here who would dance with you." I waved my hand around the room. "Why would you want to waste your time with someone as difficult as me?"

"Difficult or not, you're very beautiful. Why wouldn't I want to dance with you?" Paul's lips twitched in amusement. "Come on, don't make me beg."

"Well, I don't want you to beg. But I also don't want to dance—at least not right now."

Anna turned back around to face me then and caught me up in excited chatter on gossip I'd missed.

Paul continued to pester me for a dance, and in the end I was too exacerbated to deny him any longer, which I think was his intention. For the last half hour or so, the band had stopped playing jazz and played square-dancing music. Couples were setting themselves up in a dance I recognized so I wasn't too self-conscious as I allowed him to lead me out onto the dance floor. I took my place opposite Paul, who smiled in triumph, as though he'd won a small battle.

I gave him a pointed look but he paid no notice.

The music started up and we began to move through our steps. It wasn't long before partners were switched and Paul pouted like a child when I was swept away by another man. I laughed and relaxed into the dance, enjoying myself more than I thought I would have.

Until I glanced ahead, to see my next partner. My breath hitched when I realized it was the man from outside. The blood roared behind my ears, muffling the music, as I moved forward to dance with him.

I couldn't look at him. I didn't want him to know how much he affected me. His eyes bored into me, making my face feel like it was only an inch away from the surface of the sun. In the end, I couldn't resist for a moment longer, and flitted my gaze upward and locked directly with his.

It was too easy to peer into those eyes. He held me there by some invisible force and forbade me to pull away. I frowned, waging an internal war with myself. *Look away. No, just a minute longer, please.*

We slowed to a stop and the world came back into focus. The band stopped playing and stood closely together, smiling broadly and holding up champagne glasses.

The countdown to midnight started.

What was I going to do? I didn't know this man — didn't know what he expected. I looked around, trying to find Anna, or anybody, to use as a plausible excuse to leave this awkward situation.

Were they counting down quicker just so I didn't have time to leave? I could have just walked away — I did possess legs after all. But I couldn't stand the embarrassment. It would be obvious what I was doing. As crowded as the dance floor was, someone was bound to notice me leaving the poor man in the lurch. I was socially obliged to remain where I was, slap on a brave face, and take it like a woman.

It all seemed to happen at once.

I resisted the urge to cover my ears and look like a fool. The room burst into life, the celebration igniting the atmosphere as people kissed and laughed and cheered.

The crowd faded into the background once again as he brought my attention back to him as he clasped my hand and held me to the spot with his magnetic gaze. I couldn't understand what was happening, what changed. I was no longer afraid of what would come.

He lifted my hand to his lips, brushing the back of it with the barest of caresses with his mouth. Even though it was the lightest of touches, my hand sizzled with electricity.

I didn't know what to do, what to say.

Around us, the crowd started singing.

"Happy New Year," he said barely above a whisper, in a voice that was low and smooth. I felt it all the way down to my toes.

Lowering my hand, he looked down. He let me go and backed away into the crowd. It only took half a second to lose sight of him.

Then Anna was there, hugging me and trying to sing along to the song she didn't know the words to. A waiter walked around with trays carrying champagne cocktails. Anna grabbed two, thrust one into my hand and chinked her glass to mine.

"To sisters!" she toasted.

"To sisters!" I agreed, and took a gulp of champagne in a pointless effort to recover from what that had been.

The band started again and Anna snatched my hand, refusing to let me disappear back to our table. Deciding to throw myself into it, we danced for hours until our feet ached and we could dance no more.

We walked home at two a.m., arm in arm and laughing quietly.

I tried to lock the memory away, keeping it safe from the hands of time. I wanted to always remember us that way, even when we were old and gray.

Young, happy sisters.

Chapter Three

The farewell with Anna at the train station was tearful. I wanted to steal my sister away with me, but she was about as suited for life at Wellesley as I was to being a housewife. So, instead, we hugged and promised to talk soon.

The train to New York was packed and the connection swift, so I was rushed and frazzled by the time I made it onto the train to Boston. I searched the busy carriage for an empty seat, my face flushed with exertion.

"Hey, Barb!"

Glancing up from scanning the carriage for a desirable seat, I blinked a few times as I tried to put a name to the face. In my frantic state it took a long moment for it to register that he was Paul.

Oh, no. I was in no mood to idle chit-chat, and I hoped he wouldn't suggest we sit together for the journey. I fixed a polite smile in place, ready to rebuff whatever he might offer, but it froze as I noticed the man behind him.

My dance partner from the night before stowed a suitcase in the overhead rail. He turned around to reach for another but paused in his action as he noticed me. He skimmed over me with his eyes and a thrill shot up my spine.

"This is a pleasant surprise," Paul said with a grin. "Headed back to Beantown, huh?"

His friend swiveled around to put away the other suitcase and dropped into his seat, leaving me faced with Paul.

Freed from his magnetic pull, I closed my eyes for a second, finally able to answer. "Um, yes, I am. Excuse me—" I wanted to get past him, but he was taking up too much room in the aisle. It would have meant pressing up against him. *That* wasn't going to happen.

"Are you traveling with Anna?" Paul asked, leaning his hip against a seat and folding his arms across his chest. He didn't look as if he was moving any time soon.

"No. Can I just—" I motioned for him to let me pass.

"Oh, right, she and Kenneth are probably real busy with wedding plans now?"

I sighed and clenched my fist around the handle of my suitcase. "Right."

Paul smiled again and moved to the side to gesture to the open seat across from his friend. "Why don't you sit with us?"

"What?" I asked. *Oh, God...*

"You're alone, aren't you?"

"Yes, but—"

"But nothing, come on. I can't let a lady sit by herself."

"But nothing?" I repeated. "I can assure you I'm more than capable of traveling by myself. Besides, I have some reading I'd like to finish."

Paul sighed and finally moved out of the way. "You're breaking my heart."

"I'm sure you'll survive." My lips twitched into a smile. As I squeezed past Paul, I couldn't help but cast my glance down at his friend. His eyes locked on mine and my cheeks flushed at being caught looking. Rushing forward, I changed carriages and hoped it would be enough distance to forget about them.

It took a while, and some profound concentration, but I finally managed to lose myself in my book and force the two men out of my head. Even still, when my attention faltered, my dance partner from New Year's Eve would flash in my mind. My heart would pick up speed and my palms would sweat.

I'd never met a man who could make me uncomfortable with so little effort. Perhaps it was his quiet intensity that unnerved me. Maybe he was simply shy and I was thrown off kilter because he wasn't as obviously persistent as other men. Like Paul.

The door to my carriage opened and I glanced up as I turned the page. My pulse spiked as I saw the friend casually slope toward me, hands jammed in his pockets and eyes cast downward.

Maybe he won't see me. I stared at the words on the page so hard they began to blur.

"Good book?" His voice was alluring—smooth and easy—but I still jumped about a foot out of my skin at the sound.

"I wouldn't be reading a bad one," I answered without looking up. It came out sharper than I intended.

It didn't deter him. "What are you reading?"

"Homer's *The Iliad*."

"A fan of the classics?"

"So it would seem."

"Do you enjoy Dante?"

My eyebrows pinched together at his question. How he could possibly have known? It made me raise my eyes. He leaned against the seat in front of me, arms folded across his strong chest, an inquisitive gleam to his eyes. "Very much. Do you?"

His lips curled into a subtle smile. "*Inferno* is a personal favorite."

Was he flirting? Pretending he enjoyed my favorite author? Well, we would soon find out. I closed my book and placed it on my lap. "Favorite canto?" I'd bet just about anything he wouldn't have an answer.

"Fifth, the second circle."

"Really?" I asked, unable to keep the shock from registering on my face.

His smile widened, as though he knew he'd smashed my preconceived notions. "*No hope ever comforts them, not of repose, but even of less pain.*" He chuckled and glanced down as if embarrassed. "Impressed?"

Completely. Not that I would give him the satisfaction of knowing. "Anyone can find a quote if they really want to. To try to impress someone, for instance."

"All right, give me your favorite canto," he said in a challenging tone and straightening his stance.

"The Gates of Hell," I replied without thinking.

"*This way a good soul never passes...*" he said with another confident smile.

I could only stare at him. Whatever battle this had been, clearly, he'd won.

"What's the matter? Disappointed?"

"In what?" I asked with a frown, not understanding the question.

"Me," he said with a quiet laugh. "Disappointed that you didn't get a chance to embarrass me, since you thought your knowledge of the *Divine Comedy* was more superior to mine?"

I felt flustered and embarrassed. "I—"

"Mind if I sit?" He pointed to the empty seat across from me.

"Yes," I said, a little too quickly.

The smile spread wider over his face. "Yes, what? Yes, I can sit, or yes, you mind?"

"Yes, I mind." My cheeks burned and I knew I looked as flustered as I felt. This man was something else—he confused me, set me on edge, surprised me... Even made me curious.

"Too bad, I was looking forward to teaching you more." Smiling still, he sauntered out of the carriage.

His words taunted me, repeating themselves in my head for the rest of the godforsaken journey. He'd wormed his way beneath my skin and I hated it. I couldn't understand what game he was playing. I didn't know how to play, whatever it was, and I certainly didn't know the rules.

Still, annoyed as I was, I didn't ever have to lay eyes on him again. I could only assume he went to Harvard with Paul, and I had no plans to visit. Wellesley was far enough away, and Boston was a big enough city, that I didn't have to worry about running into him.

No, we would never see each other again. The thought did little to comfort me as I struggled to I push all thoughts of him, and Dante, out of my head.

As I left the station, I kept my eyes forward, not daring to look up in case I locked eyes with either of them. I breathed a sigh of relief once in a cab and heading away from the train station, going back to where I belonged.

* * * *

To say I was excited to see Lois would be an understatement. She returned the day after I did, which left me rattling around our room and counting down the hours until she was back. If anyone saw me, I would surely resemble my sister on Christmas as she awaited Kenneth to make the announcement of their engagement.

Lois burst into our room and dropped her luggage where she stood. I was on my feet in a heartbeat, hugging her as tight as I could. We laughed and wished each other a happy New Year and kissed each other's cheeks.

Lois threw herself onto her bed. "Give me a cigarette, quickly now, before I die!"

Laughing, I tossed her one and took one for myself.

"Better?" I asked, smiling.

"You have no idea," she said, leaning back against the pillows. "When did you get back?"

"Yesterday." I sat cross-legged beside her on the bed. "Anna got engaged."

Lois pushed herself up, lifting her eyebrows. "Is she happy about it?"

"Ecstatic." I rolled my eyes. "She's practically floating."

"That won't impress you," Lois commented.

I frowned and picked at the quilt. "No, I'm happy for her. She's making the right choice. She loves him very much."

"You're singing a different tune." Lois laughed. "Did you meet any boys on your trip that changed your perspective?"

"No!" I sat bolt upright and my cheeks warmed. *Damn it.*

Lois laughed harder at the fierceness of my answer. "What happened?"

"Nothing."

"You're a terrible liar, Ms. Howell."

"And you're an insufferable gossip, Ms. Dubbs."

"You're right about that. But I still want to know what happened. Who did you meet?"

I groaned. "All right, I met a man, but don't get all excited. I didn't like him. He was…peculiar."

"Peculiar." Lois' smile softened. "Of course you didn't like him, you hate all men."

"I do not hate all men." I huffed.

Lois looked positively gleeful. "Just the ones who try to make conversation with you."

I glowered at her.

"All right, all right, I'm sorry, okay? So what did the *peculiar* man do?"

"He was infuriating. He— He acted like he knew what was best for me, told me I should be wearing a jacket, like he's, I don't know, my *father*, and he danced with me, and, and…" All my pent-up frustration poured out of my mouth. And not in a comprehensible manner. "And he was there at midnight. I don't know how he did it, but he must have fashioned it that way, the sneak. Oh! And he sought me out on the train, just to insult my intelligence!"

Lois looked at me with a mixture of amusement and confusion. "Really? He was that bad?"

"And he has terrible taste in friends," I mumbled around my cigarette.

"Most would say you do too." Lois nudged me with her foot.

I smiled. "Actually, his friend was a lot like you, only he wore pants instead of dresses."

Lois laughed. "Wonderful! You must set up a meeting."

My smile was replaced with a frown. "No! No, I-I doubt I'll see either of them ever again."

The smile Lois gave me was coy and knowing. With another huff, I whacked her with a pillow. That night we toasted our reunion at the Dragon and swapped horror stories of our Christmas vacation.

It was good to be home.

* * * *

"Hi, Dad." It was in early March I got the news I'd dreaded. I called home once a fortnight to tell my parents how my studies were going and to ask how the wedding plans were coming along.

"Barbara! It's good to hear from you, kid."

A smile twitched the corners of my lips. If I had to guess, Dad was being driven mad by all the wedding preparations. I doubted my mother would have given him a moment's peace. "How are things?"

"Oh, you know. The usual."

I laughed. "That bad, huh?"

His voice dropped to a hushed whisper. "You have no idea."

"I can only presume you refer to Mother." I leaned against the wall and couldn't help but smile. Poor Dad.

"She's even enlisted Evelyn to help with wedding plans. I wish she would leave that woman in peace. She does enough, you know?"

I knew only too well how much Evelyn did for us.

The Evelyn my father referred to was my aunt Evelyn. My mother's younger, and far less severe, sister. Aunt Evelyn was part of the high society in New York and had all the right connections. Anna and I stayed with her every summer vacation, and we always looked forward to it. Except now it would just be me who visited.

We went with my mother's encouragement, as Evelyn knew everyone who mattered—and their unwed sons. Mom, of course, hoped in vain that their charisma and financial prospects would catch my eye. Anna never fell for any of them either, but everyone knew she wouldn't be a problem. *I*, on the other hand, would be.

I groaned. "Poor Evelyn, she'll be at her very end."

"At least Evie is in New York, I have to live with the woman," Dad grumbled. "Evie's secured the country club at Yellow Sands for the reception. Thank God I'll get a decent golf game out of the fiasco."

It didn't come as a shock that the wedding would be held at Yellow Sands, the small but wealthy little town outside New York, where the rich could play in the summertime. It was an idyllic place with a beautiful beach and luxurious golf courses.

I was used to spending one week out of each year at Yellow Sands and I didn't mind it. It got a little overwhelming at times. The rich snobbery always wore down my patience. But it would provide my sister with the fairy-tale wedding she deserved.

"Is that Barb?"

"What was that?" I asked, not sure I wanted the answer.

Dad sighed. "That would be the creature that has taken over your darling sister."

"Is that Barb?" Anna screeched again.

I held the phone away from my ear before I went completely deaf.

"Yes, Anna, for goodness' sake. Hold on a minute, will you?" My dad sighed. "I think your sister would like a word. Call again soon, okay?"

"Two weeks, just like always." I promised.

"Take care, kid."

There was barely a pause between my father's farewell and Anna's almost indistinguishable ramblings.

"Barb-I-have-the-most-wonderful-news!" Anna gushed in one breath.

"What?"

I could visualize Anna standing in the kitchen, probably damn near ripping the cord out of the phone and dancing in excitement. "I-need-to-ask-you-a-question-and-so-help-me-Barb-if-you-say — "

"Whoa! Anna, slow down." I laughed. "Just ask me. And, for God's sake, breathe."

Anna released a long breath. "Will you be my maid of honor?" she asked with deliberate slowness.

A moment passed.

And another.

And another, until I realized I couldn't hear Anna breathing.

The last thing in the world I wanted was to be a bridesmaid...and maid of honor sounded like a lot of responsibility. It wasn't that I was self-conscious, but I hated the thought of all those eyes on me, silently judging and weighing me up beside my flawless sister. And, of course, the question I'd be plagued with the entire day — *when will it be your turn, Barbara?*

So, for my sister's sake, I closed my eyes and tried to find the actress who — hopefully — lived inside me. "Really? Oh, Anna, of course!"

Anna burst into tears.

I clutched the phone tighter. "Honey, what's the matter? I thought you wanted me to do this." Had I read the situation wrong? Did she want me to say no? Had she only asked me to keep Mom happy?

"I do," she sobbed. "I'm. Just. So. *Happy*!"

I bit my lip so as not to laugh and waited for a few minutes for her to stop crying.

Anna sniffed. "You've made me so happy, Barb. I really thought you'd put up a huge fight about it."

I should have known. Anna knew me entirely too well. "You're my sister, therefore your wish is my command. I have to go now, but I'll talk again in two weeks."

"Before you go" — Anna cleared her throat — "I've already found a dressmaker for you in Boston. She has all the details for the dress, so all you have to do is show up. I thought it would be easier for you, so you don't have to keep traveling up here."

"That's really considerate of you, Anna, thank you." I paused. "Wait a minute — how did you know I was going to say yes?"

Anna laughed. "I trusted you to be the wonderful sister I know you are."

"You knew Mom would bully me into it if I said no, didn't you?"

"Yes."

Rolling my eyes, I said, "Goodbye, Anna."

"Bye, baby sister."

Hanging up the phone, I couldn't help but cringe. *Bridesmaid!*

Lois, of course, found the news hilarious. I told her I was being supportive of my elder sister, and it would be nice if she in turn would be supportive of my support. Realizing how important Anna's happiness was to me, Lois did no more mocking on the subject. All she asked in return was an invitation to the event itself.

I'd rather she carried on with the mocking.

But in the end, Anna beat me to the punch. When I called a fortnight later, she informed me Lois' invite was in the pile along with everyone else's.

* * * *

The rest of the school year fell away in a blur. I was so focused on my exams, time began to mean very little. I sat each exam with a flutter of nerves, but some deep-routed confidence. I knew I'd put in hard work throughout the year, and that was bound to show up in my exams.

All at once, they were finished. The student body began to breathe easy once again, and summer was upon us. The hallways were filled with suitcases and bodies.

I promised to spend one week with Lois and her family before we went to Yellow Sands for the wedding. I could hardly believe the wedding was here already. I'd been so focused on my exams, everything else had faded into the background. When Lois and I boarded the train to go to her family's home, it was only a week away. The final dress fitting took place to make sure it was in order, so there was nothing left to do but wait for the day to arrive. The dressmaker was sending it straight to my mother at her request. She didn't trust me enough to insure its safety throughout the journey.

I loved my dress. I owed Anna a huge favor for reeling my mother in and not letting her go crazy with the design. Cut from the finest silk and the palest lavender, it was elegantly simple.

Chapter Four

Lois regaled me with tales of her family as we began our travels. I was nervous about meeting them. When we'd first met, Lois had assured me her parents were like mine in wanting her to settle down and marry. But Lois had such a laid-back, bohemian attitude, I could only imagine her parents were the same. She told me about her younger brother, Sterling, whom she adored, and the adventures they'd had when they were little. I had to wonder just how old she had been, as Lois didn't seem the type of person to let age get in the way of mischief.

Lois grew up in New Bedford, a considerably larger city than I had. It suited her big personality and I knew I wouldn't be bored.

And I was right.

As soon as we dropped our suitcases in Lois' room, she grabbed my hand and led me outside. She took me to a little café, which she loved, and to all her old haunts. Lois had so many friends. It seemed everywhere we went, someone was there to hug and greet her. I wasn't surprised. Lois had natural charisma and people were drawn to her.

We went to shows, bars and anything else that took Lois' fancy. She rarely gave her parents any information, and they rarely asked for it. I wasn't sure if they were being especially relaxed because I was there, or if it was the norm for them. Either way, it seemed to work for everyone and caused very little arguments. Unlike my own house where hostility was as common as the promise of another tomorrow.

Lois grew increasingly excited about the wedding. The day we traveled to Yellow Sands she could barely sit still. She wanted to do everything all at once, explore and experience all that was possible. In the end, Lois settled for meeting my sister. This, she assured me, was what she'd looked forward to the most. Anna and Lois hit it off immediately. They laughed for hours, sharing stories and talking about me…thankfully never in a bad way.

Even my mother found Lois charming—a breath of fresh air she'd called her. Mom advised I could learn a thing or two from Lois. I fought back a laugh as I imagined the things Lois would *really* love to teach me.

* * * *

The night before the wedding, all us girls enjoyed a luxurious meal prepared by Mrs. Dixon and my mother. Kenneth and his friends were having his gentleman's dinner at the country club, and Anna refused to leave the house in case he accidentally saw her.

The atmosphere was light as we all giggled like schoolgirls in the lounge after dinner. Someone made a round of highballs, but Anna behaved and only had one. Even after Lois assured Anna of some foolproof tricks she knew that would rid oneself of an alcohol headache, Anna still resisted. Lois and I retreated to our beds sometime in the early morning, giggling endlessly and shushing each other to keep quiet.

I wasn't at all surprised when the door creaked open and Anna poked her head into the room. She smiled at seeing us awake and quietly closed the door behind her, before tiptoeing across the room and launching herself into my bed.

We fell asleep sometime before dawn.

The next day, Lois couldn't keep herself away from the room where we were getting ready. She offered herself around, helping girls into their dresses and holding a piece of hair here or there. She looked at me with an impressed grin once I was ready and told me the dress really suited me. I did have to admit that it was stunning.

It was sleeveless with a corseted bodice, which ran down into a skirt that flared out at my hips and came down to just past my knees. A satin sash cut across the waist in a darker shade of lavender than the rest of the dress. The hairstylist rolled my long, thick hair into beautiful pin curls and fastened my small lavender hat with its birdcage veil in place.

Even I was impressed with the outcome.

"How are you feeling?" Anna asked from behind me as I stared at the glamorous results in the full-length mirror.

I laughed. "How am *I* feeling?"

Anna smiled. "I know what your nerves are like, little sister."

My heart burst with pride. She was a wonderful sister. I turned around to hug her, taking care not to spoil her dress or hair. "Don't worry about me, Anna."

"I have faith in you, you'll be fine." Anna said, her eyebrows pinching together in concern.

"Hey," I said with a soft laugh. "Shouldn't I be the one to calm you down?"

Anna smiled. "Probably. But we've never played by the traditional rules, have we?"

"No, I guess not." I hugged her again. "You look beautiful, Anna. I'm so proud of you."

* * * *

Unable to resist, I opened a side door a tiny crack to sneak a look at the mass of people who had come to watch the wedding.

And immediately wished I hadn't.

Nerves tumbled in my lower belly as I saw more people than I'd reckoned on being present. And... Lord. I had to walk down the aisle in front of them all. I'd known the number would be high—I just didn't think it would that high. I doubted even Anna knew the exact number. I guess Mom had gotten carried away with the guest list...

It was hard to pick out a few familiar faces among the mass of strangers. Scanning the rows upon rows, I was in awe of my mother. Surely she didn't know all these people. She must have sent an invitation to the entire phone book!

My body jolted as I caught sight of someone I recognized in the back pew. He looked bored and was having his ear chewed off by the man sitting next to him. *What are they doing here?* Mother must know one of their families. She had to, for them to be here. *Just what I need, another reason to make me nervous.*

I scolded myself. What did it matter if he was here? It shouldn't make me any more nervous... So why did it?

I didn't even know the man! And what I knew of him, I thoroughly disliked. It might have been easier to detest him were he not so attractive.

Maybe that's why he irritated me so much... Because I did find him attractive.

I narrowed my eyes at him from behind the safety of the door. Stupid man. Stupid, stupid man with stupid floppy hair that flopped into his stupid, beautiful eyes. Stupid.

Luck was on my side as I walked down the aisle without so much as a single stumble. As Anna and Kenneth said their vows, it took all my effort to keep my eyes on them.

I was determined not to let him know I was aware of his presence. Who was I kidding, anyway? He probably didn't even remember me. It had been six months, after all. I let that thought comfort me and prayed I was right.

So why, then, did the back of my neck burn, as though there were one set of eyes in particular, focused solely on me?

* * * *

By the time the meal had ended and the first dance was completed, I was more than ready for some fresh air...and a break from the festivities. Mom kept an eagle eye on me throughout the dance, as though she suspected I'd embarrass her at any moment.

Which, if I was honest, I sorely wanted to do, but not for her benefit.

Sandy, my dance partner, was a new breed of vile. His hand wandered to the extreme of my lower back and bordered on inappropriate. I wanted to stomp on his foot as hard as I could with my heel, but instead I smiled at him, sickly sweet, and gritted my teeth. If it weren't for the fact that we, among the other first dancers, had the attention of almost every person in the room, I'd gleefully abandon him mid-dance.

Fortunately, the dance didn't last forever, and the very second it was socially acceptable, I left the towering oaf standing on the dance floor.

The French doors opened out onto the beautifully lit patio. The cool night air washed over my skin, refreshing and cleansing. I leaned against the railing that overlooked the expansive lawns to the moon reflected in the pond by the golf course, like a bloated silver orb suspended in the sky.

"Penny for your thoughts?"

I jumped at the voice, both from the sudden break in the quiet, and that I knew the owner in a heartbeat. I twisted around and he kept his eyes on me as he leaned beside me against the railing. He shoved his hands in his pockets and I hated that I was already so familiar with the action.

"Are you having a good time?" he asked.

"Does anyone at these things?"

"Some people do. My friend, for instance, can't resist a good wedding." He smiled and pointed back into the ballroom where his friend was flirting with a pretty girl.

I turned to lean my back against the railing, glancing around the guests inside. "Is that why you're here — to flirt with beautiful women?" I asked without looking at him.

"I came here at Paul's request."

"His?" I was surprised by the answer. "Why does he need you here?"

"Some company, perhaps?"

"He doesn't seem too lonely," I mumbled, looking back at Paul, where it seemed he was making good progress with his partner.

"No, he doesn't, does he?" He laughed. "So, how do you know the bride?"

Turning to face him, I arched my eyebrow. If he was friends with Paul, it stood to reason that his family was also somehow familiar with mine, and should therefore know I was Anna's sister... Unless he didn't recognize me from our meeting on New Year's Eve, or the train to Boston.

I must be forgettable.

Disappointment coursed through me and I tried not to let anything show on my face. "The bride is clearly someone you don't know, or you wouldn't be asking that question."

"I don't know the bride, or the groom, for that matter."

I scoffed. "Were you even invited?"

"Yes."

"How so, if you don't know anyone?"

"Paul was invited, and then in turn invited me. But sadly, I've been neglected for most of the evening while he chases pretty girls."

"How tragic." I tried not to smile.

"Can I get you a drink?"

My heart gave an uneven thump and it made me answer pricklier than I would have normally. "I can get my own drink."

"I don't deny that you can't. I simply asked if *I* could."

"No," I said, frowning.

"All right, how about a dance then?"

I was saved from answering by my favorite blonde tornado running into me at full speed and throwing her arms around me.

"How amazing is this thing?" she asked. "I haven't stopped dancing for hours! I need to catch my breath and have a cigarette." Lois popped one in her mouth and lit it, only then noticing I wasn't alone. "Oh, hello."

"Hello," he answered, smiling at the force of nature that was Lois.

She turned to face me again. "Who's this?"

"I have absolutely no idea."

Lois looked back at my companion. "I'm Lois. Who are you, since my friend doesn't know?"

Is she flirting? My skin prickled with irritation.

"I'm —"

"Excuse me, I'm going to get a drink. I'm feeling a little…parched." *Parched? Smooth, Barb, real smooth.*

Instead of hitting the bar, I headed for the back of the room and sat as far away from everyone as I could. The conversation outside had rattled me, not unlike the time he'd sought me out on the train, and I wasn't in the mood to have polite chitchat with anyone.

My mother must have had me on her radar, as my butt was barely in my chair when she descended on me.

"What do you think you are doing?" she asked in a quiet voice that I knew meant she wasn't happy.

I lifted my eyebrows. What did she *think* I was doing? "Nothing, I'm just sitting."

"Precisely! Do you think opportunities like these happen every day?"

"What opportunities?" I asked with a frown.

"Look around you — all the eligible bachelors from the state are here tonight. So many are showing interest in you, and what are you doing? Hiding at the back of the room like a sullen little girl."

"Mom, for goodness' sake, my head is pounding from all the people I've talked to. I'll have blisters the size of pancakes on my feet tomorrow with the amount of dancing I've done. You can't say I haven't made an effort tonight, because I have."

Mom sighed as if she was all at once exhausted with me. "I am sick of arguing with you, Barbara. I hoped seeing your sister get married today would inspire you."

I swallowed the thick lump of anger that burned in my throat. Now wasn't the time to lose my temper, but Lord help me, I'd had enough. "I've told you I'm not going husband shopping just to please you. If someone comes along who I genuinely like, maybe it'll happen in the future. *In the future*, okay? I'm happy just as I am."

My mother stood like a statue, her lips smashed together. "Stop acting like a brat and make an effort. I expect to see you on that dance floor in five minutes."

I glared at her as she stomped away from me. At this rate, I was going to end up marrying some idiot just for a quiet life.

Stubbornness had always come naturally to me, so instead of doing what I was told like a good little girl, I stayed glued to my seat. Time crept by and I don't know how long I sat by myself. Mom didn't come looking for me again, a small mercy.

A drink slid in front of me and I didn't need to turn around to know who was there. "Looks like you could do with it more than me," he said.

I took a sip of the drink, a good vintage Scotch.

It was a few moments before he spoke again, his voice softer, less teasing than it had been before. "These occasions can be fairly overwhelming most of the time."

"No kidding." My voice sounded foreign to me. It was robotic, automatic, no life behind it.

"How about a dance?"

Is he serious? I couldn't believe he had the nerve. I stood up and whirled around to face him. "How dare you!" I burst, becoming angrier with each passing second. "What is it with you men? I mean really, did you think I would agree? Were you hoping I was one of those depressed bridesmaids who would be over the moon at some man paying attention to her? Guess again, friend. I don't care that I'm not the one getting married. I'm glad it's not me. The idea of spending eternity with one of you fools is enough to turn one into an alcoholic! You saw me sitting here and thought I was an easy target, a few sweet words and I would fall to your feet in gratitude."

If he was startled by my outburst, he didn't let it show. "Actually, I was on my way back to my seat, which you're sitting in, by the way, when I saw you and figured you needed distracting."

I folded my arms across my chest and glared at him. "And why would you be able to distract me?"

He smiled, showing lovely straight, white teeth. "It worked, didn't it? You're not thinking about whatever it was anymore, are you?"

He's right... Damn it. Some of the raw anger bled from my veins. "No, I'm thinking about how you have a very annoying habit of popping up everywhere." I waved a hand in his direction.

"So it worked."

"What worked?"

"My distraction."

My cheeks burned with renewed frustration. "You — You're nothing but a pest!"

He laughed.

"Don't laugh at me."

"I'm sorry, I can't help it." He tried to swallow his laughter. "Are you sure I can't tempt you with a dance?"

Does he never give up? "Hell itself will freeze over before I dance with you."

"Ah–ha! I found you!"

I cringed at the obnoxious, booming voice behind me. Jeepers, this was not my night. Fixing a smile on my face, I turned to greet someone else I'd rather have avoided. "Hi, Sandy."

"I think it's time for you and I to have that second dance," he said as he loomed over me, invading my space.

I took a step backward to put some distance between us and bumped into a chest. Thinking on my feet I said, "Actually, I just agreed to a dance, sorry." I'd likely live to regret my words, but in that moment, one man was considerably more desirable than the other.

"Sorry, friend, what can I say? I must be the lesser of two evils." He stepped between us and offered me his hand, his lips twitching in amused victory.

I shot him a poisonous look. There was no other alternative but to take his hand and let him lead me onto the dance floor. He didn't take us to the center as I thought he would. Instead, he chose a spot on the outskirts of the crowd, which backed into a secluded corner. Less of an audience and considerably more private.

The music slowed to a more intimate number and a shiver crept up my spine as he placed his hand on my waist and drew me closer to his body. I lightly held his shoulder, feeling the strength even through his tux.

"Did you bring your ice skates?" he asked, taking one of my hands and holding it to his chest.

"Excuse me?"

"Hell froze over, remember?"

I narrowed me eyes. "I'm only doing this because Sandy is a disgusting man who lets his hands wander."

"I know. I can still enjoy the moment anyway." He smiled and closed his eyes.

Good Lord, I could murder him. "Well, don't." I huffed. "You're quite possibly the most annoying man I've ever had the displeasure of meeting."

"So you do remember we've met before?" he asked. "I couldn't tell."

That meant that he also remembered me. A flutter began in my belly and I wished I could reach inside and swat them away. I gave him my sickly sweet smile. "I tried my hardest to forget, but you were such a pest it seems you made a lasting impression."

"I like that I've been on your mind." His smile widened at the shock on my face. "What were you thinking about before?"

I hadn't realized my deep thinking had been so obvious. "Nothing important. Nothing that would interest you."

"Try me," he said softly.

I sighed. How much to tell? I didn't have the energy to get into my fight with Mom all over again. Nor did I want a perfect stranger to know what the relationship between us was like. "I was just thinking how I thought, for today at least, that my mother would leave me be. Instead, she just harassed me even more."

"She does that a lot? Harass you?"

I laughed bitterly. "A lot? What an understatement."

"What does she harass you about?"

"Marriage. My life choices. *Me*," I said.

He was quiet for a few moments as though contemplating my words. "I think sometimes the people who should know us best actually know us least of all. You'll find your people, I promise you."

I couldn't help it, a small smile made its way onto my lips and I felt warmed all the way to my toes. "Thanks." I didn't notice right away that we had stopped moving. The band announced they were taking a short break and the dance floor began to empty.

"No problem," he said, returning my smile. "So, since I saved you from a fate worse than death dancing with Grabby Hands, do I get to know your name?"

I laughed only because he didn't know just how right he was. "I suppose that isn't too much to ask. You first."

"Van Judson."

"Barb Howell."

So he knew my name, and I knew his.

We were no longer strangers.

Just as he had at New Year's, he kissed my hand and said, "Thank you for the dance."

Chapter Five

Lois stayed with my aunt Evelyn and me the week after the wedding at Yellow Sands and she enjoyed it thoroughly. She wasn't short of suitors and had a date almost every night. I chose to remain elusive as usual, staying in my room and reading. My mother returned home with my father the day after the wedding, so I was free to be as boring as I liked.

The days were spent with Lois swimming and playing tennis, and in the evenings, after dinner, I got to be alone. Something I rarely got to enjoy. We parted ways in New York at the end of the short week, with Lois going back to her family's home and me going to stay with Evie in the city. We would see each other in the fall as sophomores.

I loved staying with Evie. She was beautiful and fun loving and always had some glamorous place to rush off to. In a lot of ways, she'd felt more like an elder sister to Anna and me.

Evelyn would usually arrange a few dates for me over the summer months, and I'd long suspected it was because Mom nagged her almost as much as she nagged me. So when she arranged dates for me, I went on them…but she never complained when I didn't see them again. Which, generally speaking, suited both parties just fine. The only thing the rich New York boys were interested in was themselves — that and money, of course. They vested very little interest in me, and I knew why. Those types of boys would marry the purest of stock, and the type of girls who had little or no opinions.

I was far too highly spoken for them to waste any time on.

Evelyn herself had never remarried. I think she felt too much sorrow in the loss of her husband. She didn't need to remarry — she was financially taken care of. And in my mother's opinion, that was what an independent woman was. It didn't matter if she were intelligent, only that she had the finances to help her along her way.

Halfway through the summer, Lois surprised me with a long-distance phone call. "Have you met any cute boys?"

"You're calling me to ask me about boys?"

"Would you expect anything else?" She laughed. "So answer the question!"

"Well, I met one boy called Thomas Gentry. He seems nice enough, but I can't figure him out," I said with a weary sigh. The Gentrys were longtime friends of Evelyn's, and it had always been Mrs. Gentry's wish to set me up with her son, a junior at Georgetown University, but for some reason or other, we were never in the city at the same time.

Until this summer.

Thomas routinely invited me out again and again, but there was something about him I couldn't quite put my finger on.

"Tell me more," Lois said and I could hear the smile in her voice.

"Well, he's a perfect gentleman. Too perfect. He takes me to really busy places where there's no chance of being alone. He doesn't tiptoe around me or shower me with compliments."

"Sounds like your perfect man."

I laughed. "No, he doesn't interest me that way. The only thing I feel toward him is curiosity."

"How so? Maybe he's just shy."

"No, there's definitely something strange about him." I frowned. "He took me to dinner with his parents."

"Wow! Sounds serious to me."

"Tell me about it," I mumbled. "But if you saw how he acts, you wouldn't be saying that. He can barely be bothered to be on the date we're on, yet he always arranges another at the end of the night."

"Any goodnight kisses? I get a better idea of them after a goodnight kiss."

Typical Lois Dubbs answer. I laughed. "Of course you do, Lois. But no, he hasn't even attempted to hold my hand. Normally this would thrill me, but there's something about him I just can't put my finger on."

"How was the mother at dinner?"

"Oh my God, you should have seen her." I rolled my eyes. "She was so happy I was there, I honestly thought she was going to kiss my feet."

Lois giggled. "Hmm, I can't imagine what his secret is. Maybe I should come visit for the weekend. I could seduce it out of him."

"No, that's okay." I shook my head. "I'll find it out soon enough."

* * * *

Shortly after talking with Lois, I grew tired of the strange game I was playing with Thomas. I stopped returning his phone calls and declined every offer he made. Evelyn didn't comment on my sudden change of heart—or mind—over Thomas, but my aunt had clearly told my mother about my dates with Thomas. She became considerably pleasanter in her letters and when we spoke briefly on the phone.

After a week of avoiding him, Thomas showed up at the apartment. My aunt showed him in and offered him coffee, then left us alone.

"I came to apologize," he said, looking at his hands. "My behavior, it was unacceptable."

I narrowed my eyes at him. "How so? You always behaved like a perfect gentleman."

"That's precisely what I mean. I acted with decorum, and at times, with too much. I understand my behavior is confusing, but I have enjoyed spending my time with you. By way of a peace offering, I would like to invite you to a party this evening."

I was unsure of what to do. I knew I had no romantic feelings for him, but he did intrigue me. And the more energy I focused on discovering his secret, the less time I thought about the elusive Van.

Van.

I shivered as I thought his name and mentally shook myself. He was still under my skin, his words from the wedding played in my head, though I wished they wouldn't. I forced myself to focus on the present before I became angry and vented on poor Thomas. "What kind of party?"

"My cousin's engagement party at the Plaza."

I deliberated for a moment. "All right, I'll go."

Thomas gave an odd smile and I couldn't tell if he looked relieved or not. Maybe a little. "I'll pick you up at eight." He stood and let himself out.

So I'd agreed to yet another date with him. I'd never courted someone so often like this before and now I knew why.

It was far too confusing.

* * * *

My aunt's reaction when I stepped out of my bedroom told me I had chosen the right dress. It was very fine black material, button down with a plunging neckline. It hugged my figure and made my already long legs appear longer. Thomas, however, looked neither impressed nor unimpressed, adding yet more confusion. He himself was handsome in his black tux, his white-blond hair slicked back.

He helped me out of the cab and offered his arm as we walked into the lavish party. People flocked to our sides, complimenting us and saying what an attractive couple we made.

We danced a little, mingled a little more. He retrieved glasses of punch and lit my cigarettes. Thomas was being more attentive than he had ever been and I decided to keep close tabs on him, but in the end I didn't have to. He barely left my side. "It's almost midnight and this party is showing no signs of slowing down," Thomas commented as the band started another song.

"I guess your cousin is in the mood to celebrate."

When Thomas didn't reply, or even comment, I lifted my head to look at him. His eyes were pinned on something near the staff entrance.

"Thomas?"

He snapped his head back. "Yes?"

"Are you okay?"

Thomas nodded, but was still distracted. He glanced around again and his face lightened. "There's Dad, we'd better say hello."

Thomas led me over to his father who stood with a few other important-looking men. He smiled at our approach then dipped his head to kiss my cheek.

"Barbara, you look stunning as always," Mr. Gentry said.

"Thank you."

"Hey, Dad, why don't you take Barb for a spin on the dance floor? My feet could use the break." Thomas winked at his father and I had to swallow the bite of annoyance. *Oh yeah, because it was* my *idea to dance until my toes dropped off.*

"Excellent idea, Thomas." Mr. Gentry extended his hand. "Shall we?"

With no other option but to muster up my sincerest fake smile, I accepted Mr. Gentry's hand and let him pull me back onto the dance floor that I'd clocked more time on than the happy couple themselves.

"I must say, Thomas' mother and I are very happy that he has found a nice girl like you."

I caught sight of Thomas as he weaved through the crowd, making his way to the staff entrance that had captivated his attention so thoroughly minutes before. "Yeah, he's a good friend."

Mr. Gentry chuckled. "I think Thomas has a little more than friendship on his mind."

Thomas disappeared through the double swing doors.

"Oh, I don't know. We're both young. No need to rush into anything serious."

"Don't let my wife hear you talking like that. She's practically chosen your china patterns."

His words left a sour taste in my mouth and I tried to steer the conversation away from the future Thomas' parents seemed to be mapping out for us.

When the dance finished, I all but ripped out of Mr. Gentry's hold. "Excuse me, I need to freshen up." Knowing I had to move quickly, I went through the same doors Thomas had just a few minutes before. It was dark as I crept down the narrow corridor and I could barely see where I was going. I turned corner after corner and wondered where I would end up.

Murmured voices drifted through corridor to reach me. I held my breath as I moved quietly. It was then I found him.

Slightly obscured from view by a stack of crates, he whispered to someone, leaning in and stroking their face—the entire exchange screaming with intimacy. *How rude!* Here I was, his date for all intents and purposes, and he was seducing some waitress. A breathy laugh escaped the lips of his companion and it made me gasp.

No, it can't be...

I clamped a hand over my mouth to silence myself. I retreated as quietly as I could and rejoined the party. My mind was a whirling dervish and I couldn't organize my thoughts. *Did I really see that?*

There had been whisperings of a gentleman back home, a lifelong bachelor who spent most of his time with another man. Rumors spread about them like wildfire and there was even an occasion when we saw one of them on the street. Mom crossed to the other side, tugging me along behind her with so much force she almost pulled my arm from its socket.

It wasn't something we talked about. The subject of a different kind of love was taboo in our house... Was Thomas really —

Maybe I'd misread the situation. It had been dark, after all. Though it would explain some of his behavior, why he seemed determined to have me in his life despite his seeming indifference.

It was some twenty minutes before Thomas found me again, mumbling his apologies that he got caught up with an old friend. I shot to my feet as he approached the table. "I'm tired. I want to go home," I said, my voice colder than I intended as I avoided his eyes.

He shot me a puzzled look, but nodded and gathered our things.

"What did you think you were doing tonight?" I asked him the second we were outside and away from prying eyes.

"What do you mean?" Thomas gave me a baffled look.

"I followed you down that corridor," I said, dropping my voice. "You know what I saw." Lifting my eyes, I scanned his face, waiting for any sign that what I saw really was true.

Thomas' expression slackened, as though all the fight had drained out of him. "I never meant any harm toward you, truly I didn't," he said, his voice breaking on the last word.

My eyes widened at the raw emotion he showed. It was like seeing him for the first time — the real Thomas Gentry. "Then what were you doing? Why the charade?" I asked, softening my voice.

His shoulders curled inward. "I didn't mean to lead you on, Barb, I swear. You're a wonderful person and I never meant to hurt you."

"You didn't hurt me, don't worry about that." I laughed in surprise. "I never had feelings for you, you vain oaf! And I don't care who you are *really* sweet on. It's the lying that upsets me."

"How could I have told you the truth? What would I have said?" He darted a look around me and leaned in to say under his breath, "Hi, my name is Thomas and I'm a queer. How about a date?"

Despite myself, I snorted a short laugh. "It certainly would have made an impression." Shaking my head, I placed my hand on his arm. "I just don't understand. What on earth were you doing with me?"

Thomas flashed me a sheepish smile. "Well, your reputation is well-known for being a man hater. I thought if you sensed I didn't pose a threat, you might keep going out with me." Thomas paused, giving me an apprehensive look. "But you have to admit, it worked out well for the both of us."

"How so?"

"It's no secret what your mother is like. I can only imagine she's a little more pleasant now you have a man on the scene. And my mother and father are happier now. They're delighted that I found you. Don't you see, Barb? This is the perfect situation for the both of us."

His meaning sank in. I looked down, self-pity washing through me. So this was the only way a man would want me. To pretend to be his girlfriend. The irony was not lost on me. Maybe this was what I deserved for being so headstrong.

"Look, I love that man," Thomas said with passion in his voice. "I love him more than life itself, but I'm terrified of being found out. My parents would shun me. I would disgrace my family. They nag me about settling down and finding a nice wife. Since we started spending time together, they've backed off."

I shook my head again, my mind swimming. "Thomas, this is how people get hurt. Maybe not you or I, but think of that poor man you claim to love. How must he feel to watch you out in the open with me, and skulking in the shadows with him?"

Thomas had the decency to look ashamed. "I'm aware it isn't the perfect situation. But even if we continued for the rest of the summer, that would buy me enough time. I'll be back at school in the fall and free from my parents for another year."

I could sympathize all too well with him. I was quiet for a few moments, trying to find a reason to deny him. When I couldn't find one, I sighed. "All right. Until the end of the summer. But then that is it, Thomas. I mean it."

Thomas nodded, a genuine smile lighting up his face. "You won't regret this, Barb."

Something told me I probably would.

We agreed to continue as we had been and it suited both of us to a certain extent. He would pretend to be with me on some evenings, and sneak off to be with his real love interest. And I would pretend to be smitten with him in front of everyone. I knew my mother would feel victorious at my courting Thomas, but it wasn't about her and I wouldn't spoil things for Thomas simply so I could hurt my mother.

I didn't even tell Lois his secret. I reasoned it wasn't my secret to tell. She pestered me to tell her, of course, but I told I hadn't figured it out yet.

Come the end of the summer, we had a heartfelt goodbye. I managed to cry real tears as we parted ways, a relationship no longer possible since our schools were hundreds of miles apart. He thanked me for my efforts during the charade and I wished him the best of luck with anything the future brought. He hinted at a reunion next summer, but I remained vague. I couldn't imagine committing to such a project again. We would keep in touch for although we were not romantically inclined to each other, I had made a good friend in Thomas. He told me how relieved he was at my knowing his secret, some weight lifted off his heavily burdened shoulders. I was glad to have helped him.

And so fall was here again. I stood waiting at the station for my train to Boston, and Van's face flickered past in my mind. Maybe it was because of the familiar setting of the year before. I was re-reading Dante's *Inferno* and planned to finish it on the train home. It was unintentional, but it reminded me of him all the more. I wondered if he were thinking of me, wherever he was. Thinking of the strange, rude girl he kept bumping into. I casually wondered if he was as annoyed by me as I was by him. I hoped so.

Chapter Six

I stood outside the dorm and took a deep breath of wonderful Wellesley air—full of knowledge and freedom. Had it been only a year ago I'd stood on these very steps and felt fear? A smile teased my lips. How good it was to be *home*! I ran up the steps, eager to get back to my version of normal.

Lois arrived later in the day. I heard her coming—she belted out *All Hail to the College Beautiful* at the top of her lungs as she approached our room. She threw the door open and struggled to get the last line out past her laughter. Dropping her suitcase at her feet, Lois marched over to hug me. "How good it is to be back!"

I nodded my agreement and squeezed her tight. "That was one long summer."

"Tell me about it," she said, rooting around in her pocketbook. Saving her the search, I tossed my cigarette pack at her, and she grinned. "You know me so well. So how was it? Did you figure out Mr. Gentry?"

Before leaving New York I'd decided that I definitely wouldn't talk to Lois about Thomas' secret. It would be hard as I told the girl just about everything. I shrugged. "More or less. He was a nice guy."

"And? Is a future on the cards?"

I fought back a laugh. "No. Definitely not."

Lois grinned. "I see the old Barb hasn't gone too far. I was expecting a different woman to greet me after you had a summer of love." She pinged a rubber band at me when she caught me rolling my eyes. "Have you heard about the common room?"

"No, what about it?"

"We get the use of one now, strictly for sophomores." Lois' eyes gleamed. "Some of the girls have already hid liquor behind the wall panels."

I couldn't disguise my shock as I let out a burst of laughter. "Lois Dubbs! You've only just got here — how is it you have gossip so soon?"

Lois tapped the side of her nose. "Call it an extra sense."

Once Lois had changed, we headed for the common room. It was great to be able to hang out somewhere other than our room. Girls chattered in various corners and cigarettes were passed around freely. I guessed I would be spending a fair amount of time in here.

* * * *

The first semester in my sophomore year was harder, as I knew it would be. But I rose to the challenge and was determined to do my very best. Lois didn't take her studies seriously, as she only had one or two that weren't social, aiming to turn her into a wonderful wife and mother. She hated them and mocked the tutors, but stuck with them.

Lois' parents had refused to allow her to attend college unless it was as a finishing school. So she took the opportunity to be away from home, even if it meant studying how to make the perfect pot roast.

After my summer with Thomas, I started to give men a bit of a chance and wasn't so quick to shoot them down in a blast of annoyance. Thomas had proved that some men could be more interested in my brains than my body, and could be interested in friendship.

Lois loved the change in me and insisted on going on some double dates — and didn't pay a blind of notice to my *friendship* preoccupation. She arranged one for Saturday evening and told me about it only that afternoon. Lois insisted I wear a nice dress and she took the time to do my hair.

She'd been dating Derek for a few weeks, and apparently his roommate was perfect for me. We met the boys at the Lakeside, a fine restaurant in town with food to die for. Not that Lois or I dined there often — I enjoyed the food more than the prices.

The boys were already seated when we arrived. Lois winked at me before kissing Derek on the side of the mouth.

Derek's friend rose out of his chair. Wow. The guy looked like a movie star. He had a million-dollar smile with sparkling white teeth. Glossy brown hair was styled within an inch of its life and his suit was of the latest fashion. He had an olive tone to his skin and stood a head above me. "Hello, you must be Barbara."

"Yes," I said, offering him my hand to shake.

He took it and pulled me toward him, kissing me on the cheek and lingering too long.

It was about then I decided not to like him.

"I'm Charles, it's a pleasure to meet you."

I shot Lois what I hoped was a killer look. She avoided my eyes and turned to Derek, but not before I saw her lips twitch with amusement.

The lovebirds sat closely throughout dinner, their heads pressed together and barely speaking above a murmur. Leaving me to converse with Charles alone.

"So, how's school?" Charles resorted to a safe question, since every other topic he had raised resulted in one-word answers from me.

"Fine." *Well, why change now?*

"Any favorite subjects?"

"A few."

Lois' foot connected with my shin in a none-too-subtle kick and I jumped in my seat. I glared at her, but she hadn't even looked away from Derek. I sighed and forced myself to smile. I'd never hear the end of it otherwise. "Literature and art history are a couple of my personal favorites."

"Oh really? I'm something of an art buff myself. I traveled Europe a few years ago with my family. I favored the galleries in Paris."

Maybe there was more to Charles than I initially thought. "Any particular artists catch your eye?"

"Well." Charles coughed and he fidgeted with his napkin. "Da Vinci, Picasso, Van Gough. To name a few."

I arched an eyebrow at his uncertain tone. "And what pieces of theirs did you like?"

He coughed again. "Oh, there're too many to name. I did enjoy learning about their history, of course."

"The artist's history?"

"Yes."

Leaning an elbow on the table, I rested my hand on my closed fist and peered up at Charles. "I'm writing a term paper on da Vinci's history. Any thoughts you could give me would be wonderful," I said with a bat of my eyelashes.

Lois' attention was caught—probably by my sudden interest in my date, and she and Derek turned to face us.

Charles's face flushed beetroot. I knew I smelled a rat. "Well…"

I couldn't help myself—Charles had set himself up too perfectly for me to resist knocking him down a peg or two. "So, answer me this. What do you admire him more for—being an artist or a mathematician?"

Charles laughed. "Oh, Barbara! He was no mathematician. I think you're getting confused."

I smiled and lifted my water glass. "Actually he was—along with being a writer, an inventor and architect, to name a few. Being so interested in his history, I thought you would have known that."

Charles sipped his drink and gave a nervous laugh. "I'm sorry, did I say da Vinci? I meant Picasso's history. I enjoyed learning about *his*. Though, I always wondered why he cut off his ear."

I clamped a hand to my mouth. Even Lois stared at him with a wide mouth.

Derek stuttered a laugh. "I think we should get the check and call it a night."

"Wonderful idea." I beamed. The best thing I'd heard all evening.

Derek and Charles drove us to the dorm and I kept my back turned while Lois said a very thorough goodnight. But her mood soon soured.

As we walked the hall toward our room, Lois marched ahead of me. "You could have at least been nice to him."

"Lois, he thought *Picasso* cut off his ear! He was such an idiot!"

"Maybe, but he was a *gorgeous* idiot!" she huffed.

I laughed and rushed to match pace with her. Linking my arm with hers, I leaned my head on her shoulder. "I appreciate your efforts, Lois. But next time you think you've found my dreamboat, make sure he isn't full of crap first, okay?"

Lois giggled. She could never stay mad at me for long. "Promise."

* * * *

The fire crackled and the flames danced, casting shadows on the walls. The common room was near deserted as I sat curled in an armchair, reading. Lois burst into the room like the force of nature that she was and collapsed beside me on the chair.

"Can you believe it's almost Christmas?"

I wriggled over, trying to make more room. "I know. I really wish I wasn't going home. Anna's spending the holidays with Kenneth and his family at some cabin in the mountains."

"Sounds...fun?" Lois stifled a laugh. "So it's just going to be you and your folks this year?"

I nodded glumly.

"Why don't I come?"

My face lit up. "Oh, Lois! Do you mean it?"

"Of course, I said last year I would come another time. My folks'll understand." She grinned. "And what kind of friend would I be if I let you face your mother alone?"

I managed to free one arm and threw it around her, almost knocking her to the ground. "You're the best!"

She laughed and held on to me for balance. "Remember that when you're buying my gift."

There was no one else on this green earth like Lois Dubbs — and I was better for knowing her. My little blonde tornado.

However, I should have known my savior would gripe like an irritable bear when faced with the journey to my hometown.

"Does there have to be so many people?" Lois grumbled the second we were on the cramped train.

"I suggested leaving a few days earlier. I recall it was you who procrastinated."

Lois loved Wellesley even more than I did, and hated to leave its safe walls for the outside world. "Can't they turn the heat up?"

"Stop your bellyaching."

She sat chattering her teeth and rubbing her hands together, shooting evil looks at anyone who dared bump her accidentally. I wasn't sure of who was more relieved when we finally got off the train in New York.

"That was definitely longer than the summer," Lois complained.

I sighed and left her to get some warm coffees to sip while waiting for our connection train. I feared this would be the only time Lois would travel home with me, as she clearly hated it. She barely spoke to me on the final train.

* * * *

"Mrs. Howell?" Lois said as she approached my mother in the kitchen the day before Christmas.

"Yes, Lois?"

She clasped her hands in front of her, widened her eyes and appeared far too innocent. "I'm doing housewife studies at Wellesley, and if you wouldn't mind terribly, I was wondering if I could help you prepare lunch tomorrow?"

My mother couldn't have looked more pleased than if I'd announced my own engagement. "Oh, of course you can! That's no trouble at all."

"Are you sure?" Lois asked with a wide smile. "I don't want to be in the way."

"Nonsense, I admire your desire to learn. I'm happy to assist in any way I can. It would be a pleasure for you to help me."

"Thank you, Mrs. Howell." Lois beamed at my mother. Once Mom's back was turned, Lois winked at me before skipping away victoriously, leaving me gaping in her wake.

What a minx.

My mother was so overjoyed by Lois. I think she considered adopting her and sending me to an orphanage. Lois teased me about this, saying I would have to get a job as an Apple Annie to make ends meet. I soon reminded her how much worse my mother was compared to hers, and she stopped the jokes.

* * * *

New Year's Eve, 1940

Lois snuck champagne into my room, which we drank straight from the bottle, giggling as we got ready for the night ahead. She styled my hair for me, creating perfect glory rolls. I could never have sculpted my unruly mane as well as she did.

I wore my new dress—a gorgeous navy pinstriped wiggle piece with a cinched in waist that made my figure look dynamite. Lois encouraged me to wear heels that made my legs seem longer and I knew would help my confidence.

Lois herself looked stunning as usual. She pinned up her hair and wore a very suggestive red dress, giving the impression that she was a Hollywood starlet.

The club was just as busy as it had been a year ago, but we found some empty seats at a table without too much trouble. Lois promised to try her best not to leave me, the way Anna had unconsciously done, but I told her not to be silly, she should enjoy herself. The glint in her eye let me know me she would.

Sometime later, the band played a familiar song we normally heard in the Dragon, and, laughing, we headed for the dance floor where we were each other's partner. We'd danced swing with each other before, so we knew our weights and limits, and it wasn't difficult to pull off a few simple moves. People applauded and a few joined in around us. Lois wanted to keep dancing once the song had ended, but I cried off and let a handsome young man replace me.

I wasn't missed for long.

Sinking into my chair, I fanned myself with my hand and smiled as I watched Lois have a ball.

A glass of neat Scotch was placed in front of me. My heart stuttered and a shiver crept up my spine. I knew those long, elegant fingers. I knew exactly who they belonged to. Taking the time to school my features before turning around, I was surprised, then, when I did, that there was no one there.

Had I read too much into it? Was it an innocent gesture — someone wanting to free his hand and simply forgetting about it?

But try as I might, I couldn't forget that a similar action had been performed that summer, at my sister's wedding.

Growing bored with where I sat, and with my mind going around in useless circles, I wandered the room, chatting to people here and there. I caught up with some girls from high school and shared stories of Wellesley and all her glories.

Before I knew it, midnight drew nearer and Lois showed no signs of slowing down. She was in her element on the dance floor and I guessed she would be there for the countdown to the New Year.

I would be braving it alone then.

Deciding to get a drink to give myself something to do, I pushed my way through the crowd. The bar was jam packed with bodies, and getting the bartender's attention seemed an impossible task.

"Would you like mine?"

In the crush of people, I hadn't noticed him, but even among all the other voices, I recognized his as if I heard it every day.

I squeezed my eyes shut for a beat, willing my racing heart to slow. Van wore his trademark amused smile as I slowly turned to face him.

"You could save yourself a lot of trouble if you just accepted my more than kind offer," he said.

"And you could save yourself a lot of trouble if you just left me alone," I said with a scowl. What was it about this man that brought out the very worst in me?

Not that it deterred him. He laughed. "Is that right? I think I can handle myself all right."

"And so can I."

"I never said you couldn't. Are you this friendly to everyone who tries to lend you a helping hand?"

"No, I save it especially for you."

"It's nice to know I mean so much to you." Van laughed and pushed his glass toward me. "Last chance."

It was a Scotch. I didn't have to taste it to know it would be a good one. It would be a long wait if I were to get my own, but stubbornness stood in my way.

He rolled his eyes. "It's just a drink for chrissakes."

I narrowed my eyes and picked up the glass to take a sip. "I know."

"Wasn't so hard, was it?" he asked, his tone playful.

That was it. The last straw. I'd had enough. Setting the glass down on the bar more forcibly than I'd intended, I swiveled around to face him fully. "What is your problem?"

"What?" he asked, with a blink.

"You have a very annoying habit of showing up places and being very rude to me."

Van's eyebrows shot up and he laughed, quick and loud. "I'm not the one being rude here, that would be you."

My cheeks began to warm, a sure sign of my frustration. No one could throw me off balance quite like Van could. "Well, you deserve it," I said, spluttering.

His smile widened. "Do I? Why is that?"

Oh, he was doing it on purpose. I just knew it. I pointed a finger at him. "You intentionally antagonize me, and don't deny it."

He held up his hands in mock defeat. "Caught me. The reactions are priceless."

"I'm glad I amuse you so much," I mumbled, reaching again for the Scotch. "What are you doing here anyway? You're not a local."

"I was invited."

"Again?"

"Again." Van leaned an inch toward me. "You know, it's only you who thinks of me with such low regard. Everyone else finds me charming."

I snorted—a very unladylike laugh—my mother would be mortified. "I find that hard to believe."

"Somewhat unlike yourself, of course, whom everyone finds unpleasant and hostile." A smile tugged at the corner of his lips.

I gasped. "I am not unpleasant or hostile!"

Van rolled his eyes. "Yes, you are a picture of nicety. But you could prove me wrong."

"And how would I do that?"

"You could dance with me."

I made a show of looking around me. "Why? I don't see Sandy Brock here anywhere."

He pressed a hand to his heart. "You, woman, know how to wound a man."

"Oh, please." I waved my hand in dismissal. "We both know the only reason you want to dance with me is because *I* don't want to."

"No, it's not."

"Then what is?"

"Because, believe it or not, I find *you* somewhat charming."

Confusion washed through me and, underneath, a bloom of pleasure. I shook my head. "I thought I was unpleasant and hostile."

"Maybe that's what I find charming."

My head reeled. This man brought out every prickly aspect of my personality, admitted I wasn't a very nice person, yet still wanted to spend time with me. I was caught between a dozen different emotions— annoyance at myself for letting him get to me, and for giving a terrible impression of myself—annoyance at *him* for deliberately provoking me—and irrevocable gratification that he found me charming.

"So you *will* dance with me?" he asked, startling me.

"What? I never—"

"Great." He smiled broadly. "Shall we?"

"No," I said. *Why am I so persistently stubborn?*

Van sighed and looked as if I'd taken away any future chance he had for happiness. "You shall never know how deep your words wound me."

"Is this guy bothering you, Barb?"

I twisted around to see Tony, a boy I went to high school with, leaning against the bar and glaring at Van.

I smiled and batted my eyelashes. "Always, unfortunately."

Tony hitched his thumb over his shoulder. "Hey, friend, why don't you split?"

"All I did was give her a drink and ask for a dance. She's the one getting overexcited," Van said, not taking his eyes off me.

"I am not—" I started.

"You want to me sort him out, Barb?" Tony asked, still looking at Van.

"What?" *Is he serious? Men! Barbarians, the lot of them.* I sighed and wished I'd never opened my mouth—to either of them. "No, I don't need your help, Tony."

"He's being rude," Tony said.

"No," Van said. "That would be her."

"You better shut that smart mouth of yours, friend."

"Take it easy, she's not a delicate little flower, *friend*."

Well, I can't argue with that.

Tony straightened to his full height. Tony had played football all through high school, and had a good few inches on Van... As well as several pounds of muscle. "I don't like your tone."

"Neither does she, funnily enough," Van said, not looking in the least bit concerned that Tony's face was darkening by the second.

My heart lurched. He was going to get himself a pounding. "You got a death wish or something?" I whispered in a hiss.

Van smiled and winked. "It may have to be you who saves me tonight."

I threw up my hands. "Oh, for goodness' sake! You are the living end!" Turning to face Tony, I said, "Tony, we were just messing, okay? He didn't mean any harm."

He didn't look convinced. Tony balled his hands into fists. "I think he needs to be taught some manners."

Jeepers... This won't end well. "No, he doesn't, now stop it. Didn't your mother ever tell you not to fight with people?"

"She also told me never be rude to a lady."

"What's ladylike about this girl?" Van asked, laughing.

Tony made to lunge for him, but I was in the way. I would have been knocked to the ground, but there wasn't room among the mass of bodies surrounding us.

"Hey!" Van and I shouted at the same time.

Van gripped my elbow, keeping me pinned to his side, his face a mask of anger.

"Step out of the way, Barb. I'm going to finish this clown," Tony said, his eyes locked with Van's.

"*I* am finishing this. Stupid boys!" I exclaimed, wrenching out of Van's hold to turn around and face him. "You, come on." I didn't look back to see if he was following, but I prayed he was. The last thing I wanted was for Tony's temper to get the better of him, and Van's face to pay the price.

"Guess we're even now." Van smiled as he fell into step beside me once we were free of the stifling crowd surrounding the bar.

"What was that?" I paused to look up at him. "Why were you provoking him?"

Van shook his head, his expression turning more serious than I'd ever seen it. "He provoked himself. He wanted to impress you, be the big hero."

I rolled my eyes. "No, he thought you were being an ass, which you were, by the way. He would have floored you, you know." I dropped my gaze to the ground.

"He wouldn't have gotten the chance."

"Because I was in his way!" I laughed as I headed back toward my table.

"I am sorry about that." There was honesty in Van's voice. A contriteness that wasn't there before.

It dissolved the rest of my irritation. "It's not your fault. You didn't try to hit him." We reached my table and I sat down, rooting around in my pocketbook for a cigarette. I handed one to Van, which he accepted as he sat in the empty chair next to me.

Van leaned closer and set the drink he must have grabbed while leaving the bar in front of me. "I admit I did provoke him. But it was his choice to react the way he did. Like I said, he wanted to impress you with his gentlemanly, heroic ways."

"That's not the way to impress and me."

"I know." Van leaned back in his chair.

"You do?" I asked, raising an eyebrow at him.

"Sure. You're not nearly as complex as you think you are."

"I don't think I'm complex. *You*, on the other hand, are a very complex man."

He shook his head and smiled. "Quite the opposite."

"You always talk so cryptically. You keep appearing out of the blue when I least expect it."

"I could appear more regularly if you'd like."

"I didn't say that," I said in a rush. It would kill me to admit just how appealing the thought of seeing him on a more frequent basis was.

Van smirked and dropped his arm along the back of my chair, sending a thrill up my spine. I swirled the Scotch around in the glass before finishing it in one.

"Better?" he asked.

I nodded.

"How are you feeling?"

I frowned, puzzled. "Fine. How are *you* feeling?"

He chuckled. "Fine. Just testing the waters."

"For what?"

"Asking you to dance again."

I laughed. I really had to admire his determination. "What is it with you and dancing? Honestly, what will make you stop asking me?"

"I'll stop asking." Van's smile widened. "When you say yes."

Well, I walked right into that one, I guess. "For goodness' sake," I said with a smile I couldn't suppress. "Then yes, okay? Yes."

He grinned and stood, offering his hand. For a moment, all I could do was stare at it. His hands were nice — and, as I had thought earlier, exactly as I remembered them — strong, with long, thin artistic fingers. Clean fingernails. Soft-looking palms. Looking up into his open face, his expression patient, as though he would wait a lifetime for me, I blushed and slipped my hand into his.

Van loosely clasped my hand as he guided me out onto the dance floor. He raised our hands to his chest and slid his free arm around my lower back. We were closer than we'd been at the wedding — a mutual familiarity between us.

He lowered his head to murmur in my ear, "This is twice now."

"What is?" I asked, ignoring the shiver from having his mouth so close to my skin.

"We've been dancing as the New Year comes in."

"Oh," I said softly.

Van didn't speak again as we danced, simply held me and swayed in slow, confident movements to the music. I closed my eyes and tried to imprint every sensation to memory.

What I wanted to remember most was Van's arm around me, and how secure, how protected, it made me feel. I'd never experienced anything like it in the arms of a man before and a niggling thought at the back of mind kept prodding me, that this was why everyone insisted I find myself a man.

The band finished the song and started their countdown. Van let his arm drop from my back, but kept my hand in his. I could almost see the electricity spark between our fingertips.

I spotted Lois in my peripheral vision, making eyes at the man by her side. Then she threw her arms around his neck and kissed him.

It took me a moment to realize the countdown had finished and it was a brand new year.

Van pulled my attention to him as he once again kissed the back of my hand. It only took an instant, but time seemed to stand still as he held me to the spot with nothing but the power of his eyes.

His soft brown hair flopped onto his forehead, partially shielding his dazzling electric blue eyes. Leaning closer, he touched his lips to the shell of my ear. "Happy New Year. Again."

The cat got my tongue as I stood, speechless. Warmth flooded through me, unfamiliar as it was pleasant.

"Thank you," he said, "for the dance." Van lowered his gaze as he released my hand and backed into the crowd. I watched until he disappeared.

* * * *

The world was quiet as we walked home. My mind was a hub of activity, replaying the events of the night...every word, every touch, exchanged with Van.

"I saw you dancing with that man again." Lois' voice broke the silence around us.

I laughed as if I didn't know what she was talking about. "Which one? I danced a lot."

She smiled. "I know, and your mother would be very proud. You know who I mean—the one from the wedding. It's the same guy as last year, isn't it?"

I was glad it was dark and she couldn't see me blush. "Yeah, one in the same."

"So? Do you like him? Are you going to see him again?"

I laughed. *Like* him? There wasn't a word I could think of that described how I felt about Van. "No, I don't like him. He's the epitome of annoyance. But I have a feeling that I haven't seen the last of him."

"Barb, you know I love you, but why so negative? You obviously have a thing for the guy. Why hurt yourself in denying it?"

"I don't have a thing for him!" I exclaimed. "He sneaks up on me at the most peculiar places—twice now at New Year's in my hometown *and* my sister's wedding. All he does when he sees me is insult me. He called me unpleasant and hostile this evening, and tried to pick a fight with an old friend from high school."

Lois laughed. "And the fact why this man is annoying you so much? Why he's under your skin like this? Sweetie, it's because you like him."

"Stop saying that. I don't like him," I insisted, staring hard at the ground.

Lois sighed as if only humoring me. "Whatever you say, Barb."

I didn't say anything else to her on the walk home.

Like him? Showed how well she knew me, the turncoat.

Chapter Seven

Over breakfast the following morning, Lois took great pleasure in telling my mother about the man I'd met the night before. The same man I had danced with at the wedding, she informed her. I dropped my fork with a loud chink onto the plate in front of me. My expression was the only confirmation my mother needed. Glaring at Lois, I picked my fork up and stabbed it into a helpless piece of bacon. She smiled sweetly back at me.

After breakfast, Lois followed me into my room. She threw a cigarette at me and it bounced off my nose. "At least your mother thinks you've got a sweetheart now," Lois said as she sat at the foot of my bed, smoking. "I've done you a favor."

A favor! I'd never hear the end of it from my mother. Every fortnightly phone call, I'd be pressed for details about my dreamboat. I scowled at Lois.

"It's okay to be scared." Her pretty blue eyes were wide with innocence. "You should take things as slow as you feel comfortable with. He probably already knows you're a virgin."

I grabbed the first thing my hand came into contact with — a pillow — and hurled it at her with all my might. It caught Lois off guard and she fell, sprawling off my bed.

Laughter bubbled out of me, breaking my silence. I didn't think I'd ever forget the sight of Lois lying on my bedroom floor, blonde hair splayed across her face with her legs in the air.

Once she picked herself up, she hugged me and apologized. Not that it was much of an apology. "I'm sorry, Barb. I can't help being right all the time," she said as sincerely as she was capable of.

I huffed and lit my cigarette. And thus ended our one and only feud.

Lois wanted to leave the very next day for college, which suited me fine as I was dying to get back to Wellesley. It was busy when we got to the station, but not as busy as last time. I spent the entire journey with a thick knot of nerves in my belly as I fretted over spotting Van and Paul.

But we made it all the way to Wellesley without seeing either boy.

As we walked up the steps into our dorm, I couldn't tell if I was relieved or disappointed.

* * * *

The attitude around Wellesley was carefree and happy during the week approaching spring vacation, proving that a little bit of sunshine worked wonders on the soul. Most of the girls came from rich families and so were vacationing in warmer climates. I, myself, preferred to stay where I was. And bless her heart, Lois stayed with me. Although I suspected it had more to do with the boy from town she'd been courting the last few weeks.

One particular Wednesday evening, I grew restless. Lois had been out all day with her new love interest, and I was starting to yearn for some human interaction. I decided to be brave and head to the Dragon by myself, something I'd never done.

It was busy as I walked in, but there were a few vacant stools at the bar and I took one in the corner. Joe saw me and nodded and it was moments later when he sat a highball in front of me.

"Where's your partner in crime?" Joe asked, smiling.

I shrugged. "Your guess is as good as mine."

"So you're by yourself tonight?"

"Yup."

He frowned slightly. "Not too smart, Barb."

I narrowed my eyes at him. "Oh, relax. The world isn't going to stop turning just because I'm in a bar by myself."

"Just make sure you get a cab home, okay?"

I rolled my eyes, but smiled. "Sure thing, Dad."

Joe shook his head and laughed, muttering something about headstrong women. He set a basket of peanuts in front of me, which I happily nibbled on. It wasn't long before there was an impressive pile of empty shells to one side of the small basket.

By nine p.m., the bar was lively. I remained seated on my stool, and Joe sat in front of me on his side of the bar and kept me company for most of the night. He had another boy working so he used this to his advantage not to work overly hard. Joe replaced my empty peanut basket with a new full one and I beamed at him.

"Thanks, Joe. Can I get another highball, please?"

"Sure thing, doll." Joe turned to mix my drink, but smiled when he saw a newcomer enter the bar. "Hey, Van! Good to see you!"

My stomach dropped as if I'd launched myself off a cliff with no bottom in sight. It couldn't be… There had to be more than one Van in the Boston area.

But, alas, it appeared there wasn't.

"Hi there," Van said. He stood beside me at the bar and reached over to shake Joe's hand. "How's it going?"

"Good, you?"

"Can't complain. You look busy tonight."

Joe smiled. "Nah, not really. I've seen it worse. I've got Bobby in tonight, leaving me free to keep this lovely lady company."

Van turned in my direction as I popped a peanut in my mouth. I nearly choked on the damn thing. "Well, well," Van said, his smile widening. "What are you doing here?"

"Same thing as you, I imagine." I sipped my highball to soothe my throat.

"Really? You got ditched by your friend for a member of the opposite sex?"

I frowned. "Yes, actually."

Van laughed. "I guess that makes two of us then."

"I guess it does."

Van pointed to the empty stool beside me. "Do you mind?"

"It's a free country."

"Is that a yes in your language?"

I glared at him and went back to the peanuts. I felt as if I didn't fit inside my skin and I wished I'd chosen a nicer dress. There was nothing wrong with the black short-sleeved wraparound with daisy print that I was wearing, but I'd bet the more feminine, figure-hugging dresses that Lois preferred would have made a better impression.

Not that I was trying to impress him.

Shrugging out of his jacket, Van handed it across the bar to Joe. Van kept his scarf on, the chill of the cold night air coming off his body in waves. He took the stool beside me, angling his body toward mine, as Joe placed a Scotch in front of him.

"How's school, Van?" Joe asked as he sat down again.

"Good. Few months left and then I'm done, thank God." Van laughed.

"Amen to that!" Joe toasted him with his own glass. "So what is it with you guys?" Joe asked, looking from Van to me. "Most kids are taking off for break. And you two stay around here? Guess it isn't only the smart kids who go to college after all."

I tossed a peanut at him. "Hey, you're still here."

"I, my dear, am working for my keep. Besides, who would replenish your supply of peanuts if I wasn't around?" Joe asked.

"Yes, yes, I know how invaluable you are," I replied, reaching across the bar to pinch his cheek.

"Seriously, why are you sticking around here?" he asked me with genuine curiosity as he batted my hand away.

"Seriously?" I asked. "I just saw my mother at Christmas. I don't need to see her again until next Christmas." Van and Joe laughed. I don't think they realized just how honest I was being.

"What about you, Van?" Joe asked him.

Van smirked. "Well, the family I've adopted's real son wasn't going home, so I didn't think it would be appropriate for me to go alone."

Joe looked puzzled but didn't ask for any details. Bobby called for Joe at the other end of the bar and he went to see what he wanted.

I watched Van cautiously out of the corner of my eye. He was staring at me. I turned to meet his gaze straight on. "Since when have you cared about being appropriate?" I asked.

"Since when have you cared?" he asked, grinning. His hair flopped onto his forehead and I itched to push it back. It didn't look like he'd styled it tonight, which meant it was all natural. I wondered how it felt.

I huffed and picked up my drink.

Laughing, he said, "Wow, you really are a touchy little thing, aren't you?"

"You tend to bring out that side of me," I said. Which of course he knew.

"So," Van said before sipping his Scotch. "Is your spring vacation as boring as mine?"

I laughed in shock. "My spring vacation isn't boring." Should I have been offended?

Van's eyebrows shot up. "It isn't? You actually like being stuck around here?"

"Why wouldn't I?" It hadn't occurred to me this past week that I was stuck at Wellesley. It was my home...where I belonged.

"Isn't it lonely?"

"No. Lois is here too," I said. "Well, some of the time she is."

"Okay, so you have Lois. What else do you do?"

I shrugged. "Take walks. Read. Study."

"Sounds pretty boring," Van said.

"Maybe to you it is. Not to me. There's this wonderful thing that I dream about more than anything else in the world," I said, leaning my elbow on the bar and propping my head up with my hand.

He seemed to sense my sarcasm and grinned. "And what would that be?"

I sighed, as if I were daydreaming of my most heartfelt dream. "Being left in peace."

Van chuckled. "Is that a hint? Would you like me to leave you in peace?"

"Oh, no," I said, widening my eyes. "I wouldn't like it. I'd love it."

He clutched his chest and leaned back in his stool. "Ouch, that hurts. And here I was thinking we're friends."

My mouth hung open in shock. "Us? Friends? You must be joking!"

He smiled a dazzling, lopsided smile. "Admit it. You look forward to these little meetings of ours."

"These little meetings?" I repeated, my temper rising. These little meetings? How — How on earth was it even possible to describe our interactions as little? To me they were anything but little. After a conversation with Van, my mind reeled and I couldn't help but replay it over and over in my head. Was he only teasing me? Was that what he looked forward to himself — teasing me and watching me get riled up? "Is that what you call it?"

"What would you call it?"

I glowered, once again more annoyed at myself than at him. "A series of unfortunate coincidences orchestrated for the sole purpose of irritating me and for you to go out of your way to be rude."

Van barked out a laugh. "If you weren't such a delicate female, maybe you wouldn't think I was being rude. Maybe you would realize it was banter between friends."

Delicate female! "Now you listen here, you, you — troublesome man!" I said, getting to my feet.

"Hey now, folks, what's all this about?" Joe asked, returning to us and looking between Van and me as though we were about to cause a bar brawl.

"Nothing, Joe," Van said with a smile, seemingly cool and calm while I worked myself into a frenzy. Just like always. "The woman is being deliberately perverse."

I gasped. "I am being nothing of the sort."

He laughed. "Yes, you are."

In that instant I knew I had to get out of there before I embarrassed myself. My reaction to Van, yet again, was puzzling and far too extreme. My manners were atrocious. I picked up my purse and made to storm out of the bar.

That was the plan, anyway.

In my anger and haste to be as far away from him as possible, my shoes tangled with the legs of the stool. Van was on his feet in a heartbeat, his arms wrapping around my waist as he caught me before I would have tumbled to the ground and made even more of a spectacle of myself.

He straightened me as though I weighed nothing at all, and I gripped his forearm, feeling the strong muscle beneath his shirt. Van didn't release me right away. He loosely held me, giving me every opportunity to pull free.

I couldn't seem to find the strength.

Van's bright blue eyes burned into mine. "You all right there?" he asked in a low voice, the sound washing over me.

Every part of me tingled. Our bodies barely touched but I felt him everywhere.

I wanted… I wanted… I had no idea what I wanted, but I knew that I wanted it now.

Pushing away from Van, I stumbled back into my stool. My body was on fire and I needed some distance between us to clear my head. I blew out a breath and reached for my glass, finishing the drink in one gulp. Out of the corner of my eye, I saw Van watching me. "What?" I demanded, frowning at him as I put the glass down a tad heavy-handed.

Van dropped his eyes with a chuckle. "Nothing, I'm just trying to figure something out."

"What's that?" I wasn't sure if I wanted the answer.

"If all women are this moody, or if it's just you."

I huffed at the insult and moved to close the little distance there was between us. "Why do you do this?"

"Do what?" Van asked as he frowned in confusion.

"Torment me like this." I folded my arms across my chest and scowled at him. I would get to the bottom of this if it damn well killed me. There had to be a reason behind his behavior. There had to be. If only so there was a reason behind my reactions.

"Torment you?" he repeated.

"Yes. I seem to be the punch line for all your stupid jokes and I want to know why. It's getting on my nerves and I don't enjoy being ridiculed."

"Barb, I—" Van paused and glanced at the ground before looking back at me, his eyes full of remorse. "I'm sorry. I didn't mean to make you feel that way. I thought it was fun because we seem to have a great rapport. No one argues with me like you do."

"Well, no one aggravates me like you do."

He smiled. "It's only because I know what buttons to push."

"I can't argue with that," I murmured. I sighed, all at once tired and more than ready to call it a night…before I did anything to embarrass myself. Again. Turning to Joe, I said, "Can I get that cab now, please?"

"Wait, let me walk you," Van said, touching my elbow. He looked at Joe and reached under the bar for his jacket and mine. "She doesn't need one."

Van shoved his arms into his own jacket, and held mine up for me to step into. I paused for a second, surprised by the action. Although I didn't know why, it was a perfectly normal thing to do. Snapping out of the confusion, I turned, letting him help me into my coat. Van held the bar door open for me, still being the perfect gentleman.

We walked side by side in deafening silence as we headed out into the cool night air. I didn't need to give him any directions, Van knew exactly where to go. It could have been innocent—maybe he was simply familiar with the town. But I had a different theory.

"Should I presume that you've done this before?" I asked with a smile.

"Walked you home?" he guessed with a raised eyebrow.

"No, but walked someone home. To Wellesley."

Van smirked and jammed his hands in his pockets. "I've been known to escort a Wellesley girl home on the odd occasion. Not unlike this occasion, might I add."

"Do you know a lot of Wellesley girls?" I asked, wondering why I cared.

He shrugged. "A few, I wouldn't say a lot. I'm not courting any of them, if that's what you're asking."

"I wasn't. Asking, I mean," I said, thankful that it was dark and he couldn't see my blush.

I dug my hands farther into my pockets and wished I'd dressed warmer.

"Here." Van put his hand on my arm to stop me. He took off his scarf and wrapped it around my neck. It was warm from his body heat, and smelled just like his cologne. It was intoxicating and made my head spin.

I lifted my eyes to meet his. His gaze was penetrating and all consuming. There was something of a promise in that look, as if he knew something I didn't and was just waiting for me to catch up. "Thank you," I said quietly.

"I may not be the devil incarnate after all." He grinned and rubbed the back of his neck.

"Maybe not," I agreed. "But one of his minions at the very least."

Van laughed.

We walked the rest of the way in silence, but it wasn't uncomfortable. It felt odd to walk on this dark night with Van. I was so used to arguing with him it was almost peculiar not to wait for his next teasing comment.

Wellesley loomed up into the dark sky. Lights from the pathway and windows lit up her high walls in a menacing manner. It was never a sight that made me afraid. I knew every part of her, every secret, every whisper.

"So, you're really not bored here? Not at all?" Van asked, motioning toward Wellesley.

I shook my head. "I like it when it's this quiet. Lois is here too, remember? Sure, she's out with her boyfriend a lot, but I don't mind."

Van shifted his weight. "Because, if you ever wanted to do anything, with me I mean, we could. Do that. Do something. Sometime."

I frowned. Was he asking me out? And if he was, why did that make my stomach dip and flutter?

"I don't mean a date, of course," Van said in a rush, taking a step closer to me. "Just if you wanted some company or even a ride somewhere, you know."

Definitely not a date then. That was a relief. So why am I disappointed? I forced a smile. Poor guy probably felt sorry for me, pictured me whittling away the hours in Wellesley's great hallways with nothing but the portraits for company. "I think I'll be all right. Anyway, thank you for walking me."

"It's no problem," Van said. His eyebrows pinched together. Was he disappointed? Lord, I needed Lois. She was far better at deciphering men than I was.

"I'll see you around? You do have a habit of showing up, after all."

"Right," he said, smiling wider. "So, goodnight."

A couple walked past us, huddled close together before sharing a tender embrace right in front of us. I dimly recognized the girl — a senior. Van and I looked away from them, and from each other. I felt embarrassed, but I didn't know why. We were intruding on this couple's moment.

Flushing scarlet, I gave Van a smile and an awkward wave before I darted around the couple — who didn't look as if they cared we were getting a free show — and walked into the grounds, nodding to the night watchman.

Why did I feel relieved once I was back in the safety of my little room?

I took a deep breath and leaned against the closed door. Shaking my head, I tried to shed the itchy, restless feeling that crawled over my skin. I peeled off my jacket and crossed the room to my closet, stopping to pause in front of the mirror. There was an odd flush on my cheeks, a rosy glow that didn't come from the cold air.

It was then I noticed the foreign item still wound around my neck. Van's scarf remained where he placed it. I unwound it carefully, trying to ignore the gentle stirring of his scent from the small movement.

As I undressed for bed, I couldn't get rid of the smile from my lips. He seemed different tonight, more sincere perhaps. Or was it me who was different? Had I lowered part of my solid brick wall barrier and been able to see past the rude behavior and realize it was just banter between friends after all? Questions taunted me as I fell asleep. Questions I had no answers for, but kept asking nonetheless.

Chapter Eight

The morning after Van walked me home, I woke up just as confused as when I'd fallen asleep. Lois snored in her narrow bed beside mine, and a huge part of me wanted to shake her awake and voice all the thoughts rattling around in my brain. When she woke and asked me how my night was, I opened my mouth to tell her exactly what had happened.

But nothing came out.

How could I ask Lois for advice, even vocalize what I was feeling...when I had no idea how to even put it into words?

So I told her it had been a quiet night in the Dragon, and I'd come home early. The words had barely left my mouth when she launched into a rundown of her own evening. It seemed this new boy in Lois' life was making an impression with my crazy friend.

I decided that morning not to repeat my actions of the night before, and started to avoid the Dragon at all costs. Lois was becoming less and less available in the evenings anyway, so it wasn't really a problem to keep it from her. I told myself it was only for the duration of spring vacation.

Surely Van would be too preoccupied with his own schoolwork by then, wouldn't he?

In the end, avoiding the Dragon hadn't been necessary. I'd taken myself on a walk into town one afternoon, and met him walking toward me.

On seeing me, Van's mouth split into a wide, surprised smile. "Well, hello there."

"Hello," I said, unable to stop my answering smile. Or ignore the butterflies in my belly. "What are you doing here again?"

"I was going for lunch with a friend but I got dumped at the last minute."

"So you're going by yourself?"

Van nodded. "I have reservations, so I may as well. I have to eat after all."

"That's too bad. Where are you going?"

"The Lakeside," Van said. "Would you like to come with me? Save me the embarrassment of eating alone?"

I hesitated, the butterflies working up to a tornado. "Um, okay, thanks. That would be nice."

Van's smile widened and he laughed. "Wow, that was unexpected. It normally takes quite a few attempts to persuade you to do anything with me."

I smiled. "Would you like me to change my mind? It could be arranged very easily."

"No, that's all right," Van said in a rush. "Do you need to do anything first? Can we go now? The reservations are soon and I'm starved."

"Now is fine."

We walked in easy silence to the restaurant. I hadn't been since the disastrous double date with Lois, but I had a feeling this time would be better. The sun shone high in the sky and I enjoyed the delicious rays warming my face and shoulders as we sat in the decked area beside the lake.

I glanced around the handful of couples occupying the restaurant, and smiled to one in particular. I wondered who they were, why they were there. Were they confused by their date as I was?

For our meal, Van recommended the steak, and I went with his advice. He had been right. Each morsel was delightful, succulent, pleasing to my ever-grateful tongue. My knife slid through the vegetables like butter and I continued eating long after I was full.

We fell into companionable silence as we let our food settle. I dug around in my purse for a cigarette. I offered one to Van and he took it.

"Another drink?" Van asked as he tipped the wine bottle up and found it empty.

"I really shouldn't," I said. "I don't do very well with drinking wine."

He nodded and asked the waitress for a soda for me and a scotch for him.

The sun had begun its slow decent to the ground when the time made itself known. I couldn't believe I'd lost track, and was surprised at how easy it was to be around Van…now that I realized he wasn't trying to ridicule me at every opportunity, and I wasn't taking offense to everything that came out of his mouth. Instead, I found he was smart and very charming. He seemed genuine and interested in the things I had to say, asking in-depth questions and listening attentively.

He remained elusive when it came to his own background, dodging questions and answering them with questions of his own. I didn't pry too much, as I knew how irritating it was for me when people didn't know when to leave well enough alone.

The sun almost disappeared from sight when I first shivered. The thin sweater draped over my bare shoulders proved insufficient against the rapidly cooling air. I'd lost hours and hours that afternoon sitting with Van, though it was as if five minutes had past. I halfheartedly rose from my seat. "Well, I should get going."

"Can I give you a ride?" Van asked, standing also. "I left my car in town. I could give you a ride from there."

"No, it's fine, really. I told Lois I might drop into the Dragon anyways."

"Right," Van said, his smile not as sure as it had been a few minutes before. He disappeared inside the restaurant to take care of the check and I loitered out front.

Time had gone too quickly. As we walked back into town, I found myself purposely dawdling, trying to stretch out the last few minutes I had with him. We reached a crossroads and both paused.

"My car is that way." Van pointed to his left.

"I'm going that way." I pointed to my right. *Get it together, Howell!* I didn't want this — whatever *this* was — to end, so why wasn't I doing everything to ensure it didn't? I inhaled sharply and clenched my hands into fists. "Do you want to come for a drink?" I asked, my stomach fluttering. "To let me say thank you for lunch, I mean."

"Hey, you did me the favor, remember?" Van said, giving me a lopsided smile. "But, I don't think I could refuse, even if I wanted to."

I flushed with pleasure and couldn't stop from releasing a relieved breath. Van grinned at my response and jerked his head in the direction of the Dragon.

Lois was sitting in a booth with a man I didn't recognize when we arrived. She looked up and spotted us. "Barb! Over here!" she yelled across the bar, waving us over. Lois rose to kiss me on the cheek as I reached her.

"How long have you been in here?" I asked her, sliding into the booth.

Lois giggled. "A while."

Van touched my shoulder and hitched his thumb to the bar. "Usual?"

I smiled. "Yes, please."

He glanced at what Lois and her companion were drinking, and made his way to get us drinks.

Lois, thankfully, waited until he was out of earshot before turning her Cheshire Cat grin my way. "Well, well, what have you been doing all day?"

A blush made its way onto my cheeks. "We went for lunch."

Lois laughed. "Barb! Lunchtime ended hours ago!"

I shrugged. "So? We were talking."

"About?"

"Lots of things."

"Like?"

"My annoying roommate who asks too many questions."

Lois laughed louder and turned to her friend. "Do you see what I mean? She's priceless!"

It was then that Van arrived and slid a tray of drinks onto the table, effectively ending the questions being fired my way.

I could have kissed him.

My cheeks scorched.

"Hi there," Lois said as Van sat beside me.

"Hello," he said with a smile.

"Who are you?"

Van turned to look at me. "You know, you Wellesley girls sure know how to bruise a man's ego."

"Why? Because you would like to think of yourself as notorious, when you're simply forgettable?" I asked sweetly.

Lois then gasped and jumped up and down on her seat, pointing at Van. "I remember you! The guy from the wedding! And New Year's! I remember!" She collapsed against the back of the booth in a fit of laughter.

"Maybe I'm exactly as notorious as I think I am," Van murmured in my ear. And to Lois he said, "I'm getting the impression that you girls have discussed me a little."

Lois' eyebrows shot up into her hairline. "A little? Barb would get so worked up after seeing you! She would obsess over it for— Ouch!"

I had subtly kicked her under the table while keeping a smile fixed on my lips.

Van looked at me in amusement.

Maybe I wasn't all that subtle.

I gave her a pointed look. "Aren't you forgetting your manners, Lois? You haven't introduced us to *your* friend."

"Oh, right," Lois said, as though she remembered that was there with someone. "Barb, Van, this is Doug Norton. Doug Norton, this is Barb and Van."

We exchanged hellos, although the heavy set of Doug's forehead told me he resented the disruption of his time with Lois.

The men fell into near silence as we girls dominated the conversation. I stayed for one more drink then made my excuses to leave. Lois was having none of it. "Come on, one more drink, Barb!"

"Another time. I'll see you later." I kissed her cheek as I stood to leave. On my way out, I slid some money across the bar to Joe and he winked at me.

Once outside Van asked, "What was that about?"

"I give him money for a cab for Lois. She tends to forget to save some for getting home. Joe calls a cab for her and pays it and then tells her she ordered it hours ago for that time and gave him the money to keep for her." I smiled. "I know, it's stupid, but it makes me worry a whole lot less. Some of the guys she goes out with would love her to be stranded."

Van peered at me with an odd expression.

I frowned as I tried to work out what it meant. "What?"

He chuckled and shook his head. "Nothing, it doesn't matter. Come on, I'll give you a ride home."

"Oh, that's okay, really. I'm fine walking."

It looked as though Van had a lot to say, but stopped himself at the last moment. "Please, Barb?" Van offered me his elbow and after a moment's hesitation, I took it. We walked in silence to his car and on the drive to Wellesley, the soft crooning of a singer through the wireless was the only sound.

Van shut off the engine outside the college gates and dropped his hands from the steering wheel.

"You seem to have a lot on your mind," I said. My insides twisted. Had I done something wrong?

He turned his head to face me, his eyes soft yet probing. "I'm just thinking how hypocritical you are."

I gasped in shock, but before I could launch into a tirade, he held his hand up to stop me.

"I'm not trying to offend you."

"Yet you somehow manage it well enough," I said with a huff.

"I just meant it's funny how you worry about someone else's wellbeing when you have complete disregard for your own."

Curiosity piqued and blew holes in the prickly irritation I'd felt moments before. "What do you mean?"

"What you did for Lois, paying the cab fare so you know she'll get home safely. You worry about her."

I narrowed my eyes. "And why is that bad?"

"It isn't. You care about her, and that is a beautiful thing," he said. "I just don't understand how you can care about her safety so much, and yet your own doesn't even get considered. You would have walked home the other night from the bar, and tonight, if I'd let you."

"I can take care of myself."

"That's exactly my point, Barb." Van shook his head and his expression softened. "You don't have to put up this harsh exterior to the world. Anyone can see how extraordinary you are. You don't need to be reckless to do it."

I tried to make sense of his words. It was one of those situations where I could have flown off the handle, but, as I took the time to let what he had said sink in, I realized it came from a genuine place of concern. "I don't know what to say," I admitted.

"You don't have to say anything," Van said quietly. "Thank you for lunch today. I had a really good time with you."

My face warmed and I bit my lip. "I did too."

"I'll see you again?" he asked.

I smiled. "Seems inevitable, doesn't it?" Before I could overthink it, I leaned across to press a kiss to his cheek before all but throwing myself out of his car.

* * * *

Spring vacation finished with no more sightings of Van. A few times in the Dragon, I would turn to the door when the bell above it signaled a new customer. The disappointment stung every time when it wasn't him.

Soon after my classes started back up, I received a letter from Anna, asking what my plans were for the summer. Kenneth was taking her to Yellow Sands for an anniversary treat and wanted to coincide our dates that I'd be there with Evelyn so we could get to spend some time together.

I called her that very same day.

"Anna!" I gushed when she answered.

"Barb! Great to hear from you!"

"I just got your letter, but I wanted to make sure you're okay with this." I glanced at her letter still clutched in my hand. "Don't you want it to be just you and Kenneth? Doesn't he mind?"

Anna laughed. "Actually, it was Kenneth's idea. There'll be some potential clients there, and he wants to try to impress them. He said he might be busy, so suggested you come along and then I wouldn't be bored!"

My heart swelled at this. Maybe Kenneth wasn't as bad as I thought. "Wow, that's pretty decent of him. I'm going to write to Evelyn now, and see what she thinks. I'll be in touch."

"Okay, I have to go now anyway, I'm trying to ice a cake and I keep messing it up."

"Um, okay, well — good luck with that."

My handwriting was barely legible as I scribbled a letter to Aunt Evelyn. She was always out at some event or another, my beautiful social butterfly of an aunt, and therefore impossible to get hold of on the phone. It was an agonizing two weeks before I had her reply, which stated she would be more than happy to go when I pleased. On receiving my letter, she booked our cottage right away, so the holiday was set. In her letter she also told me my old friend Thomas Gentry would be summering there at that time, so it would be a treat for everyone.

I groaned at this. I held no malice over Thomas but I certainly didn't want a repeat of last summer. I would have to talk to him and tell him I wouldn't be his distraction to his parents this year.

But soon summer and all its plans were pushed from my mind as it became exam time again, which occupied my attention.

The weather warmed with each passing week, steadily growing more and more summerlike. Wellesley was a flurry of activity as everyone darted around, preparing themselves for the upcoming exams.

Lois seemed to take them more seriously this year, and it became more common for her to be in the library rather than the Dragon. Weekends were spent locked away, scribbling notes instead of flirting with the latest love interest.

I followed her good example and stayed clear of any and all distractions. I didn't call home or write any letters, knowing they would bring news I that neither cared for, nor was interested in. My family would understand. They knew the pressures of the exams and how I needed to focus. Although my mother still sent the weekly engagement notices from the local paper, and eventually I stopped opening envelops with her handwriting.

The whole school seemed to take a deep breath and relax once the year was over, and the students got into the summer mood. Exams were finished and packing was done. We sat through one last assembly and we were free to leave.

"Write me, okay?"

"Of course. I'll let you know the address of the hotels we'll be staying at in my first letter," Lois said, throwing her arms around me as we said our goodbyes until we would meet again as college juniors.

The lucky thing was going on a trip across the country! I wasn't too envious, though. I looked forward to spending time with Anna, and I loved my summers in the city with Evelyn.

"Good." Tears pricked my eyes at our goodbye. "I'm going to miss you, Dubbs."

"Same here, Howell."

We laughed through our tears and had one final hug. I broke free and hopped into my waiting cab. It would be a long wait till I saw her again.

Chapter Nine

My aunt and I arrived the day before Anna and Kenneth. The air was cleaner at Yellow Sands, helping to refresh and rejuvenate me. It was a long wait to see my sister — we arranged to meet for lunch on the day of their arrival. Months of separation, and it was the final day. I was the most impatient as I counted down the minutes.

The morning saw me hopping from foot to foot, waiting for the lunch hour to come. I busied myself in front of the mirror, painting my eyelids and my lips. I even wore my new navy button-down day dress and finished off my outfit with a pair of heels. I'm not sure who I was dressing up for, Anna knew what I looked like and didn't care how much effort I put in. I told myself it was for the opening of the season. It was good to set an appropriate tone.

I rushed my aunt out of our cottage, insisting we'd be late if we didn't leave that very second. It was only a five-minute walk to the club's restaurant, and there was still forty-five minutes before we were expected.

The sun shone in the clear blue sky as we walked toward the restaurant, warm and bright. We had been strolling for a few minutes when I heard my name called. Squinting, I shielded my eyes with my hand so I could see who had called me.

A familiar frame jogged toward me. "Barb! I was hoping I would run into you."

"Hello, Thomas," I said as I smiled at my old friend.

"Are you headed to lunch? Can I escort you?" His smile was wide and sincere, and it made me feel guilty that I was about to turn him down.

"Yes, we're going to lunch, but we're meeting family. Another time perhaps."

Evelyn tapped me on the arm with her pocketbook. "Barbara, don't be so cruel to poor Thomas. I imagine he has been looking forward to this meeting since last September," she scolded.

I shot Thomas a pointed look and folded my arms across my chest. "I'm sure he's had other thoughts to occupy himself with."

"Quite the opposite, I've looked forward to seeing you," Thomas said, his grin widening.

Evelyn chuckled under her breath. "I have a headache coming, I can feel it. You two young people go and enjoy this wonderful day. Give my regards to Mr. and Mrs. Dixon." With that, my aunt turned on her heels and retreated back toward our cottage, leaving me to attend this bizarre double date.

It was a flurry of excitement when Anna came in, lots of hugging and kissing and even a few tears. I hugged Kenneth, more to his surprise than mine. When I introduced Thomas, recognition flared in Anna's eyes and she turned to smile at me, her face full of excitement.

"*The* Thomas? From last summer?" she asked.

I nodded and he slipped his arm around my waist. My smile was so wide it hurt my cheeks. But it was better to smile than stomp on his foot and ask just what the hell he was doing.

"How wonderful—a summer love reunion!" Anna gushed.

Oh dear Lord, she'll have our wedding china picked out by the end of this meal... "Hardly," I scoffed before checking myself. "Shall we sit?"

We were seated on the decked area outside. Throughout the meal, Anna and I chatted about everything, our voices growing more and more excited as we made up for all the lost months.

The four of us stayed long after most of the other diners left, until Anna stifled a yawn and I knew I could keep her no longer.

"I'm sorry I'm such a bore, Barb. You know how I get after traveling," Anna apologized as we headed out of the restaurant.

"Don't give it another thought," I said, hugging her. "Go lie down. I'll see you tomorrow."

Kenneth nodded to me as he turned away with his arm around Anna's waist.

"So, what's on the cards for us now?" Thomas asked.

"For us, nothing. For me, a walk perhaps."

Thomas laughed. "Come on, silly girl. Let's get out of here." He took my hand and placed it in the crook of his arm and held it there with his other hand, leading us in the general direction of a small wooded area.

"I think a conversation is needed, Thomas," I said after a few steps. He had to know... I had to make it perfectly clear that this summer would not be spent like the last one.

"Oh? And what sort of conversation is that?" he asked.

"I'm not prepared to put on a show like last year. I won't say anything, you know that. But I cannot devote another whole summer to your charade."

Thomas chuckled. "So stern, Barb. What makes you think I need you?"

"I—" I started, suddenly feeling big-headed and foolish. Had I read the entire situation wrong? "I'm sorry, you just seemed very eager to see me, that's all."

"I was eager to see you. You are still my friend, are you not?"

"Of course."

"Well then, I see no problem."

"If anyone asks if you're courting me, I'll deny it."

"So will I." He seemed sincere enough. "But, I can have the pleasure of your company every once in a while, can I not? Just as friends, of course."

I smiled. "Of course."

We strolled for a further hour before we parted ways. The talk with Thomas helped me to relax, and I could enjoy his company without worrying he took it to mean more than it did. He walked me to my door and kissed my hand with a wink, making me giggle at his faux gallant behavior.

Evelyn must have been telling the truth when she'd said she had a headache coming, as sure enough she was lying on her bed with the curtains drawn.

I would have made myself a sandwich for supper that evening, but Thomas called round and insisted on taking me out. I couldn't deny him now that everything had been straightened out, and it would be nice to have some company.

There wasn't another soul in the restaurant that I knew, and Anna must still be sleeping off her journey. Dancing began soon after dinner and I found myself having a good time with Thomas. There was no pressure in our relationship and certainly no confusion, so I was free to be myself without discrimination. He was a very good dance partner and loved the swing numbers, and could throw me about with ease.

I liked the familiarity of Thomas. He knew what made me laugh and was very pleasant company. He was a great friend — just like Lois.

As I danced with Thomas, I thought of Van.

He was never far from my thoughts these days, thought I couldn't pinpoint the reason. I decided it was because we were becoming friends and were finally moving away from the aggression that seemed to stalk me whenever I was near him. Yes, he was a friend, that was the reason. Glancing at Thomas' handsome face, I wondered why it wasn't all my friends who gave me delicious shivers.

* * * *

The sun beamed through my sheer white drapes, coaxing me awake. The brightness of the day beckoned me, and I threw back the sheets and jumped from my bed, anxious to get a head start on the day. I sang loudly — and out of tune — in the shower and continued to hum to myself as I dressed in my white halter playsuit.

There were a few people milling around, despite the early hour. The heat of the sun warmed my back as I walked toward the tennis courts. A few of the club's trainers were ready and waiting when I arrived — they must start work at dawn, ready to accommodate the ridiculously eager tourists.

But who was I to talk? There I was — ridiculously eager myself.

A large, athletic woman offered to play me and I accepted with apprehension. She lumbered toward me, her muscular thighs could make any male envious. It had been a while since I played and I was terrified what this woman would do to me.

My muscles recalled the movements far clearer than my mind. It was like riding a bicycle, and soon enough, I had my swing back. Despite her heavy build, my coach moved effortlessly. She was an easy partner, starting with simple serves then challenging me when she knew I could handle it.

My serve grew stronger and she began to sweat. We got a good volley going, the ball flying back and forth between us. The muscles in my legs stretched and came back to life as I flew across the court. My feet moved with unfamiliar grace as I lunged to meet her furious back swing.

"Barb?"

I turned unconsciously at the sound of my name, some distant part of my mind knowing the owner before seeing who had spoken. It was then what felt like a brick smacked me on the head, and the next thing I knew, the sun dazzled me as I looked up at the sky from the ground.

Why am I on the ground?

A face shaded mine from the blinding rays of the sunlight and I squinted, trying, and failing, to focus.

"Barb? You all right there?"

"Ouch," I said, raising my hand to hold my head. "What the heck was that?"

"The ball. It was moving pretty fast—"

"Move back please. Oh yes, she'll be fine. Come on, sugar, walk it off. No harm done." The face was pushed aside and I was back on my feet. A hand cupped my elbow as I swayed from the sudden movement.

The world came back into focus and I turned to the idiot who had called me. *Of course!* "You!" I exclaimed. Van flashed a cringing smile that made my stomach flip.

"Sorry," Van said sheepishly.

The coach snatched the racket from my hand. "That should do for today, I think." And with that she marched from the court, leaving Van and I blinking in her wake.

Van released my elbow, bringing my attention back to him. "Can I buy you a cup of coffee, by way of an apology?"

I smiled and gently touched the side of my head. "Make it an aspirin and you've got a deal."

Van grinned. "Deal." We left the courts, wandering with no rush to reach our destination. He chuckled and rubbed the back of his neck. "How about that coach? Her backswing would shame any man's."

I laughed and pointed to the side of my head. "Yeah, I know, and I was the one who had to play her." I nudged him in the side with my elbow. "I almost made it out unscathed."

"You're a braver soul than I am," Van said, shaking his head.

"What are you doing here anyway? Are you with your friend's family again?" I asked.

Van nodded. "Yeah. Just for the week. You?"

A thrill went through me. *He's here for a whole week…* "Two. Anna and Kenneth are here and invited my aunt and me. We come every year anyway, but it's nice to spend time with Anna as well."

"That's nice of you, to come with your aunt every year."

"It's more her vacation than mine. Anna and I stayed with her every summer since we were little, now it's just me of course, but it's good for her to get out of the city." I laughed. "It's not like she needs me for company — that woman's social calendar is so full I'm surprised it hasn't burst."

Van nodded. "You must get along well, to spend so much time with her."

I smiled, thinking of all the ways I adored Evelyn. "She's a wonderful woman, a far nicer version of my mother."

"So, what do you normally do for fun around here?"

"Nothing you would consider fun," I said with a laugh. "I walk, swim and play tennis. I read — no surprise there, of course."

He shoved his hands in his shorts pockets. "What about in the evenings? Do you date?"

I shrugged. "Not really. Maybe if I'm asked, but that doesn't happen very often."

Van frowned. "Why not?"

I smiled at him. "Because, strangely enough, you aren't the first to think me unpleasant and hostile."

Van cringed as I repeated the words he had said to me at New Year's in a joking, but not untrue, fashion. "I don't think you're unpleasant or hostile."

"Maybe not now, but a lot of people do. I don't have a great deal of tolerance for the male species. Word tends to spread that you needn't bother asking."

"You shouldn't be so harsh on yourself. I bet tons of men would summersault backward just to get a date with you."

I laughed in surprise. "I very much doubt that. My aunt sets me up from time to time and I go to keep her happy. Mostly I just don't have the patience."

"For?"

"You ask a great deal of questions, has anyone ever told you that?" I asked, nudging him again.

"Yes. Didn't I ever tell you I'm pre-law?" Van answered with a grin. "So why don't you have patience for dating?"

Releasing a heavy sigh, I had to wonder that once I told Van the truth, if he'd think me just as peculiar as everyone else did. "When I was a little girl, my mother told me the only thing in life that was expected of me was to become a good wife and mother. And from then, I've fought against it."

Frowning, Van asked, "What are you fighting against? Your mother, or marriage itself?"

"A little of both, I think. We both know how stubborn I can be, and my mother is just the same. She wants me married. I don't. I haven't had a great deal of experience with men, but what I have seen is enough to put me off for life. Most are disgusting little trolls who only think of one thing and others only want a wife to replace their darling mothers. Then there are the ones so self-absorbed in themselves, I don't know how it would be possible for them to spend their life with another," I exclaimed, breathing heavily. I hadn't meant to get so worked up.

Van didn't seem perturbed by my outburst. "It sounds like you've been dating the wrong men."

"I doubt it," I mumbled. "I've met enough to know I can't imagine spending a lifetime with one of you menfolk."

He laughed. "You should give us a break. You can be pretty intimidating."

"My point exactly," I said, smiling sweetly. "How could I seriously consider someone if they're too cowardly to come back a second time?"

Van chuckled. "I see your point."

I decided then that I loved his laugh. Full and rich, it was completely inviting and made me want to smile in return. Warm, friendly and caused my heart to thump. It was as alluring to me as the flower was to the bee. *Jeepers… That ball must have hit me harder than I thought…* I waved my hand at him. "Enough of this talk. Summer's meant to be fun, not serious. Didn't you say something about coffee?"

Van took me to a quaint little café in town, away from the main resort, where we sat for most of the morning. "Do you have any plans for the rest of your day?" Van asked once the small town started to get busier.

"No. I barely saw Anna yesterday, so I imagine we'll do something. Will you be having dinner at the club tonight?"

"I expect so."

"Us too. See you at the bar?" I smiled.

"Count on it." He grinned.

Faces passed me by in a blur as I walked home and I was unable to keep the smile from my lips. I was glad Van and I were friends. The more time I spent with him, the more I realized how much I liked him. Our banter still continued, which was fun. It was a relief to be able to speak freely with someone without the fear of upsetting them.

With Van…I was myself.

And the best part… I think he liked it.

Chapter Ten

That evening I dressed with extra care and ignored the voice in my head that told me why I was putting in so much effort. I attempted to put my hair up, but every time I tried, it caused the bump that had formed after my tennis mishap to protest and pain to sear through my skull. In the end I gave up and left it down in its usual waves. I wore a fitted green dress with a mandarin collar and buttons down the front.

Evelyn and I arranged to meet Kenneth and Anna for dinner, and we arrived around the same time and were seated. I scanned the room for Van but caught no sight of him. Anna noticed me looking, so I ceased my search. She'd only get overly excited if I told her I was looking for a man, and wouldn't believe me if I told her he was nothing but a friend.

Soon after we finished eating and our table had been cleared, I felt a hand on my shoulder. My lips twitched into a smile and I turned, only to be faced with Thomas Gentry. I was surprised to feel disappointment.

"Thomas," Evelyn said with a smile.

Anna turned to look at the newcomer. She beamed at Thomas and me.

I burned scarlet. I'd never get a moment's peace for the rest of the vacation.

"Good evening, everyone," Thomas said with a charming smile. "Barb, I was wondering if you'd like to dance?"

"Oh. Maybe in a little while, Thomas, I'm still full from dinner." I hated being put in such an awkward position, even more so when his wide smile fell. *I bet his parents are watching.*

"Go on, Barb," Anna said. "It'll help your digestion."

I shot her a poisonous look. "I said in a little while."

"Of course, I understand," Thomas said, not even trying to hide his disappointment.

Evelyn huffed and gave me a scolding look. "Sit down, Thomas. I'm sure Barb will be more in the mood in a few minutes." She signaled to the wait staff to bring another chair for him.

Biting the inside of my cheek to keep from protesting, I knew my face would be almost puce with mortification. I had nothing against Thomas, but he was only fueling my family's belief in our relationship.

He winked at me as he sat down a little too closely and slung his arm around the back of my chair. *Oh, he is doing this on purpose, the sneak.*

In no time at all, Thomas held my aunt and sister in the palm of his hand. He told them about his courses and life at his own college at Georgetown University. He turned to smile at me often, making Anna and Evelyn swoon.

I made my excuses to leave the table, needing a break. Evelyn's cocktail glass was almost empty, and I selflessly offered to fetch another. As I waited for the bartender, the stench of stale alcohol and cigarettes overwhelmed my nose. A man stood close to me and as I glanced at him, he roamed his gaze over my body.

I sucked in a breath and hoped if I ignored him, he would go away.

Instead, he leaned in closer. "How about a dance?"

"I don't think so," I said, stepping away.

"Why not? I think you might like it." The drunk followed me for every step I retreated. "Come on, beautiful."

"No."

"Why? Don't you like dancing? How about a walk then? My cottage is nearby..." A particularly strong waft of his disgusting breath hit me in the face and I struggled not to gag.

Maybe this is why it's a good idea to have a boyfriend... Someone to ward off undesirables.

The bartender moved to stand in front of me and he shot a disapproving look at the drunk, who leaned unsteadily against the bar. "What can I get you?"

I ordered quickly, and left even quicker.

No one at the table noticed my exchange with the drunk, and when Thomas asked again if I'd dance, I took him up on the offer before the words were even fully out of his mouth. I shook off the dirty feeling the man had left, and focused on enjoying myself with my friend.

We danced three more times before I cried off and told Thomas I was going outside for a cigarette. And it was only once I was out on the patio that I realized I'd forgotten my lighter.

"Need a light?"

My pulse quickened at the sound of the familiar voice. Turning, I saw Van leaning against the wall behind me, half encased in the darkness. I walked toward him and he flicked his lighter open.

"Thanks," I said as I leaned in toward the small flame.

"Having a good night?" Van asked, tucking the lighter back into his pants pocket.

I moved to his side and leaned against the wall so our shoulders touched. "So-so. You?"

"Can't complain."

"It's so hot in there. I had to come out for air."

"Dancing will do that to you."

"Were you watching me?" I asked, my eyebrows shooting up.

"Just a glance, I promise." He smirked. "How's your head?"

"Feel for yourself." I took his hand and guided his hand over the bump under my hair. His fingers skimmed over it, and chills shot down my body. It was an innocent gesture, hardly risqué...but I felt bold and daring. Our faces were close and I could see every fleck of color in Van's bright blue eyes.

I wonder what it would feel like to –

"Hey, hey, lookie who I found."

Ripped out of the moment with Van, I whirled around to see the drunk from the bar coming toward us, stumbling with every step he took.

"Friend of yours?" Van murmured. He pushed off the wall and turned his body. It took a moment to realize that he was shielding me.

"Ready for that dance?" the man asked, coming closer.

I wasn't the kind of girl to hide, and as Van had pointed out once before, I had a bad habit of being stubborn and insisting that I could take care of myself. But I found myself stepping closer to Van, and peered at the guy from the safety of Van's tall body. "No. But thank you for asking."

He trailed his gaze over my body again, making my skin prickle with unease. "Seems to me that you like a bit of male attention. Well, here I am, giving you attention. Would you rather go somewhere more private?"

"I'd like you to leave me alone," I said.

He narrowed his eyes and took a menacing step forward. "So I'm not good enough for you? You spread yourself around the other men plenty, what's wrong with me?"

"Hey now," Van said, anger filling his voice. "That's about enough."

The guy sneered at Van. "I wasn't talking to you. Leave us alone, college boy."

"I can't do that, friend. Why don't you go back inside and get a cup of coffee."

"I'm not going anywhere." The drunk looked me up and down again. "Come on, how about it, beautiful? Your boyfriend here won't mind if I borrow you for a while. Everyone else has had a turn tonight."

Van moved so quickly he almost blurred. His hand curled into a fist and he landed a punch on the drunk's chin, sending him sprawling backward and landing flat on his back.

It had only just registered that Van had hit him when he pulled me back inside, away from the drunk and before we drew any more attention. "Are you all right?" Van asked, his eyes searching mine.

"I—" I stopped and took a steadying breath. My heart pounded along with my head. "Yes, are *you*?"

Van shook his hand out. "Yeah, boy, that hurt. I've never hit anyone before."

"Why did you?"

He glanced at the ground before returning his gaze back to me. Van looked apologetic, but not regretful.

"He was being disgusting, Barb. I'm sorry. I shouldn't have reacted that way. He got me angry, is all."

I stepped closer and touched his arm. "Don't be sorry, I'm glad you did it. He was being a creep. He deserved it."

He scanned me with his eyes, as though trying to see a lie that wasn't there. After a moment, Van blew out a breath. "Come on, I'll walk you home. The fresh air will help your head."

"The cottage is a five minute walk from here," I said with a laugh.

Van smiled. "Okay, then we'll go the long way."

* * * *

I made my apologies to my family and blamed my pounding head for my early departure. They accepted the excuse and I could barely get out of there fast enough. My heart thumped unevenly as I saw Van standing under the beam of the streetlamp.

Our pace was slow. I wasn't in a rush, and from his relaxed stroll, I guess Van wasn't either. Away from the noise of the club, it was as if we were the only two people on the entire resort. Ankle-high lights lit up the path for us as gravel crunched under our feet.

Van remained quiet as we walked, and I couldn't help but wonder if he was mad at me for getting him into a fight. I was nothing but a troublesome woman.

"I didn't see you at the club. Until I was outside, of course," I said, finally breaking our silence.

"You were a little busy with dancing." Van flashed me a lopsided smile.

"I thought you only glanced." I prodded him in the arm with my elbow.

"I did — each time." Van grinned. "We came in late and sat near the back, that's probably why you didn't see me."

"Ah," I nodded. "Why weren't you dancing?"

"Well, every time I came to ask, you were already taken," Van teased.

"Oh, poor you!" I cried with a laugh.

"Yes, poor me. How will you make it up to me?"

"That depends on what you want." Anticipation pulled at me, confusing me once more.

"Hmm…" He rubbed his chin and didn't take his eyes from my face. "I think a lunch date will do."

"Oh, is that all?" I lifted my eyebrows and ignored the butterflies that had taken flight in my belly.

Van's smile widened. "Better make it two lunch dates."

"Didn't your mother ever tell you to take what you can get and not push your luck?"

He looked down. "Actually my mother taught me to see what I want and go for it, and never mind what anyone else thinks." A moment passed. A serious tone fell on the conversation, but I didn't understand why. Eventually Van shook his head. "So who was your friend, anyway?"

"What friend?" I asked, puzzled. My head was still working over his previous statement.

"What friend, she asks!" Van repeated while laughing. "Only the one you were with all evening."

"Oh, *that* friend." I shrugged. "That was Thomas Gentry. I met him last summer."

There was a heavy pause before Van spoke again, his voice a note quieter. "Are you courting him?"

"If there was a word stronger than *no*, I would use it here." It was on the tip of my tongue to explain to Van why there would never be anything more than friendship between Thomas and me. But I couldn't betray Thomas' trust, not even to reassure Van. Which I wanted to do. A lot. "What are you doing with the rest of your summer?" I asked, changing the subject.

"I have an internship with a big law firm in New York. This is the one week of my vacation where I get to relax and won't be working."

I pulled a face. "Sounds awful."

Van shrugged. "Depends how you look at it. On one hand, it would be great to spend the summer doing whatever I wanted. On the other hand, I'm getting the necessary experience to help carry me through studying law. Plus I'm getting paid."

"It sounds like you are very focused," I said, smiling. I liked that he was dedicated and hardworking. It showed how strong his character was.

Van pinned me with his gaze. "You have to be to get what you want."

"And what is it that you want?" I asked quietly. It felt like a dangerous question.

He grinned but it didn't meet his blue eyes. "I thought there was to be no serious discussions during summer?"

I sighed as if it didn't bother me one little bit that he hadn't answered the question. "Fine, don't tell me."

Van had been telling the truth when he had said we would take the long way back to my cottage. It was a couple of hours later before we arrived at the gate, though it felt like only minutes. If anything, I was disappointed it hadn't taken us longer.

"Sleep well, Barb," Van said as he opened the gate for me.

"You too." I headed up the short walk in front of the house before turning back around. "Van? Thank you, for what you did tonight."

He narrowed his eyes in confusion. "I don't—"

"With that awful man. No one's ever taken up for me like that before. It meant a lot."

Van's face softened and the barest of smiles touched his lips. "Any time, Barb."

I turned and hurried up the rest of the walk.

Sleep took me that night with the image of Van in my head.

* * * *

My first week of vacation drew to a close and Van had walked me home most nights after dinner. We fell into an unusual, but pleasant routine that I looked forward to more each day.

On his last night at Yellow Sands, Van handed me a scrap of paper when we arrived at the gate of my cottage.

"What's this?" I asked, unfolding the square of paper.

"My New York number." Van shoved his hands in pockets. I was beginning to recognize the action to mean he was nervous. "I'd like it if you'd call when you get back to the city. If you want to, that is."

I glanced at the paper in my hand and a flush of pleasure warmed me from the inside out that he wished to see more of me. I'd lowered almost all my barriers this past week, and had truly relaxed in his company. But he'd made me greedy. With every meeting I wanted more, wanted longer with him. I tried to smile but it wobbled at the edges. "Of course I do."

Van grinned, quick and relieved. "Good. So I'll hear from you in a week or so?"

I nodded. And before I could change my mind, I kissed his cheek then turned and darted up the path. I closed the door behind me and let out a shaky breath, my heart thumping and my head spinning.

It was late — the house was quiet and my aunt long in bed. Moving into the front room, I twitched the drape back a fraction and saw Van still staring at the house.

Chapter Eleven

"Call more often." Anna's voice broke.

"You too." I sniffed, my eyes stinging.

"And visit whenever you can, you hear me?"

I laughed. "I hear you."

"Stop leaving it so long."

"Okay."

"Anna, sweetie, we have to go. The cab is—"

She broke Kenneth off midsentence. "I know!"

"Go, Anna," I whispered, giving her a gentle nudge toward Kenneth.

Anna let out a sob. She threw her arms around me and I fought to breathe. "Stop being so damn stubborn, Barb. Thomas is a nice boy. You could do a lot worse."

I bit my tongue and nodded.

Like always, my farewell with Anna was filled with tears and heartbreak. Seeing my big sister served only to remind me just how much I missed her. It would be a long wait until our next reunion.

The day after Evelyn and I returned to the city, I was busy unpacking my things. The day after that, Evelyn took me to an art gallery, desperate to show me the work of some new artist she'd discovered.

She kept me so busy that it was a full week arriving in New York that I got a chance to call Van.

"Van? Hi, it's Barb." I wondered if the nervousness sounded as clear to him as it did to me.

"Barb," he said, his voice filling with surprise. "I was beginning to think you were too chicken to tell me to my face you never planned on calling."

I laughed softly. "Don't be ridiculous, I've been busy."

"What are you doing right now? You feel like getting a drink?"

I'd counted on this and was already dressed to go out. He told me the name of a bar in the Village and I agreed to meet him there in a half hour.

He was almost twenty minutes late due to the fact that he took a wrong corner somewhere and found himself hopelessly lost. I teased him and promised I'd pick him up next time.

We slipped back into our friendly ways and again hours passed by like nothing at all. I was more safety conscious in the city, so I didn't argue with him when he insisted on sharing a cab home.

"Are you busy tomorrow?" Van asked as he walked me to my building's foyer.

"Just in the morning. Evelyn and I have brunch every Sunday at the Tavern." There was a tiny flutter in my stomach. "We could do something after, if you want to?"

Van grinned. "Yes, absolutely."

"Okay, meet me at the Tavern around noon?"

He agreed and wished me goodnight.

Tomorrow couldn't come fast enough.

* * * *

The day was like any other — warm and pleasant. But there was something in the air — a lightness to my steps that I'd have been a fool to think had anything to do with the good weather. The Tavern was busy as it always was, and the food was delicious. I smeared cream cheese over my bagel and savored every bite.

"Any plans for the rest of the day, Barb?" Evelyn asked as she finished up her bacon and eggs.

I dabbed my mouth with a napkin before replying. "Yes, I'm meeting a friend after brunch. I'm not sure what we're doing, we didn't decide on anything."

She nodded. "Is it a boy you're meeting?"

"He's a friend, Evie," I said, giving her a reproachful look.

Evelyn smiled at my reaction. "What about Thomas? Do you have any plans to see him?"

"No."

"I'm afraid you do now."

My shoulders sagged. "Oh, what have you done?"

Evelyn laughed and reached for her water glass. "Me? Not a thing, dear. I met his parents at the theater the other week and they asked if you were in town. When I confirmed, they invited us over for dinner."

"When?"

"Tonight."

"Tonight? Oh, Evie!"

Evelyn frowned. "What's the matter? I thought you liked Thomas and his parents."

"I do, but a lot has changed since last summer. Thomas and I are strictly friends. I don't want his mother to get her hopes up, that's all."

The hostess approached our table and told me there was a gentleman waiting to see me. Evelyn instructed her to send him through.

I arched an eyebrow at her once the hostess had left. "You and Mrs. Gentry aren't trying to be matchmakers again, are you? I don't want to hurt her feelings when it's made clear that there will never be anything serious between me and Thomas."

Evelyn tutted. "It's only you who reads too far into things. She has no expectations for you and her son. She likes your company and I think you'll survive one little dinner, Barbara. It's not as if you're announcing your engagement."

The conversation halted with the arrival of Van.

I could have kissed him for his timing.

"Van." I grinned as I stood up to welcome him. "Sit, please."

Evelyn's eyes flitted between my handsome friend and me a few times before she schooled her features. "Hello." When I didn't catch the introduction cue right away, she gave me a pointed look.

"Oh, I'm sorry," I said. "Van, this is my aunt Evelyn. Evie, this is my friend Van."

"It's a pleasure to meet you. I've heard a great deal about you," Van said, shaking her hand.

Evelyn's eyes sparkled with mischief. "I wish I could say the same. I only learned of your existence this morning."

"I think Barb likes to keep our friendship secret." Van smiled at me.

"She never was a child for sharing," Evelyn agreed.

I gasped and the two of them laughed at me. Traitors.

Aunt Evie insisted that Van stay for some food, and ordered him bacon and eggs. Once he was finished eating, Van and I waited with Evelyn until her cab arrived. "Remember our plans," she said as she kissed my cheek.

I nodded and closed the door of the cab for her.

Van and I walked into the heart of the park and I couldn't help but admire its natural beauty. I loved Central Park and how a place of calm could exist in such a busy city. But I suppose that was its charm.

"Shall we sit?" Van asked after a half-hour of idle walking and small talk. He carried a thin jacket, which he spread out on the grass of the great lawn. Van then sprawled next to it.

I shook my head as I laughed at him and took off my shoes before sitting on his jacket. Van lay with his arms behind his head and closed his eyes. He remained silent for so long I began to think he'd fallen asleep.

Curious, I leaned over him to try to figure out if he had in fact drifted off. My head cast a shadow over his face and he opened one eye to look at me. My cheeks flushed with embarrassment, but I didn't move away.

"What?" he asked, a small smile touching his lips.

"I thought you were sleeping."

"Why would I waste time sleeping when I have the pleasure of your company?"

I laughed. "I'm not all that fascinating."

Van propped himself up with his elbow. "On the contrary. I find you extremely fascinating." He looked away from me and his eyes roamed over the vastness of the park. "I can't get used to this."

"Me neither," I said, partly grateful that he had released me from the hold of his eyes. "I love it here."

"So what are your plans tonight?" Van asked. "I heard your aunt remind you."

"Dinner with friends of the family."

He nodded in acknowledgment. "Anyone I know?"

I arched an eyebrow. "I doubt it."

"Try me." Van sat up and leaned with his palms behind him on the grass.

"The Gentrys."

"Sure, I've heard of them."

My eyebrows shot up in surprise. "You have?"

"Well, only one, really. Their son." He smiled crookedly. "I heard about your love affair with him last summer."

I laughed. "My love affair?"

"What else would you call it?"

"I don't know, friendship?"

Van peered up at me. "Like you're friends with me?"

Frowning now, I didn't know how to explain to him without betraying Thomas. "No, not like us."

"You courted him, you were more than friends." It wasn't a question.

"Yes, I suppose we were." There were so many things I wanted, but couldn't say. And not just because I wouldn't betray Thomas. There were things I wanted to tell Van that I could barely even admit to myself.

"And now?"

"And now we're friends — only friends. My aunt sees his parents regularly, sometimes I have no choice but to socialize with them."

"Just be careful of him, Barb," Van said in a low voice.

"What do you mean?"

He shook his head and seemed to decide against whatever he was going to warn me about. Van pinched the bridge of his nose. "Nothing, I'm sorry. I think I'm just tired."

"Have you been working too hard?"

"Any work is too hard," Van said with a grin. He shrugged. "It's a good experience. I suppose I'm just not used to the long hours."

"What's the office like?"

"It's really neat, busy. Just like you would expect it to be."

"I'd love to see it. I've never been inside a law office before."

Van offered to take me out to lunch on Tuesday and would show me around the office afterward. After I accepted, he remained quiet for a while and I left him to his thoughts in peace.

"Walk with me?" Van asked, a little while later.

"Now?"

"It's a good a time as any." Van jumped up and held out his hand for me. He pulled me to my feet and let me place a hand on his shoulder to steady myself while simultaneously pulling on my shoes and trying to ignore the closeness between us. Giving it too much thought would no doubt result in me losing my rigidly held balance.

The sun was warm on my face as we walked around the park. We paused in the middle of Bow Bridge that stretched across the lake. Ducks swam below us, dipping their heads under the water.

"Are you looking forward to dinner?" Van asked as he leaned against the railing.

I frowned at his bizarre question and joined him at the railing. "As much as I look forward to any meal."

Van rubbed the back of his neck. "I suppose I mean more of the company you'll be keeping, rather than the meal itself."

"The Gentrys are pleasant enough people." I glanced down at the railing, at my hands, so close to Van's. Less than a centimeter separated our fingers. All I needed to do was stretch out my pinkie and we'd be touching. Van's hands seemed strong. They didn't appear rough and labored, but soft and caring. A shudder ran down my spine as I imagined the feel of his fingertips on my cheek.

"And Thomas? You enjoy his company?" Van asked, snapping me out of daydream.

"Yes. I wouldn't be friends with him otherwise."

Van's eyebrows pulled together. "You don't have to water anything down for my sake, Barb. I don't give two hoots if you have feelings for the boy."

The coldness of his words shocked me. "Why don't you just say whatever's on your mind instead of asking me all these silly questions?"

He shook his head. "I don't have any more."

I didn't believe him for a second. "Are you jealous of my friendship with Thomas?" I asked, teasing. "I do have other friends aside from you, Van. You never have seemed to mind my being in the company of Lois, for instance."

Van smiled at my joke, but it didn't meet his eyes. "Forget it. I'm sorry I even brought the matter up."

"You certainly are an odd creature," I murmured. I looked at my watch and saw it was almost three in the afternoon. "I should go. I don't know what time we're expected this evening."

Van nodded and jerked his head, shoving his hands in his pockets. "Come on, I'll get you a cab." It was the last he spoke until we were out of the park. He hailed me a cab and opened the door, but I couldn't bring myself to get inside.

"Van, are you okay?" I asked, with my hand on the cab door.

Van frowned but nodded. "I'm fine, why?"

"I don't know. It seems like there's a lot on your mind."

He forced a smile. "I'm fine," he repeated. "I'll see you Tuesday."

There was conflict in his eyes as he shut the cab door after me and I didn't understand why. But I hated leaving him there when there was something clearly wrong. For the rest of the afternoon, my mind raced with unanswered questions over Van's strange behavior.

* * * *

Aunt Evelyn was wealthy by anyone's standards, but the Gentrys were in an entirely different league. They lived in the penthouse of one of the most prestigious buildings on the Upper East Side and had phenomenal views over the park.

Mrs. Gentry had fine taste, which was evident in the exquisite paintings decorating the many walls of the apartment. The furnishings were only the best, nothing else would do. Rugs from India, silks from China, fabrics from France... Mrs. Gentry had never met a price tag she didn't like.

To say that Mrs. Gentry was pleased to see us would be an extreme understatement. We were shown into the lounge by a member of her staff and she enveloped me in a hug, holding me so tight I'd smell of her perfume for weeks.

Evelyn looked amused as I talked openly about other boys throughout the meal, which was beautifully served on bone china with silver platters adorning the table. I felt incredibly rude, but it had to be made clear that I didn't see Mr. and Mrs. Gentry as prospective in-laws.

The dinner dishes were cleared away and we were moved into the lounge and each sat nursing a Scotch. A look pass between Mr. and Mrs. Gentry, which was quickly followed by an enquiry to Evelyn if she would care to see the new painting they'd just purchased.

Thomas winked at me and I rolled my eyes. "I'd say I'm sorry about my mother, but it's actually entertaining to watch," he whispered as he moved to sit beside me on the stiff, uncomfortable couch.

I elbowed him playfully in the ribs. "So, how are things?"

"Great." Thomas darted a look around him, and on seeing the coast was clear, whispered in an excited voice, "I met someone. His name is Charles."

"That's great! I'm happy for you," I said, thrilled that my friend was so happy. "How are you seeing him?"

"He lives near my college. We're writing over the summer."

"Aren't you worried someone will find the letters?"

Thomas grinned, his eyes sparkling. "There's a loose floorboard in my room. I've hidden them under there."

I laughed. "Nice. I'm impressed."

Thomas' smile lasted another few seconds before his face turned serious. "I have to tell you something, and I've been avoiding it."

"This can't be good," I murmured. "What is it?"

"I've heard some rumors. About you. And me."

I arched an eyebrow. "What kind of rumors?"

"The engagement kind," Thomas said, twisting his hands together. He looked down. "That isn't the worst part. I haven't done anything to stop them. I've been letting the rumor spread."

"Thomas Gentry —" I started, my blood simmering.

He winced. "I know, I know. I should have denied it from the start."

"Well, I insist you find the culprit responsible for starting the stupid rumor and dispose of them in the cruelest way possible," I said with a hiss.

"I think that might be a tad difficult." A smile twitched on his lips. "I have a feeling the culprit may in fact be my mother."

I groaned and held my head in my hands. "You have to talk to her, Thomas. I mean it."

"I will! I promise."

Well, it certainly explained Mrs. Gentry's behavior.

* * * *

The following day I met a few café society girls for a late lunch, which turned into early drinks and a very late night. I enjoyed their company. I'd been craving female conversation, which proved how much I missed Lois. She sent me many letters and postcards, making me green with envy, but I was pleased she was enjoying herself.

My late night meant I struggled to get out of bed on Tuesday morning, and the only reason I did was because I had plans to meet Van. I showered for as long as the water ran hot, and once dressed I made myself a strong cup of coffee. I took greater care than usual when applying my makeup, ensuring the black circles under my eyes couldn't be seen. I rolled my hair into pin curls to keep it off my neck, and felt like a million bucks in my new red pencil dress.

It was a long walk to Van's office, but I had been sure sitting in the back of a burning hot cab would make me ill. I asked at reception for Van, and the woman told me where to go. I took the elevator up to the appropriate floor and was greeted by a new receptionist when I stepped out. I told her who I was looking for and she pointed me toward a small office near the back of the room.

I paused in the doorway, my hand raised to knock. But the sight of Van had me frozen to the spot. The jacket of his suit was unbuttoned, showing a matching vest and crisp white shirt. He'd slicked his hair back, and I knew that when he looked at me I'd be hit with the full-force of those dazzling eyes. The very sight of him had butterflies erupting in my belly.

He was seated at a desk crammed with files and paperwork. The office itself was tiny, with hardly any room at all, not even a window. A plant drooped in one corner, turning a deathly brown color. But he lit up the space, made it appealing because he was in it.

Shaking myself out of my stupor, I tapped on the open door.

Van jerked his head up and a smile spread across his lips. "Hi," he said.

"Hi. Am I too early?"

He rose from his chair and came around his desk. "No, your timing couldn't be more perfect. I'm starved. Do you have anywhere in mind for lunch?"

"I'm open for suggestions."

He grinned and led me out.

"I thought you were going to show me the office," I protested as we walked to the elevator.

"After lunch, I promise. I'm so hungry, Barbara, I could eat your hat."

"Well, by all means let's go. I like my hat."

Van took me to a little French restaurant I'd never been to before. A few other couples were scattered throughout the room and soft piano music tinkled delicately in the background. Tea light candles flickered on the tables adorned with blue and white checked tablecloths.

"How was your day yesterday?" Van asked as he accepted his menu from the waitress.

"Fun, I met some of the girls I haven't seen since last summer. We went to lunch and then for some drinks."

"That does sound fun. Where'd you go?"

"Um, a few bars. I can't remember their names. I had a few too many cocktails. I didn't get home till after two."

Van laughed. "And how do you feel today?"

"Much better now. I was terrible when I first woke up. You're lucky, I almost canceled our plans."

"Well, I do feel honored," Van said, smiling.

His lunch hour was over far too fast for my liking, but I was pleased to have seen him, for however long I'd gotten. And at least it was extended somewhat by the tour he'd promised.

I couldn't believe how large the office was. And that was only the floor he worked on, there were many others. The library was huge — stocked full of books, and people scurried here and there, carrying cups, files and an assortment of items.

"As much as I hate to say it, I really should get back to work," Van said as we arrived at his small room.

"What is it you're doing exactly?" I asked, eyeing the colossal mountain of paper.

"Mainly filing, exciting, huh? But it gives me the chance to look over the files and have a better understanding of the cases. I get to go to court to watch too, that's more exciting."

I nodded. "Okay, I'll get out of your way. Thanks for lunch." As I turned to leave, I bumped into a tall gentleman and sent a stack of papers flying from his hands. "Oh, gosh, I'm sorry. I wasn't looking where I was going." I bent to retrieve the paper for him, but he was already collecting them. I handed over what I'd picked up and straightened myself.

"That's all right, a pretty girl like you can bump into me any time." His eyes twinkled. He was friendly in a fatherly or uncle kind of way, and I knew he was only teasing.

I smiled at him, relieved he hadn't bitten my head off. "Thank you."

He nodded and looked into the office to Van. "Is this a friend of yours?"

"Yes, Mr. Tate, this is Barbara Howell." Van stepped forward to introduce us.

"Hello, Barbara," Mr. Tate said, shaking my hand. "But don't call me Mr. Tate, it's Jack to you, all right?"

I laughed. "All right. And it's just Barb."

He smiled and looked back at Van. "She's delightful. How long have you two known each other?"

"A year or two," Van said, shooting me a wink.

"Wonderful. Any signs of wedding bells?"

I choked back a nervous laugh. "We're just friends."

"Oh, I see." He winked at Van. "Don't leave it too long, she might meet someone else."

"She already has."

Jack's smile faltered but he quickly recovered. "Oh. Well, I'm sure you can sway her decision. Have you invited her to the party Saturday?"

Van shook his head. "I wasn't sure if she was free."

Jack looked at me. "Do you have plans for Saturday evening?"

"Not that I am aware of."

"The firm has its annual summer ball this Saturday, if you'd be interested in coming? We old folks can let our hair down, and it's also a good opportunity to impress clients and get to know our staff a little better."

"It sounds wonderful," I said. And it did. A ball...Van in a tux... Except, he hadn't invited me, Jack had. What if Van didn't want me there?

"Excellent. Van has all the details. I look forward to seeing you both there." Jack smiled and carried on his original route.

"I'm sorry," I said as I took a few steps into Van's office. "Did you have someone else you wanted to take? I won't go of course, he won't remember me."

Van sat on the edge of his desk, his eyes intent on mine. "No, I haven't asked anyone else. I was going to ask you."

"Oh." I frowned. "Why didn't you? I'd love to go with you."

"I thought you might have plans with Thomas. Saturday night is typically a date night."

"Why would I—" I paused and it dawned on me what he'd said before. "What did you mean 'she already has'?"

"Excuse me?" Van frowned.

"When Jack said I might meet someone else, you replied I already had."

"Yes. It's the truth, isn't it?"

"Far from it. Who am I supposedly courting?"

"Thomas Gentry. Who else?"

I laughed. "What on earth gave you the idea that I'm courting Thomas Gentry?"

"Maybe because the news of your impending engagement is all over New York," Van said, pushing off his desk and rifling through some of his paperwork.

Taking a step closer to him, I touched his arm until he turned to face me again. "Van, I am not marrying Thomas Gentry. I have no intentions of marrying that man."

He looked up at me. "You're not? You don't?"

"No. Is this why you keep questioning me about him?" My brows furrowed together. "Why didn't you just ask me out right? I would have told you."

Van shifted on his feet. "The answer seemed clear to me. I heard all the way back in Boston about your last summer with him. He was at Yellow Sands with you, and you're always with him here."

I squeezed his arm, realizing I was still touching him. "First of all, yes, we did court most of last summer, but in a very different way from what you're thinking. Second of all, he wasn't *with* me at Yellow Sands. I was there, and he happened to be there at the same time. Not unlike yourself. He's my friend, so of course I see him now that we're both back in the city. He doesn't have much to do and neither do I. My other friend works during the day." I crossed my arms and looked pointedly at him. I wondered if he could hear the unsteady thump of my hyperactive heart. Why had I felt the need to clarify everything so fully?

"Oh," he said softly. "I'm sorry, Barb. It was none of my business."

"I don't understand why you care so much," I said quietly. More than anything I wanted him to explain to me why he did.

"Let's forget all about it."

I nodded, swallowing my disappointment. "So, are you sure about taking me to the party?"

Van laughed. "Of course! Who else would I take?"

I waved my hand toward the pool of typists in the outer office. "You must have tons of girls around here dying to go on a date with you."

"Maybe, but I wouldn't have anywhere near as much fun if I went with one of them." Van smiled. "Do you know who that was before?"

"Who, Jack?" I asked. "I have no idea, why?"

"He's Jack Tate. As in Johnston, Tate and Brown, attorneys at law. Senior partner."

I gasped... *Jeepers.* "I didn't embarrass you, did I?"

He smiled, the action full of affection. "Far from it."

Breathing a sigh of relief, I said, "Oh, good. Anyway, I should let you work."

"Is it all right to pick you up at seven on Saturday?"

"Seven is fine." *Seven is perfect.*

"Good."

"See you then."

I floated home.

Chapter Twelve

The rest of the week dragged its heels. Time passed with excruciating slowness as my excitement grew with each passing day. Evelyn and I went shopping for a new dress, and I found the perfect one. It was cream colored with a long skirt and small train and a corseted top. Evelyn took me to have my hair fixed on Saturday morning and I loved the new style. It was swept off my face and curled down my back.

I fidgeted as the hour drew closer to seven and could barely stand still. I was repainting my lips in my dressing table mirror when the soft ring of the doorbell rang through the apartment.

Evelyn's heels clacked on the hardwood floor as she rushed to answer the door and I heard her show Van into the lounge to wait for me. She practically ran into my bedroom to tell me he was here, and clutched my hand in excitement as she said how handsome he looked.

With a deep breath, I ventured out.

Van stood with his back to me, looking out of the window. Evelyn coughed behind me, making him turn.

His eyes widened for a beat as he scanned me from head to toe and set my blood on fire. His breath left him in a rush and he took one long stride toward me before stopping. "Wow, Barb," he said uneasily.

I took in every detail of him and marveled at how attractive he looked. His hair was slicked back off his face again, letting the full penetration of his electrifying blue eyes hit me. The black tuxedo fit him perfectly, flowing over his strong, sculpted shoulders and running down to his tapered waist. Even in heels, I only reached his chin. He made me feel small, delicate, feminine. "You too," I said with a shy smile.

"Yes, yes, you both look beautiful. You'll be late if you stand there staring at each other," Evelyn cried. She stopped us at the door to take our picture. Van held out his arm for me to take and I slid my hand into the crook of his elbow. The flash was blinding...but I'd already been dazzled.

Van was the perfect gentleman as he opened doors for me and helped me into the black car waiting to take us to the party. We said very little on the drive and it took every ounce of self-control not to twitch and fidget. It felt as if I didn't fit inside my own skin. Whatever calming ease I'd built up with Van had been smashed to pieces and the very air around us crackled with tension. And infuriatingly, I couldn't read Van at all. He stared out of his window, his face a blank canvas. I had no idea what was going on in his mind.

Jack and the other partners greeted the guests as they walked into the ballroom of the hotel. He smiled warmly at me and made me promise I would save him at least one dance.

"I knew this was a bad idea," Van whispered in my ear as he led me to a table.

My stomach fell in disappointment. "Why?"

His lips twitched with amusement. "I'm not going to get one dance with you tonight. I think a line for you has already started forming."

I laughed and swatted him on the arm, taking the seat Van pulled out for me. The ballroom was exquisite, and I didn't think I'd ever been in such a fairy-tale-like room. A great chandelier hung from the ceiling, it's thousands of crystals sparkling. The lights were low but weren't overly romantic. A band dressed smartly in white tuxedos occupied the stage, and wait staff in the same attire carried trays of entrées and champagne.

The band played classical ballroom dances all evening, so no swing for me tonight. Not that I could have managed it in my gown. Jack sought me out for a few dances, as did a few of Van's colleagues. I didn't really want to dance with any of them, but I didn't want to embarrass Van or give them reason to mock him come Monday.

I took a break from dancing to enjoy a drink and cigarette, and my date, of course. The moment I finished, Van stood and said, "All right, I think it's about time you earned your invite and dance with me."

Fighting a smile, I stood and took his hand. He led us to the center of the dance floor and pulled me into his arms. I didn't recognize the music as we danced, but it didn't matter. It natural to me now, to dance with Van. There was no awkwardness that there once had been, and being with him, in any capacity, was simply…right.

"This is weird," Van said, smiling, "to dance with you close to me, and not have a huge distance between us."

I laughed. "I barely knew you. I was hardly going to be inappropriate." My heart thumped loudly — surely he would be able to feel it.

"Well, I'm glad we know each other now." His eyes were warm as he peered down at me, and he tightened his arm around my waist. "You look wonderful tonight, Barb."

My pulse raced at his words. "Thank you. You don't look half bad yourself," I teased.

He lowered his head and his mouth touched the shell of my ear. "I didn't think I'd get you to myself all night. I didn't like having to share."

"I didn't like having to be shared," I admitted. "I only danced with those other men to be polite."

Van chuckled, the sound sending shivers down my spine. "You and your manners. You were never that polite to me when we first met."

"You never used to be polite in the first place so why should I have been? All you did at first was insult me," I said, squeezing his shoulder to let him know I wasn't being serious.

"I never openly insulted you. You only took it that way because you're so prickly in nature."

I gasped. "What a contradictory sentence."

He laughed. "I'm just teasing, Barb."

"Which is the only reason why I haven't deserted you yet."

Van lifted his head to look down at me. "Yet? Are you planning to?"

"Depends on how much you decide to tease me," I said with a wide smile.

He sighed. "All right, I promise. No more teasing."

I rolled my eyes. "Impossible. You can't help yourself." Deep down, I loved Van's teasing side. If nothing else, it kept me on my toes. Especially now that I didn't take what he meant seriously.

"I can. I honestly promise, from the bottom of my heart, I will do no more teasing. Tonight."

"And tomorrow you will be back to your old bantering self?"

"More than likely."

"That's a relief. I don't think I could tolerate a polite Van for long."

He raised his eyebrows at me. "Oh! I don't think that's very fair! If I'm not going to tease for the rest of the night, then you shouldn't be allowed to, either."

"I don't think that's fair."

Van squeezed my waist. "Then do as you please, Barb. I'm sure you would regardless."

I grinned. "Most likely."

Van answered my smile with one of his own. He scanned my face, seeming to gauge my mood before speaking again. "What does Thomas think of you being here with me?"

Why is he talking about Thomas again? "Why would he care?"

Van shrugged and avoided my eyes. "I suppose I'd care if it was the other way around."

"Why?"

He let out a soft laugh and shook his head, looking at me as if the answer should have been obvious. "Look at you, Barb. You might not see how incredible you are, but every man in here does."

I had no reply for him. Van seemed sincere, and I wanted to believe him. But, if he really believed what he said, wouldn't he have made more romantic intentions clear by now?

And how would I get past the disappointment that got stronger every day he didn't?

Van saved me from floundering in trying to come up with a response. "Drink?"

I sighed in relief. "Yes, please."

When we returned to our table with our drinks, Van's neighbor asked him how he was enjoying his internship. It wasn't long before they were in a full-fledged debate over a Harvard or Yale education.

I was asked to dance again and I accepted. Van was still debating education with his neighbor so I was sure he wouldn't miss me.

Within a few minutes, I knew I'd made a mistake in dancing with the man. Regret along with nervousness fluttered in the pit of my stomach. There was something about his touch that unsettled me, his hold a bit too firm, body too close for new acquaintances.

His rat-like features were not something any woman would find attractive and my skin crawled as his hand crept south down my back and perched indiscreetly over my buttock. "Do you want to get out of here?" he whispered in my ear.

I wrinkled my nose as his breath wafted at my face. "Excuse me?"

"I'm staying in the hotel tonight and I have a suite upstairs. I'm sure you'd like it."

I searched the room for Van, praying that he would see my angry face and realize I wasn't having a good time with this cretin. But he was nowhere in sight. He must have left the room for some reason or other...

Last summer flashed in my head, of losing my date and finding him in a shocking position. *No... Could – ? No. There is no way that Van...*

I couldn't bring myself to finish the thought.

A hand clamped down onto my dance partner's shoulder and I looked over to see Jack Tate. Relief washed through my like a tidal wave. "Mr. Robins, a pleasure. How are you enjoying the party this evening?"

"Very much," Mr. Robins said, not taking his eyes off me.

Jack smiled. "I'm pleased to hear it. I must give you my apologies, however, as I have to steal this young lady. I believe someone is looking for her." Jack was not a man to be argued with, and so Mr. Robins had no choice but to let me go without protest. Jack pressed his hand to the small of my back as he led me off the dance floor and toward the bar. "I can't speak ill of Mr. Robins. He's a good client who brings my firm a lot of business. Unfortunately, he lacks decorum and favors young women. I wouldn't recommend him as a dance partner to anyone."

I shuddered once again at the memory of his hands on me. If Jack Tate was nothing else, he was a man of exceptional timing. "I had no idea he was such a creep. Thank you, for helping me."

"My pleasure. Can I get you a drink?"

"Please. Scotch," I said. "So is Van looking for me?"

Jack ordered our drinks and turned to me with a chuckle. "No, that was just an excuse to relieve you of Mr. Robins. Drink this, then I think it would be wise to call it a night."

"Sounds like a wonderful idea," I said. "Thank you, Jack. I'm glad I met you."

He smiled and gave me a nod before disappearing into the crowd.

I took my drink and went to find Van. He was still talking to the same man, and smiled over his head as he saw me coming. Van stood up to pull out a chair for me, but I touched his arm to stop him. "I'm getting tired. I think I'm going to go home. You stay, have fun." The last thing I wanted was to drag poor Van out of the party when he was having a good time. Besides, it was beneficial for him to socialize with the firm's clients and his colleagues.

He smiled and shook his head. "I don't think so, Barb. Come on, let's get out of here."

Secretly I was thrilled he wanted to leave with me — that I was more important to him than furthering his social standing within the firm. We walked out of the ballroom, and Van kept his hand to my back. My skin burned under his touch.

What flush of pleasure I had from Van, was doused with ice-cold dread when I spotted Mr. Robins loitering in the lobby. I didn't look at him or even acknowledge him as we walked past.

It didn't stop him calling out to me. "I'm here for three nights, if you change your mind."

Van twisted to look at Mr. Robins, a confused frown puckering his forehead. I clutched his arm and hurried him forward until we were safely on the street. "What was that? Do you know him?"

I shook my head. "Let's walk. I don't want to get a cab."

There was a tremble to my voice, and Van picked up on it, his expressive blue eyes widening in concern. "Barb, hey. What's wrong?" He reached for my arm but I jerked out of reach.

Flashing him an unconvincing smile, I said, "I'm fine, okay? I just want to get home."

But Van wouldn't let it go. Not that I blamed him, really. "Did that guy bother you?"

"A little," I admitted. "But it doesn't matter."

He managed to stop me this time as he cupped my elbow and stepped into my space. "Yes, it does, Barb."

I sighed and shook my head. "It's taken care of, okay? No harm done. Van, let it go. Please." I tugged on his arm to get us moving again and was surprised when he came willingly.

We walked in silence but I could feel the anger radiating from Van in thick, hot waves. I snuck a few glances at him but his expression was stoic and unreadable.

It was a beautiful night in the city. Despite the lateness of the hour, it was still lively. Lights flickered from bars and theater lights illuminated the sidewalk, making it feel magical. The tension between us kept me from truly enjoying it.

Had I spoiled the evening? The entire thing — getting dressed up, the ball, dancing, this beautiful night... It was the most romantic setting I'd ever been in... And I'd made it awkward and edgy. If I'd never danced with Mr. Robins, would this be a different kind of walk entirely? Would he hold my hand... Lean in to —

The thought I'd had while dancing with the vile Mr. Robins flared to life again in my mind when I'd been unable to spot Van. It was entirely possible that he was like Thomas, that he saw me as nothing more than a friend or someone he could use to disguise his true nature.

I was so lost in my own ramblings, I barely realized we were outside my apartment building until Van stopped walking and shoved his hands in his pockets. Glancing up at the building with a blink, I forced my mind to the present. Mumbling a distracted thanks, I turned to head inside.

"Barb, you can't leave it like this," Van called after me.

I twisted back around to face him and my heart raced that little bit faster. "Like what?"

"You have to tell me what happened with that man tonight. If you don't, I'll only imagine the worst."

It wasn't fair to keep him guessing and drive himself crazy with wondering. But I was terrified that once he knew he'd do something stupid, like try to defend my honor or something. "If I tell you, do you promise to go straight home and forget about it? Not make a big deal over it?"

Van hesitated before blowing out a breath. "I promise."

"Fine, then." I gulped in some air. "He was a cretin, that's all. He asked me to dance and I agreed. It was soon after that he began propositioning me — the kind where he'd take me upstairs to his hotel room."

Anger flashed across Van's face and his fists balled up.

"You promised you wouldn't get worked up over this." I frowned and stepped closer to him. "I told him no, and it was about then that Jack stepped in. He said the guy was a creep and best to stay clear of him. He's an important client, though, Van. That's why I didn't tell you. You can't do anything about this, okay? Promise me you'll just forget all about it."

Van rubbed the back of his neck and glared at the sidewalk as if he wanted to take his frustration out on it. When he finally looked back at me, his eyes were tortured, conflicted.

Reaching out, I laid my hand on his forearm. "I'm okay. I'm not worried about the jerk. You want to know what I was worried about?"

"Enlighten me," he mumbled.

"You. I was worried you would overreact and mess up your entire future. You, my friend, have a habit of letting your anger get away from you."

His eyes softened fractionally at this and relief washed through me that I hadn't made him react irrationally.

I'm not sure what made me do it, but I threw myself into his arms and held him as tightly as I could. "Thank you," I whispered.

"For what?" he asked, bringing his arms around me to pin my body to his.

"Listening to me."

Van chuckled and I felt the sound all the way down to my toes. "It's you who doesn't listen to me, remember?"

For a second I squeezed my eyes shut and relished being in his arms before I knew I had to pull away. It was heady, being so close to Van. My senses were full to the brink of him. "Thank you for a wonderful night, Van," I said as I looked up into his eyes.

"Thank you for making it wonderful," he said, a small smile touching his lips.

Surely this was the appropriate moment for a goodnight kiss? My heart thumped and I was lightheaded and was so nervous I almost didn't want him to try to kiss me...but I *did*. I stared up at him and he stared back.

Seconds ticked past and he didn't move.

My cheeks burned with mortification that I had completely read the situation wrong. So I turned on my heels and fled into the building.

* * * *

Evelyn was keen for details the following morning over brunch. I remained vague, simply saying that it was a charming party filled with charming people. I was far too embarrassed to try to tell Evelyn stories. Every time I thought of Van, my stomach dropped and my face blushed.

I'd made a fool of myself. Last night Van had made it clear he had no romantic inclination toward me. Outside my building had been the perfect opportunity for a goodnight kiss, and he hadn't even tried. His behavior was becoming more and more like Thomas', only further confirming my suspicions.

The insecure, saddened part of me whispered that it was my own fault…what I deserved. All these years I'd rebelled against love and relationships, only to be rejected when a man who I could actually see myself with came along.

I picked at my eggs, not feeling hungry. My eyes stung, not for the first time that morning. A mixture of disappointment, embarrassment and exhaustion. When I'd gone to bed the night before, I had tossed and turned so much poor Evelyn probably heard me on the other side of the apartment.

"Morning, Barb."

I snapped my head around in the direction of the achingly familiar voice. Van stood on the other side of the railing beside our table, as though he'd passed us on his walk. "Van," I acknowledged with a tight smile.

"Hello, Van!" Evelyn greeted him. "Come join us, I insist."

Van winked at me and hopped over the railing to sit in the empty seat at our table.

Evelyn giggled at his theatrics. "Barbara has been regaling me with tales from last night's party."

"Has she now?" Van asked, his smile amused.

She tutted. "No, the exact opposite. She's being irritatingly vague."

"Sounds like Barb," Van said.

"She's being oddly quiet this morning. Take her for a walk, Van. See if the fresh air will loosen her jaw."

"I'd love to," Van said, standing.

"I'm eating," I cried in protest.

"Barbara, you've barely eaten two mouthfuls this entire time. Go now, before you put everyone off their food with that sour face of yours."

I gasped at her and Van stifled a laugh. There was no other option but to follow him out of the door... Not over the railing.

"What's bugging you?" Van asked, stuffing his hands into his pockets.

"Nothing."

"You're an appalling actress, Barb," Van said with a sigh. "I need coffee, come on, I'll take you to my apartment."

I made no objections as Van guided us out of the park. He bundled us into a cab and headed for the Upper West Side. We didn't talk. Why was I even doing this to myself? If Van really was a homosexual, why bother torturing myself? He would never want me, that wouldn't change.

Maybe I was a masochist, and so long as I got to be around him, in whatever capacity, then I'd take it regardless of the pain.

"It isn't much," Van said as he led me up the stairs to his apartment. "It's just for the summer."

Van's apartment was almost completely bare. A waist-high partition separated the open-plan kitchen and living room, where there was only a couch and a radio. The kitchen held the basics only, and an open door showed a tiny bedroom with a mattress on the floor, surrounded by dozens of books and notepads.

I perched on the edge of the couch as Van puttered in the kitchen, brewing coffee.

"What's going on in that head, Barb?" Van handed me a cup and sat at the other end of the couch.

"Nothing important." I feigned a smile.

"Jack called me this morning," Van said while lighting a cigarette. He offered me his pack and I took one.

My heart skipped a beat. Had Jack been angry? What if he'd only been nice to my face last night, and inwardly he was furious with me and had taken it out on Van? I schooled my features and tried to appear calm at least. "Oh?"

"He wanted to make sure you were all right. And to make sure you wouldn't say anything about last night."

"What?"

Van nodded. "He said it would look bad on the firm if you started badmouthing Robins and telling people what happened at the party."

I frowned. I had absolutely no intention of speaking about last night every again. And not just because of Mr. Robins. "That's ridiculous. Of course I won't say anything."

Van took a hard pull on his cigarette, his shoulders rigid with tension. My words were doing absolutely nothing to reassure him. "Talk to me, Barb," Van pleaded. "I know last night affected you more than you're letting on."

"No, it really hasn't. I promise. I'm just—I'm so worried I've screwed up your internship. Was Jack mad?"

He stubbed out his cigarette and wrung his hands. "No. But I'm pissed at him for putting that idiot before you." Van stood and turned on the radio that was on the counter.

A familiar song filled the room. I stubbed out my cigarette and moved across the room to the window. People looked so small and insignificant from such a great height. They were moving to the beat of their own lives, their own thoughts, and their own destinies. And

I was up here, with no idea where mine was leading me.

"Dance with me," Van said from behind me.

My pulse picked up speed as I turned around to face him. "Here?"

"Why not?"

I frowned. "Why?"

He reached for my hand to pull me closer to him. "Because it'll take my mind off last night." Van drew me into his body, holding one of my hands to his chest and looping his other arm around my back. "It was supposed to— Last night should have been different. It should have been about you and me. No one else. Nothing else."

His words made my eyes sting but I didn't know why. I laid my head against his shoulder and slid my hand up his strong arm to cup his neck and hold onto him. He let out a breath and rested his cheek against mine.

Van and I were a perfect fit. He smelled wonderful, like coffee and soap and something made up of purely him. It didn't feel strange to be dancing in his apartment. Instead it was completely natural, as though there wasn't another thing in the world that we should be doing.

I knew I shouldn't let myself feel this way for him. I'd only get hurt. But I couldn't help it. Was this why I'd had so much anger toward him during the first few times we'd met? Because I knew what he could potentially mean to me?

I had to stop this. I couldn't dally in this strange world any longer. Yet I couldn't bring myself to pull away from him. As though sensing my tumultuous emotions, Van tightened his hold on me, as if the last thing he wanted was for me to leave.

Despite holding me, despite being in his arms, Van was an unreachable dream.

Is this what a broken heart feels like?

A shrill ring from a telephone in another room startled us both. Van smiled in apology and dropped his arms as he went to answer it. "Hello?"

There was a pause as the other person spoke.

"I'm sorry, I can't right now. Tomorrow?"

"Of course I want to, I just—" Van glanced up and saw me staring. I flushed and he turned his back and lowered his voice.

Whirling around, I faced the window again and tried not to listen. Which, of course, was impossible in an apartment so small.

"I just can't right now, I have company. I promise I'll see you tomorrow, okay?" He released a breath, as though he was relieved. "Okay, bye."

Van smiled as he came back into the room. "Sorry about that. Where were we?"

"I should go," I said in a rush. How could he expect me to stay when I'd just overheard him arranging a tryst? I picked up my pocketbook and headed for the door. Twisting the handle, I yanked on it with all my might, but had no success in opening it.

"You have to jimmy the lock," Van explained as he came to help me. He pressed so close I could smell his skin.

An electric look passed between us. It was so powerful I very nearly leaned into him. Our eyes were locked for an eternity as we stood in the doorway. But when he didn't move, I once again had my answer.

So I turned and left before he could see the hurt that would no doubt be blazing in my eyes.

Chapter Thirteen

I felt sick and stupid as I stomped home. People I passed on the street must have thought I was crazy as I muttered under my breath.

How could I have been so blind? Of course he was like Thomas. It all made perfect sense now. He behaved exactly as Thomas had last summer. He was making me his deception. *Not this time,* I told myself. I wouldn't stand for it again.

Before I could change my mind, I let my anger fuel me back to Van's apartment to say my peace. A delivery boy was leaving the building as I arrived and he held the door for me. I marched up the many flights of stairs with single-minded purpose and hammered on his door with my fist.

Van threw open his door, his eyebrows pinched together. His eyes widened in surprise when he realized that it was me. "Barb, what—"

"Don't talk, I have something to say." I brushed past him into the apartment, where I paced like a tiger locked in a cage too small to contain its power.

"Don't you always?" Van closed the door behind me.

In the living room, I whirled around to face him. My body shook with adrenaline and I clenched my hands into fists. "I've figured you out, and I want nothing to do with any of it."

"Excuse me?" Van asked, his eyebrows shooting up.

"I refuse to be anything for you, Van. I've done this once before, and I will not do it again."

He took a step toward me, confusion written all over his face. "Barb, what are you talking about?"

My eyes stung again and I swallowed the emotion that lodged in my throat. "I'm talking about your secret and why you act so strange. I want you to know that I know what it is, and I want nothing to do with it."

Van's face fell. "I see."

"I'm glad you do. You made a serious lapse in judgment the day you thought I would be perfect to act out this charade with you. I mean, what is it with your kind of men? I must be truly repulsive, if this is the only capacity in which a man will be with me." I heaved in a breath, my heart hammering. "What is it about me? Is it just because of my views on marriage? You all think I'm a safe choice because I won't actually fall for any of you? Or is it just because any sane girl would have figured you out by now and not kept your secret?"

"Barb, I'm sorry —" Van's eyes filled with sorrow, his expression crestfallen.

"No, I'm the one that's sorry." Angry tears pricked my eyes but I refused to let him see me cry. "I'm sorry that I ever met you. I'm sorry that I *ever* gave you a chance. But mostly, I'm sorry for thinking about what your intentions toward me might have been."

Van dropped his eyes to the ground, his shoulders slumped. I hated that I felt terrible for causing him any kind of pain.

"I don't know how I didn't figure it out sooner." I laughed with no humor. "You were always so sarcastic, you didn't care about my feelings and you never complimented me. Then once you'd wormed your way into my life, you dug in your claws to make sure you stayed there. You knew all the right things to say and never actually asked me on official dates. Never attempted a goodnight kiss! You even arranged a secret tryst while I was in the next room."

At this something inside me broke. All the heightened emotion that coursed through me burst, and the first tear slid down my cheek. "At least this time I didn't have to see for myself what you really were. This is hard enough without having the image of you kissing a man burned into my memory to torment me at every turn."

Van's head snapped up. "*Man*?" He took one quick step closer. "Barb, do you think I'm a fruit?" he asked incredulously, his eyebrows disappearing into his hairline.

I folded my arms across my chest. "Don't deny it. I know it's true."

He laughed quietly and shook his head. "Nothing could be further from the truth. Is that what all of this has been about? You thought that I've been making it look like we were involved, in an attempt to avoid scrutiny into my personal life?"

"It would certainly fit the pattern. Well, I've said what I came to say. I never want to hear from you ever again."

Van blocked my path when I tried to leave. "Barb, you silly thing. You, who overthinks every little thing, has let your imagination go too far this time."

I couldn't look at him. I knew the tears would come if I dared meet his eyes. My heart squeezed at how genuine his words sounded.

"I'm not a homosexual, Barb. All this — everything that has ever passed between us — is because a long time ago I told myself if anything should happen with us, it would be on your terms, not mine. You would dictate the terms of this relationship, friendship, whatever you want to call it."

Mustering my last ounce of courage, I looked up into his eyes to find them pleading with me. More than anything I wanted to believe him. Wanted to believe that I was wrong.

Van shifted an inch closer. "We've talked before about why we acted the way we did, those first few times. No, I'm not afraid to hurt your feelings just like you aren't afraid to hurt mine — it isn't cruel, it's banter, and it's fun. You're outspoken and free-spirited. That is a wonderful thing, Barb. And when we were finally friends? I wasn't about to ruin what we had by presuming you wanted more. I took things at the pace you made clear you wanted. Oh, and the phone call? My mother. But that is a whole different conversation."

"And last night?" I whispered.

He frowned. "You mean why didn't I kiss you goodnight? Simple. I wasn't sure you would want me to. For chrissakes, you'd just been pawed by that cretin. The last thing I thought you wanted was me to come at you like a hormonal teenage boy."

My breath left me in a rush. "And if you knew I wanted you to?"

Van's eyes searched mine for the longest moment. Time stood still as I swam in his hypnotic gaze. I was held there for I don't know how long, before he cupped my cheeks between his soft and strong hands.

I think my heart stopped dead when he bent his head to brush my mouth with his. Van's lips were silky-soft and warm, the pressure so blissful I'm sure I touched the heavens.

Van pressed his forehead to mine, his breath tickling my face. A single tear slid down my cheek and he wiped it away with his thumb. Van moved his hand into my hair, sliding his fingers through the strands, sending a delicious shiver down my body. "Do you believe me now?" he whispered.

There had been no lie in his kiss, that much I knew for certain. I nodded, not knowing if I could speak even if I wanted to.

Van chuckled and held me closer. "I've ached to tell you for so long."

I clutched his wrists. "Why didn't you?"

He sighed. "Fear, I suppose. I decided I'd rather take the pain of only being your friend, than have the loss of not having you in my life at all."

Pulling away, I scanned his face. "So, all this time —"

Van nodded.

Years.

Van had felt this way for *years*.

And I'd hurt him, over and over again, by being prickly and difficult and obtuse. The thought of causing him pain for so long physically hurt. My heart ached for him.

This time it was me who closed the tiny distance between us. I knotted my hands in his hair, holding him to me. My lips searched his and were not left disappointed. At first we were timid as we explored each other. I moved my mouth over his and when he increased the pressure, my lips parted in a gasp. Van gently coaxed my tongue with his, igniting a low ache in my body that was every bit intoxicating as it was foreign.

The hunger between us grew. Van's arms coiled around my waist, pinning my body to his. I wanted, *needed*, closer to him.

There would never be an experience like it again. Kissing Van was like standing on the edge of a cliff with the wind touching my face. I'd never been so exhilarated or alive.

When we broke the kiss, I fell against him, burrowing my face into his neck and breathing heavily. The building could have collapsed around us and I'm sure we wouldn't have noticed.

His chest rumbled with a quiet laugh as he held me closer still to him.

"What's so funny?" I asked.

"Nothing, I—" Van paused. "I guess I've been imagining our first kiss for so long. I just never imagined it would be in a dirty little apartment like this."

A laugh bubbled in my throat. "That's what you're thinking about right now?"

He squeezed my waist. "Among other things."

I didn't need to ask what they were. "What did you imagine it would be like?" I asked as I pulled back so I could see his face. "Our first kiss, I mean."

Van shrugged. "There were a lot of different scenarios. After a romantic date, I think, was the most common."

"Are you disappointed?"

Van grinned and dipped his head to kiss me quick. "Not in the least."

The radio played in the background but I couldn't say what song it was. It was as though we were meeting again for the first time. I was nervous and awkward and unsure on what to do. Which was ridiculous, we were still the same people. I was still Barb and he was still Van. But so much had changed. We could never go back to what we were before. Not that I wanted to.

"Can I ask you something?" Van sat beside me on the couch, pulling to me his side.

"Anything."

"When you said you wouldn't let yourself be used again, is that what happened with Thomas last summer?"

Horror washed over me when I realized what I'd done. In my moment of defending my honor, I'd betrayed my friend. "Please don't say anything to anyone," I said in a rush. "I feel awful. I can't believe I sold him down the river."

Van shook his head and squeezed my hand. "Of course I won't. I'd always had my suspicions about him, that's why I told you to be careful. As much as it pained me to think of you with anyone else, I knew you'd get hurt if you were too invested with Thomas."

I nodded. "I never felt anything for him, even before I found out the truth. I was curious because I knew he was hiding something. He paraded me around in front of his friends and family, yet he was almost indifferent when we were alone. When I found out, I agreed to see it through until the end of the summer, mostly to give us both peace from our pestering families. He's a good friend now, and I made it clear when we met earlier in the summer that I wouldn't be a part of the lie."

"What about the rumors, though? Something must have got them going."

I smiled. "Thomas thinks it was his mother."

"Whoever the source, I'm glad it isn't true." Van rose from the couch and pulled me to my feet. "Come on, it's too beautiful a day to be cooped up in here."

"Where are we going?" I asked as he led me out of the apartment.

"The park?" Van suggested.

"Perfect." I slipped my arm into the crook of his and walked close to his side. It felt strange and wonderful all at the same time. This man, this extraordinary man, who'd been my friend for a while now, was suddenly something much more intimate. I snuck a look at him from under my lashes. His beauty really was extraordinary. What on earth was he doing with such a dull person as me?

"You never talk about girls to me," I said, the thought popping into my head.

Van laughed. "Do you want me to?"

I shrugged. "The thought just occurred to me."

"Didn't you think it was because there haven't been any girls to talk about?"

"Ever?" I asked, lifting my eyebrows in shock.

He laughed again. "No, not never, Barb. But once you stopped hating me so passionately, I stopped noticing any other girls."

"Were there a lot? While I still hated you?" I asked, unsure if I wanted the answer.

"I wouldn't say a lot. I was never like Paul, if that's what you're getting at. You filled my head completely, Barb, and I could think of nothing else. I hoped I'd get over my obsession, but none of the girls I dated ever had half the hold on me like you do."

I flushed from head to toe with pleasure.

"And you?"

"And me what?" I asked.

"Have there been many men?"

"I would have thought that was obvious."

"Not at all."

"Oh." I frowned. "I... I didn't have any time for men, much to my mother's disgust, of course. I never met anyone I wanted to get to know further. After what happened with Thomas, I realized that not every man only wanted either a wife or a good-time girl, but they could be interested in personality and friendship too. I started to give some a bit of a chance, but none really stuck around. I must be frightening to anyone except you."

Van grinned. "How lucky for me."

I nudged him in the ribs with my elbow.

"I'm serious. Did it all start as a means of upsetting your mother?"

"It didn't help," I said with a sigh. "All I've heard since I was a little girl is that my only role in this world is to be a wife and mother. Even now, she mails me the wedding announcements from the local paper."

Van threw his head back and let out a loud laugh.

"Even though none of the boys at home interested me anyway, I grew more stubborn because of my mother. I didn't even bother getting to know anyone new. Eventually it became known not to waste time asking me on dates, because the answer would always be no."

"What did Anna think of your views on courting and marriage?" Van asked.

"That I was strange, just like everyone else." I laughed. "She was a sweetheart, though. She'd get frustrated at me sometimes, like if she wanted to double date. But she knew I would never be like the other girls, whose only dream was to find a rich husband. I told her and my mother that it wouldn't be marriage that would settle me down, it would be the man himself. If I found someone who could love me for who I was and not try and tame me, then I wouldn't be opposed to sharing my life with him. Until that happened, I certainly wasn't going to accept the first proposal that came my way."

Van nodded. "Did your mother ever try to change you?"

"Of course!" I laughed as memories came to mind. "She would traipse me around town, introducing me to girls who'd recently gotten engaged, and they would tell me how wonderfully magical it all was. She didn't realize it only made me even more adamant that I'd never marry. She would find young men who were visiting relations in our area and parade me in front of them so they could size me up the way farmers do at livestock auctions. That's why I come to New York, you know."

"What do you mean?" Van asked.

"My mother would send Anna and me here every summer because my aunt has terrific connections with the right kind of people. She hoped someone would find me charming and convince me a comfortable life wouldn't be so bad. Evelyn, though, was never as severe as my mother. She didn't mind if I didn't have a date every night of the week. From time to time she'd arrange dates for me, more to keep my mother happy than anything else."

Van smiled. "Sounds like a good woman. Did she herself never marry?"

"Oh yes. She fell in love with a wonderful man. He worked on Wall Street and gave her everything she ever wanted."

"What happened?"

"He died. Heart problems at thirty-eight, can you believe it? She never got over it. Who would? He left her his fortune, so she's well taken care of."

"That's too bad," Van said, quietly.

I nodded. "Anyway, let's not go into a somber mood. Don't you have any cheerful questions for me?"

A mischievous glint flashed in his eyes. "When are you going to introduce me to your parents?"

That I was not expecting... "What? I don't know — I don't particularly want to scare you away."

He laughed. "You didn't, so I think I'd handle it all right."

I huffed at him and waved the subject away with a flick of my hand. "Let's not think about that. You met Evie, isn't that enough for now?"

"I met her as your friend. Aren't I more than that now?"

"Yes." Glancing at him, I realized that I did want him to meet Evelyn again, this time as someone much more important. I wanted to show him off — to let the world know that this amazing man wanted to be with me...

We entered the park and Van guided us to a large tree on the lawn. He sprawled out on the grass, keeping his head in the shade of the tree. I sat down and leaned against the thick brown trunk.

"I wish every day was Sunday," Van said with his eyes closed.

"Why is that?"

"No one rushes anywhere, nothing is hurried."

I thought about it. "I loathe Sundays."

He opened one eye to look at me. "Any particular reason?"

"Well, Saturdays tend to be busy and full of plans. But usually I spend Sundays waiting for Monday to come around."

Van laughed. "That is the most miserable description of a Sunday I've ever heard. You don't do anything on Sundays? Nothing at all?"

I shrugged. "Not when I'm at Wellesley. During vacations it's different, I suppose. At Yellow Sands it's like any other day of the week. When I'm here, I have brunch with my aunt and now you have developed a pattern of appearing." He grinned at my last remark. "But normally, yes, my Sundays are boring. I read, or I'm suffering the effects from the night before, having spent most of the night with Lois in the Dragon."

Van propped himself up on his side. "How about from today onward, Sunday is our day. Even if we do nothing at all, we spend it together."

"What do you mean, even if we do nothing at all?"

"I mean, if you want to have your beautiful nose hidden in a book, then you can, just as long as I can be with you while you do it."

I smiled. "All right. I can live with that."

"Good." He sat up fully and brushed my face with his fingertips. Van pulled me toward him. My heart thudded so hard I was sure it would burst from my chest at any moment. And as softly as he had the first time, he kissed me.

I was sure I could spend all my days kissing Van without ever growing tired of it. Was this what I'd been missing out on all along? Was this why Anna, Lois, my mother, all nagged me to meet a man, because they knew the pleasures it could bring?

No, it wouldn't have felt the same with anyone other than Van.

We stayed in the park so long it became time for dinner. Van took me to a tiny little out-of-the-way place. Cozy, with a certain amount of privacy. We talked in hushed voices and teased each other's fingers across the table.

On the walk home, we dawdled so much that it took over an hour to travel the short distance. We said goodbye under the canopy of my building and shared a delicious kiss. Van said it would only be polite to escort me to the elevator, to make sure I got in the building safely since the doorman was on a break. Once at the elevator, I said he might as well make the trip with me.

We stood outside my front door for a further half hour, neither of us ready to say goodbye.

Our goodnight kiss was chaste and proper with both of us all too aware of nosy neighbors and their peepholes. We wished each other goodnight and Van promised to call the following evening.

I floated to my bedroom in a haze, seeing nothing but Van's glorious face behind my eyelids. I thought I'd lie awake for hours, but sleep took me surprisingly quickly. I slept fitfully and dreamlessly, and at this, I was disappointed. I'd hoped that since we couldn't be together in person, my dreams would have taken me to him.

Chapter Fourteen

Evelyn noticed my agitated state the following day when I couldn't sit still for more than five minutes at a time. She eventually kicked me out of the house with a shopping list and told me not to return for at least an hour. I didn't tell her the reason behind my behavior, as though it would somehow ruin the feeling by saying it aloud.

On my return, she decided it was as good a time as any for me to learn how to cook a roast dinner. She set me to work peeling vegetables and chopping things. It was good to have something to occupy my mind. If I paused, even for a second, my thoughts were flooded with Van and it seemed as if time moved backward.

When I finished one job, Evelyn was ready with another. By the end, I was proud with the result. I'd made a salad and dessert, prepared vegetables for the main course and helped Evelyn ready the meat. She gave me a duster and motioned for me to dust anything that looked like it needed it. To be honest, nothing looked like it needed it at all, but I dusted and polished every visible surface just for something to do.

Come six that night, I'd grown increasingly impatient and I'd still not heard a word from Van. I didn't expect to until later, I knew he'd be working hard. But it was an agonizing wait, nonetheless. I went for a long hot bath to try to relax myself then dressed for dinner in a loose-fitting blouse and slacks.

I walked into the dining room and was confused at what I found. The table was laid for three, not two, and Evelyn had elaborately decorated the table the way she only did when she was expecting company.

"Evie?" I called, heading for the lounge to look for her. "Are you expecting someone? I can keep out of your hair if you are."

Her voice came from the kitchen and I followed it. "That would defeat the point of who I invited."

"Who did you invite?"

"Go see for yourself." Evelyn placed three cocktails onto a tray and handed it to me, shooing me into the other room where our guest was.

Van sat on one of the couches and rose when he saw me entering the room.

"Oh," I said, before breaking out into a grin and enjoying the pleasant dip of my stomach.

"Evening," he said with a wicked smile on his face.

I turned to my aunt. She smiled knowingly. "You've been restless all day, child. You didn't have to be a genius to figure it out."

I laughed and shook my head at her. Evelyn was more perceptive than I gave her credit for.

"I'm going to check on dinner. Barb, I'm sure you'll entertain our guest."

My face flushed at this, though Evelyn was only being polite. She disappeared from the room, leaving me alone with Van.

He rose to relieve me of the tray and placed it on the table in the center of the room. Van returned to my side and took my hand in his. "Do you mind me being here? I would have called but I didn't get time and I think your aunt wanted it to be a surprise."

I smiled. "Of course I don't mind. It's a wonderful surprise." Moving closer to him, I whispered, "I've thought about you all day."

Van grinned. "Me too. I've barely been able to concentrate on my work." He pulled me toward the couch and we sat down as close to each other as was possible.

I glanced toward the doorway and saw no sight of my aunt, so felt safe to lean in and kiss Van. It was so tender a kiss I was sure I would remember the moment forever. I touched his forehead with mine and closed my eyes. He traced my cheek with his fingertips, making me break out in goosebumps.

Dinner passed smoothly with Evelyn quizzing Van on his life. Work, housing, education and such things. He always replied with the utmost politeness and when confident enough, he would gently tease her.

When the table had been cleared, Evelyn poured Van and I each a Scotch and asked us to move into the other room where we would be more comfortable. Evelyn sat in a chair while Van and I took the couch, sitting with an appropriate distance between us.

Before long Evelyn made her excuses to leave. I didn't know what her rules of etiquette with male guests in her house would be, as I'd never had anyone over before who wasn't a friend. I didn't feel comfortable in asking Van into my bedroom, yet sitting here felt so formal and stiff.

So I suggested taking our drinks onto the terrace and Van agreed. The terrace itself was large enough for a set of table and chairs. The comfortable silence continued while we sipped our drinks and listened to the steady stream of traffic emanating from the street below.

When my glass was empty, I stood and leaned on the thick stone railing and took in the marvelous sights before me, letting the city wash away any thoughts.

Van's chair scraped against the stone floor. He pressed in behind me, his front against my back. My stomach flipped as I turned in his arms. It only took seconds for his lips to find mine. Hesitant at first, then more passionate as our confidence grew. Our hands were everywhere — in each other's hair, touching faces, holding our bodies tightly together. A cry escaped my lips and I was flung back to the present. The kiss was broken and Van took a step away from me. He shook his head and rubbed the back of his neck, mumbling something about 'a highly dangerous creature'.

He passed me a cigarette from the open pack on the table and lit one for himself, sinking back into the chair he'd occupied minutes before. I stayed standing and leaned with my back against the railing. My heart raced and my face was still flushed red.

"Barb, you know that we can take this as slow as you're comfortable with, don't you?"

I frowned. "What do you mean?"

"I mean that I'm fine with whatever pace you want to go at." He paused and looked me straight in the eye. "I know that this is all new to you, and I don't want you to feel pressured in anyway. I'm not going to mess this up by going too fast. Promise me you won't give a single thought to what you might think I want, okay? I want what you want. It's as simple as that."

The sincerity in his eyes was overwhelming and I couldn't deny he was speaking true. I lowered myself onto his lap and wrapped my arms around his shoulders. "You're too wonderful, Van," I whispered.

"Oh, I'm not that great," he said, ducking his head.

"I think you are," I said as I broke away from him.

He smiled and stroked his hand down my hair. "I think maybe you're biased."

"Maybe a little."

Van glanced at his watch. Sighing, he said, "As much as I hate to say it—"

"Then don't," I interrupted.

He gave me a small smile that didn't reach his eyes. "I really should go. I got no sleep last night because I couldn't stop thinking about a certain someone, and I have a busy day tomorrow."

Even with dawdling as best I could, the short walk to the front door was over far too quickly. He kissed my cheek and ducked out—gone before I could even utter goodnight. I knew it was for the best. I knew only too well how long we could prolong our goodnight kiss.

I ran back to the terrace and leaned over so I could see the sidewalk beneath me.

Moments later Van appeared from under the canopy and flagged down a cab. My heart gave a little jolt at the sight of him. He didn't look up at the building as he got in and disappeared into the night.

Sighing to myself, I gathered the paraphernalia from the table and took it inside. I kept the cigarettes with me as I shut myself away in my room. Sitting at my desk in front of a blank sheet of paper, I planned to write a letter to Lois. No words would come and an hour later the paper still remained untouched. I longed to talk to Lois and tell her what I was feeling, Anna also. I knew both women would be over the moon with happiness for me, so why couldn't I write anything? Maybe because I didn't know what words to use, to describe the intensity of what flowed through my veins. Anything I said would only sound dramatic.

As much as I longed for Lois and her company, I ached for Van. I wanted to feel his touch, see his eyes and kiss his lips. I yearned for the feel of his strong arms wrapped around me, shielding me completely from any outside forces.

* * * *

"Any plans for today?" Evelyn asked over breakfast.

I shook my head in reply.

"Why not call in and see Thomas? I'm sure he'd like it." Evelyn cleared her throat. "His mother called last night while you were getting ready for dinner."

I froze. That couldn't mean anything good. "What did she want?"

"She wanted to know if you would have lunch with her this week."

I groaned and let my toast fall onto my plate. "Oh, Evie, couldn't you have said I was sick or something?

Evelyn narrowed her eyes. "Barbara, I will not lie for you. You're an adult—it shouldn't be too hard to meet someone like Mrs. Gentry for lunch."

I rolled my eyes. "You know why she wants to meet me."

Her lips twitched. "I have my suspicions, but your feelings for her son, or lack thereof, shouldn't stand in the way of the friendship you have with her."

What friendship? She's still convinced I'm going to marry her son! "I'd feel like I was giving her false hope."

"You just have to subtly tell her you have no intentions of getting involved with Thomas."

"As simple as that?"

Aunt Evelyn smiled. "Yes, as simple as that."

"Then will you come too?" I asked with a hopeful smile.

She laughed. "Oh no, this is for you to take care of."

"Fine, I'll call her after breakfast and arrange something." Flashing Evelyn a look, I said, "But don't blame me when she flips out when she hears I've got a boyfriend."

* * * *

Mrs. Gentry was ecstatic when I called her to accept the offer of lunch. She was eager to meet me right away, but I told her I'd not long finished breakfast. Coffee then, she negotiated. It became clear I was not going to escape the phone call without arranging a date with her for that very same day. I agreed to meet her at a little café a few blocks away in an hour.

I dressed in a simple cream dress that was loose-fitting and cool in the heatwave that had hovered over the city these past few weeks. I arrived before Mrs. Gentry, and secured us a table outside in the shade. She was full of smiles when she finally showed up and kissed my cheek by way of a greeting.

"I'm delighted you could meet with me, Barbara," she said as she sat down opposite me.

"It's no trouble at all. Was there a particular reason for the meeting?"

"Not at all. It occurred to me last night that it had been a while since we'd chatted."

I nodded and tried to keep the smile fixed on my face.

Mrs. Gentry dragged the coffee out to three cups and an apple Danish. For the most part we made awkward small talk, and it wasn't until we'd been sitting at the café for almost two hours that she finally said what was on her mind.

"You don't seem to be around as much as you used to," Mrs. Gentry said.

"I've been busy this summer," I said, choosing my words carefully. Though I had no interest in letting Mrs. Gentry continue to think there was still hope for me and Thomas, I didn't want to hurt her feelings. "I have a lot of friends in the city that I don't get to see a great deal of. I try and divide my time as equally as possible."

"Of course." She nodded. "However, last summer it seemed like you and Thomas were inseparable, seeing each other almost every day."

"A few things have changed since then," I said, shifting in my chair. "We courted last summer and that is not the case this year. Thomas and I are different people now."

She laughed. "Don't be ridiculous, the boy adores you."

I smiled softly. "And so do I. But as a friend."

"*Friend.*" Mrs. Gentry brushed the word off with a wave of her hand. "He would love to be your boyfriend again."

"That isn't possible." I sucked in a breath. *Here it comes...* "I already have a boyfriend."

"Oh, I see." Mrs. Gentry blinked. She couldn't mask her shock, but soon shrugged it off. "A summer romance never lasts though, dear. Thomas is a good choice for the long term."

I looked down and focused on keeping my temper in check. My patience waned. "May I remind you that Thomas was a summer romance last year? Mrs. Gentry, I appreciate your intentions, but I just don't have any romantic feelings toward Thomas. He and I are friends, and that is as far as either of us wish to take our relationship."

"Thomas can provide security for you. You wouldn't need to continue in your education, he could give you a lovely home and full life," Mrs. Gentry said, trying a different tactic.

"Mrs. Gentry, I don't know how to say this without hurting your feelings, but I don't want to marry Thomas and he doesn't want to marry me."

"And this other boy does?"

My heart fluttered. "I have no idea. We haven't discussed any future possibilities."

"You would be a wonderful daughter-in-law," she said in a quiet voice.

I smiled. "And you will make a lovely mother-in-law one day. You just won't be mine."

Her eyes filled with tears and I couldn't help but cringe. As soon as she had her emotions under control, I hailed her a cab and sent her on her way. Relief washed over me as the taxi disappeared from sight.

My afternoon picked up considerably when I arrived home. Van had left a message for me with Evelyn. Jack and his wife wanted to take us out for dinner that night. There was a bounce in my step that I hadn't felt since childhood as I headed for my room to select an outfit for the evening.

* * * *

Van picked me up at seven-thirty sharp for dinner, looking dashing in a gray suit. I wore a fitted burgundy dress and left my hair down in natural waves. There was a cab waiting for us downstairs to take us to the restaurant.

Butterflies flitted in my belly as we walked into the restaurant, but Jack was just as friendly as the last time

I'd seen him, and his wife, Camilla, was as lovely as Evelyn.

Camilla had also attended Wellesley College and so we found a lot to talk about. We laughed about grumpy professors and the tiny dorm rooms. She told me hilarious stories about what she and her friends had gotten up to, and when the boys from a nearby college had plotted and managed to pull off a panty raid on her dormitory.

I laughed harder when I learned that Jack had been one of the guilty party.

After the dessert dishes had been taken away, Jack turned to me. "So, Barb. How's that other boyfriend of yours? Have you saw sense yet and broke it off so you can get together with Van?"

A look passed between Van and me, which confirmed this for him.

"Marvelous!" Jack bellowed, clapping his hands together. "When did this happen?"

"A few days ago," Van replied, placing his hand on top of mine.

"What did I tell you? It was the party, wasn't it? No need to thank me, my boy. It was my pleasure." Jack laughed. He turned to his wife. "This is all my doing."

"Yes, dear," she said, humoring him. Camilla flashed me a wink.

"Have you ever seen a couple who was better suited for one another?" Jack asked Camilla.

"They do make a handsome pair," Camilla agreed.

I was saved from further embarrassment as the waiter brought over after-dinner brandy for everyone. We didn't stay too late, and soon said goodnight to Jack and Camilla.

"Do you want to come to my apartment for a nightcap?" Van asked.

"I'd love to," I said.

Van put the radio on when we got to his apartment and poured us both a highball.

He handed me mine as I stood by the breeze of the open window. Van then sprawled himself on the couch, stretching his lean body.

I sat beside him on the edge of the couch and pushed his hair off his face. "Are you tired?"

"No," he said through a yawn, his eyes already halfway closed.

I finished my drink and put the glass in the kitchen sink. When I turned back around, Van was snoring softly.

A soft smile pulled at my lips. I tiptoed back to the couch and pulled off his shoes. I kissed his forehead and left a scribbled note on the kitchen counter for him saying I'd gone home and I'd see him tomorrow.

* * * *

During brunch the following day, Evelyn asked when I was seeing Van. I told her I didn't know, as we hadn't made any definitive plans the night before. I almost expected him to appear midway through the meal as he'd done twice now, but he never came.

Once Evelyn had left in a cab, I bought some fresh bagels and took them across to Van's apartment. There was no answer when I knocked on his door and I banged for so long I started to think that maybe he'd gone out somewhere.

But eventually the door opened and Van stood blinking at me, his eyes barely open slits, and his hair poking every which way.

"Oh!" I cried, when I took in his appearance. "I'm sorry, I didn't think you'd still be sleeping, do you want me to come back later?"

He reached for my hand and pulled me inside the apartment and greeted me with a sleepy kiss. "Of course not, this is the best way to wake up."

"Hungry?" I asked, holding up the paper bag from the bakery.

His forehead puckered in confusion. "Aren't you having brunch with Evie?"

"I already have, it's after noon, Van," I said, laughing as I walked into the kitchen.

"Really? Wow, I was dead to the world. Did you do that?" He pointed to the shoes.

"Well, it certainly wasn't the maid," I threw over my shoulder. "You were exhausted, poor thing."

"Did you get home okay?"

I nodded and smeared cream cheese on two halves of a bagel and handed it to him on a small plate before brewing some coffee and tidying up the mess I'd made.

"You are incredible," Van said as he took a huge bite. He finished his bagel and coffee in record time and stretched his body fully before slouching on the couch. He yawned as I moved to sit beside him.

"Are you still tired?" I asked.

"You have to be kidding me. How could I be tired when I have you here?"

I laughed. "You passed out after I'd been here for five minutes last night. I didn't realize I was such a bore."

"Well, I didn't want to tell you," Van teased. He pulled me closer to him and I rested my head on his chest. I loved the feel of his body pressed against mine — him hard in all the places I was soft.

"Do you want to do anything today?"

"I'm already doing it." There was a smile in his voice. "And I plan on doing nothing else at all."

I pushed myself up and looked at him. He was being deadly serious. "Nothing at all?"

"Nothing at all." He confirmed.

"So this is really all we're going to do today?"

Van groaned. "Yes, woman. Now stop complaining."

"Aren't you bored?"

Van laughed. "In some parts of the world, people enjoy relaxing. Why don't you try it? You might like it."

"I do relax. I just can't sit here with nothing to do."

Sighing, Van got up and left the room. He returned a moment later and dropped a book into my lap. Dante's *Inferno*. I smiled at him.

"I'm going to run down to the corner to get a paper. Do you need anything?"

I shook my head, already thumbing through the pages to get to the beginning of the book.

When Van returned, he lay down with his head in my lap to read the paper while I lost myself in Dante's world. He made us a snack a few hours later and we sat in the sunshine on the fire escape to eat it.

After, we moved back to the couch, but there was an itch under my skin and I couldn't concentrate on my book. I dropped it to the floor and threw myself onto Van. We kissed for hours and I could feel all my inhibitions slipping away. Van wouldn't let it go very far before he would break it off and let us cool down before starting up again. He really did want to take things slow, I realized, and let things progress at a lazy pace so as to enjoy each and every moment.

Our perfect Sunday soon crept into the early hours of Monday, and I knew I ought to go home. All I wanted was to fall asleep with him, but I forced myself into a cab around one a.m.

Chapter Fifteen

It felt as if I'd been sleeping my entire life. I'd been lying dormant like a volcano and life now exploded out of me. My whole world became Van. I lived and breathed for him and everything else faded to a background.

Word got back to my mother about Van and she insisted on meeting him. I should have known it wouldn't take long. I delayed the inevitable as much as possible, but there was no avoiding it. My mother and father were coming to New York for the weekend and said there was no time like the present. I was mortified. Thank God for my father, though. I knew he would make it somewhat bearable.

My nerves were shot to hell the day of the dinner.

Van tried his best to soothe me throughout the day, but no sooner had I calmed down than my nerves escalated once again. Van left me to get ready and promised to be back once he himself was dressed. We were having dinner in the Plaza. My parents had never taken me anywhere so fancy, and I guessed it was more to impress Van, rather than a treat for me.

I fidgeted with my hands in the cab. What if Mom was rude to Van? My mother was so cruel to me at the best of times and I hated to imagine what she would be like to Van if she didn't like him. And most of all, I was terrified Van would have a different opinion of me once he got to know what my mother was like.

Mom and Dad were already seated when we arrived. It was my father who saw us coming first and rose out of his seat. He hugged me and whispered for me to relax.

I squeezed Van's arm as I smiled up at him, never prouder than I was in that moment. "Dad, Mom, this is Van Judson."

Dad extended his hand to Van, a warm, open smile on his lips. "Van, good to meet you, son. Is it Vance? Do you go by Van?"

Van nodded and shook Dad's hand. "Yessir, Van suits me just fine." He smiled at Mom and dipped to kiss her cheek. "Ma'am."

If I didn't know better, I'd swear that Mom blushed and may have even, dare I say it—giggled.

Not that I could blame her. Van was every bit as handsome as he had been the night of the party. He wore a black suit and had slicked back his hair again. He looked like a well-groomed young man and I secretly challenged my mother to try to find a fault in him.

We all took our seats and Van threaded his fingers with mine under the table.

"How are you enjoying the summer with Evelyn?" Dad asked, finally breaking the silence.

I grinned. "As much as ever. You know, Evie. She's a popular woman and she gets invited to everything."

Dad chuckled. "Yes, she always did like to socialize."

"Van and Evelyn get on tremendously well," I said.

"Oh?" My father looked at Van.

"Yessir, she's a charming woman. I think anyone would find it hard to not like Evelyn," Van said.

"How has your summer been, Dad?" I asked. "It seems I've barely spoken to you since Christmas."

He shrugged. "It's been okay, steady as always."

"And you, Mom?" I looked at her and she stared back at me.

Her face softened and she smiled as she spoke. "Oh, you know, Barb. I've just been supporting your father whenever he's needed me. The way a good wife does."

"And the café society?" I asked, lifting my eyebrows. "They haven't missed you while you've been performing your wifely duties? Or have you allocated a slot of time dedicated to cakes and gossip?"

My father cleared his throat to conceal a laugh. "Your mother has been very kind to me this summer, Barb. She's been helping in the office as much as she can, typing and what not."

"And your summer, Barb?" my mother asked, her eyes flashing. "Have you been occupying the bars again, as you do when you are at that college of yours?"

"Of course, someone has to help keep the barmen in employment." I smiled.

Mom sighed, but seemed to realize I wasn't going to back down to her. "Have you been helping Evelyn?"

"When does Evelyn need any help?" I asked with a smile. "I give her my opinion when she asks for it, about art for example. I do her grocery shopping and run errands whenever she asks. Mainly it's company I provide."

"It's good for her to have company in that big apartment of hers. And you still have time for her? Despite now having a distraction in your life?" There was no malice in her question.

"Yes, I'll always have time for my family. Instead of going out, some nights Van and I stay in and we play board games with Evelyn. Every Sunday morning I still have brunch with her. She keeps herself busy also, and disappears off to parties and benefits without telling me."

"Yes, she always was like that," Mom said, nodding. "Do the two of you go on drives to the country? I'm sure she would appreciate that, you could take her some weekday when it's quiet."

"I don't drive, Mother," I reminded her.

"Doesn't Van?" she asked, looking at him.

"He works," I said.

This caught both my parents' attention.

"Oh? A summer job?" Dad asked.

"Just an internship," Van said with a smile. He was modest, and not the type to brag. "At Johnson, Tate and Brown."

"The law office?" my father asked.

"Yessir."

Dad lifted his eyebrows and sat back in his chair. If I didn't know any better, I'd say Van had just knocked his socks off. "I've heard those internships are very elusive. How did you come about getting it?"

"I suppose I was the right man for the job," Van said with a small smile. "It's where my interests lie, and I start Harvard Law in the fall."

Mom and Dad exchanged a look, both of them seeming impressed.

"Wait," Dad said, "did Barb say your surname is Judson? Your father wouldn't be Jeffrey Judson, would he?"

Van's smile faltered. No one else would have noticed it, but because I knew all his smiles, all his expressions so well, I knew the conversation had just made Van uncomfortable. "Yessir."

"Who is that? Do you know him?" Mom asked.

"Yes, you could say that," Dad said. "Jeffrey Judson is better known as Chief Justice — of the Supreme Court."

"Oh..." My mother's eyes lit up at this information.

I glanced at Van out of the corner of my eye. He rarely talked about his family and was vague when he did.

"Are you following in your father's footsteps, Van?" Dad asked. I wished he would drop the subject. I had no idea what the beef was between Van and his father, but it was enough to put him on edge.

Van took a sip from his water glass. "I've always taken a keen interest in the law. I like to think I would be making a difference, to represent people who can't do it themselves."

Dad nodded. "And is he helping you on your way? Is that how you got the internship?"

Van's body tensed. "I like to make my own way in the world and not ride on the coattails of others. I can only assume my surname helps me, but I've never dropped my father's name in the chance of bettering myself. I'd like to think I was chosen for the internship because I was the best man for it."

I'd never heard Van speak in that tone before. It wasn't cold, but somehow detached. He remained polite as ever and the change wasn't obvious to anyone but me. "Van is very popular with Mr. Tate, one of the senior partners." I threw in to help move the conversation away from what was making Van uncomfortable.

"Really? I heard he was a difficult man to impress," Dad said.

Van chuckled. "I believe it was Barb who warmed him to me."

My father laughed. "How so?"

Swatting Van on the arm, I rolled my eyes at Dad. "I bumped into him and made him drop the papers he was carrying."

Not surprisingly, Mom tsked at my clumsiness.

"He was so charmed by her he invited her on the spot to the firm's annual summer ball," Van continued. "We had dinner with Jack and his wife a few weeks ago."

My parents looked at me incredulously.

I smiled so widely it hurt, and willed the waiter to hurry up so we could get this meal over with.

That night Van did a better job of impressing my parents during one meal than I had in my lifetime. Once off the subject of his father, Van broke out the charm and I swear, Mom even giggled at one point.

He made lifelong fans in my parents.

At the end of the evening, Dad asked if we wanted to share a cab with him and my mother back to Evelyn's but Mom hushed him, saying he was ruining the romance of the evening as she was sure Van would like to walk me. I laughed at my parents and agreed with my mother that a walk would be lovely.

Once goodnights were said and Van had promised to make a trip with me to visit my parents, I was finally alone with him. We walked along the crowded streets with his arm around my waist and with me tucked in close to him.

There were so many questions I wanted to ask Van, but had no idea where to start.

"Do you think they liked me?" Van asked, squeezing my waist.

I laughed. "Are you kidding? You couldn't have been anymore charming if you tried. What did you think of them? My mother—" I started.

"Your family are golden, Barb. They created you and helped shape who you are today. I have to love them for that."

"You always know what to say," I said, kissing his cheek.

We went back to Van's apartment for a nightcap. He turned the radio on as normal and we danced in his tiny living room, feeling like the happiest couple in the world.

* * * *

It was as if my mother had changed personalities overnight. She'd never been kinder toward me. I wasn't so big a fool not to know why there was a drastic change in her character. After years of pestering, she thought she'd won the battle. I overheard a conversation she had with Evelyn, who defended me to my overbearing mother. Evelyn said she always knew I would get serious about a man, it just had to be the right man, and at least I wasn't foolish to dally about with men that held no real interest. But my mother's happy and superior bubble couldn't be burst by anyone.

Mom joined Evelyn and me for brunch the morning after dinner with Van, and kept up her friendly chatter. "Would you like to go shopping today, Barb? We could get you some new clothes to go back to school with."

Evelyn smiled and shot me a wink. "Oh, you won't see Barb after this, Florence. She and Van spend every Sunday afternoon together."

"How lovely. What do you do?" Mom asked me.

I shrugged. "Sometimes we take a walk through the park or around the city. Most of the time we just read, or talk. Spend time just the two of us."

"That doesn't sound very exciting." My mother frowned. "There are lots of things you could be doing."

"It's how we like to spend our Sundays, Mother."

Mom sighed but pushed me no further.

Van surprised us three women that midmorning by showing up at the Tavern, something he hadn't done for a long time. It was a lovely surprise, and I suspected he did it to earn me points with my mother... But the gesture was appreciated all the same.

When we left my mother and aunt to finish their gossiping, Van informed me that he had an ulterior motive for stealing me from them. Van had borrowed a car from someone at the office, as he left his in Boston, not wanting to spend so much money on gas driving it to New York. He was taking me to a restaurant upstate.

Van took the top down, making the drive refreshing and warm as the sun kissed my skin. The wind blew all thoughts from my head as I watched the scenery around me changed from bustling city life to the green and empty hills of the country.

We drove through a small town and though it seemed to be nothing spectacular in its scale, the grandeur of the houses indicated only the wealthy must live there. The houses disappeared into the backdrop and for a while there was nothing at all. Not before long, Van pulled into a small parking lot beside a restaurant that looked like a converted mill.

The drive itself had taken almost two hours and it felt good to get out of the car and stretch my legs. A small stream ran behind the restaurant where ducks lingered, warming their backs in the sunlight. Van led me inside and it was clear we were in for a long wait.

The hostess led us into a comfortable lounge where we could wait until there was a table ready. Van remained quiet, as he had during the journey. I'd thought it was because with the wind in our faces, conversation would have been difficult without shouting, but maybe he'd had something on his mind. I didn't want to push him into talking — he'd do it when he was ready.

Our wait wasn't too severe, only forty-five minutes, which was no time at all when I was with Van. He placed his hand on the small of my back as we walked to our table. It made me feel safe and secure, but most of all it made me proud. Proud that I had been the one to attract his eye. I saw looks from young women when we passed them by and the hope in their eyes that one day they themselves may find someone who adored them as much as Van obviously adored me. Secret looks flitted between Van and myself that no other person in the world could interpret. We were an elusive club, with room for only two members.

The room could have been empty for the amount of attention we paid to the other patrons. The noise died down to a quiet whisper to our ears only, and all the other faces became a blur. There wasn't much more conversation during the meal itself, but there didn't have to be. We were so comfortable with each other now that constant chatter wasn't needed.

With one look, Van told me it was time to leave. He settled the bill and we made our way outside. The sun was beginning to set, sinking low in the sky. The light was almost blinding as it kissed the tops of the trees. It was the time when things slowed to a close and grew lazy. Van walked ahead of me with his hands jammed in his pockets.

I paused, for no reason at all, other than to take in everything around me. The birds chirped and sang in the trees and a heron stood patiently in the water, getting ready to catch an unsuspecting fish. A breeze teased the long, drooping branches of the weeping willow, stirring it to life.

As I had with Anna that New Year's Eve that now seemed so many, many years ago, I wished with more desperation than I'd ever known to remember every detail of that moment.

Van must have realized I wasn't by his side, and turned to face me. A small, secret smile formed on his lips and he held out his hand for me to catch up to and take.

In that moment, I knew I was looking at my future. I wondered if Anna looked that way at Kenneth when she knew they would forever be together. I wondered if every woman was this certain on the man she wanted to marry.

Of course, my mother would rejoice and thank the heavens if she knew what I was thinking. The stubborn part of me still wanted to deny her this truth. My future was Van after all—I didn't have to marry him to enjoy him for the rest of my days. But I wouldn't embarrass my family by living in sin.

As surely as I knew how much I wanted Van, I also knew how much I didn't want to marry him, not yet at least. Years and years had still to pass before I'd be ready, but at least I knew I was on the road toward it. And that was plenty enough for me.

With a goofy smile, I rushed toward him. He took my hand and kissed the top of my head. It was brief and routine, something he did often. Yet I was convinced there had been no more romantic gesture in the history of the world.

In the car, I closed the distance between us and Van put his arm around my shoulder and held me to him. Sleep could have taken me easily. But I was determined not to miss a single second of that day.

Chapter Sixteen

Whatever it was that was playing on Van's mind, it grew larger and more dominant on the drive back to the city. I yearned to know what it was, not for the simple reason of knowing, but for the opportunity to comfort him somehow.

I got my wish eventually. Van pulled off the road and stopped the car. The road was quiet that Sunday evening and not one car passed by us. "What's the matter?" I asked, pulling back so I could see his face.

Van cleared his throat and stared out of the front windshield. "I wanted to talk to you today, and I keep finding excuses not to. The drive too noisy, the restaurant too crowded. I thought now would do."

I lifted my eyebrows. "Here?"

An uneasy smile pulled at his full lips. "Why not?" Van got out of the car and left his door open.

Van paced back and forth, running his hand through his hair a few times as though trying to put his thoughts in order. I wanted to help him, to shoulder this terrible burden, whatever it was.

"Van? You know you can say anything to me." I assured him.

At my voice, he stopped. A soft sigh escaped his lips as he faced me. I scooted to the edge of the seat and let my legs dangle over the side.

Van took a deep breath and jumped in. "I didn't sleep a wink last night thinking about some of the things your father said. It brought things to mind that I'd rather not think about. You know how I feel about you, and for that reason I can't stand for anything to be unknown between us. I want you to know everything there is to know about me—the good and bad."

Van paced again. "Your father asked some questions about my family. I don't doubt that you caught my reluctance in answering, and I know you've picked up on the fact that I very rarely talk about my family. Because I'd sooner say that I had no father than admit to the one I do have. My father disgusts me."

Van spat the words as though they tasted like poison in his mouth. "He disgusts me and I hate that I'm tied to him by blood. When I was a child, he wasn't ever around much. He was too busy bettering his career to bother himself with a son. My father provided well for me—I got the best education, clothes and anything else I asked for. On my acceptance to Harvard, he sent a big fat check covering housing and tuition for all four years to the school itself, so I didn't get a chance to rip it up and mail him the shreds."

I wanted to ask what his father had done to deserve such harsh words, but I doubted Van would hear me. He was wrapped up in his head, and would be until his story was told.

"My mother was the opposite of my father. She was loving and kind and interested in everything you had to say. She tolerated her husband with the patience of a saint. She was understanding when he didn't deserve it, and always accepted his excuses for his absence without question. During my senior year of high school, my mother became ill. She kept to her bed and started acting strangely. I came home one day and found her hat in the refrigerator. Another day she walked to the next town, which was more than ten miles away."

Van caught my puzzled expression and realized he wasn't explaining himself very well. "My father was away in the city as usual, so I called the doctor. He couldn't explain it, and sent her to the hospital for a round of tests. It came back that she had a brain tumor, which was what caused her odd behavior. That day she walked so far was because she forgot where she lived. She forgot she was married with a son in our town, and was walking to her family home where she'd lived with her parents. They were both long dead, but she thought she was still a girl and had to return home. The tumor was affecting her memory more and more, until everyday life slipped away from her and she became a danger to herself."

Van's face clouded over and was so stormy I knew to expect an outburst. "My father could more than afford to pay for some live-in help, a nurse or something, but he refused. Instead, he packed her off to a care home. The doctors told us there was no treatment available for my mother. There were some pills prescribed, but they did nothing. Maybe I expected too much of them. So my father sent her away where no one would ever see her again. She became an embarrassment for him and he no longer wished to bother himself with her needs. Now he lives in the city with the woman he'd been sleeping with behind my mother's back for ten years. All the while, his wife rots in a care home far enough away that she would never be a problem for him. Her illness never made public in his social circles. I suppose powerful men always have their wives in the suburbs and their pieces in the city." Van smirked coldly. "Because as reluctant as I am about talking about my family, my father is even less so. Not one person knows of my mother's illness, at least no one who would reveal the dark family secret my father is so ashamed of. The day he cut my mother from his life was the day I cut him from mine. He paid for my college tuition and I had no option but to accept. I need my education to be independent from him, but I haven't accepted anything from him in four years. I haven't even set eyes on him, let alone spoken to him."

Van's voice softened, the adrenaline no longer keeping his body rigid. "When my mother's parents died, they left a small sum to me. Together with my allowance, which I meticulously saved, I had enough for my tuition for law school, rent and a few other luxuries. I work at a bar when I'm at school and that helps keep me going. Everyone knows who I am — the surname and likeness between my father's face and mine are undisputable. But I take nothing from him and I want absolutely nothing to do with him."

He stopped moving and leaned against the car. I waited a few moments to make sure he was finished. With my heart aching in my chest for all the pain he must feel, I got up from where I sat and moved to stand in front of him.

"So now you know. My deep, dark secret." Van rolled his eyes, and despite the lightness of his tone, the words were laced with pain. I knew it had taken a great deal for him to speak of his past... His present. "You're the only person I've told, and most likely ever will."

I took a step forward and placed my hand over his heart. Van clasped it with his own and rested his forehead against mine. With my free hand, I touched his cheek and found it damp. He turned his face toward my hand, his breath hot against my palm.

A tap on my head jolted me back to the present. Then another, and another, until we were in the middle of a downpour. Van and I stared at each other in shock for a second or two before laughing. Van pushed me into the car and turned to struggle with getting the top up. I hopped into the back seat to try to help him.

By the time we managed to get the wretched thing up, we were both soaked to the bone. Van jumped into the car and tried to start it to get the heater on. The engine clicked over and refused to jump to life. He folded his arms over the steering wheel and rested his head on them. "Is there no luck for me tonight?"

I scooted forward from my seat in the back and wrapped my arms around his shoulders. I kissed his cheek then whispered in his ear, "Rest easy, Van. I can think of worse people to be stranded with."

Van laughed under his breath. He jumped over the seat to sit by my side and all at once looked exhausted.

"Are you okay?" I asked quietly, knowing he was anything but.

He gave a halfhearted shrug. "I've only said aloud what I've thought countless times."

"I can't imagine having to shoulder all that. You're a strong man."

Van let out a rueful laugh. "For not abandoning my mother, yeah, I'm a superhero."

"You shouldn't be so hard on yourself."

"I can't help it. I always think that if I'd been more observant, we could have caught her illness in time and maybe she would still have her memory. At least, it could have been more intact."

"How —" I paused for a moment, unsure how to ask the question. "How severe is it? Does she —"

Van caught my meaning. "Does she recognize me? Some days she does. Some days she's almost her old self. She contacts me when those days occur. Remember, she called my apartment a while ago? Other days she thinks I'm one of the staff where she lives."

My heart physically hurt for him. I wanted to take away his pain, to soothe his suffering somehow. "I can't imagine how awful it must be for you."

Van sighed. "It isn't me you should feel sorry for. I still remember my mother and all the things she did for me. She lived a life that could now belong to a stranger for all she knows. She deserves your sympathy far more than I do."

"Has your father tried to contact you?"

"He did at first, but he hasn't bothered in the last couple of years. It's a relief more than anything. When he'd try and call or write, everything would get dragged up again and make the pain fresh. It's better this way."

"Do you visit your mother often?" I asked, reaching to take his hand. I laced our fingers together.

Van squeezed my hand. "When I can."

I swallowed a ball of nervousness and glanced at him from beneath my lashes. "I'd like to go with you, the next time you go."

Van's head snapped up to look at me. "You would?"

"Of course," I said with a hesitant smile. "Even if you don't want me to actually go in with you, I want to at least make the trip with you. You shoulder this even though it was never asked of you. You care so much for your mother and take care of her as best you can. But who is taking care of you?"

Van looked at me with a strange sense of longing. He let out a shaky breath and leaned forward to touch his forehead to mine. He cupped my jaw, stroking my cheek with his long fingers. "Barbara Howell, you are undoubtedly the most extraordinary women I've ever met. I'm completely and utterly in love with you."

He caught my legs behind the knees and tugged them over his lap. Van brushed away a few loose tendrils of hair. He looked at me so intensely I wondered if he was trying to remember every single tiny insignificant detail of my face.

The rain pounded on the roof of the car and I leaned a fraction closer and planted a kiss on his lips. "I love you, Van. And I'm unconditionally yours."

* * * *

I spent my first night with Van that night. Our lips barely separated and our skin always touched. I wanted to progress our love to the next level, but Van halted my advances. He refused for us to give in this way. He wanted everything to be perfect, including the setting. And the back seat of a car that didn't even belong to him, he said, just didn't make the cut.

As much as I wanted him, all of him, I did have to admit that I wanted it to be perfect too. I wanted the perfect bed, the perfect room, the perfect everything. I'd been frustrated at first with him, but I knew he was right. And the more I'd thought about it, the more perfect I knew it would be, when it was finally time for us.

We fell asleep some hours later, the rain ceasing sometime in the night. The car started the first time Van tried it in the morning, and we made our way—unwillingly—back to reality. Van found a payphone at a gas station along the way and called the office to explain his absence. They understood and told him to make it in to the office when he could.

We were back in New York by eleven a.m. and Van dropped me off outside my building. I couldn't keep the smile from my face as I kissed him goodbye. I sighed, knowing this man belonged to me body and soul. We made no arrangements to see each other. There was no need. I doubted a day would pass from here on out that we didn't see or speak to each other.

Evelyn arched an eyebrow questioningly at me when she took in my knotted hair and crumpled clothes.

"It's not what you think, Evie," I said as I slumped in a chair in the lounge. "We got caught in the rain last night, and the car wouldn't start. We were in the middle of nowhere."

Evelyn nodded. "I understand. I had a few 'stranded' nights of my own, back in the day. I'm only surprised it didn't happen earlier." She winked at me before returning to the paper she had been reading.

"We didn't—" I started. *Oh, God. I'm going to have to say it out loud.*

Evelyn sighed. "I'm not your mother, Barb. I don't need any details you don't want to give. If you're happy, I'm happy."

I didn't think I could have explained to anyone what had passed between Van and me last night. So instead of trying, I rose from the chair and disappeared into my room. I took a shower, letting the hot water undo the muscle pain in my shoulders.

Van called from the office after dinner. He felt guilty for being late that morning and was putting in extra hours to make up the difference. I hid my disappointment, but was pleased by his integrity.

When I went to bed that night, every sentence that passed between us the night before played in my head. I thought back to a time when he'd told me of his 'adoptive family' who invited him everywhere. I felt a stabbing pain of realization in my heart. He said no one apart from me knew the truth of his family, and so he'd definitely not told his friend. So that was why he'd always been with him. He had nowhere else to go. He was lucky to have such a good friend who didn't ask questions and whose actions were unconsciously kind. Ache tore through my body as I thought of Van spending holiday seasons alone and vowed from that second on, he would never feel loneliness again.

* * * *

Summer passed in a blur. My days were spent waiting to see Van, and making the most of the time I got with him. Evelyn barely saw me in the evenings and on weekends as I was forever dashing out of the door to see him. Dates became more intimate and Van laughed at me when I told him I preferred the dates we had in his tiny kitchen, to the ones where he would take me to the theater or anywhere else public.

The last week of summer vacation held a few surprises. The first, possibly the best one of all, was that Jack had ended his internship one week early, to give him 'time to be a kid', he said. Summer was a time for play, not work. We had one week before real life came back for the fall. One week where the days belonged solely to us and could be spent them any way we pleased.

The second surprise was Van got tickets to see the New York City Ballet. We got dressed up and mingled with the rich and high society. The performance of Concerto Barocco was beautiful, and I couldn't believe that I cried. I would remember that date above all others for its beauty.

And the third surprise Van had in store for me was a trip to see his mother. He didn't want me to stay in the car, he wanted me to meet her for myself.

We met unintentionally, as it turned out. I stood by a bay window, which looked over the lake, while Van met with his mother's doctor to see how she had been doing.

"Do you like the view?"

I turned to see a woman who joined me at the window. Giving her a smile, I said, "I do."

"I look out at this lake every day. I never tire of it." Her face grew warm and a beautiful smile lit up her already pretty features. "You are lovely."

I blushed. "Oh, thank you."

"Don't be shy, I'm just being honest." She patted my arm. "My son would fall for you in two seconds flat. You must let me introduce you to him."

I didn't want to be rude. The people here were sick, and the last thing I wanted was to upset this poor woman.

Her face softened at my hesitation. "You already have a boyfriend. Of course, a pretty girl like you, why wouldn't you?"

"I see you two have already met." We both turned to face Van. His smile was amused before his mother reached for him, pulling him in for a fierce hug. "Mom," Van said once she had released him. "I'd like you to meet Barb."

Mrs. Judson looked at me with surprise. "Oh! You should have said that your boyfriend *was* my son."

I laughed. "I didn't know he was."

Mrs. Judson chided Van for not bringing me to meet her sooner.

It turned out we'd come on a good day when she was almost completely lucid. She knew who Van was and asked him how school was going. She thought he was still in high school, but Van had said it was one of the best days he'd seen her have. We chatted for hours and I found that I truly loved the woman.

Sadness enveloped me when we left, but the day grew late and she'd started *sun downing,* as the doctor called it. Van wanted to leave before it was painful for any of us, and as we left, she hugged me tightly and made me promise I would come back and see her.

Van held my hand as we walked to the car, and he lifted it to press a kiss to the back of it.

* * * *

Our bags were packed and the station awaited us. Van had purchased first-class tickets, and so we had a compartment all to ourselves. Over four hours in private on the train with Van. The train was packed full of bodies as was normal for this time of year, with everyone making their way back to their lives, and so it was a relief that we wouldn't have to contend with it. We could sit in comfort and take it easy.

We began the journey normally enough, with Van reading a paper and me reading a book. Halfway into our travels, a food trolley trundled through the corridor and Van grabbed a few sandwiches for us. After lunch, I stared out of the window, watching the rolling countryside appear and disappear in front of me.

Feeling his eyes on me, I turned my head to find Van staring. I smiled before surprising him with a kiss.

The rest of the distance was over far too quickly after that.

My mood was gloomy as we stepped onto the platform at Boston. Each step I took felt sluggish and slow as I tried to delay the inevitable. Van carried most of our things despite my protests. He found me a cab and helped the driver put my suitcases in the trunk. He kissed me quickly and promised we'd see each other soon. The distance between Wellesley and Boston was nothing really, yet it was so much farther than I cared for. I loved being able to walk to his apartment and see him, and I no longer had that luxury.

A thick lump of emotion lodged in my throat when he closed the cab door. He waved in a way that was more cheerful than I knew he was feeling. I smiled and knew it wouldn't convince him, but I refused to be one of those pathetic girls who couldn't function without her boyfriend, but I also knew that deep down I was one of them.

Once Van was out of sight, but most definitely not out of mind, I focused on the positive things. I would see Lois soon! I missed my friend dearly and knew we would have a wonderful time reuniting and sharing stories from our summer apart.

Chapter Seventeen

Wellesley hadn't changed as much as I had in our separation. I was now a junior, but the change went deeper than that. A line of freshman girls waited with their suitcases to be shown around their new dorm and I felt a pang of pity for them. I remembered all too well how daunting it was arriving on my first day. If they had any luck at all, they would land a roommate who was as refreshing as mine, and made the transition that much easier.

Lois and I were rooming again this year, only with two other girls. We decided at the end of last year to get housing off campus since we would be juniors, and had secured a four-bedroom house in the college housing district in the town of Wellesley. The same rules applied that were in place at the dorms, no overnight guests, no boys, et cetera, and there was a warden who lived close by who could check that the rules were being enforced.

But it would give us a bigger sense of freedom and for that we were happy. It would be nice to have a room to myself for some solitude and privacy.

I picked up my schedule, book list for the coming term and collected my new house key and walked into town to find my new home. All the houses in the area looked more or less the same, having been constructed for housing students only. I knocked on the door first before walking in, and chaos met me when I did.

The smoke was thick and the radio blared as loud as the girls dared. I guessed I was the last to arrive. The house was on three levels, the bottom being for the kitchen and living area, the middle for three bedrooms and bathroom and the third being an attic bedroom.

Since I was last to arrive, I was awarded the punishment of getting the attic room. I didn't mind, it had character. Its slanted walls meant you had to duck before you hit your head on a beam in certain areas, but I'd get used to it. There was enough room for a bed and bedside table, a desk and chair, which would have to double as a dressing table. A small walk-in closet had been built in the back of the room.

I dumped my suitcases and ran downstairs so I could see Lois. She'd been in the shower when I'd arrived, so I'd been told by one of the other girls. I knocked on Lois' bedroom door and I heard her shout over her radio to come in.

I threw open the door, and Lois screamed in excitement. We danced and hugged, both of us talking over each other. Once the exuberant greeting had played out, Lois handed me a cigarette and we sat on her window seat to gossip.

She told me all about her summer and it sounded fabulous. She'd seen all the sights around the country and had loved every second of it. Lois swooned and sighed as she told her stories of romance and showed me letters she'd already received from her lovers of

California, Hawaii, Florida and every other state she had visited.

"Enough of me. What did you do?"

I shrugged. I still hadn't told Lois about Van. "I kept my aunt company — "

Lois interrupted me with a sharp laugh. "Barb Howell, you are the most boring creature! Summering in New York City should be exciting and all you did was sit about with your aunt."

I swatted her on the arm. "I did other things, too."

"Like what? Did you see that boy Thomas again?"

"Yes, a little." I groaned. "You should have seen his mother. The second she knew I was back in town, she thought Thomas was going to propose."

Lois collapsed in a fit of giggles. "What did you do?"

"I had to assure her that I had no intentions of ever marrying her son. I mentioned other boys at every possible opportunity but she just wouldn't listen."

"What other boys? Did you date a lot? Why didn't you tell me in your letters?" Lois demanded.

A blush crept up my cheeks. "Yes, I dated other boys."

Her eyes widened. "Wow, must have been something, look at that blush! Tell me every detail. How many boys? How cute were they? Do you have any pictures? Are you going to see any of them again?"

"Well, it wasn't a lot of boys, just one, really."

Lois' face softened a little at this. She must have detected my hesitancy. "Oh. Go on, tell me about him."

"You kind of know him." I glanced down. "It was Van."

Lois screeched so loudly I jumped in my seat.

"Shh!" I hissed.

Lois laughed. "I'm sorry, you have no idea how long I've waited for this."

I narrowed my eyes at her. "Telling you about me and Van?"

"Yes, in a way." She grinned. "Honey, remember when you told me about him after Christmas a few years ago? Well, I had a feeling it was the beginning of something. And I was right."

Lois and her feelings... I rolled my eyes. "You did not know something would happen. Come on, I hated him."

"Yes—too much. He got under your skin and he stayed there, admit it." She held her hand up. "No, wait, don't. I want to hear all about this summer. Don't miss out a single detail."

And so I told her about us meeting at Yellow Sands and finding out he would be in the city for the summer. I told her all about the ball and what it made me realize. I smiled as I remembered some details. Lois looked fit to cry when I told her some of the romantic dates he had taken me on. I never told her of the night we broke down on the side of the road, but I did say we had exchanged our proclamations of love to each other.

It was easier talking about it all to Lois than I'd thought it would be. Of course, some things were kept private. She didn't need to know everything. Plus I wanted some things to belong only to me and Van.

"I'm so happy for you," Lois gushed when I finally finished.

I smiled at her. "I'm glad. I can't believe how I feel about him. I can't believe it's happening to me."

She laughed. "I know—I was beginning to think you would end up an old maid."

Huffing, I whacked her with a pillow.

"I'm kidding! I knew you'd find it, Barb. I never doubted you the way everyone else did. I just knew it would have to be someone pretty spectacular is all."

I threw my arms around Lois. "I've missed you, friend."

"That makes two of us." Lois broke away from me. "Come on, let's hit the Dragon. I'll bet they missed us."

"I'll catch you up. I want to unpack first."

Lois rolled her eyes at me but agreed.

I sat on my bed in my little room and looked around me. How much smaller this room seemed, in comparison to the room I had at Evelyn's. I preferred this one, though. I could put my personal touches on it.

I unpacked my clothes and books and other paraphernalia. At the bottom of one of my suitcases full of clothes that had come from storage, a foreign item caught my notice. I dug it out, recognizing the color and pattern immediately, though the item wasn't even mine.

Van's scarf.

Memories flooded back to me. The moment he had slipped this inoffensive item around my neck, a gesture at the time made in friendship, but that I now took to be one of love. How had I not seen it, even then? How had his true feelings evaded me?

I remember packing the scarf before I had left for the summer. I could remember, as I put it into this very suitcase, my confusion over why I was keeping it. I could easily have thrown it away. It wasn't as though I was ever likely to wear it—I had my own scarves for that, after all. But I'd kept it nonetheless.

Raising the scarf to my nose, I inhaled. Mostly it smelled of the bar of soap I'd placed among the clothes in the suitcase to try to keep the musty smell off of them, but among the soapy smell was the tiniest trace of him. I smiled, and neatly folded the scarf and laid it in my bedside table drawer.

I caught a glimpse of myself in the mirror that hung on the wall next to the door. My face was drained and I realized how tired I was. My body argued with my mind when I decided it was time to go meet Lois. Sighing, I knew I had made a promise and gathered myself together to make the short walk to the Dragon.

* * * *

Finding a balancing act for all the things in life can be a tiresome chore. Lectures, classes, schoolwork, studying, seeing Van, eating, seeing Lois, sleeping…something had to give. One month into my fall semester and I felt like the walking dead. I tried to do everything all at once. I studied between classes, saw Lois for an hour or two, went out with Van, came home to eat and try to do some homework assignments, and if I was really lucky, squeeze in a few hours of sleep before I woke and started everything all over again. I was reprimanded often for handing in work that was not my usual standard, and when I fell asleep after seeing Van for only five minutes one evening, we knew something had to give.

Van was under tremendous pressure at law school, even more than I could comprehend. He couldn't carry on the way we had been without consequences, and so we made the awful decision to see each other at weekends only. We also vowed to be honest with each other when it came to schoolwork. If we had any to do, it would take priority before we could be with the other.

I'd grown far too spoiled over the summer but I knew it had to be done. Van's future was so important I wouldn't let him jeopardize it for me, and he felt exactly the same away about mine, so we kept each other motivated in our own little ways.

I announced my major at the beginning of the school year—English literature. I figured I was already a dedicated reader, I may as well get a degree out of it. Along with complying with her mother's request to keep up her housewife courses, Lois decided she was going to study nursing. The growing terror in Europe made her believe our country would need all the nurses it could get...should Hitler and his Nazi thugs shift their gaze to our continent.

I chose not to dwell on things that would never happen. But that was our Lois. Dramatic to the end. Secretly, I think she just wanted the uniform.

Chapter Eighteen

The leaves soon started to change from the luscious greens and vibrant colors of the summer, to the subtle yellows and browns of fall. I loved fall, almost as much as summer and the only thing I didn't like about it was the cooler weather it brought. Then it was a subtle transition from fall to winter.

My classes were going well, though I found the work a lot harder. Thanksgiving would be a welcome break. Most of the girls went home for Thanksgiving, including me and Lois, but this year, I had something else in mind.

I'd rented a tiny cottage about an hour away, nestled in the woods and overlooking a lake. I bought all the groceries we would need and hid them in a large trunk. I packed my suitcase and waited on the front stoop for Van to pick me up. I'd told him no details, simply to pick me up the morning after school broke up for with a few changes of clothes. I remained vague and managed to avoid his prying questions.

I could barely sit still in the car as we drove. The car kept to the narrow, twisty road and the trees around us grew denser, blocking a lot of the natural light. The lake came into view and I told Van where to turn off. A small dirt-track road led us to the cottage, hidden away entirely from civilization.

Van arched an eyebrow at me as he pulled the car to a stop in front of the cottage. I got out and walked up the front steps and peered through a window. Van collected the bags from the car and followed me inside as I unlocked the door.

He set the bags down and looked around. We stood in a cozy living room, with an open-plan kitchen to the right. A doorway at the rear of the kitchen led to the small dining room, and down the hall from where we stood was a staircase, which took you up to a loft bedroom. A bathroom was at the rear of the house sporting a new shower and bath.

I thought it was perfect for us. Something tiny for us to share, something that was just ours, for however brief the period was.

"Barb—" Van began as he looked around him and took a few tentative steps forward.

"Surprise," I said, biting my bottom lip.

"I don't get it, are your friends joining us? Family?"

"Nope. It's just us."

"*Us?*" Van repeated incredulous.

I nodded, my body thrumming with nervous energy. What if he hated the idea? What if he thought I was too forward? I grabbed the trunk and dragged it into the kitchen and started unloading the groceries onto the kitchen worktops and transferring them to cupboard and fridge.

"Barb," Van said gently, walking to my side and taking my hand, stopping my preoccupation with the groceries.

"I wanted us to have Thanksgiving together," I said quietly.

Van gave me a tiny smile. "I don't know what to say. This is the best thing anyone has ever done for me."

"Really?"

"This is perfect. Really." Van smiled wider, putting me more at ease.

"I think I brought far too many groceries," I said as I eyed the overcrowded worktop.

"We can handle them," Van said, grinning. He looked around him again. "I can't believe you did all this. It's really just us?"

I nodded. "For the whole week."

Van swept me up in his arms and twirled me around the kitchen. "You are incredible, Barb." He stopped spinning but didn't put me on my feet. He kissed me, long and slow, making my toes curl in pleasure. When he set me down, Van went to investigate the rest of the cottage. I heard him go upstairs and down again then disappear out of the back door.

I finished putting away all the groceries and took my suitcase upstairs to unpack it. I hung up my dresses in the closet and slid the suitcase under the bed out of the way. I wondered when Van would mention the sleeping arrangements, as I knew he eventually would.

When I came back down, Van was in front of the fireplace in the living room stacking wood up at the side. I made us sandwiches for lunch then we went for a walk around the lake and surrounding area. Van wanted to chop more wood when we got back to the cottage so we had a good supply, and I let him have his manly moment and lazed on the luxuriously comfortable and long couch. The fresh air had worked wonders for me and cleared the cobwebs away. It made me drowsy, and I fell asleep on the couch for a while.

Van was sitting by my head, stroking my hair, when I woke up and found him watching me. "Hi," I said with a sleepy smile. "How long was I sleeping?"

"A few hours."

I sat up and saw darkness creeping in around the house. I scooted closer to Van and he held his arm up, waiting for me nestle into his chest. It was the best feeling to be so close to him, and was something I never grew tired of. I would have been happy to lie there all night, but my stomach let out an embarrassing growl, indicating it was perhaps time for me to get dinner started.

Van grinned at me as I stood and he followed me into the kitchen, and wouldn't take no for an answer when he asked to be put to good use. We cooked together in sync. Van chopped and cooked the vegetables and I took care of the steaks. I set the table and put out two bottles of beer for us.

After dinner, Van winked and got up from the table. As I cleared the dinner things away, he got the fire started, and I could soon hear the crackle and snaps as it flickered to life. I sat on the couch and watched him tend it. When it was roaring with life, Van moved to sit with me. He stretched and sprawled his lean frame on the couch, resting his head in my lap.

I teased his dark locks with my fingers as I read my book.

"Barb?"

"Hmm?"

"I—" Van paused for a moment. "I want to ask you something, but I don't want you to get upset." Van sat up and swiveled around to face me. "I couldn't help but notice the number of bedrooms. Do you want me to sleep on the couch? I could—"

My laughter broke his sentence. "Oh, Van! Don't be so silly."

His eyes flickered to mine, but he didn't say anything.

"We're two grown people, Van, and I trust you. I know it isn't exactly appropriate... But I think we're more than capable of sharing a bed without it resulting in..."

Van placed his fingers under my chin he lifted my face so I looked at him. "I know, Barb. I just didn't want to presume anything. You know?"

I nodded. "So you don't mind?"

Van laughed. "Do I mind having to share a bed with the most breathtaking creature I've ever laid eyes on? Somehow, Barb, I think it'll be tolerable."

As the hour grew late, I began to relax. My overactive mind had ceased activity for the time being and the words on the page of my book began to revert back to a language I understood. When I was fully relaxed and back to normal, Van announced he was going for a shower before bed. My heart spluttered again and I tried to keep a nonchalant look on my face, but I probably just looked deranged.

I grabbed my opportunity to undress and get into bed before he emerged from the shower. I all but ran up the stairs and stripped off my clothes. In my nervous state, I struggled with the buttons on my dress and so it took longer than I'd hoped it would.

Pulling the soft material of my long, fitted nightgown over my head, I took a few deep breaths and tried to calm my racing heart. I turned on the lamp beside the bed, creating a soft glow. There was a dressing table at the side of the room, and I sat on the stool and began to take down my hair. As I placed the pins in front of me, the sound of the bathroom door opening and closing again drifted upstairs.

"Barb?" Van called from downstairs.

"I'm up here." My voice shook as I spoke. Why was I so nervous? I wasn't going to initiate anything and Van certainly wasn't going to, so why the panic? Maybe because it was the first planned full night we were going to spend together.

Van padded around downstairs for a few minutes before I heard the stairs creak under his weight.

He appeared in the mirror as he reached the top, my heart jolting at the sight of him in an undershirt and skivvies. His look softened when he saw me. Van approached me and kissed the top of my head. He smelled fantastic—warm and clean from the shower. With a saucy wink, Van pulled back the bedclothes and climbed into bed.

I sucked in a calming breath and followed him. The sheets were cool as I slid between them and it wasn't even a conscious thought as I curled against Van with my head on his chest. He wrapped an arm around my shoulders, and it felt like the most natural thing in the world.

Van reached with his other arm and turned off the lamp, letting the darkness envelop us. A faint glow from the fire below danced on the ceiling above us.

"Goodnight, Barb." Van's voice was barely a whisper and yet I couldn't have heard it more clearly if he had shouted the words.

"Goodnight," I replied.

Van's fingers lightly traced lines up and down my arm that I had draped across his chest. I relished the touch and it was the last thing I was aware of before slipping into sleep.

* * * *

Pale sunlight entered the cottage as I slowly woke. Van was still sleeping as I stretched to look at him. We hadn't moved an inch the entire night.

I considered getting up and making breakfast for Van, but the temptation to stay where it was warm won out. Plus the fact that I was curled around Van's beautiful body helped tip the scales. I closed my eyes and tried to imprint in my memory everything about that morning. How his cheek rested against the top of my head. His fingers laced with mine. How smooth his and firm chest was under my hand, rising and falling with each breath he took.

Perhaps because I was so aware of the soft movement, I was instantly aware when its rhythm changed. I smiled, knowing that he was awake. Nothing was said for an eternity. Van hadn't moved a millimeter but I could hear his heart thud under my ear. I could bare the silence no longer.

"I know you're awake," I whispered. "How long are you going to try to get away with faking sleep?"

He chuckled and kissed the top of my head. "I wasn't faking anything, just enjoying the moment." Van stretched his long frame and rolled onto his side. He propped himself up on his elbow and peered down at me. "Good morning."

"Good morning," I said, unable to keep my grin from spreading.

"Did you sleep okay?"

"Like the dead."

"Good." Van lowered his head and kissed me. "I'm going to wash up and then start breakfast. Any preferences?"

I shook my head.

Van pulled himself out of bed and headed down the stairs. Once he had disappeared from view, I sat up and hugged my knees, surprised at the quietness of my usually overactive mind. I stayed like that until I heard Van opening and closing cupboards in the kitchen.

I crept downstairs with a fresh change of clothes and locked myself in the bathroom. The hot water from the shower worked wonders on my body, undoing the tightest of knots in my back. Unfortunately the hot water didn't last forever, and I had to get out. I ran a brush through my wet locks and pulled on a simple day dress.

The smell of breakfast wafted through the house as I emerged from the bathroom. The dining room table was covered with food. Toast, eggs, bacon, sausage, cereals, juice, coffee. The sight was incredulous and I was impressed Van had gone to so much trouble.

He gave me that beautiful, lopsided grin that I loved as I walked into the room. "Hope you're hungry." Van served an enormous plate with a little bit of everything, but I somehow managed to put it all away. I vowed not to eat again until our Thanksgiving lunch, which might have to put off to Thanksgiving dinner. We both had to lie down for a little while after breakfast. Van had outdone himself.

* * * *

Preparing dinner was a fiasco. Neither Van nor I had ever cooked a large meal, so we were at a bit of a loss. Van poured us both a large glass of wine when we realized we hadn't put the potatoes in enough water and they stuck to the bottom of the pan. We had another glass when we realized we hadn't actually turned the oven on, so there wasn't enough time to cook the turkey unless we wanted to eat in the middle of the night.

When all the countertops were covered with half-prepared food and the entire kitchen looked like a bombsite, we admitted defeat. So half-drunk on wine on our very first Thanksgiving together, we ate cheese sandwiches in front of a roaring fire. And it couldn't have been more perfect.

The day was over before we knew it. Van pulled a thick blanket from the couch and spread it out on the floor in front of the fire. He motioned for me to join him on it, and when I did he gathered me into his arms as we leaned against the couch.

He read some of Dante's *Inferno* to me as we shared a glass of Scotch. I'd never been more relaxed than I was at that very moment. After a while, he placed the book down and held me a little bit tighter. I snuck a glance up at him and found his eyes closed. I knew he wasn't asleep.

"This has been perfect, Barb." Van's voice was barely above a whisper when he eventually broke the silence.

I laughed under my breath. "Even if I ruined dinner?"

"You didn't. I've never enjoyed a Thanksgiving as much as I'm enjoying this one. It isn't about the food that's served, but who you spend it with. And for that, it's been perfect."

I smiled. "I know what you mean."

Van laughed quietly. "Besides, it'll be a fun story for the future, when we had cheese sandwiches and Scotch for our first Thanksgiving dinner."

My heart began to race, my mind wrapping around the words — *the future, first Thanksgiving, our*. Ecstatic as I now felt, I also dreaded what he might say next. I recalled Lois saying something about people choosing holiday's to announce engagements. Looking from the darkened windows and into the crackling fire, the setting was overtly romantic. It was completely plausible that he might ask me, but I prayed he wouldn't.

I knew I wasn't ready and I would have to refuse him. People could have long engagements, they always have. You could get engaged and not get married for years, but I knew how my mother would react when the news reached her, and there would be no force strong enough to stop her. She had Anna married within six months, and that was with Anna restraining her as much as was possible. There was still so much I wanted to do with my life. It was entirely plausible to be married *and* have a career, but I'd seen how things gradually slip away to the background, and eventually the dream is forgotten.

My eyes flitted to Van's face and saw he was watching me. How could I possibly hurt him? I didn't know if I had the heart to do it.

"What's the matter?" he asked as he stroked my cheek with one finger. "You look scared to death."

"No, I'm fine. I think I need a cigarette."

Van hopped up and searched some down. When he brought them back to me, I stood and circled the room, puffing on my cigarette as though it could somehow solve everything.

"Barb, you don't have to worry, I'm not going to ask."

I swiveled around to face him. "I don't know what you mean."

He smiled. "Yes, you do, and it's okay." Van rose from his spot on the floor and crossed the room to where I stood. "I'm going to ask you to marry me, Barb. One day, I will ask you to marry me. But today is not that day. You don't have to worry about this. Don't give it another thought. When the day does come, it will be when you are one hundred percent ready for me to ask."

I swallowed a lump of fear. "And if I'm never ready?"

"Then I'll never ask." There was nothing but truth in his words, or his eyes.

A slow sigh of relief escaped me. I felt ridiculous for overreacting, but also relieved. The man knew me so well and for that I was grateful. A rush of love for him jolted through me and I thanked God that I'd found him. I didn't deserve him.

Van kept the situation light. He kissed my cheek and resumed his position on the blanket. I lit a fresh cigarette and by the time I stubbed it out my nerves had returned to normal.

To put the finishing touches on this day, Van filled the bathtub with hot water and bubbles and lit some candles around the bathroom. He kissed the top of my head and shut the door behind him.

Chapter Nineteen

The hot water was amazing and I stayed submerged for as long as I could. I hadn't brought my nightgown with me, but there was a short robe on the back of the door, which I pulled on once I'd dried myself.

The door creaked as I opened it, and found there was very little light. The fire was dying and I knew Van must have gone upstairs to bed. My feet were cold as I walked across the wooden floor and up the stairs. The small bedside lamp cast a dim glow across the room and glinted off the mirror at the dressing table. I scanned the room for Van but couldn't see him.

A floorboard behind me squeaked and made me jump. Spinning around, I was face-to-face with Van. *Of course,* I scolded myself, *who else would it be?*

Van smiled crookedly at me. "Sorry." He tried not to look so amused. "I was checking the locks. Are you okay? I didn't mean to scare you."

"Yes." The rush of irrational fear had been replaced by a different set of emotions entirely.

I'd seen Van in his best suit and an expensive tux with his hair slicked back. I'd seen him in casual slacks and shirt... But he'd never looked as attractive as he did now. He only wore his skivvies and an undershirt and his hair was messy, natural, but there was something about him that made him more agreeable to me now than he'd ever been before.

I moved toward him before I even realized. I wrapped my arms around his neck and pressed my forehead to his.

"Barb?"

I answered him with my kiss.

There was something different in his kiss. Some new longing I hadn't experienced before. I kissed him harder, my breath growing ragged. Our lips broke apart, both of us gasping for air. There was a hunger in his eyes and a smile tugged the corner of his mouth as he glanced down my body. "You certainly look tempting this evening."

"Don't I always?" I teased.

"Yes, but this robe does"—his fingers traced a line on my thigh where the robe ended—"have a certain charm."

I arched an eyebrow at him and he laughed.

He kissed the tip of my nose. "You are a dangerous female." Van moved past me quickly toward the bed.

"Van—" I stared. *What am I going to say?* Anyone who knew me could attest to how outspoken I was. But now I was at a loss for words.

He turned to face me. I approached him slowly, not breaking eye contact. I placed both hands on his chest and kissed him, quick and dry. His eyes were questioning when I pulled back.

"I love you," I whispered.

He smiled and returned the kiss, knotting his fingers in my hair. "I love you, too."

I didn't trust myself to speak. Trailing my hands down his sides until they reached the hem of his vest, I tugged it upward until Van stopped me.

"What—"

I silenced him with one finger against his mouth. He let me pull the vest off him and I kissed him again. My hands shook as I moved them to the tie of my robe. Somehow I managed to undo the knot and let the robe fall open, revealing myself to him.

"Barb—" Van's voice was husky and the nervousness was evident on his face. "I thought— Don't you want to wait…" His eyes searched mine.

"For what?" I asked with a breathy laugh. "Marriage? Van, I know I want you. I want to be with you forever and there is nothing that can change that. I love you — so much—I want us to express it." The determination and surety of my tone surprised me. Van, too, as his gaze softened as he realized this was what I really wanted. "You said earlier how perfect today has been… I want to end it perfectly too."

Van sighed and pressed his forehead to mine. His hand quivered as I reached for it and guided it toward my body. I placed it on my breast and my skin came alive at his touch. My mouth found his and it told him everything he needed to know.

In that one kiss he knew how much I loved him. Van was my future, and my future began today.

I shrugged the robe off my shoulders and let it drop to the floor. Van scooped me up in his arms and carried me to the bed. He laid me on the mattress as though I were made of glass, his eyes drifting over me.

For the first time since I'd met him, Van seemed unsure of himself. Moving cautiously, he lay beside me, hovering over me. He stroked my face, and I bit my lip, feeling unsettled at the scrutiny.

It was as though Van fought with himself. A few times he started to say something, only to stop himself before a single word could escape. His innocence was almost childlike and I considered the irony of the situation—he was so much more experienced at physical love than me, yet it was as though I was the one reassuring him, the one who had to take the lead. I reached up and brushed a lock of hair from his eyes and pulled his head down so my lips could find his.

His breath was hot on my face and our breathing both became uneven. Our lips barely touched, and it felt all the more electric. A tiny cry broke free from me as his tongue teased my bottom lip.

That cry seemed to awaken us both. Van's mouth broke away from mine and moved to my eyelid, my cheek, my earlobe, my neck. He moved farther down my body, kissing every inch of flesh he could find.

My body crackled like a live wire and when he reached the southernmost point of me and kissed my toe, I thought I would combust. Van worked his way back up my body. He held my gaze as he hitched my leg up and stroked the underside of my knee and up my thigh.

A warmth between my legs spread through my body, seeming to ignite every cell within me. I was close to grabbing him and throwing myself at him. He took his time, but it was taking too long. My head was a mixture of confusion and I didn't know what to do—I was desperate for him, all of him, but the gradualness of what he was doing was mind-blowing.

Every sense had been heightened and I became hyperaware of every touch, every breath.

Van brought himself up to full height above my frame and allowed me to feel only a portion of his weight. I wanted to pull him down so I could feel the full weight of him, but I knew there was no point in trying, he wouldn't let me, and was so much stronger.

There was a fire in his eyes and they seemed alive with excitement. He cleared his throat and when he spoke, his voice was hoarse. "Are you — are you okay?"

I nodded and took his face between my hands and kissed him as if I'd never get the chance to do it again. The kiss brought a new level of hunger and he grasped my leg.

He lifted his face, his eyes never leaving mine as he slowly entered me.

I couldn't help the wince of pain from the fullness of him, the dull ache as he stretched me. Van's breath raced and he held himself still and rigid as my body accommodated him.

"Barb," he whispered.

"I'm okay," I said, clasping his face between my hands. "I'm okay." I tugged his face back down so I could reach his mouth. Van groaned and started to move, barely at first until he built up a delicious rhythm.

A gasp of pleasure burst from my lips as I lost myself to him. Each movement he made brought with it a new wave of ecstasy. My hips moved with his, my body somehow knowing what my mind had no idea. I sank my nails into his back, his shoulders, as I clung to him.

We were in perfect sync, our breathing becoming more and more ragged. With one final, powerful thrust, we were finished. Van dropped his head onto my shoulder, both of us panting. He placed a tiny kiss on my collarbone, and sank onto me fully, and I wrapped my arms around his shoulders, my hot cheek pressed against his. My entire body tingled. We stayed that way for a long time, locked together and whispering contented words.

When our bodies returned to normalcy, Van rolled to the side so I no longer supported his weight. He studied every inch of my face, but not at any point was I nervous or self-conscious. Van made me feel like the most beautiful woman alive, and to him, I was.

We fit together perfectly and I was thrilled. A satisfied smile took up residence on my lips and I kissed him, lazy and sated.

* * * *

The same hazy glow still surrounded me when I awoke the following morning. I tried to get back to sleep, but my mind was too active. Images from the night before flashed in my memory, and they proved far too interesting to be ignored.

Wrapped in Van's arms, I struggled free and sat up. My muscles ached as I stretched. Leaning on one elbow, I stared down at Van's peaceful face as a quiet snore blew from his mouth. I ran my fingers across his brow and he twitched in his sleep. I kissed him and a tiny smile teased his lips. But no, my efforts appeared fruitless. Nothing was waking the man.

Sighing, I got out of bed and pulled on the robe still lying discarded on the floor, picked up a fresh set of clothes and made my way to the bathroom.

My messy hair stuck up all over the place as I took note of it in the mirror. I stared at my reflection, trying to see some invisible sign. I looked the picture of good health. My eyes were bright and my cheeks were rosy pink. I felt older, taller somehow.

More than anything, I felt more certain that I was on the right path toward my fate. Van and I had been perfect last night, slotting together as if we'd been made for each other. He was my missing puzzle piece and I would never feel whole again unless we were together.

After my shower, I checked on Van again but found him still sleeping, so I moseyed out through the back door for a walk. The morning mist was only beginning to lift, the air fresh and chilly. I walked around the side of the lake and took in the tranquil setting. The surface a glassy mirror, reflecting the image above it. Geese called in the distance and small birds in the foreground.

The weak sun rose higher and my thoughts returned back to the cottage where Van would soon be waking. He'd get a start if he woke and realized I wasn't there. Kicking up leaves on my way back, I quickened my pace to cover the distance faster.

The rear of the cottage came into view, still a distance away. A loud noise pierced the quietness around me and birds took to the air with a start. A few moments passed and it came again. It was then I realized it was the voice a man. He was shouting, but what? A few more times he shouted and on the last, I realized he was shouting "Barb".

I strained my eyes and could just make out the tall frame of a man walking in my direction. *Van.* Cursing my stupidity for not leaving a note or something, I ran toward him.

"Barb!" Van's voice shattered the silence once again. Relief flooded his face when he saw me and rushed to my side. Van pressed me to him so hard it was almost painful. "You scared the shit out of me, you know that?"

"I'm sorry," I murmured into his neck. "I didn't want to wake you."

"What were you doing out here?" He pushed me away from him so he could read my face.

"I couldn't sleep, so I thought I'd take a walk, but I guess I went a little farther than I intended."

His eyebrows knitted together. "I figured you were out walking, so I waited. But you were gone for so long, I-I thought something had happened to you."

As guilty as I felt, I was secretly thrilled at his concern. "I'm fine." It was then I noticed his appearance. He wore a pair of boots, the skivvies from the night before and a long jacket, which hung open, offering no protection from the frigid air. I pressed a hand to his chest and found it ice cold. "Van, how long have you been out here like this?"

He shrugged. "I don't know. I was looking for you out front at first and then came and looked around out here."

"You're freezing, come on." I led us back into the warmth of the cottage. Forcing Van into a hot bath, I built a fire and made breakfast. I hummed to myself as I worked, scrambling eggs in a pan and turning the bacon. I pulled a carton of orange juice from the refrigerator and nearly dropped the damn thing when I turned and found Van leaning against the worktop staring at me.

He smirked at me with his arms folded. I scowled at him for scaring me as I transferred the juice to two glasses. Tossing the empty carton into the garbage, I refused to look at him. Van grabbed my hand and pulled me to him, locking his arms around my waist so I couldn't escape. He kissed the corner of my mouth, my cheek, my jaw and planted delicate little kisses along neck until he reached my ear. His hot breath sent a delicious shiver down my spine as he whispered, "I'm sorry, love."

I lasted a fraction of a second before I was putty in his hands.

"Am I forgiven?"

"Always," I whispered, sliding my hands up his arms. I sealed the promise with a kiss and finished preparing breakfast.

"How are you, Barb?" Van's question caught me off guard. I'd just sat with him on the couch with my feet in his lap after clearing away the breakfast things. He didn't look at me and kept his focus on my toes.

"What do you mean?"

"After last night."

"I'm fine," I said with a confused frown.

"Are you sure?" Van lifted his gaze to meet mine, and I was shocked to find it full of pain. "Did I do something wrong?"

I scooted along the couch so I was by his side. Placing a hand on his face, I said, "Of course not, why would you think that?"

Van shrugged and tried to smile. "I guess, just with you taking off this morning."

Shaking my head softly, I stroked his cheek. "I wasn't taking off. I woke up early and I didn't want to wake you, so I went for a walk to get some fresh air, that's all. Van, last night was the best night of my life. I mean, I understand if it wasn't for you—"

His head snapped up. "Why would you think that?"

"I-I suppose because of the way you're reading into it, assuming I didn't enjoy it or something." I sighed. "We both know you have more experience with this sort of thing, so I understand if it wasn't fantastic for you."

Van chuckled. "Barb, don't you see? Last night I was just as inexperienced."

"But I thought— Haven't you...?"

"Well, yes, I have." He took my hands. "But I've never felt this way before, Barb. You're the only girl I've ever loved and last night—last night was amazing. I've never been with a girl I felt that way about, so it was completely new to me. I was so scared of hurting you, of doing something wrong. And then this morning to wake up and find you gone... I thought I must have ruined everything."

"No, you could never ruin anything," I assured him. "Van, it was perfect. I can't imagine anything better than what it was." Leaning forward, I pressed my mouth against his. Van looped his arm around my middle and tugged me closer to him. I smiled and kissed him harder.

Van took my lead and let me pull him to the floor where we made love in front of the fire. All afternoon we lay naked in each other's arms, exploring and probing. We were in our own personal slice of heaven and I never wanted it to end.

* * * *

It was easy to forget about the outside world. Van had always dominated my thoughts, but now I seemed unable to part from his side even for a moment. I needed him like I needed air to breathe and my appetite for him did nothing but continue to grow.

Our week in the cottage was over far too quickly, and I contemplated staying for another but I knew Van wouldn't let me miss any school, and he had his commitments also.

I remained quiet during the drive back to Wellesley. It felt worse than it had at the end of summer. We'd seen each other regularly then, but we'd been in constant contact this past week and I didn't want it to end. When would I see him again? Be with him again? I didn't have any answers and neither did he. Van wouldn't be willing for us to have a few minutes of cramped and frantic sex in the back seat of his car — he'd think it demeaning for me.

He carried my bags up the steps outside my house. When he turned to face me, he jammed his hands into his pockets. My mood was stormy and I knew it would show on my face — I'd worn a perpetual scowl since hitting the outskirts of town. Van didn't give me a chance to vent my grumpiness. He reached for me and pulled me close. "Soon, okay?" he whispered.

I couldn't speak. A lump formed in my throat and tears stung my eyes, threatening to fall. Van planted a soft and somewhat shaky kiss on my lips before releasing me and heading back to his car.

"Wait!" I shouted after him and flew down the walk to him. I threw myself into his arms and kissed him as though he were about to disappear at any second...which to me he was. "Sorry," I whispered once I let him go.

Van laughed and squeezed my hand. "Never apologize for a kiss like that."

Despite my mood, I smiled. Van gave me a parting kiss and promised to call.

I refused to cry.

I couldn't unpack my bags right away. It would make it too real, that our little vacation together was officially over.

Lois found me sitting on my bed, hugging my knees. "Oh God, he dumped you, didn't he?"

"What?" I asked her, shocked.

"Did he finish things? I bet he thought it was all a bit much, the whole Thanksgiving love nest thing. Never mind, hun, you have the taste for boys now! Grab your coat, I'm treating you to a cocktail at the Dragon. A new man is just what you need to forget about an old one."

I rolled my eyes and let myself fall back against my pillows. "He didn't dump me, Lois. But I appreciate your confidence in me."

Lois laughed and turned red. "Oops, sorry. But look at you— You look like someone died." She paused and took a short step toward the bed. "Oh God, no one died, did they?"

"I don't know, hand me a knife and I'll tell you in a minute," I mumbled.

Lois hit me with a cushion and sat cross-legged beside me. "So, if he didn't dump you, and nobody died, what the hell is wrong with you?"

I shrugged and picked at an invisible thread on my skirt. "I'm just sad it's over, that's all."

Lois rolled her eyes. "You get more and more tragic every time you see him!"

"I do not!" I protested.

"I'm sorry to be the one to tell you, but you really do." Lois' tone was soft, but her eyes danced with amusement. She laughed. "You just get so caught up with him, it's like you're only going through the motions of everyday life just to get to the part when you're with him. Sweetie, there's more to life than a man. Wasn't that your motto before you met him?"

"Yeah, I know." I dropped my eyes, feeling every bit the hypocrite.

She sighed and reached over to pat my leg. "I think it's fantastic you met him, Barb. He's brought more out of you than you'll ever realize. You're a different woman now, and in a very good way. I think it's a confidence thing."

"So what's the problem? Why are you picking on me?" I asked as I sat up and pushed my hair out of my face.

"I just think you should try to balance things a little more evenly. Put the same kind of energy into the rest of your life. Before the summer, you and I used to do lots of things together."

I laughed. "You were always on dates!"

She rolled her eyes. "Okay, so when I wasn't on dates we used to do a lot together. Now… It's like, if it's not Van you're with, why bother?"

"Oh, Lois, I—"

Lois held her hand up to stop me. "Don't dare apologize because I do the exact same thing. All I'm asking for is a little bit of the energy you reserve for him. That's all."

I looked down at my lap. What a horrible friend I'd become. "I'm one of those girls, aren't I?"

She laughed. "Oh, Barb. You'll never be one of those girls. But you have lost your way. You used to talk about books and art and allsorts before, let's have a bit of that Barb back. You know, you can be in love and have other interests."

I hit her with a pillow.

"So how did it go, anyway? The hideaway cottage?" Lois asked with a laugh as she dodged out of reach. "Did you pull off the feast?"

I laughed. "Not at all! We ended up having Scotch and cheese sandwiches."

Lois collapsed in giggles. "I wish I'd been there. So tell me, did he try anything? You're always preaching about what a perfect gentleman he is, so did he live up to it? Or did he try and sneak a peek every time you were in the shower?"

My cheeks burned. You could always count on Lois to speak her mind. "No!" I laughed. "Don't be ridiculous, Van would never do that."

Lois narrowed her eyes, scanning me from head to toe. Her eyebrows puckered together before her eyes widened and she gasped. "You!"

"Me what?" I was really confused now.

"You! You started it!" Lois threw her arms around me with such force we fell backward onto the bed. "I'm so proud of you! Why was that not the first thing you told me?"

"I'm hardly going to run through the house singing it at the top of my voice," I said, rolling my eyes.

"So…" Lois drawled. "How was it?"

I couldn't help the goofy smile that spread across my lips. "I've never felt anything like it, Lois."

Her eyes lit up. "That good, huh? Lucky you, my first time was awful."

"He was so, so gentle and considerate of everything. He made me feel like the most beautiful woman in the world."

Lois nodded. "It's always better second time around. Did you get a second time?"

I laughed and covered my face with my hands. "A few more than that. I had difficulty keeping my clothes on."

"Wow! Barb, I had no idea you had that sort of passion in you." Lois cackled her delight. "Gee whiz, no wonder you looked so depressed. What made you go for it?"

I shrugged. "I couldn't imagine it being with anyone else, and I'm so sure of our future it didn't feel right to wait anymore."

"You're serious, aren't you? You really know that Van is the guy for you," Lois asked, her voice quiet and full of curiosity. "How do you know he's the one?"

"I don't know how to explain it." I narrowed my eyes, trying to find the words. "It's like I've seen the future, and he's it. Nothing else is certain except for us. So imagine seeing that, knowing it...but now you have to go about everyday life and wait for the time to come when you finally get to have it."

Lois blew out a long breath. "Wow, no wonder you're always so keen to see him."

It was a relief she understood. There would be no more teasing from her. Well, for now at least. I jumped up off the bed and pulled Lois to her feet. "Come on."

"Where are we going?" Lois asked as we left the room.

"Didn't you say something about cocktails at the Dragon?"

Her face lit up. "I'll get my coat."

Chapter Twenty

The first week after Thanksgiving was the hardest. Sleep, especially. Van had ruined me for sleeping alone after having had a whole week of his arms wrapped around me.

My need for Van didn't lessen over time. Instead, it grew like a fire burning deep inside me. Juggling all my commitments did become easier. I gradually returned to a normal way of life. I attended classes and got my homework done on time.

It was evident that Van couldn't bear not knowing when we could properly be together again either, as shortly after Thanksgiving he moved out of the dorm and into a shared house off campus. I spent every weekend there.

But just when I thought I had my life in a somewhat manageable order, the rug was pulled out from under all of us.

I'll never forget that day, not even if I live to be a hundred years old.

Van and I walked back from a long Sunday lunch at our favorite restaurant near his house. The cold seeped into our bones and we huddled together for warmth. The light of the day faded, only four o'clock in the afternoon, but it was December, and the darkness fell earlier each day. I pulled my scarf a little tighter and rubbed my hands together. Everything was normal.

Van held me close as we walked, trying to shelter me from the bitter cold. The streetlights flickered on above us. A few people passed by. I was gloriously happy, as I always was when Van and I were together.

The day drew to a close. It was time to return to everyday life. As much as I loved Sundays with Van, I dreaded the end of them. I always found an excuse to stay a little longer. It's too cold, let's have another cup of tea first. No one will be home, please don't make me sit in that big house all by myself. I have a headache, I really can't move yet. I had tried them all.

When my excuses were exhausted, I admitted defeat and let Van drive me home.

We turned onto my street and for the first time during the drive, I paid attention to my surroundings. My forehead puckered in confusion. Women cried, people dashed from house to house, banging on doors.

Van normally said goodbye to me in the car, all too aware of how people liked to curtain twitch in the neighborhood — the product of too many college girls living in such close proximity. But today he shut off the engine and got out of the car.

A young boy sprinted toward us.

"Hey, kid!" Van shouted. "What's going on?"

The boy halted to a stop in front of us. He crouched over and put his hands on his knees, sucking in deep gulps of air. "The Japs... Damn filthy... Pearl..."

Van placed a hand on the boy's shoulder. "Whoa, calm down. Get your breath back."

The boy righted himself. "Pearl Harbor's been hit by the Japs."

There was no way to describe how I felt when those words were spoken. I vaguely wondered how my legs still held me up because I thought I was going to keel over. Dimly aware of Van grasping my hand, he hauled me up the front steps and into the house. In the back of my mind, I was shocked at this. The rules flickered past in my mind. He'd never attempted to sneak in before, let alone brazenly march right in, in full view of everyone.

The quietness of my house scared me to death. Our house was always the epitome of life, and a somber mood was cast over it. A crackly voice came from the kitchen, and we followed the sound.

The girls sat around the table. A radio was in the middle, looking like an idol being worshiped, despite the horrific things coming out of it. Lois saw me. Her chair scrapped against the linoleum as she stood. I'd never seen Lois cry before. It was an awful sight—one I never wanted to see again. I held her. I didn't have any words of consolation.

No alcohol was passed around. No cigarettes lit. There was only deathly silence with the exception of the voice on the radio.

Van stood with his hand on my shoulder.

So Lois had been right.

World War II had found us.

* * * *

Van stayed with me that night. No rules mattered that day and we knew no one would check, not tonight. Lying in the darkness with Van's strong arms guarding me from harm, fear wrapped itself around my heart. I'd never felt anything like it before... It paralyzed me.

For the first time, I allowed the meaning of it all to sink in. In just under two hours, the Japanese Imperial Army had crippled us. The body count wasn't in, but we knew it was high.

Guilt tortured me. I was lying there, safe and warm. Families up and down the country would not have such a setting. They would be receiving news that no person deserves to receive. As much pain as I felt for the families who knew their sons would never walk through the front door again, I ached for those who were awaiting the news.

My head pounded when I woke. Nobody felt well rested as we yet again took up our vigil at the kitchen table. The front door opened and closed several times throughout the day. Girls who didn't have their own radio came to listen to ours.

When President Roosevelt made his speech, our kitchen had reached bursting point. Not a whisper was uttered. The room was thick with smoke, making my eyes stream. Like I needed another reason.

"Mr. Vice President, Mr. Speaker, Members of the Senate, and of the House of Representatives: Yesterday, December 7th, 1941 – a date which will live in infamy – the United States of America was suddenly and deliberately attacked by naval and air forces of the Empire of Japan..."

We listened to his speech, growing more emotional as it went on. Hearing his voice, how sure it sounded, should have relieved me. Instead, the fear in my heart was too thick to allow it. America was at war.

How would we survive it?

It wasn't anywhere close to being a level playing field.

The weeks following the attack on Pearl Harbor showed mixed responses from the public. Women around me howled daily. Others were angry and bitter. Some young men were excited, eager to defend their country. Hundreds of thousands of American men flooded the recruitment offices, determined to do their bit.

Some of us, myself included, were simply afraid. President Roosevelt assured the country we would never be attacked that way again, but we watched the skies just in case.

Though we attended college, the numbers dwindled day by day. Girls were being taken back home. I wasn't surprised. A lot of girls had family in the navy and army. Some had been given terrible news. Others parents simply felt better with their children back home. Some had to say goodbye to the men in their family who were now venturing into the unknown to fight the enemy.

We all tried to keep going, but we didn't know how to get back to normal. Our teachers relaxed and didn't scold as often as they once had. That first week they even turned a blind eye to homework not handed in on time.

We went to a special Sunday assembly exactly one week after the hit on Pearl. There wasn't a dry eye in the house by the time it was finished. My art history professor sang the national anthem, trying to get us geared up and patriotic. It only made me cry more.

* * * *

The night before Christmas vacation, Lois returned home with cheeks rosy from the bitter weather, and cursing like a sailor. "Bad night?" I asked from my warm seat by the radiator, nursing a cup of tea between my hands.

"I just came from an extra-credit lesson. How to cross and uncross your ankles. Can you believe it?" she asked, rolling her eyes.

Biting my tongue, I thought it unwise to tease Lois. "Tea?"

She scoffed and headed for the liquor cabinet to pour herself a large glass of Scotch. Gulping a mouthful down, she shuddered. "God, I am *freezing*!"

I gave her a shawl from the back of my chair and she wrapped it around her shoulders. "You all packed?" I asked when she'd finished her drink and no longer resembled a cat whose tail had been trod on.

She nodded. "You?"

"Of course."

"Nervous?"

"A little."

Lois' face softened. "Don't be. Your mother will be on her best behavior with Van."

"I know. Doesn't make it any less scary."

"I can't believe she invited him to stay for the whole of Christmas break." Lois shook her head. "I'm more surprised that he said no."

"I'm glad he did," I said with a smile. "He's coming to lunch, but I can't imagine him being that close and not being able to do anything. You just know my mother would catch me sneaking across the hall. Besides, it's kind of tradition for him to spend the break with Paul's family. They love him to death."

Lois sighed. "And I'll be at home... Alone... Miserable..."

I rolled my eyes at her. "Lois, I offered for you to come but you said no. You'll hardly be alone."

"Not the point." She laughed. "Okay, maybe I'm exaggerating. I do have a few old boyfriends I'm sure would love to hear from me."

"See!" I exclaimed. "There's the loveable siren we all know."

Lois gave me a withering look.

"I'm worried what it'll be like." I glanced at Lois. "Home. It's bound to be different."

"Just like everywhere else I suppose. We're all different now, Barb." Lois looked down into her empty glass. "You know, a few boys I went to high school with were based at Pearl."

"Really? Have you — Do you know if…"

Lois shook her head. "I haven't heard. I don't think my mom would tell me over the phone anyway, you know? I'll just have to wait till I get home to find out."

Again, there was nothing I could say to console her. Anything I said would just be false hope.

"When are you back?"

I shrugged. "We haven't decided. Probably not until the day before the new term starts."

Lois nodded. "I just don't want to come back and you not be here." She was showing a softer side of herself. I'd known Lois for two and a half years now, and this was the first I'd seen it. It was painful to see her like this — raw and vulnerable to the harsh realities of the world. Sensing the shift in atmosphere, Lois tipped back the glass to get a last tiny sip. She stood and marched upstairs.

Chapter Twenty-One

I was hardly the picture of patience as I waited on the front stoop for Van to pick me up. The second his car rolled into view I all but ran to greet him. I was thankful when I saw the empty back seat. I'd wondered if Van would want to travel with Paul since he was going to be staying with him.

Van caught me looking. He chuckled. "Relax, Barb. Paul left yesterday."

"I wasn't worried," I lied.

Van didn't say anything as he put my suitcase into the trunk and drove us to the train station.

The journey was less comfortable than it had been at the end of summer. No first class for us this time. Van was less frivolous with his money since he had moved into the new house, which was far more expensive than the dorm.

My parents met us at the other end. Mother was charming as always in front of Van. We drove Van to Paul's house and arranged to see him the following day.

I sat with my mom and dad at the kitchen table, nursing a cup of tea. Three boys from our town had been killed in the air raid at Pearl. I didn't know them personally, but I grieved for them nonetheless.

We tried to be cheerful, but the Christmas spirit just didn't find us this year. In light of recent events, my father decided now was a time more than ever to have your family around you. Anna and Kenneth would come for Christmas lunch along with Kenneth's parents. Van had been invited anyway, but it touched my heart that my father thought of him and included him in the family.

One afternoon while Anna and I were out for a walk, we saw one the mothers who'd lost a son walking down the street. The people nearby gawked, as if the poor woman needed to be treated like a circus act.

Anna noticed, too, and rushed to help her. "Mrs. Parson, let me help you." The woman was loaded with grocery bags, and Anna relieved her of a few.

"Oh, Anna, thank you, dear." She managed a tiny smile, but it soon fell.

Mrs. Parson looked as though she'd barely slept, her red-rimmed eyes accentuated by black circles.

"It's no problem," Anna assured her.

"Is this your sister?" Mrs. Parson asked, noticing me trail behind them.

"Yes, this is Barbara."

"It's lovely to meet you," I said, blushing furiously. I wanted to scream my apologies and offer my condolences. Like they would mean anything. How does one recover from the kind of loss she has experienced?

"Why are you out doing this, Mrs. Parson?" Anna asked quietly. "I'm sure you have someone who could do this for you."

Mrs. Parson forced a smile. "I can't avoid the world forever. Besides, it's nice to get a little fresh air."

"Well, if you ever need anything, anything at all, will you please call me?"

"Of course." The look in Mrs. Parson's eye told us Anna shouldn't expect a phone call anytime soon. We slowed to a stop at her gate. "Thank you for your help." Mrs. Parson took the bags from Anna and disappeared inside her house.

"Poor woman," Anna murmured as we carried on home. "Can you imagine feeling that much loss? I don't think I could bear it."

"No." I could barely comprehend it, let alone imagine the actual pain. Seeing a direct result of the devastation was a real wake up call. The events at Pearl Harbor affected us all, but it was a hundred times worse for others like Mrs. Parson.

It surprised everyone, and no one had a chance to say goodbye. My thoughts leaped to those who had been given a chance to say goodbye. Some of our boys had already been shipped out. Would they ever see their families again? When would we finally get the answers we all desperately needed to know?

* * * *

Everyone made an effort on Christmas Day. We ate to bursting point, our glasses never reaching empty. A permanent cigarette cloud lingered — all too symbolic of the black cloud that now blocked our country from the healing rays of the sun.

The world was injured, but we had one another.

"I have something to tell you," Anna whispered.

"Oh?" I raised an eyebrow.

Anna glanced behind her and scooted closer to me on the piano stool. Her fingers glided effortlessly over the keys, no set piece being played. Her melody took a more decided turn, the piece now familiar. "I'm pregnant."

I froze. It was instinct to throw my arms around her, but I knew she wanted no reaction from me. "Anna!" I gushed. "I— Congratulations!"

"Shh." Anna giggled, her eyes widening.

"Sorry! I'm really happy for you." A wide grin spread, taking over my face. I squeezed her knee and leaned in a fraction. "I'll try to act as surprised as possible when you announce it later."

Anna peered out from under her long lashes and gave me a wink. Kenneth hovered at the other end of the piano, and I took this as my cue to leave and found my usual spot by Van's side.

A look was passed between Anna and Kenneth, followed by a sharp cough. "Could I please have everyone's attention?"

All eyes darted to the couple now standing elegantly by the piano.

"I'm aware we chose this as the perfect setting to announce our engagement." Kenneth grinned. "And it is my immense pleasure to now inform you of another event to be celebrated. In August, our family will welcome a new member."

I clasped my hands to the side of my face, praying to God that my look was authentic. Van fought back a laugh as Mom and Mrs. Dixon began their fight to hug and congratulate the new parents-to-be.

It was just the thing we needed. The fake cheeriness was shattered, replaced by a far sincerer joy. My father dug out the good Scotch and held his glass up in a toast.

"To Anna and Kenneth, who will both make wonderful parents. I could not be happier for you both."

We all sipped our drinks in unison. Somehow Anna managed to wriggle free from the clutches of Mother and Mrs. Dixon and fought her way toward me.

"I'm so happy for you, Anna." I placed a hand on her still-flat stomach. "I'm going to be the best aunt in the world."

Anna held her hand over mine, keeping it there. "Yes, you are. And you've just signed yourself up for babysitting duties."

I laughed. "Of course, any time at all."

Anna leaned in closer. "I'm a little nervous," she admitted.

"Oh, sweetie, why? As long as you don't take any pointers from Mom, you will be fine!"

Anna's confident smile slipped. "I know. I'm just scared something bad will happen, or that I won't be a good mother."

I squeezed her hand. "Don't even think it, not for a second. You're going to be wonderful, Anna."

She released my hand and hugged me. "Thanks, little sister."

"No problem," I whispered.

Anna was dragged back into conversations regarding wool color, which I ardently avoided.

The night carried on, the good mood lifting everyone's spirits. Tales of childhood were shared, ranging from the sweet to the unbelievable. My father regaled everyone with the story of when I convinced Anna that our next door neighbor was a witch, and you had to hold your breath while walking past her house in order to avoid any spells being cast on you.

"I can remember Halloween, the year she told me that," Anna said, struggling to speak through her giggles. "She dared me to ding-dong-ditch the woman's house."

Laughter bubbled out of me, the memory flooding back. "She chased you off her porch with a broom!"

"It just confirmed your story!"

Even Mom laughed at this. "I remember that. Anna ran straight up to her room. She was terrified for weeks."

"That was our Barb," Dad said, nudging me. "She could convince anyone of anything."

The evening ended, all of us warmed from the inside out. The hour grew late and it was time for everyone to leave. Mom insisted Kenneth and Anna stay, to save Anna a trip out into the cold. She also insisted that Van stay, and he could take the couch.

It was a long wait while I made sure everyone was sleeping before creeping down the stairs. Van lay on his back with one arm tucked under his head. He smiled when he saw me sneak into the room, and lifted his blanket, letting me in to his warm embrace.

"Were you expecting me, Mr. Judson?"

"Maybe," Van murmured in my ear.

I snuggled close to him and took a deep breath. I still wasn't immune to his intoxicating scent. I wished I could bottle it and have it with me always.

Van stroked my hair, lulling me to sleep. "Barb…"

"Hmm?" I asked, my eyelids drooping even more.

"It wouldn't be a very good idea for you to fall asleep down here."

I forced my eyes open, struggling to focus on his. "Don't make me then."

Van smiled. He only had to move his head a fraction to kiss me. Softly at first, then with a hint of urgency creeping in. "Better?" he mumbled against my lips.

"Much…" I curled my body around his. Any cautious thoughts halted the moment his tongue teased mine. All my inhibitions vanished as my body responded to his kiss.

He laughed against my mouth. "Barb…"

"What?" I breathed.

Van started to pull away from me, but I didn't let him get far. My lips captured his, disobeying all the logical rules. He shifted us — pinning me down with his body. His kiss grew hungry and he grasped folds of my nightgown. "Woman, you are too appealing for your own good." Van sighed and raised himself up.

"What are you doing?" I asked, as he shifted off me.

He stroked his thumb over my lip. "Not this."

"Why?" I asked, twisting so I could take his earlobe between my teeth.

He groaned. It really wasn't fair of me to target his weak spot. "Barb, anyone could walk in."

That halted my advances dead in their tracks. It was too easy to forget my sleeping parents one floor above our heads.

"Well, that was very cruel of you." I huffed. "Leading me on like that."

Van laughed. "You led yourself."

We drew quiet. We didn't need words. When the heat from our passionate embrace subsided, I relished in the comfort of simply lying in his arms. My head danced with thoughts of him, but my sister pushed her way to the forefront.

I think we all needed her news — it helped us realize it wasn't only death happening around us. Life carried on.

* * * *

New Year's Eve, 1941

The irony didn't evade me as I pulled my new black pencil dress over my head that it would be the third consecutive year Van and I spent New Year's Eve together…the only difference was this year, it was intentional.

We were, surprise, surprise, attending the same party as before and Kenneth and Anna were coming with us. Anna decided she wasn't going to let her condition stop her from having fun, and she wasn't showing yet, so people would be none the wiser.

Lois would be sore that she was missing the party. She'd thoroughly enjoyed it last year. She also loved Anna's company and would be upset at having missed out on spending an evening with her.

The doorbell rang and I cursed. I quickly applied my lip stain, stepped into my shoes and rushed downstairs.

"Calm down, Barbara," Mom scolded me. She couldn't ruin my excitement—nothing could. Van was in the lounge with my father, sipping a Scotch. He'd left his hair natural, flopping across his forehead, just the way I liked it. He looked handsome in his black suit… *How could this beautiful man want me?*

Mom took a few pictures of us before I pulled Van out of the door, keen to start the night. We arrived before Anna and Kenneth, so we hunted down a free table but they weren't far behind.

As Anna and I greeted each other, Van and Kenneth exchanged a look and headed for the bar.

"So, how is it in the land of love?" Anna asked, her eyes wide with excitement.

I grinned. "Incredible."

"I'm so glad. I'm truly pleased you found each other. So..." Anna puckered her lips. "Any sign of...?" She wiggled her ring finger.

"Wha— *No!*" I spluttered. "You're getting as bad as Mom."

The insult twisted her face. "I am not. That wasn't nice, Barb."

"Doesn't make it untrue," I said with a wicked smile.

Anna rolled her eyes. "All right, I'm sorry I asked." She was saved by the men, who brought our drinks.

Van pulled me onto the dance floor the second we finished them. Of course, it had set a bad precedent, as I was then hounded with dance offers.

"Don't they realize I'm with you?" I groaned as one unfortunate stalked off, stinging with rejection.

Van looked amused. "Maybe they just think the Ice Queen has had her cold heart melted, and is now open to dance offers."

I gasped. "That is an awful thing to say!"

He squeezed my waist. "I'm kidding."

Shooting him a hard look, I remained silent. Until he kissed me and I had no choice but to forgive him.

The room grew fuller with each passing hour. The mass of bodies sent temperatures soaring, forcing me outside often for fresh air. Anna and Kenneth were the picture of marital bliss all evening. Kenneth waited on her hand and foot, fetching drinks and snacks at the drop of a hat. I couldn't take my eyes off them. Their happiness drew me in, warming me from head to toe.

Kenneth stood and offered his hand to Anna. He led her out to dance, looking exactly as they had at their wedding. Their bubble was back and no one was getting in.

Van motioned to them with his thumb. "Shall we?"

I nodded and took the hand he offered.

There really was no other feeling like it in the world. Moving slowly in time with the music, I tried to savor every second of the moment with Van. He held my hand over his heart, and I could feel its rhythmic beat through the soft material of his shirt.

Van had his head to mine, his mouth inches away from my ear. "This is definitely an improvement from last year."

"Mmm," I agreed. My eyes closed, shutting out the rest of the world.

"It's almost midnight," he whispered.

A delicious shiver crept down my spine from his tickling breath. "We're keeping the tradition alive, then."

"I'm a lucky man to have had you in my arms on the stroke of midnight at this party three times now." I knew every tone, every inflection of Van's voice. I'd have thought his words would sound bold, almost cocky, with a hint of a smile. Instead... He sounded morose, apologetic.

Fear crawled up my spine. "You have me forever," I whispered. Van was quiet for a moment and I was almost too afraid to question him. "Van?"

Van took a deep breath. "Do you mean that—forever?"

I lifted my head so I could look at him. My eyebrows pulled together and I flattened my palm against his chest. "Of course, forever, and whatever comes after that."

His eyes searched mine. "Even if forever has to be put off for a little while?"

"Van, I don't understand," I said quietly.

Van closed his eyes and shook his head. He trembled and tightened his hold on me. "I don't want to do this now… Here. But the thought of starting a new year without you knowing… I don't know if I can do it."

My heart raced. Whatever he was building toward, it was something big. Huge. Life-altering. The little girl in me wanted to plug my ears so I couldn't ever find out. Because if it was this hard to say…it wouldn't be easy to hear. "Knowing what? What are you trying to tell me?"

He glanced at the floor. "I'm not going to be with you for very long once the new year comes in."

"Why not?"

"There's something I have to do."

"Why? Don't do it, if it means you have to leave." My eyes stung and it was all I could do just to keep myself together.

"I have to." Van's voice shook. "Please don't get upset. This is already killing me, Barb."

I looked up to find unrelenting agony in his eyes. It was then the truth hit me like freight train. *No… Please let me be wrong.* "You're—you're enlisting, aren't you?"

Van managed the tiniest of nods.

A sob broke free of my throat. "Why? Why would you do this?"

He lifted his eyebrows, as though he wasn't expecting the question. "I have to, Barb. I can't stand idly by and not fight for my country."

"But what about us?" My voice broke. "Why can't you fight for *us*?"

"I will be," Van said. "Every single day."

The music stopped. The dancing ceased.

I barely heard the countdown. I couldn't look at Van. With one finger, he raised my chin until my eyes locked with his. A tear rolled down my cheek. My vision blurred but I saw his pain was as agonizing as mine.

"Happy New Year," he mumbled, making a dim attempt at a smile.

The breath was knocked out of me and I threw myself at the mercy of his kiss. I snaked my arms around his neck, unwilling to let him go. Harder, harder I kissed him.

Van broke out of my hold. He clutched my hand and led me out to the quietness of the street. Cheer erupted everywhere, yet my world crumbled around me. A few drunken louts sang *Auld Lang Syne*, badly and out of tune.

He swung me around to face him, wiping the tears now streaming down my face. "Barb, please—"

"What? This is what you want!" I flung my words at him. "You can't expect me not to be hurt over that."

"I know, I know," he whispered. "But please understand why I am doing this."

"Well, I can't." I stared hard at him—steeling myself even though he had never looked more vulnerable. "How can I? How can you expect me to understand that you are swapping our future for a death sentence?"

Van's eyes were mournful. He stepped toward me. "It doesn't have to be like that, Barb. You don't know I'm going to die out there."

"It's war, Van," I snapped. "People just don't come back from that."

"I might," he said softly.

"And if you don't, then what? What am I supposed to do?" My voice broke and all the fight drained out of me.

Van cupped my cheeks, bringing our faces close. "I need you to fight for us."

"Why?" I whispered. "When you won't?"

"Barb, it is for us that I am doing this. To be a part of a better future," Van said, his voice low and gravelly with thick emotion.

I squeezed my eyes shut. Why couldn't he see what he was doing? He was talking about the future — making it better... But for who? "There won't be a future for us."

"Stop it!" Van shouted, giving me a little shake. "Stop making this harder than it has to be."

A sob broke free from my mouth. Whatever control I'd had over my emotions crumpled, and they all poured out of me.

Van's eyes held a world of heartache, and a part of me hated myself for putting it there. "Please..."

I groaned and ripped out of his hold. "This is exactly what you wanted!" I shouted through my tears. "You wanted me! You wanted me, and you got me. You made me fall in love with you, and now you're leaving me."

"This, none of this, I ever had a choice on," Van said, slicing his hand through the night air. "Do you know that I saw you long before we ever even talked? I saw you walking down a street and from that day you owned me. I didn't see you again for eight months. When I did it was at the station, a few days before I got my first chance to talk to you. That was New Year's three years ago, Barb. Now do you understand? Finally?

"My heart has belonged to you for almost four years now. I could never give up, not even when it seemed like there was no hope. *That's* why you never scared me off. I didn't have a choice."

I fell against him, my tears soaking his thin shirt. "So don't do this, please, Van. Don't leave me."

He held me so tightly I struggled to breathe. I could barely hear anything apart from my sobs. Van choked back his own emotion. He whispered, "I'm sorry." His voice cracked on the words.

This was why I never wanted to fall in love, I now knew. I never wanted to feel this way. I was lost, with no hope of going home again.

Chapter Twenty-Two

To say I reacted badly to Van's news would be a severe understatement... I should have been supportive, but I just couldn't muster the energy. The anger that coursed through my veins was potent and unrelenting. Deep down, I knew he was being honorable. But I couldn't see past what felt an awful lot like betrayal. Van chased me, got me and was now leaving me. He didn't have to do this. It was his choice, yet he was acting as if he didn't have one.

On the journey back to Wellesley, I mostly stared out of the window. Van tried to talk to me a few times, but his efforts were fruitless. Every time I looked into those eyes, a new wave of pain washed through me. When we arrived at Boston, I wouldn't let him take me back to Wellesley — I insisted on going alone.

My anger hurt him.

I couldn't find a way to stop it.

Lois was her vibrant self when I got home, eager to know the details from my trip. Not up for recounting New Year's, I told her I was sick. My color hadn't fully returned since Van told me his news and it didn't take too much to convince Lois I was ill.

Sleep evaded me again that night and come the morning I knew it was pointless to go to my classes. Lying in bed, I let the misery wash over me.

Early in the afternoon, Lois burst into my room. "Why didn't you go to school today?" I rolled over to face her, and I must have looked worse than I realized as she crossed the room to sit beside me on the bed. "What happened over Christmas, Barb? And don't give me the crap about being sick."

"Van's enlisting," I said, my voice void of any and all emotion.

Lois' face softened as she reached out to touch my shoulder. "Oh shit, Barb. I'm sorry. When is he leaving?"

I shrugged. "I don't even know when he's going to the recruitment office."

Her eyebrows shot up. "So what the hell are you doing moping around here? You should be with him."

"I can't even look at him."

Lois stood and folded her arms across her chest. "Barb, I know you're hurting, but now is not the time for your insecurities to make a reappearance."

I rolled away from her, facing the wall. "I'm so angry at him, Lois. How can he do this?"

"Because he has to!" Lois shouted, her patience gone. "It's his patriotic duty to stand up and fight. You shouldn't stand in his way, or make him feel guilty. You should be with him right now, not moping around here feeling sorry for yourself."

I knew she was right. It was probably why I hadn't wanted to talk to her the night before, because I knew that for once she would be the rational one. Her words struck a raw nerve and the pain, the worry that had shaken me to my very core on New Year's once again returned.

Lois jumped onto the bed and wrapped her arms around me. "I know it hurts, I know. But you know he's doing the right thing. Don't make him feel guilty about it." She kissed my cheek and disappeared from the room only to return a few minutes later. "Go wash your face. I've called a cab for you. It'll be here soon."

* * * *

The forty-minute cab ride gave me a good chance to think. It felt as if I was split in two. I couldn't understand the logic behind his decision—couldn't understand why he was causing both of us so much unnecessary pain. He thought he was making the right choice…the honorable choice, and a part of me did get it.

But Lois was right. I couldn't make him feel guilty about it. And if our days were numbered, did I really want to spend them being angry with him? Or did I want to make them count?

There was no answer as I banged on his front door. The cab had already left and the rain poured. I hugged myself, trying to keep warm. The rain dripped down my face when I eventually saw his car approach. He parked and leaped out, running up the front steps. "What the hell are you doing?" Van demanded. "You're freezing!"

"I had to see you," I said as I stood shivering in my soaking wet clothes.

"What about school?"

"What about it?" I tried to laugh, but it stuck in my throat.

"I was coming to see you, I—" Van looked down. "I have a week."

A week... Steeling myself, I looked into his sad, blue eyes and decided to let go of everything. School, the confusion I felt over his decision, the hurt. "Then I'm not going anywhere."

Van unlocked the door and pulled me inside. Peeling my wet coat from my shoulders, he said, "Come on, I'll get you some clothes."

I followed him up to his room where I gratefully peeled off the dripping wet clothes. My skin broke out in goosebumps as I stood shivering in my slip.

Van returned with an armful of clothes. He dropped them on his bed and rubbed my arms to try to warm them. He seemed unsure of himself when he quietly spoke again, "Can I ask what brought on the change?"

"I was selfish before," I said, taking his hand. "I shouldn't have reacted that way. It wasn't fair."

Van attempted a small smile. "At least it let me see that you do kind of like me."

I pressed my hand over his heart, wondering if it felt cracked as mine did. "Be serious."

He took my hand and kissed it, his eyes turning sober. It made my chest squeeze. "I don't want to leave you."

I bit my tongue from answering *Then don't.* Instead I forced a smile that I knew wasn't fooling either of us. "I'm not going anywhere until you do."

He shook his head. "Barb, you can't. School—"

"School can wait." I reached up to kiss him. "We can't."

Van wrapped his arms around me and lifted me clear off my feet. He kissed me so fully I thought our bodies might fuse together. He set me back down and pulled my slip up over my head, letting it drop to the floor. Frantically tugging at his shirt, I all but ripped it open.

Van rid himself of the rest of his clothes and drew me to the bed. Settling himself between my legs, he was in me before I could draw breath. Our lovemaking was frantic, desperate. We needed each other and there was no time to take things slowly.

It was over quickly — our desire didn't allow it to be drawn out. Van collapsed against me, panting. Part of the desperate ache that had darkened my heart subsided — Van a balm to my wounded soul. I squeezed my eyes shut, remembering exactly how this felt — to have Van's body against mine, the sensation of him inside me.

Van rolled to the side, pulling me to face him. He kissed me — soft, habitual.

I stroked his face and tried to remember every detail.

"You are so beautiful," Van murmured. He kissed me again and sighed. "Did you really mean what you said? You're staying here till I leave?"

I inched closer to him, snaking my leg around his. My lips were millimeters away from his. "Where else would I be? You're what I live for."

Van pushed my wet hair from my face and pressed his forehead to mine. "I feel like I can't breathe without you."

"I know I can't," I whispered. Would this be one of my last memories of Van? Panic rose in my throat. Forcing it back down, I brushed my mouth over his. "Remember this, Van. Lock it in your heart and keep it with you always."

He closed his eyes. "I remember everything," Van said, his voice low and gravelly.

I kissed his collarbone, his throat, his earlobe. He shuddered with pleasure at my kisses and leaned into me. His arousal stirred, pressing tight against my thigh.

An ache throbbed between my legs and I needed him more desperately than before.

But I wouldn't let myself get carried away again. I was determined to prolong it until I thought I would burst with anticipation. Van's eyes shot open in excitement as I hitched my thigh over his hip and pushed him onto his back. I moved on top of him, laying my body flush against his.

I rocked my hips and lowered my head to catch his mouth with mine. I'd never been so bold with him before. I teased him, didn't allow the kiss to deepen when I could almost taste his hunger. I rocked harder, creating delicious friction that made my lower belly clench with need.

Van grasped my thighs and he lifted his hips, adding to the pressure building. With one last rock, Van could take no more. He pushed up into a sitting position, pulling my legs behind him. I gasped as he filled me. We locked eyes as I moved, losing ourselves in the act.

We finished together, in perfect sync. We had been made for this — for each other. We fit so perfectly, it was ridiculous to think otherwise.

I clung to him long after arousal left us.

* * * *

I barely left Van's side all week. I called Lois and she informed the school a family member was enlisting and to please forgive my absence. At the end of the week, Van was leaving for Fort Niagara, New York, a reception center to give him a taste of army life before he left for basic training. We didn't talk about the looming separation. It was too painful to think about.

We tried to act like normal, but now and then I would catch him watching me. I would be doing something routine, yet he watched, engrossed. As soon as I caught him, his eyes would laugh off the heaviness of the situation.

The day before he left brought a wave of hysteria. I'd been thinking of Anna, wondering how she was feeling. It then occurred to me that I would be saying goodbye not only to Van, but to my entire future, too. The dish I was drying slipped from my hand, shattering into pieces like my fragile heart.

Van took me by the shoulders. "Barb, what's wrong?"

"I can't do this." I trembled. "I can't lose you."

"You're not losing me, I'm coming back to you." Van's voice was so certain as though he truly believed it.

It wasn't that easy for me. I couldn't take it on faith…couldn't get past the mental block that Van leaving for war was as final as if I stood by his graveside. "What if you don't? I can't breathe without you. I—"

"No, Barb." Van shoved his hands into my hair, bringing my face closer to his. "I'm coming back to you… To us."

My eyes burned and that panic I'd kept at bay most of the week bubbled to the surface. "It feels like you're slipping through my fingers and I can't keep hold."

Van dragged his thumb across my cheek. "You don't have to. Listen to me, Barb. There is a future for us — we just have to be patient. Just for a little while."

"No, I can't," I said, shaking my head. Hysteria coursed through my veins and my loosely held control was shattering like the dish at my feet. "I was meant to have everything with you."

"You still will," Van whispered.

"No, I need it now." As soon as the words were out, clarity hit me like a ton of bricks. I knew what I needed — the only thing that could dull this pain...the only thing that could potentially bring him back to me.

"Barb, what are you saying?" Van asked, his forehead marred with a frown.

"Marry me." Lifting my eyes, I held his gaze. "Marry me, Van. Today."

He sighed, looking utterly bone-tired. I knew I was being unfair. He didn't need this extra strain. But the thought of him leaving without being tied to me in every way possible terrified me almost as much as the thought of him never returning.

"Barb..." He pressed our heads together. "No."

A sob rose in my throat. "Please... Van, I'm ready. You said at Thanksgiving we would wait until I was ready and I'm ready now."

"I believe you," Van whispered. "But I can't marry you like this, as a way to console you." The fight drained out of me and I broke down in his arms. He lowered me to the floor, pulling me onto his lap. Van stroked my hair in an attempt to soothe me. "I will marry you, Barb, you can count on that. But it won't be today. Not like this."

It was like being promised something impossible. It only made me more distraught. "Don't you love me?"

"I love you more than anything else in this world." The pain in Van's voice chilled me and broke my heart all over again. And it was all my fault... "When I get back, the first thing I'm doing is proposing. I promise. You will have that day, Barb. You'll wear an over the top white dress, Lois and Anna will be bridesmaids and Anna's child will be a flower girl, or pageboy. Your mother is going to drive you within an inch of your sanity, but you'll forgive her." Van held me tighter, as though the strength of his arms could cement his words. "We are going to have a long and happy life together, Barb. We're going to hate each other at times, but that love will never die. I'm going to watch you grow big as you carry our children, and I'm going to see you do the best job in raising them. Have faith, Barb."

His shirt was drenched with my tears by the end of his speech. I could see it all so clearly... Yet it was so far away.

* * * *

I don't know when Van packed his bag. He didn't let me see. We walked hand in hand to the station, any excuse for a few extra minutes together. His train was boarding when we got there. The steam blew at my skirts as we approached the train.

Van turned to face me with worry in his eyes.

"I'm not going to cry, I promise." I meant it. This day was hard enough on both of us. I couldn't make it harder for him by being an inconsolable female. "I have something for you. I reached into my purse and pulled out the small photograph. It had been Lois who'd insisted that I take one with me when I left our house a week ago to be with Van. She had helped me choose the nicest one, though I didn't take her advice and kiss the back of it to stain it with my lipstick.

He accepted the photograph, a soft smile touching his lips. "You think it's possible for me to forget your face? Not possible, Barb. But thank you. I'll keep it with me always." Van took my hand and planted the tiniest of kisses in the palm of it.

Terror vibrated through me, but I refrained from shaking. My eyes threatened to well up, but I didn't let them. He closed my hand and pulled me into his tight embrace. There were no more words to say—we had said them all. My heart couldn't bear to hear them again, not now. Not here.

I took a deep breath, wishing I could bottle his scent and keep it with me always. His hands were in my hair, twisting into knots. He buried his face into my neck, breathing me in, just as I had done.

Van unwound his fingers from my hair and pulled back to look at me. He tucked a lock behind my ear and caressed my cheek. He smiled my favorite lopsided smile and my stomach flipped.

Ever so gently, our lips met. It was so sweet and tender I could feel my heart breaking as a direct result.

The train conductor blew his whistle. It was time.

No! I kept the smile fixed on my face, determined not to break.

Van opened his mouth to say something, hesitated, and kissed me instead.

With a final caress of my cheek, he broke free and jumped on the train. I didn't see where he sat.

He was gone.

Gone.

The train wheezed and groaned as it pulled out of the station. It took all my might not to run after it screaming. I searched each window as they gradually sped past me.

I never saw him.

It was masochistic, but I watched until the train disappeared. When it was out of sight, I felt empty — completely drained, like there was nothing left inside me.

I need to get out of here... Rushing for the exit, my feet picked up speed until I finally reached the doors. I threw them open and burst into the fresh air. My body physically ached.

A pair of arms wrapped around me and a mass of blonde hair blocked my sight. "It's okay, honey. It's okay," Lois soothed. She held me upright as I sobbed in her arms. How was it possible to have tears left after this week?

It must have been the shock of saying goodbye to Van, because I didn't even think to question her sudden appearance.

I was dimly aware of Lois guiding me into a cab. She didn't let me go the whole way home. She held my head against her shoulder, stroking my hair and shushing me.

Lois took me straight upstairs to my room where I lay exhausted on the bed, not bothering to take off my shoes or coat. She curled behind me, holding me close. Pure exhaustion led me to a dreamless sleep. I felt stiff and uncomfortable when I woke, gray light coming through my small window.

Lois' arms were still draped over me, a soft snore blowing past her lips. My heart swelled at her compassion. She was such a loyal friend. I rolled over to face her.

My movement stirred her from sleep and she cracked one painted eyelid open. After a moment, both eyes flew open and she was a flurry of nerves. "Oh! Barb, are you—"

I smiled weakly. "I'll be fine."

Lois sighed.

"How did you know?" I asked, realization finally dawning on me.

"Van called me a few days ago." She smiled and tears filled her eyes. "He thought you might need someone to help you home."

My heart broke all over again at this. He knew me so well. When I was hurting, there was one person who would take the pain away. What was I going to do now, when he, in essence, was the source of my agony?

Lois stayed with me the rest of the day and night. She brought me highballs and cigarettes and a constant stream of cheerful chatter. She didn't mind that I barely joined in and kept it up nonetheless.

I went back to classes the next day—my departure forgiven. Apparently a lot of girls disappeared for a few weeks for the same reason.

Lois used her housewife skills to keep me in some kind of order. She forced me to shower even when I didn't feel like it, and encouraged me to eat. It was Lois who made sure I got up in the morning, although there was no need for this. Lying in silence only made the pain ache more. Surrounded by people, I found my thoughts could be heard less.

Van wrote almost every day, telling me of his training and what some of the other boys were like and how they were all being prepared for life in the army. I tried to be enthusiastic in my replies, but how could I, when my sun had disappeared from the sky...and only darkness remained?

He was safe for the time being, so I kept telling myself. I was merely missing him. But there was no *merely* about it. I craved him.

Two weeks after Van had left for the reception center at Fort Niagara, he was shipped off to basic training in Missouri. It was only a few weeks after that he was on the move again to Salt Lake City for advanced training.

It was all happening much quicker than I'd thought. They needed our boys abroad, and couldn't afford to procrastinate.

* * * *

The days blended into one another, weeks becoming months. I was sitting in my usual cloud of smoke in my room when Lois burst in. She grabbed my hand and hauled me down the stairs.

"Lois, what are you doing?" I demanded. As we came down the last flight of stairs, I spotted a familiar tall frame in the sitting room.

Wearing an army uniform.

I clumsily rushed in, throwing my arms around him as he turned.

He felt harder, stronger.

Van picked me up off my feet, crushing me to him so tight my bones complained. "God, you smell good," Van murmured. He set me back on my feet but I didn't release my viselike grip, terrified he would disappear. "You want to get out of here?"

I didn't need asking twice.

Van had a room at a bed-and-breakfast in town. Locking ourselves away, we made up for lost time. When my need for him subsided, he mixed us a highball each and brought a fresh pack of cigarettes. I scooted into his warm embrace the second he was back in bed.

"How did you get here? Did they give you leave or something?"

Van looked down. "I'm to report tomorrow morning at a nearby base to ship out. They gave us an extra few days of travel time, so it's sort of like unofficial leave."

The familiar dread coursed through me. "So soon?"

"We're needed in the Pacific."

I willed the tears that were so close to go away, so I wouldn't hurt him again. I steeled myself. I wouldn't cry. We would be happy with this gift of time.

So I told him all about Anna and her expanding belly. He told me nothing of the army. We could have gone somewhere, did something exciting. But why waste time? We could enjoy each other better here, alone.

The hours slipped away, the light outside darkening. I lay on my side, tracing Van's smooth, flawless naked chest with my fingertip. "I wish I could force myself to remember every single thing. How you feel. How you smell." I peered up at him, my lips twitching with amusement. "How you look at me when I'm being difficult."

Van's chest rumbled with laughter. "That shouldn't be too hard to remember — you see it often enough."

I sighed and pressed a kiss to his collarbone.

He stroked a hand down the length of my hair. "Have I ever told you about the first time I saw you?"

Pulling back so I could see him better, I said, "No. Not really. You mentioned something at New Year's, I think."

Van smiled and touched my bottom lip. "I was with Paul for spring break. He was in a department store, putting the moves on a counter girl. I was standing outside, bored out of my mind... And there you were. You walked toward me and I swear to God, I felt something inside of me change. You had me frozen to the spot and completely mute. Then you were gone. Afterward, I thought about all the ways I could have tried to talk to you. I hoped to run into you again, and I did. Little did I know that it would take eight goddamn months, though."

My heart soared, expanded and threatened to burst from my chest with the fullness of it. I hid my face in the crook of his neck. "But how could I have not seen you?"

Van shrugged. "You had blinders on when it came to men for years. You weren't the type of girl to scan the streets for a potential date."

A laugh bubbled in my throat. "That's true. Oh, Van, I wish I had, though. I wish I'd seen you."

He kissed the top of my head. "Relax, Barb. We're here now. That's all that matters. You know, it was the first time in ages that I took something on faith – and that was us. It's your turn now."

I nodded and swallowed the emotion that rose. I forced a smile. "Anyway, I think maybe your memory is faulty. There's no way you reacted like that when you saw me."

Van grinned and dipped his head to kiss me. "One day I'll prove it."

Wrinkling my nose in confusion, I shot him a disbelieving look. "I'd like to forget how I felt when I first met you. I'd never been so annoyed at a man before."

He chuckled. "You must have thought I was an overbearing oaf."

"I did." I grinned.

"Do you want me to tell you about our future? I have it all planned, you know."

Releasing a breath, I wriggled further into Van's embrace. I laid my head over his heart, letting the constant thump soothe my own. "Yes."

Van talked until his voice grew raspy and low. He told me what our wedding would be like and we argued over the details. Van wanted big and extravagant. I wanted small and intimate. We ignored the immediate future and what it meant and instead concentrated on the big payoff at the finish line.

We talked until the sun came up and just like that, it was time for Van to leave me again. I didn't get hysterical, I didn't even cry. His visit assured me he was ready, mentally and physically, for the coming trials. Sure, it wasn't as long as you would train under normal circumstances, but there was nothing *normal* about war. He was being briefed on the way out on the enemy. He swore to me there was no way he was being left behind on foreign soil. He was an American, born and bred. This was where he would be laid to rest, when he was a withered and frail old man.

I wanted to believe him.

Chapter Twenty-Three

Shortly after Van shipped out, summer vacation rolled around again. I dreaded it. Last summer had been so perfect, how could this year even compare? Evelyn was desperate to see me. She'd heard of the news and wanted to see how I was doing. Lois came with me. Whether it was because she wanted to, or was still worried about me, I didn't know. I was grateful for her nonetheless.

I introduced Lois and Thomas that summer. I encouraged their friendship. It made me feel less guilty that Lois was having such a boring summer because of me.

In mid-August, Anna gave birth to a healthy baby boy. Lois and I visited her in the hospital. He was beautiful—tiny, pink and perfect. Luckily for him, he had all of Anna's looks and none of Kenneth's. Robert Howell Dixon was going to be the most spoiled little boy the world had ever seen, judging by the way Lois and I fought about who loved him the most.

"He's my nephew too," Lois said with her hands on her hips.

"Yes, but he's mine by *blood*." I smiled.

"Details," Lois said.

Anna laughed. "I think it's safe to say he will be loved equally by the two of you."

We went shopping later the same day and spent a ridiculous amount of money on the tiny child. I couldn't wait to see him grow and develop into a little man.

I tried not to let Anna's happiness have the opposite effect on me. When Kenneth perched beside my sister on the bed, both looking adoringly at their son, the jealousy roared through my veins. I blocked all negative thoughts and only allowed positive ones. It would be my turn with Van one day... One day.

The silence from Van was agonizing. I knew it took a long time to reach their destination, wherever it was. I thought of him daily. As soon as a moment of quiet came, my mind would be flooded of him. As painful as they were, I clung to them. My memory was all I had of him for now.

Between Lois, Thomas and Evelyn, the three of them managed to keep me occupied. Even still, it was a strain to get out of bed in the morning. All I wanted to do was wallow in self-pity. The days melted into each other, the next no distinguishable from the last. The summer ended with no excitement. I didn't even try to make an effort.

* * * *

Lois and I had the same house for our senior year. One more year, then what would I do? Wellesley was my home. I dreaded having to leave. Where would I go? No career prospects tempted me. Because of Van, I hated the thought of leaving more than ever. Wellesley reminded me every day of him. We had so many memories here…it was at Wellesley I'd first let him in, allowed myself to drop the barriers I'd held.

The fall months brought word from Van. He had arrived safely! He couldn't write in any detail of where he was or what he was doing. Instead, he wrote of his new comrades, as though he were at summer camp, not the most dangerous place in the world.

I dedicated a few hours at the end of each day to write him back. Sitting at my small desk in a cloud of cigarette smoke, I told him about my classes and how I was progressing with my studies. Robert was a happy topic and I found I didn't need to try to sound happy when I wrote of him. I remained cheerful, even when the tearstains would tell him this was not the case.

His letters didn't come frequently, often a dozen or so arrived together. In one of his letters, Van reported a few of the other boys didn't write to anyone—perhaps I could arrange for a few Wellesley girls to put pen to paper?

"Lois, how do you feel about being a soldier's pen-friend?" I leaned against the sideboard, watching as she scrubbed a pan in the sink. "Van wrote me. A few guys he knows don't have anyone to write to. I thought maybe you'd like to."

"Me? Write to a soldier?"

I nodded.

She shrieked and grasped my arms with her bubble-covered hands. "Imagine it! Oh, Barb, I'll be the best pen-friend. Wow, a soldier." Lois danced around the kitchen, clasping her hands together. "We could start a torrid love affair—by paper. We'll fall in love… I must send a picture!"

As Lois tore from the room and bounded up the stairs, I smiled wistfully after her. Poor Lois. There was nothing romantic about war or a soldier's life.

* * * *

As was the tradition, I visited my parents for the holidays. I'd been dreading the slow approach, knowing it would be especially difficult.

Lois couldn't come with me and I was almost grateful. She'd become my bodyguard at Wellesley, protecting me, shielding me. I wanted her to enjoy the holidays, not have to look at my sour puss. My mother would leave me be, this I knew. After all, I'd finally earned her love by getting serious about a boy. I could only imagine how much she must brag now she had a soldier in the family.

Anna was enjoying her first Christmas with her now larger family. She promised to visit, but wouldn't stay for long. I didn't blame her. Had the roles been reversed, I would lock myself away with Van for eternity.

It was only my father who greeted me at the station. He hugged me awkwardly and took my suitcase without a word. The house was quiet. Every footstep seemed to echo.

My room comforted me as I lay on the familiar narrow bed. I closed my eyes and tried to imagine Van lying there also, wrapping his arms around me.

A sharp knock on my bedroom door shattered my fantasy. Dinner was being served.

"Any word from Van, Barb?" my father asked, cutting into steak.

I nodded.

My mother cleared her throat, a signal that if I didn't make more of an effort I'd be in for a scolding.

Sighing, I looked up. "Yes, Dad. He writes when he can. It isn't frequent."

"How are things going out there? Are we gaining any momentum?"

"He can't say."

"Not even a little?"

"It gets edited."

"Oh."

Mother's laugh was forced. "Oh, for heaven's sake. This talk is too depressing. Van will be back soon enough and then they will be married."

Even when war was involved, my mother still found a way to include marriage.

* * * *

New Year's Eve, 1942

I faked a headache.

By ten-thirty p.m. I was tucked up in bed, reading my old tattered copy of *Inferno* and hearing Van's voice. Van had read it to me often and it was no struggle to recall him speaking Dante's words.

Mom and Dad tried to talk me into going to the New Year's party, but nothing would change my mind. I had no one to go with anyway, and all it would do would remind me of previous years.

My parents danced in the lounge. I heard their happy giggling and the glasses clinking together as they toasted the New Year. Never in my life did I think I would be jealous of my parents. They had each other, and for that simple reason I envied them.

Before falling asleep, I sent up a silent prayer. Squeezing my eyes shut, I tried to force love out of me and into Van's heart. I wished more than anything that we were together. Had it been a year already? One painful year since he'd told me of his intentions to enlist.

I vowed the new year would be happier. It couldn't be any worse.

Chapter Twenty-Four

The day was so beautiful I almost enjoyed it. Spring colors bloomed in the trees, the sun warmed my face and the air was clear in my lungs. Birds sang, their melodic voices cheerful as they rolled and dipped in the skies. Children shrieked, their sounds of play filling the air. To anyone else the day would be perfect. But everything would always be just short of perfection for me, and it would remain that way until Van was home.

Classes were over for the day, earlier than normal. Thursdays I only had a half-day, and it meant that for a few hours, I didn't have to pretend to be fine. Lois was scared to death I was having some kind of mental break because I was still so broken over Van's absence. So for the most part I pretended I was hurt but manageable, holding up just like every other woman whose man was in the services.

But inside, I screamed like a banshee whose pain could never subside...the only balm to my anguish thousands of miles away in constant mortal peril.

I turned onto my street, the house coming into view. As I strolled closer, I spotted a figure on the porch swing. A suitor for Lois, no doubt—unaware she wouldn't be home for hours.

I pushed open the gate and sauntered up the steps.

The swing squeaked as he stood up, rigidly holding his tall frame. He stepped out of the shadow and his face came into view.

Van...

The books I carried fell out of my hand, a lump lodged in my throat. My heart pounded. He hurried to me, eager to help. His hair was slicked back and I wondered if it was because he saw this as a special occasion.

It was when he was right in front of me that my momentary flash of happiness was shattered—it wasn't him. Bitter, aching disappointment replaced the thrill of seeing him. How quick my mind wanted to trick me into believing he had returned.

"Mr. Judson?" I asked with a frown.

"Hello, Barbara, is it?"

I nodded meekly, struggling to get over the shock. I would pay for this mistake later when I was alone. Thinking Van was back from war was a dangerous dream.

I dimly recalled Van telling me the likeness he and his father shared. I had no way of knowing just how true that was. Mr. Judson was Van looking at me, only his jet-black hair was salt and peppered with gray. His face was much harsher than Van's, his eyes more severe. But he was still Van...

"Can we talk inside?" he asked.

I nodded again, feeling an idiot for staring. My hands shook as I turned the key in the lock and pushed open the door. Mr. Judson walked ahead of me. The man was nothing close to shy. He stood in front of the liquor cabinet in the sitting room, pausing to light a cigarette.

His hands trembled. "Can I pour us a drink? Do you like Scotch, or would you prefer something else?" Mr. Judson asked, keeping his back to me.

I stood by the window, dreading whatever was about to come. Because whatever the reason was... I swallowed. "Mr. Judson, I don't mean to be rude, but could you perhaps tell me what you're doing here?"

He turned and a small, faraway smile tugged at his lips. "Straight to the point. You're a very direct woman, Ms. Howell. I can see why my son favors you."

"He would also tell you I'm not known for my patience," I said, folding my arms across my chest. If my mother were present, she would spank me raw for being so insolent to an elder, and the father of my boyfriend. In those moments, manners were the last thing on my mind. I simply wanted him to get to whatever point he had and leave—this man brought the love of my life nothing but pain.

Mr. Judson sighed and shoved his hands into his pants pockets—an achingly familiar motion. "I didn't know Vance enlisted, not until I received an automated army postcard informing me he'd shipped out."

"I'm not surprised he didn't tell you. Why would he?" I asked, my voice cold and distant.

Mr. Judson shot me an angry look but held his tongue.

Oh yeah, buddy, I know all about you... "Is that why you're here?" I continued without waiting for a response. "You want me to tell you why he kept this from you?"

Mr. Judson looked down at the hardwood floor. "I was shocked, of course, when I learned of his enlistment. But above that, I was surprised he'd listed me as next of kin. I didn't think he would admit I was his father."

The truth was, it shocked me too. I'd always assumed he'd listed Paul's parents as his next of kin—he sure as heck wouldn't have listed his mother… She wouldn't have been able to handle the news even if she understood what it meant. Where was Mr. Judson going with this? Did he want me to tell him why Van had enlisted? Where he was? What news I had of him?

"I don't know the details. I can only assume he filled out a form stating his wishes, should anything happen, and someone back home needed to be notified." Mr. Judson sucked on his cigarette until it burned down. He stubbed it out and took a step toward me. Every step he advanced, I retreated.

At those words, my eardrums started ringing in a high-pitched frequency that made me lightheaded. I prayed it was loud enough that I wouldn't hear what was coming. My stomach dropped. I couldn't speak. I couldn't think. Terror held me prisoner. My body shook, my eardrums rang louder.

The first tear escaped, running down my cheek.

"He didn't want you to go through the pain of having the telegram delivered." Mr. Judson's voice broke. "He hated me, but he loved you more."

I shook my head, mumbling, "No, no," over and over again.

"I have no words of consolation," Mr. Judson said. "But I am so very sorry." Reaching into his breast pocket, he pulled out a rectangular piece of yellow paper and a notebook.

"Leave," I whispered.

"Barbara—" Mr. Judson took another step toward me.

"Leave!" I screamed, surprised at the power of my voice.

Mr. Judson flinched as though I slapped him. He placed the paper and notebook on the coffee table and walked around me to the door.

I didn't see him leave, but I heard the door click behind him. I was unable to move, my feet rooted to the spot. Staring ahead, I saw nothing. I was aware my body shook, but I couldn't stop it.

It was as though I looked down on myself, and saw my movements disjointedly. I crossed the room to the liquor cabinet Mr. Judson had stood beside just moments before. With trembling hands, I poured a large glass of Scotch. I gulped it down, hoping the alcohol would numb me.

Placing the glass down, I straightened up. A stream of sunlight filtered into the room, falling on the coffee table. Dust motes hung in the air, caught in the sunshine, dancing, floating. The light illuminated the small piece of yellow paper. Such an innocent item, yet it brought with it so much grief. I couldn't tear my eyes from it.

I picked the glass up and hurled it as hard as I could toward the wall, shattering it into hundreds of glistening pieces. My sobs came out as inhumane screams. I fell to the floor, pounding the wooden floorboards with my fists. My nails broke as I clawed at the floor, making my fingers bleed. I wanted to match the agony of my heart, to materialize the pain that racked through my body, ripping me apart piece by piece.

I let the pain take me.

I didn't try to fight back.

* * * *

Lois found me sometime after. My throat was raw from my sobbing screams that had been reduced to breathy whimpers. She fell to my side and grasped my shoulder.

A curtain-twitching neighbor saw me enter the house with a strange man and heard the commotion. They knew Lois and me well, and called the college office to fetch her, she told me.

"Barb, my God, what's happened?"

I couldn't answer her. I wanted to bang my head against the hard floor and stop all thoughts.

Lois pulled me up, holding me by the shoulders. "Barb, sweetie, you're scaring me. I need you to tell me what's wrong."

Lifting my eyes to meet hers felt like the hardest thing in the world. When I told her, when she knew... The worry was clear in her eyes as she wiped my hair off my face. A fresh sob broke out. My tears blurred her from my vision.

Lois scrubbed my face and made a helpless noise in her throat. She looked around the room, trying to find a clue as to what had happened. "Have you been drinking? Did you break a glass?" She rose from my side and took a step toward the coffee table. "Barb," Lois whispered, her eyes locked on the yellow paper.

It wasn't until she made to lift it that I snapped back to reality. "Don't touch it!"

Lois jumped and jerked her hand back.

"Get away from it!" I sounded possessed, and probably looked it, too, as I forced my agony-ridden body up into a standing position.

"Barb..." Lois' voice broke. She reached for me.

I let her catch me before I fell again. Like at the train station, she held me to her. Lois rocked me back and forth and allowed me to scratch her arms in frustration when I wanted to break free. She stroked my hair and sobbed with me. She was my best friend and loved me. We were in harmony with each other. She could feel my pain, and my pain was killing me.

Chapter Twenty-Five

The tears dried, my sobbing stopped. I continued to whimper, gasping for breath until eventually I grew still. Lois didn't say anything. There was nothing she could. She stopped rocking me. I heard her crying stop also.

Sometime later, Lois wrapped her arm around my waist and pulled me up. She didn't take me to my room, she took me to hers. I curled into a tight ball on her bed.

Lois sat a full glass of Scotch in front of me and placed cigarettes nearby. She sat in her chair in the corner and watched me.

The room darkened but she didn't turn on the light. She didn't even move.

* * * *

I surfaced. Glancing at her clock, it was after three in the morning. The room was lit only from the clear, bright moon.

Lois still watched.

Once I gulped down the Scotch, I lit a cigarette.
She took a breath.
I closed my eyes. "Don't."

* * * *

Lois let me stay in her room as long as I needed. She never left me.

She'd gathered the items from downstairs and brought them up, leaving them on the bedside table.

I watched them for hours. I didn't have the courage to pick them up right away. Each time I thought of its contents, a fresh batch of sobbing began. Eventually my body, my mind, was so exhausted I think I was numb. I could put it off no more.

Lois didn't move to sit by me.

I reread the words countless times before they began to make sense.

The telegram was cold, unforgiving:

Deeply regret to inform you that your son VanCE Judson is captured and presumed killed stop will send you further particulars when available STOP please accept our sincerest CONDOLENCES STOP

Tears dripped onto the telegram. I made no effort to stop them. I read it over and over, searching in vain for a glimmer of hope.

Lois darted across the room to envelop me in a tight hug when she saw my shaking begin again.

* * * *

I became aware only of the pain. The days passed with no meaning. Lois brought food, which I ignored. When up to it, I would drink and smoke until my head swam and my body numbed. Those bouts didn't last long. I felt guilty for being able to bear my pain. I shouldn't be allowed to separate myself from it, not even for a second. The guilt never failed to bring the agony back with new force.

Lois tried to be as supportive as she could, but I shunned her efforts.

I left her room and locked myself away in mine. I hid under my covers, clutching Van's scarf.

Five days passed. I finally gave in to sleep. I managed a few minutes here and there, but the nightmares always jerked me awake. Pure exhaustion took me with no permission. I didn't dream. I was thankful.

The day was bright when I cracked my weary eyelids open.

I was aware of a presence beside me. I sat up.

Lois stroked my hair.

"How long have I slept?" I asked, my voice gruff.

"Two days," Lois said, handing me a glass of water.

I sipped at it, my throat in agony. "Have you been here the entire time?" I handed her the glass back.

She shook her head. "I checked in on you from time to time. About an hour ago, you started getting restless, tossing and turning. I thought I'd wait."

"You're a dear friend, Lois."

Her smile was frail…apprehensive.

Puffing out my cheeks, I released a slow breath.

Lois waited.

"I don't know how—" My voice caught. I very nearly got my sentence out.

Lois leaned her head against mine. "Shh. You don't have to say anything."

319

We were quiet for a long time. The tears flowed silently. I was grateful the violence was gone from my sobbing. My body was in agony.

"You should see this, Barb," Lois said, getting up. She walked to my desk where she retrieved the thing I desired to see least in the world. "There was more than one telegram. Van didn't have his personal effects with him when he was captured." Lois sat beside me on the bed, taking my hand. "They don't know if he was made to drop it, or if for some reason his pack had been left where they camped that night. Either way, a few of his things were found and sent home. This must have been one."

Lois laid the worn brown leather notebook in my lap.

"I haven't looked at it. But when you're ready, you will." Lois kissed my forehead. "I'll be downstairs."

I touched the cool leather, hand visibly shaking. I wasn't ready. I didn't think I would ever be. My misery rose, and again I put up no fight to it. The pain came in waves, sometimes slow and almost calm, other times fierce and strong.

Placing the notebook on the quilt, I stood up and moved around the room, my body grateful for the muscles being stretched. My skin itched. I sat at my desk and smoked for hours, never taking my eyes off the brown notebook.

Realization stabbed at my heart. This was the last piece of Van I had. It didn't matter how much it hurt—I had to have him. Retrieving the notebook, I brought it back to my desk.

Slowly and carefully, I opened the front cover. Pressed between the cover the first page was a small, familiar photograph. A lump lodged in my throat as I picked it up. The image was worn and faded, as though it had been taken out often.

On the inside page in his beautiful script was his name. I didn't know what I expected to find when I opened the notebook's pages, but it wasn't what I found. Van had never written in it in front of me, yet it was clearly something he treasured. It was worn not from neglect, but from years of companionship.

The first few entries were sporadic, a brief recount of Christmas and a semester of college. But then...

One entry leaped off the page, achingly familiar—a time Van once told me about.

It was us. The beginning of our story.

Van had kept a journal.

April 25th, 1939

I saw a girl today.
The best damn looking girl I've ever seen in my life...

* * * *

At the end of his first entry, I scrubbed at the rivulet of tears that streaked down my cheeks. I slowly pushed my chair back and rose from the desk. I took two shaky steps away and sucked in a breath. Van's words swam before my eyes, in his quick, careless scrawl.

As I had read, it was as though he were there with me, whispering his innermost thoughts in his smooth voice that I adored so, so much. I craved to hear it again, just once, just once so I could listen closer, hear every tone and dip and lift of his voice that made me melt and my heart stumble.

My soul was a shredded mess. How could I have caused such an extreme reaction in him? I was just a regular girl, and he was extraordinary. But in his eyes...so was I.

His words... His script on the page was like having him with me again, a piece of him that could never be taken away.

The journal lay open on my desk to taunt me. I paced back and forth, never taking my eyes from it. I longed to read more but fear wouldn't allow it. At some point, Van would write about our first interaction, where I had acted like a rude, indignant girl.

Oh, Van, I wish I could go back to that night...

He'd told me the night we'd stayed in the bed and breakfast before he had shipped out of the first time he'd laid eyes on me, said that one day he would prove it to me. I hadn't believed him. Couldn't believe that I wielded so much power over another person. Yet there the evidence lay, in his handwriting before my very eyes.

And he had been right.

Van had proved what I had doubted. He really had such a reaction.

I knew what awaited me when I turned to our next entry — the ugliest side of my personality. The side I wished above all things I could change, to change it for something sweet and far less cynical.

How much time had I wasted in ignoring my true feelings for Van?

I hadn't thought it mattered all too much — we'd gotten there in the end. At one time I'd thought it was a good thing I'd been so reluctant. We'd gotten to know each other properly before jumping headfirst into something. With every ounce of my being, I knew Van was the man for me. He pushed my buttons within an inch of his life, drew out awful reactions in me, yet never deterred from his feelings for me.

Not once.

I had refused and denied for months, but he'd had enough faith that our day would come. He'd never made a move, never asked me out and never expected anything from me at all. Van had told me once that if something were to happen with us, it would be on my terms.

Why couldn't I have realized my feelings sooner?

I cursed my mother for being pushy and overbearing, for trying to dominant me. Because of her, I'd never allowed myself to accidentally fall in love.

How much time had I wasted in denying him? Too much time... Time that could have been spent in his arms, kissing his glorious mouth. I would never have him back. He was gone from me forever.

The sun had set on our time together, and would never again rise to bring with it a new day. I was left alone in cold and cruel darkness, never moving forward and unable to go back.

Chapter Twenty-Six

Hindsight became my worst enemy. I thought about all the things I'd have done differently. I would have told him at every opportunity how much I loved him, how he was my world, my air. I would have kissed him a hundred thousand times.

Above all, I'd have ignored all the reasons in my head that told me he was condescending and arrogant, that very first time we spoke outside the club so many New Year's Eves ago. The moment my ears heard his silken voice, I would have given myself to him. I would have stepped into his arms and it would have been like going home.

How many times had my heart spluttered frantically? How many times had he given me chills? The electricity sparked between us so often it should have created blackouts across the country. How could I have ignored all of these things?

But the thing I looked back on most was the cottage at Thanksgiving. Our wonderful cottage that held so many blissful memories also held a lifetime of regret. How clearly I saw it all now. The timing, setting and mood. It had all been perfect. A perfect time for a proposal.

I'd let my overactive mind run away — convincing myself I wasn't ready. Had I known then what I knew now, I would have dragged him to the closest church and said I do then and there. Maybe then, when Pearl Harbor had devastated us all, our marriage may have been enough to keep him here.

Like I said, hindsight became my worst enemy.

* * * *

The days passed with no change.

I stopped counting them.

What was the point? I had nothing to look forward to. Nothing would cure this agony. I stopped drinking. I stopped smoking. I stopped everything. The pain had taken me before, but now I invited it.

How could a person feel this...all this hurt and anguish and unbearable heartache, and survive?

Lois sat with me sometimes, as I lay unseeing on my bed, staring into nothingness. Van's scarf was wrapped tightly around my throat and wrists, restraining me from ever letting it go.

The sun made me ache with sorrow. On one of the rare occasions I rose from my bed, I looked out of the window to find that life continued. My world had ended, but it hadn't for anyone else. Couples still courted, children played and the sun still rose every morning.

Dickens once wrote, '*Suffering has been stronger than all other teaching, and has taught me to understand what your heart used to be. I have been bent and broken, but — I hope — into a better shape.*' How true his words were to describe my heart — bent and broken. It was not into a better shape. I was broken, every inch of me broken into a different shape. I had been mangled. In place of what was once a woman now stood a monster.

The phone rang often. Its shrill ring reverberated all the way up to my room where I held myself captive.

Lois' voice always dropped to a murmur. She never called on me.

When my eyes ran dry and my body felt spent, I knew it was time to get up. The world wouldn't wait for me to be ready, because I never would be. I would always hurt. It would be something as continuous as a heartbeat.

The simple act of moving my body was enough to bring about fresh, raw emotion. I hugged my knees as I sat under the flow of water from the shower. I felt guilt for being alive, for daring to move. It took all my might just to get out and drag myself back to my room.

A timid knock stirred me from the black hole I'd disappeared into again, though I didn't get up. My bedroom door creaked as it opened. I made no effort to look.

Heels clicked across the wooden floor until they reached me. The bed dipped and I felt the tiniest amount of pressure from a hand on my shoulder. A familiar perfume teased my nostrils.

Mom brushed the hair from my face, revealing the blotchy and swollen skin to her. She drew in a sharp breath, not from shock, but from her own sobs.

Forcing myself to sit up and face her, fresh tears rolled down my cheeks. "Mom?"

Her arms were around me before I could blink, trying to take my pain. "Shh, baby. Don't say anything. It's going to be okay now."

The familiar racking sobs found me. I soaked her blouse but not once did she move me. She held me till I grew quiet.

"It's time to go home, Barb," Mom said, pulling me to my feet.

Longing flooded me. Family. My childhood bed — familiar and safe.

She filled suitcases with my belongings. I gathered Van's things myself, not allowing her to touch them. Lois loitered in the doorjamb, watching with sad eyes. We hugged long and tight, not wanting to let the other go. "It's for the best," she whispered.

I nodded, unable to speak.

"I'll see you soon."

The train was the worst. Being near so many people was unbearable. But it didn't last forever. What was one day out of the thousands that now faced me?

It was on the train going home that afternoon I first saw Van.

He walked past my compartment with hands in his pockets, hair flopped across his forehead. Somewhere, deep in the quiet recesses of my broken mind, I knew it wasn't him. There was no way it could be him.

But rational thinking wasn't something I was capable of.

With no warning, I leaped from my seat and yanked the sliding door back with so much force it rattled in the jamb. I pushed my way past the people in the corridor, desperate to catch him up.

I never found him.

Back in my old bed, I felt neither safe nor comforted. My childhood home was no peaceful sanctuary. Everything was a reminder. The couch where I behaved so brazenly with him, right under my parents' noses. The table where I dressed before attending the

New Year's parties. The picture of Anna and me at her wedding that hung above the fireplace — the wedding that Van had also attended.

None of it was fair, and all of it hurt. I didn't see how I could ever get past this.

Maybe I wouldn't.

Maybe this was my life now.

My pain was all that held me to Van. That and his journal, which I still hadn't dared touch again. Those were all I had, and I could part with neither.

* * * *

With the summer months approaching, the temperature rose day by day. Despite the heat, my heart remained cold and untouched. My grief gently slipped into anger and bitterness. I found it painful to be around normal people, and their ungrateful happiness.

Lois called once a week, not that I talked to her. Anna came when she could but never stayed long. Her face was always guilty, though I could never reason why.

I received my college diploma, having been sent by the dean. Wellesley allowed many early graduations that year. It saw many of its women throwing themselves into the heat of battle to act as nurses on the front line. Many women, like me, experienced loss of family members and loved ones, and could no longer function well enough to carry on with day-to-day life.

I'd always been a studious person, and this helped me have enough credits to graduate early. I didn't care.

My room was my only sanctuary. I stayed there almost all day long. A few days after returning home, I began sitting with my parents at the kitchen table to pick lifelessly at the food placed in front of me. My room was the only place I didn't see Van. On the rare occasions I ventured outdoors, he was everywhere. I saw him walking down the street, sitting in the backyard, under my window, looking up at the house.

My mother never showed her caring side again. I didn't want to see it. Even through my grief, it unsettled me. Dad didn't know how to deal with me. He tried the soft approach, and when that didn't work, he tried being overly friendly and joking.

Anna's little boy, Robert, was the only one who could stir emotion in me. He turned one year old, and I could only just bring myself to go to the birthday party Anna and Kenneth held for him.

He crawled around the lounge, tasting anything he found and seeking everything out. I loved how pure he was — untouched by the cruel twists of life. He loved unconditionally and always migrated toward me. I would pick him up and breathe in his delicious baby smell. Robert would sit on my lap and suck his chubby thumb, while holding mine with his other hand.

Robert made me smile, and the pain seemed unable to reach me in his company. My only source of light in constant darkness. My visits couldn't last forever, but I always looked forward to the next one.

In the daylight, I could avoid thinking, to a certain extent. But when night fell and sheer exhaustion snatched me into sleep, I was haunted with images of Van. I saw him lying in puddles of blood, surrounded by Japanese soldiers and being dragged away screaming. The nightmares were awful, but the dreams were impossible to endure. The dreams brought his arms, his kisses, his gentle whispers that tickled my ear. It was the dreams that continued to hurt me, long after waking from them.

As the summer months gently slipped into fall, I was offered no relief from the ever-present agony.

Everything felt like an effort, nothing felt natural. Every word uttered was laced with pain. The slightest thing would spark a tearful episode, from which there was no return for hours. I was trying my mother's patience and wearing it thin. Before, I would have enjoyed it, now I couldn't help but cause it. She and my father argued about me almost daily.

"For chrissakes, Florence. The girl is grieving, leave her alone."

"She has been mollycoddled long enough. She needs to face things."

"Mollycoddled? Who has mollycoddled her? I'm just trying to make things a little easier on her, the least you could do is acknowledge the pain she is in."

"She needs to realize she has to move on. He isn't coming back, yet she still waits for him."

"And so you would be able to just move on, were I to die?"

She tsked at him. "Don't be ridiculous. It isn't the same thing."

"Why not? She loved him."

"She doesn't know what love is."

"I used to think that deep down you gave Barb such a hard time because you only wanted the best for her. Now, I just think you envy her."

"Envy her?"

"Either that or resent her. It doesn't matter which, it's still wrong, Florence. She's your daughter. If it were Anna, you would be bending over backward to do everything you could. But because it's Barb, she has to pick herself up and brush off the dust."

"You don't know what you're talking about."

It was painful to hear. My heart went out to my father who always defended me. I felt bad for the continuous strain I was placing on the household, and figured there was only one remedy for it.

* * * *

I gave no warning before turning up at Evelyn's apartment. Her eyes welled up the moment she saw me. I let her hold me, barely returning the gesture. She scolded me for not telling her of my visit, she would have made up my room. Evelyn relieved me of my solitary suitcase and guided me to the bathroom, telling to me to take a long bath and only come out when I was ready.

There was a fresh set of clothes laid out on the bed for me. Evelyn had taken great care in making up my room and my heart swelled with love for her. She handed me a Scotch and a cigarette when I found her in the lounge. I curled up at one end of the long couch, drawing my knees up to my chest.

"I called your father, he was worried sick. You didn't even tell him you were leaving," Evelyn said, nursing her own drink.

"Goodbyes aren't exactly my friend right now." I picked at an invisible thread on the cushion I held in a death grip. "I'm sorry," I whispered. "I was making them so unhappy. I figured if someone could deal with me, it would be you."

Evelyn moved to sit beside me and I rested my head on her shoulder. "Oh, Barb. I never wished the pain I felt after Henry passed on anyone. I still feel it to this day. I wish there was some sweet words of consolation I could give you, but there aren't any."

I sighed, fighting back the tears threatening to fall once again.

"It gets easier, that I will say. But, baby, you be as sad as you want to be. Everyone told me I had to get up and live my life. Some days I did, others I couldn't even get out of bed. You take your time. You'll get there at your own pace."

A few tears escaped and ran off the end of my nose. I knew I'd made the right decision in coming to Evelyn.

Chapter Twenty-Seven

My parents didn't collect me from Evelyn's to take me home as they had done from Wellesley. Many months passed, and the only thing that changed was the weather, which now matched my feelings and moods perfectly.

Evelyn did as she'd said. She never once forced me to do anything. She did, however, make me eat regularly and made sure it was always something of sustenance. I'd lost so much weight since that fateful day in April that I was a ghost of my former self.

December brought the beginning of a line of visitors. Anna was first, with little Robert, who was soon becoming big Robert! He was a charming child and enjoyed provoking smiles in me. Anna was doing an amazing job as a mother and it got easier to be around her happiness.

The most frequent visitor was Thomas. He'd avoided being drafted. Even he didn't know how he'd been so lucky. He seemed immune to my pain and not once did he acknowledge it. Thomas chatted to me, whether I answered or not.

Thomas became a good influence on me and dragged me out of the house regularly. It was with Thomas that I first laughed again. We'd taken a walk in Central Park with his mother's obscenely tiny dog, which had relieved itself on the leg of Thomas' designer suit. The sight of him jumping around in an angry and disgusted frenzy aroused the bubbling laughter in my throat.

Most surprising wasn't that I'd finally laughed again, but that I didn't feel guilty. Locking myself in my room with a few packs of cigarettes, I knew I'd been feeling guilty for all the wrong reasons. Van would never want me to live my life like this. He would be ashamed of me, were he able to see what I had become.

A simple thing such as laughing felt natural, but also wrong. How could there be laughter in a world that no longer held Van? He was my sun, my air, my life… And he was gone. He was gone but not forgotten. I had his journal for that.

The day I laughed again was the day I picked up his journal, for a fresh stabbing of delicious pain.

December 22nd, 1939

What did I say!!!

Today Paul and I traveled back to his hometown for the holidays, and while we were waiting for our connection at Penn Station, I looked over and there she was.

The girl was back.

How long has it been? Eight months… Eight long months since that glimpse. That week at Paul's I'd looked for her everywhere – in store windows, at the malt shop, the drug store, on the street. Nothing.

And there, in Penn Station, she was.

She was every bit as gorgeous as I remembered. I had thought that maybe I'd exaggerated her looks in my mind over the months, that she wasn't as remarkable, wasn't as stunning. What an idiot... She was better. She was a goddess.

She stood beside a small suitcase, looking a little lost, and it seemed like she was making an effort not to play with her hair, which was loosely gathered down her back.

It took all my self-control not to rush to her side, to offer her help in whatever way she'd accept it. I almost fell down dead when she got the cutest look of determination on her face, picked up her suitcase and marched toward me...and marched right on by to the departure board.

I knew I had to take my chance. Fate had smiled on me twice now... Would she a third time? I was all set for approaching her, even had a killer opening line that I now can't remember – until Paul, the jackass, punched me in the arm and commented brashly on the beauty of a passing girl. And when I'd looked back to my girl, she was gone again.

My best friend is lucky he's still breathing.

So here I am, Fate... On my hands and knees, praying you'll give me a third chance. I swear, this time I won't screw it up.

December 31st, 1939

Well, tonight didn't disappoint

All week long Paul had talked about the dance party he went to every year, and promised it would be a night to remember. Well, he damn well owed me after letting the future Mrs. Judson get away for the second time. Truth be told, I looked forward to the distraction – a few hours of fun, drinks and dancing.

Paul looked forward to the girls. And he knew a lot of them. He tried to introduce me to a few, but my head was too full with one in particular to flirt with some skirt I'd never see again.

I lost track of Paul after a while. It was his hometown – he knew a lot of people. The dance hall was packed when we *arrived, and it had only swelled in numbers in the hours since. Even still... I must have been under the same roof as her for most of the night and the idiot that I am hadn't even realized.*

I'd gone outside for some air, could only have been out there a few minutes when I heard a soft sigh behind me. I turned around...and there she was. Wearing a red wraparound dress, she looked like a million bucks. It set off her dark hair and creamy skin and I was a goner. For all my determination that if I got another chance then I'd damn well make it count, all I could do was stare. Jesus, she was beautiful.

She shivered in the cold night air, and I stepped forward and said, "It's cold out here, you should have a jacket."

My grand opening... What a jackass. But still, I'd done it. I'd actually spoken to her. Not that it did me any good. She turned those big brown eyes my way and sized me up. Then told me I should have one too and went back inside without a backward glance.

At least this time, I knew where she was. She hadn't disappeared on a street corner or a train station – she'd gone inside the building to the party. All was not lost and I took off after her.

There was no sign of her in the crowd. I checked the bar, scanned the many tables but came up empty every time. I couldn't even find Paul – who was getting a big fat kiss for bringing me to the dance. He was redeemed for the Penn Station incident.

Midnight approached and I wondered if she had a sweetheart she'd be dancing with.

Oh... She had a partner all right... But I was damned if he'd become her sweetheart. Paul, the eager beaver, stood with her on the dance floor. So I grabbed a girl, gave her a wink, and positioned us for the dance. I'd have my girl in my arms soon enough.

It took forever. Countless girls passed by me before it was her turn. She didn't pay me any attention as she slipped easily into my arms. I wanted to pull her closer, to fill the space between our bodies. I wanted to know how she felt pressed against me. It was a miracle I remembered the steps to the dance – I couldn't take my eyes off her, could think of nothing but the feel of her hand in mine.

She finally shifted her gaze from the floor to my face, meeting my eyes. I was caught staring. She tilted her head, narrowing her eyes as she frowned at me. A look that would have decreased the beauty in any other face, only made hers more enchanting. It must be a look that spent a lot of time on her face, as it seemed perfectly at home there. I smiled crookedly at her, sending her a silent apology. She didn't look away as I thought she would. Her eyes held me, forbidding me from looking away. She wasn't a shy one, this girl.

The music stopped.

The countdown to midnight began.

"Ten!"

She was there...with me. This was it... My chance.

"Nine!"

Her eyes darted around, looking for an escape route? Was I repulsive to her? She was having the opposite reaction I was – I wanted her forever, she wanted to flee. I couldn't get enough of her, and I was her personal level of hell.

"Eight."

She looked around her again, what was she looking for? Boyfriend? Husband?

"Seven!"

Maybe she was just shy. We were, after all, strangers, save one informal exchange.

"Six!"

I had to ready myself. Make sure I didn't become too keen when the moment came.

"Five!"

What was I thinking? I couldn't do this – I'd earn myself a slap in the face if I moved in for a kiss. This wasn't your typical girl, she was different... Special.

"Four!"

But...

"Three!"

Oh Lord, help me....

"Two!"

I couldn't breathe....

"One!"

This was it....

"Happy New Year!"

The room exploded with cheer. All around us people kissed, hugged and laughed. I only saw her.

Her hand was still loosely held in mine from when we danced. Raising it slowly, her eyes met mine. I kissed the back of it — that smooth, soft hand — barely even grazing her skin. I lowered her hand, freeing her.

"Happy New Year," I whispered.

She looked at me with a puzzled expression. Like she was trying to figure me out but couldn't quite manage it.

I knew then, that even if I had chased her down that first time I'd seen her, it wouldn't have made a difference. This girl is so different from any I'd met before. She's a rare breed and typical charm won't work on her. If I'd approached her, asked her out, even inquired after her health, I had no doubt she'd have shot me down and refused to give me the time of day.

I'll see her again. I have no doubt. And when I do not only will she remember me, but she'll never forget me.

I left soon after, not trusting myself to not seek her out. I wanted to be somewhere warm and homely, with someone waiting for me, to ask me how my evening was. Offer me a warm drink to take the chill off the night. I have no such person. It didn't stop me imagining one...with the face of a beauty I'd danced with at midnight.

Chapter Twenty-Eight

Why couldn't he have been selfish? Why couldn't he have stolen that New Year's kiss? That kiss would have told me everything I'd needed to know! Time wouldn't have been wasted.

I sighed and lit yet another cigarette. I was lying to myself. All this desperate pleading with the past didn't do any good—most of it was lies. Had Van kissed me that night, I most likely would have hit him and never given him the time of day again. I would never have allowed him to become my friend, and we would never have fallen in love. *But then I'd never be feeling like this…*

I shook my head to rid it of the blasphemous thought. I'd take this pain any day over the alternative of never knowing him. Van had touched my life in such a beautiful way… I could never regret that.

A knock on my door interrupted my thoughts.

I tried to speak but it caught in my throat. After clearing it, I tried again. "What is it?"

The door slowly opened, wide enough eventually for Lois to be seen in the doorway. "Hi," she whispered.

I tried to smile, I didn't quite manage it.

* * * *

Lois linked arms with me as we walked through the park. The lawn was coated white, the tree branches loaded down with heavy snow. "This place is beautiful, even in the winter."

"This is when I like it best," I said. "Everything is dead, but you know it's only a matter of time before it all comes back."

Lois cut her eyes to me and paused before speaking again. "So what do you want to do? Lunch? Movie?"

"Nothing, this is fine."

She squeezed my arm. "I *know* you want a drink."

"No, really. I'm fine," I said with a smile. I knew it looked false but she didn't check me on it.

"Have you seen much of Thomas?"

"A little. He comes by from time to time."

"And Anna? Robert?"

I prickled. "Stop it, Lois."

Her eyebrows shot up. She could pull the innocent look all she wanted, but I knew her too well not to know what she was going. "Stop what? I'm only asking if you have seen Anna for chrissakes."

"No, you're asking in your own way if I'm moving on."

Lois sighed. "That wouldn't be a bad thing, Barb."

I paused, unlinking her arm from mine. The park developed a dark edge to it, or maybe it was just me. Anger boiled in the pit of my stomach.

"Barb, I know how much this is hurting you, but you know that you have to get on with things now."

"What the hell do you know? It's *my* pain, Lois." My temper rose, heating my blood and scalding my cheeks. She had no idea what she was talking about… No idea.

If she did...there was no way she would be telling me to move on, because she would know it wasn't something possible.

"Yes, I know, but you can't keep yourself locked up forever," she insisted, all softness gone from her face. She sounded like my mother.

I walked away from her, storming ahead. If I hadn't, I'd have said something I didn't mean in the heat of things. People dodged out of my way, shouting complaints to my back. My cheeks burned as I got more and more worked up.

Lois tugged on my arm, spinning me around to face her. "Wait, Barb. I didn't come here to argue with you."

"So why did you?"

Her eyes widened with hurt. "I was worried about you. Christ, Barb, I haven't heard from you in months."

"I've had other things on my mind."

"No, you've had *one* thing on your mind." Lois sighed. "Barb, it's time to —"

"Don't you dare say move on," I bit out through clenched teeth.

"But it is!" Lois cried. "Barb, it's been nearly a year — do you realize that? A whole year, and you're still as broken as the day you found out."

I groaned, throwing my arms out to the sides. How did she not see? How could no one see? "How else should I be? How can you expect me to be okay? You say it's nearly been a year, like that means *anything*. One year — big deal. I'm facing the rest of my life without him."

She reached for my hand but I yanked out of her grasp. "Sweetie, I know, but he wouldn't want this. He would want —"

"He wouldn't want me to be with someone else, so don't you dare say it." My head swam... Surely we weren't having this conversation in the middle of the park. The love of my life was dead… I didn't even get the chance to say goodbye. I would never have a place to mourn him, no grave, nothing. He was dead and she wanted me to go on a date?

"But he would. Deep down you know that. Van would never want you to be this unhappy."

I snapped. She'd gone too far. "Don't say his name. You have no right—"

"No, Barb. I *do* have the right. He was my friend, too, all right? I miss him too. But more than that, I miss *you*. I miss my friend who was happy, who didn't need any guy—"

I gasped.

"Okay, I didn't mean that. I just— Before Van, you didn't need anyone, that's all I'm trying to say. You didn't need anyone then, and you don't now. You have the strength to move past this."

My eyes were hard on her face. I loved this girl to death, but in that moment, I think I hated her.

"Look, people aren't going to put up with this forever," Lois said, her patience finally worn down. "You're going to wake up one day to find everyone gave up on you a long time ago. You can't expect people to wait around for you to come out of your grief-induced coma."

"Good," I said in a cold voice. "I don't want anyone to wait for me. I want to be left alone."

"Well, guess what, that isn't happening! People care about you, Barb. Think what this is doing to them."

I sucked in a deep breath, trying to get a hold on my anger.

"Barb, Van died, okay? He's dead and he isn't coming back. You have to stop waiting for him. He died, but you didn't. *You* are still here, so get on with your life."

I didn't even think about what I was doing. It was done before I'd even realized it was happening. In a disjointed sort of way, I saw my hand lift and connect with her cheek. My palm stung and fury built up inside me, even as she clutched her reddened cheek, looking at me with tears in her eyes. "How dare you," I whispered, my own eyes filling. "You know how much I loved him, Lois. You should know that just because he isn't here anymore, doesn't make that love disappear. He died, and so did I. I feel dead, Lois. There is no life for me without him. If you were my friend, you would realize that."

I left her there in Central Park, holding her face while I ran from the ugliest scene of my life.

* * * *

It took hours, but my anger subsided. I was horrified with myself when it did. I'd never struck another person in my life, never mind Lois, who I loved like my own sister. It could have been the shock of having such a raging argument that pulled me out of my own grief long enough for me think clearly for the first time in months, or it could just have been I was finally ready.

Whatever the reason, when I woke the next morning after a restless night's sleep, I knew it was time to face my life.

Boarding the train to Boston, my argument with Lois played over and over again in my head. I felt awful, yet I couldn't bring myself to apologize. Lois had hurt me deeper than I'd ever thought her capable of, even if she believed tough love was the cure I needed. She had no right to talk to me like that, but I also had no right reacting the way I did. Yes, I was hurting and in a very fragile place, but what I did was unforgivable.

Scenery passed by my window in an unseeing blur as I hugged my arms around myself. My stomach rattled with nerves and a huge part of me thought I was making a terrible mistake. But one thing Lois said was true—I *did* have to move on. Moving on was a part of life, and I had to go back to finally be able to go forward.

* * * *

His house was empty, the windows black and cold. I'd found out his roommate had left soon after Van had, and no one had ever taken it over. I wondered if the owner perhaps enlisted himself, and was no longer around to oversee maintenance.

I stood on the sidewalk, shivering in the cold wind, staring at the house for a long time before I found enough courage to move across the street and come closer to my past. The hideaway key still remained under the eave. I slid the key into the lock and turned it until I heard the click. A chill crept down my spine and I peeked over my shoulder. Van watched me from the very spot I'd stood in across the street.

I squeezed my eyes shut, and he was gone when I pried them open. Taking a deep breath, I pushed the door and stepped inside.

It was dark. The dim winter light filtering through the cloudy windows was not enough to make the rooms as bright as they had once been. My shoes left footprints in the dust that coated the floorboards as I moved deeper into the heart of the house.

All the furniture remained, covered with white sheets to protect from absent time. The house was different from the one I remembered, which had been so bright and full of life.

My feet led me up the stairs, which creaked under my weight. Turning at the top of the stairs, I kept my eyes locked ahead, staring at the closed wooden door.

I trailed my fingers along the railing as I made my way toward what had once been my slice of heaven, but now lay in the middle of hell. The brass doorknob beckoned for me to turn it. It gave off a high-pitched screech, groaning with underuse. I shuddered and gritted my teeth.

A familiar smell teased my nostrils as I opened the door. There was a musty undertone from abandonment, but time had not rid this room of Van.

He was everywhere.

He was on the bed, arms folded behind his head and giving me a suggestive smile. He was at his desk, scratching his pen across a pad to meet a deadline for a term paper. He was holding me at the window, whispering delicious promises of what our future held.

I ran my hands on the bed frame, the coolness of the metal grounding me to the present. Moving around the bed, I noticed something near the head of the bed, peeking out from where it lay on the floor. Bending, I reached under the bed to pick it up. My fingers met a familiar shape and as I rose with it in my hand, tears welled in my eyes as I dusted off the cover.

Van hadn't left a single piece of himself in this house. No possessions, nothing. What he'd done with them, when he'd arranged it…I had no idea. But this…this I knew. I knew exactly how it had been forgotten, despite it being precious to both Van and I.

It was Sunday morning, one of many I'd woken up after staying with Van. I lay naked in bed with my nose in a book. Van nudged the door open with his shoulder, a mug of coffee in each hand.

He laughed and rolled his eyes. "What did I tell you? No reading! You've read that thing hundreds of times."

I looked up at him and batted my eyelashes. "But you were gone so long, and it is one of my favorites."

"I was not." Van set the mugs down on the nightstand. He gave me a lopsided smile. "Put it down."

"Hmm...no." I grinned, snuggling deeper into the bed.

Van stared at me, as if he were best deciding how to handle my insolent behavior. With no warning, he leaped into action, jumping onto the bed and tickling me until tears rolled down my cheeks.

He didn't relent until I was writhing beneath him, and his touch turned to a caress. Van kissed my throat and the laughter died. My body responded to his kiss and I arched into him. He trailed featherlight kisses up my neck and hovered above my lips.

And ripped the book still clutched in my hand from my grasp and tossed it under the bed.

"Hey," I protested, struggling to sit up.

Van looked at me with a wicked smile. He pinned me down with his strong body. "Do you want it back?"

I pretended to consider for a moment before slipping my arms around his neck and drawing him closer. "No."

It was *Inferno*, of course, dusty and neglected. That had been the week before Christmas, shortly before he'd announced his life-altering news. It had lain there untouched all this time.

Anger boiled inside me. All the rage I'd felt over the last few months threatened to spill out of me. Staring at the book in my hand, I was reminded of too many happy memories. With a small scream, I threw it with as much strengthen as I had. It was a hardback edition and it sailed straight through the window, shattering the glass.

"How could you leave me?" I screamed, unable to hold anything in any longer. "How could you leave me here alone? You selfish bastard, you left me! I hate you! I hate you! I hate... I hate... I...miss...you... I..." My voice croaked till it faded to silence and only sobs remained.

I wrapped my arms around my middle, trying to hold myself together as I broke for the hundredth time. As the adrenaline diminished, realization hit me and I rushed to the window.

Leaning on the sill, I peered out. Pain sliced my hand and I wrenched it back. A piece of glass cut into my palm. I pulled it out and clenched my wounded hand into a fist. Blood dripped down and hit the floor in delicate crimson droplets. I took a handkerchief from my purse and wrapped it around my slashed hand.

I ran out of the room and out into the backyard. It took some time, but I found the book. Tucking it into my coat, I retreated back to the station. The rain ran freely down my face. I didn't bother to keep dry or wipe my face. I thought it might mask my misery.

* * * *

I must have looked worse than I thought. Evelyn's face morphed from relief to horror as I dragged my weary body through the apartment to my bedroom. "Barb, where have you been? Oh my God, look at you! You're soaked through..."

In the safety of my room, I carefully removed the book and hid it along with Van's journal and the telegrams, which, for some morbid reason, I couldn't part with.

"Barb, honey, you don't look well. You know I don't pry, but..."

"I cut my hand," I mumbled, lifting my gaze to meet hers as I unwound my blood-red hanky.

"Good Lord!" Evelyn rushed across the room and took my hand, examining the wound. "This is filthy. Get your coat on. You need stitches at least."

I protested for as long as possible, but it was no use, Evelyn wasn't budging. She got a cab for us and we sat in the emergency room for over three hours. "This is ridiculous," I hissed under my breath, hyperaware of all the people around me.

"No, it isn't, now be quiet," she said, not looking up from her magazine.

I continued my silent fuming at Evelyn and almost missed my name being called.

With my hand stitched and bandaged and a prescription for antibiotics to keep infection at bay, Evelyn finally let me retreat to my room. I lay on my bed, fully dressed, and stared at my mummified hand.

This was my wake up call. I was burning too many bridges and if I didn't do something about it soon, some of them would be damaged beyond repair.

Chapter Twenty-Nine

I pushed open the window and breathed in the smoggy air. Not quite as purifying as it could have been, but the action was all I really needed. A deep breath of air cleaner than my stuffy, smoke-ridden bedroom was the purpose. I breathed deeply again, closing my eyes. This was part of my healing process, or so I told myself.

I needed to purify my wretched soul.

It was a Sunday, the day that was always the hardest. I needed guidance, and there was only place I could think to go.

Broadway teemed with people as it always did. I moved quickly through the crowds, afraid I would lose my nerve. A few parishioners were knelt in prayer as the noise from my heels on the stone floor echoed throughout the room. I scanned the place, not sure where to place myself.

"Can I help you?"

I jumped at the voice behind me and whirled around to see a clergyman. He gave me a warm, encouraging smile.

"I-I'm not sure."

"Have you been here before?" he asked.

"Um, I think a few times when I was little." I cursed myself, feeling incredibly stupid. "Is that a— I mean, do you need to be a member?"

His smiled remained. "No, not unless you want to be."

"I don't really know why I'm here," I admitted. My voice broke and I fought to push back my emotion. I was here to move forward, not wallow in my past.

"Would you like to take confession?"

My eyes widened. "I haven't done anything wrong."

He chuckled. "All right, how about a chat? It's somewhat less formal." He motioned for a nearby pew away from the other parishioners.

I followed him and sat twisting my fingers in my lap.

"My name is Father Morgan. I will be of as much help as I can."

"Well, my name is Barb. Barbara. Barb. I— My— I lost someone."

Father Morgan nodded in understanding. "So far eighty-two members of our Mission House are serving in the armed services. These are very difficult times we live in."

I let out a shaky breath. "It was—my Van. He was captured and killed by the Japanese. It's been almost a year."

"Was he your husband?"

I let out a rueful laugh. "He was going to be, one day."

"Do you seek guidance through your grief?"

I nodded. "I'm pushing my family away. I don't mean to, I just—"

"It can be hard for our loved ones to see us grieve."

"They all keep telling me it's time to let go." I stared at my hands and held my purse so tight my knuckles turned white. "I know they're right. I know if Van could see me like this, it would make him so unhappy."

Father Morgan seemed to choose his next words carefully. "Letting go can only happen when your heart is ready. Trying to do so before will only cause you more pain. You have to be sure."

"How can I know?" I asked in a whisper.

"You will know, when the time is right, you will know." Father Morgan shifted in his seat. "It can take a little longer, given your situation. You never got a proper goodbye. It can make the separation process all the more difficult."

"So that's what I need to do? Say goodbye?" Could I do that? Despite everything else that had happened, it seemed so...final. Absolute.

"It varies from person to person."

"I don't want to say goodbye," I whispered, my eyes stinging. "I don't want to let him go."

Father Morgan reached over to pat my hand. "That is what you need to come to terms with. Saying goodbye alone won't heal you. You have to mean it."

I nodded. "Thank you, for speaking with me."

"The church is always here for you, should you feel the need to seek us out." Father Morgan helped me up and showed me to the door. "Our Lord works in mysterious ways, we may not agree or understand it at times. God has a plan for you. This is part of that plan."

I shook Father Morgan's hand and walked quickly away. The sky threatened rain again, so I hailed a cab. As I went to give Evelyn's address, a new thought occurred to me. "Do you go upstate?" I asked the driver, mentally calculating how much money I had with me.

"You got money, I go anywhere," the cabbie replied in a thick Russian accent.

I gave him the address and settled into the soft seat.

* * * *

The care home looked depressing as the cab slowed to a stop. It hadn't seemed so bad in the summer, but in the winter it gave off a cold impression. The flowers that had once decorated the boxes along the front wall were long dead. The double oak doors reminded me of a mouth of a monster, beckoning his victims to enter, walking through the jaws of death with free will.

I introduced myself to an orderly who secured me a visitor's badge. Standing in the main room, I swept my gaze over the residents, the solitary people sitting alone. Some looked forlornly out of the windows, while others wept in corners.

But then I saw her in a chair near the window that overlooked the lake. "Mrs. Judson?"

Van's mother turned at my voice. "I don't mind the rain. Not like some people. It feeds my lake—look."

"I see." My eyes pricked but I mentally shook myself. It didn't matter how emotional this was for me. I refused to confuse or hurt this poor woman.

But being the wonderful, motherly woman she was, knew right away there was something wrong. "What's the matter, dear? You look sad."

I smiled and prayed it looked genuine. "No, I'm fine. How are you? Are you okay?" I placed my hand on her arm and stood a little closer.

"I'm fine, same as every other day." She smiled and looked back out over her lake. "It is beautiful, isn't it?"

"Very," I agreed.

"Have you seen it before?"

"A couple of times."

Mrs. Judson turned back to face me. She stroked my cheek. "You're very pretty, I would remember your pretty face."

"Thank you."

She laughed, her smile widening. "My son would like your pretty face."

I laughed. Mrs. Judson had no idea how right she was. "I think he would."

Her eyes glazed for a moment. She pulled her arm free from my gentle hold. "Where is my son?"

A lump lodged in my throat. I didn't want to lie to her, could hardly stand the thought of it. But telling her the truth was so much worse. "He's away for now."

"Will he be back soon?"

I smiled and tried to look reassuring. "Yes, he'll come back soon."

Her face relaxed as she let out a breath. "Good, I miss him."

My heart broke a little bit more in that second. "Me too."

I found us a cup of tea each and she seemed happy to sit with me. She had to remember me vaguely, even if she didn't realize it. Van had told me she got scared around strangers. She'd been comfortable with me when we first met, something she'd apparently never done before. But I'd been there with Van, so that had relaxed her.

Mrs. Judson seemed happy to sit and chat with me, and asked lots of questions about myself. Like Van, she listened attentively, not missing one word.

Occasionally she interrupted me with questions about him. It got easier as the hours passed, to hear his name, and gradually easier to talk about him. Mrs. Judson told me stories from his childhood, making me laugh harder than I had in a long time.

She talked of me, without realizing it. Van had told her of the first time he'd seen me, the first time we'd danced and the first time we'd kissed. She remembered almost our entire relationship, and said she couldn't wait until our inevitable wedding day.

It cut me like a thousand swords, stabbing my battered heart. Knowing that day would never come was just one of the many ways I ached. I didn't let it show on my face. The moment passed without her even realizing how distraught it made me.

I survived one of the seemingly impossible obstacles on my road to letting go. I relived a lot of Van that wintry afternoon and survived to tell the tale. My body and mind felt weak and frail as I left—physically exhausted from holding my emotions close to my heart.

As I signed out at the reception desk, the last person I ever expected to see drew up beside me. We looked at each other in shock for a moment before looking away. My heart skipped a beat as I cursed the likeness once again between Van and his father.

I took a step away from him, and another, until I was out of the door. Not looking behind me as I ran toward my waiting cab, the realization of where I had seen him didn't hit me until we were almost back in the city.

* * * *

Lois avoided my phone calls. I didn't blame her. Evelyn had told me she was staying at a nearby hotel for a few weeks before starting her new job. When it was clear she wasn't going to talk to me over the phone, I showed up at her hotel. My heartbeat pounded in my ears as the elevator pulled me upward for the scariest apology of my life.

The only other thing that came close was when I'd had to own up to my mother for breaking her favorite vase — not entirely by accident — when I was six years old.

Lois didn't respond to my gentle tap at the door. I knew she was in there, the receptionist told me so. I knocked harder, but still got no response.

With my frustration mounting, I called through the door to her. "Lois, I know you're in there! Open up!" I let a moment pass before hammering on the door with the palm of my hand. Searing pain shot into my hand, forgetting I'd battered the door with my injured palm. "Ouch! Son of a bitch!" I hissed.

The door flew open and a blonde storm of anger faced me. "Do you mind not swearing outside my hotel room, please? This is a nice place."

"Sorry," I mumbled. "I hurt my damn hand."

Lois glanced down at my bandaged hand. Her eyes flickered with worry for a moment, but she quickly recovered herself.

"I only came to say I'm sorry." I spoke in a rush before she could slam the door in my face. "I didn't mean to hit you. I was just so angry, Lois. Those things you said, they really hurt me."

She lifted a perfectly maintained eyebrow. "Good. They were meant to."

I couldn't help but flinch. "You don't mean that."

"Yes, I do. But you didn't let me finish." Lois' eyes were still hard as she folded her arms across her chest and moved sideways, to let me into her room.

I rushed into the room and unbuttoned my coat, tossing it over the back of a chair littered with Lois' own clothes.

Some things never change.

Lois sighed. "I wanted those things to hurt you. You need to snap out of this, Barb. You needed to get angry so you could start seeing things again. You know I'm right, don't you?"

Nodding, I lifted my gaze to hers.

Her face had softened and her eyes were no longer hard. Lois laughed without humor. "Though, had I known the slap was coming, I may have chosen a better tactic."

I let out a startled laugh.

Lois crossed the room and pulled me into a fierce hug. "I'm sorry."

"No, I am," I said, sniffling.

We laughed together and hugged all the more tighter. Relief washed through me. I had my friend back. Lois poured us drinks and fetched cigarettes as I told her how I got my cut. I edited a lot of the details. I decided not to tell her about the priest or visiting Van's mother and running into his father.

I felt better than I had in months, as if the fog had finally cleared. My sun still hadn't returned to the skies, but things were definitely clearing.

Lois called Thomas to invite him over and he agreed, rushing over within the hour. He'd also graduated from college and was now mooching around his parents' apartment.

It seemed Lois and Thomas had kept in contact since their meeting last summer. I found it easier when it was three of us, I didn't feel so strained to keep up happy chatter. But between the two of them, they did a good job of getting me back on my feet. We went everywhere together, out for drinks, meals, trips to the movies and the theater.

I slowly began to feel myself healing. Like stitches coming together, I knitted back together again. Thomas and I planned a big night out for Lois, who was leaving us for her first real job. She'd finished her nurses training and was going to a veterans' hospital in Washington. It had been Lois who'd agreed with Van's decision to be patriotic, so it came as no surprise when she wanted to help with the war effort in some way.

Rivers of tears were shed as we said our goodbyes. It hurt less than I thought it would and I no longer felt so dependent on her. Lois had been my crutch, but I could walk again. Thomas needed a great deal of consoling when Lois' cab disappeared into the throng of traffic.

We had each other, I told him.

* * * *

New Year's Eve, 1943

It was my second New Year's without him. Next year, I'd have been without him for as long as I'd been with him. The year after that...the former would officially outnumber the latter.

Thomas tried his best to convince me to go out with him. He knew a dozen parties we could lose ourselves in, but I declined. When that didn't work, he even offered to stay in with me. He was a dear friend. I was lucky to have him in my life.

I wanted to be alone with my thoughts, with my grief that was becoming an old acquaintance. I sat on the balcony wrapped in a wool blanket and listened to the revelries on the street.

That night I didn't cry. Maybe my tears had finally run dry...or maybe it was the highball-induced numbness I'd soaked myself in.

I lifted my glass to the sky in a toast when the New Year came in and threw the rest of the drink down my throat. Below the balcony, people cheered and laughed, singing badly and out of tune. Shaking off the blanket, I walked to the ledge and placed my hands on the cool stone.

"Happy New Year's, Van," I whispered. The stars weren't visible, but I saw them nonetheless — blazing across the sky like the night we spent stranded in the broken down car. I'd give anything to go back to that night, to any night, with him.

God, I miss you.

It didn't hurt as much to remember him, to remember times we'd spent together. His smile, his easy confidence, how much he loved me.

Lois was right — he'd hate the person I'd become.

As a rule, I never made resolutions on New Year's, but that would change this year.

I vowed that this was the year I said goodbye. It might not be today or tomorrow, but I would find a way to do it this year. Van would be so unhappy if he could see me. My pain made me feel connected to him, and to part with it would mean parting with him. But it was worth giving up, if it would make Van happy, wherever he was.

I would also read Van's entire journal. Sometimes when he wrote something really personal, I'd feel as if I was intruding on his soul. Van never kept secrets from me, but he didn't over share any details either. I knew how he felt about me, but his words in the journal were the innermost workings of his heart. Something he never intended for me to see.

Chapter Thirty

Thomas and I spent so much time together the rumors of our impending engagement rose again. We laughed them off, but no one took us seriously. I owed a great deal of gratitude to Thomas. In Lois' absence he proved an excellent friend. He was sensitive to the fact that some days I just needed someone to sit with. Other days he knew when I needed distracted and we'd do silly things like go for a boat ride in Central Park, or visit the zoo.

Though she never said it, I felt like I was taking advantage of Evelyn. I decided to get a job to give her some rent money. The only problem was, I didn't know what I wanted to do. I didn't really have any skills apart from reading. My first obvious calling was to the library, but they wouldn't hire me.

One option stared me in the face, but I was unsure if I could take the pain it would cause daily. There would be no escaping Van if I went through with it—I associated the place with him above anything else. But if I was serious about moving forward, then I couldn't avoid every little thing that reminded me of him.

I'd have to go to... I don't know, Alaska or something, to find a place that wasn't immersed with memories of Van. But I'd bet there would still be something, the sneak.

I took a deep breath as the elevator lurched skyward. My legs trembled when I disembarked, and was asked to wait by the receptionist. It was only a few minutes before Jack appeared, his face marred with emotion as he guided me to his office.

Jack motioned to a chair and he leaned against his desk, crossing his legs at the ankles. "I know this is probably the last thing you want to hear, but Van was an honorable man. He's greatly missed."

Taking the offered seat, I smiled and ignored the rising lump in my throat. "I know."

"What can I do for you? Something tells me this isn't a social call," Jack said with a smile.

"I have a favor to ask." *Here goes nothing...* "I need a job. As a senior partner in one of the most reputable law firms in the city, I figured it was worth a shot coming straight to you."

Jack laughed, his eyebrows shooting up. "Not what I expected, but okay. What kind of job?"

"Any. I've got an English literature degree from Wellesley. I'm smart, I learn fast, I won't get in anyone's way—"

"Whoa, slow down a minute." Jack held up his hands. "Can you type? Answer phones? Make coffee?"

It should have been an idea to prepare a list of my actual talents before ambushing him. Now that I was there, it was painfully obvious I was lacking in secretarial skills. "Um, I can learn to type. But the rest I can do." Which was more or less true. Lois and I spent enough time talking on the phone... Surely that counted?

Jack nodded. "Then I think we can work something out."

Relief washed through me and my shoulders relaxed. "Thank you, but, can I ask one more thing?"

He chuckled. "Shoot."

"I don't want anyone to know who I am. You're probably the only one who would think to link me to Van. But just in case, I'd prefer not to have condolences every day."

Jack's face softened. "Of course, I understand. Okay, how about you start on Monday and we'll take it from there? We'll find where you fit, Barb."

"Perfect. Thanks, Jack." I rose from the chair, but paused before heading out of the door. "You were his role model, you know. He really respected you."

Pain streaked across Jack's normally warm and friendly eyes. He gave me a tight smile and walked me out of his office.

I couldn't help myself. In the main atrium, I dragged my gaze across the room to the back wall where a cramped little office remained littered with files. The only difference was it was someone new behind the desk.

So I'd survived another challenge. But I still had a journal full of them waiting for me at home. After dinner with Evelyn, where I told her all about my newfound work ethic, I took up my usual spot on the terrace. Wrapped in a blanket and a cigarette in hand, I opened the journal where I had last left it.

January 1st, 1940

I don't know what I've done to deserve the favor of the gods, but she was there – on the train back to New York. It all makes sense now. Her parents must live in Paul's hometown.

That's why she was at the New Year's party, and at Penn Station. She would have been on the same train as me. I'd been so close to her...

Paul – lazy bum that he was, had shoved our cases at me to stow away in the overhead rails. My back was turned when I heard him greet someone, and I wasn't intending paying a blind bit of notice, until her familiar voice reached my ears. I whirled around pretty damn fast and watched her goddess-like frame saunter down the aisle toward us. Paul stepped in front of her like a tame gorilla. And Christ... I really needed to talk to him about reading signals, because all he was doing was irritating her with his banter.

He asked her to sit with us and made the mistake of insinuating it would be better for her if she did. She cut him down without breaking a sweat, and even Paul had the decency to look admonished. The girl was not one to be underestimated. Maybe that's where I'd gone wrong on New Year's. I'd told her she should have a jacket, and it woke some demon in the pit of her belly. No, the girl doesn't like to be taken care of. Why? What happened to make her so fierce and independent?

After she'd escaped – because there wasn't any other word for it... Jesus, Paul – I questioned Paul about her.

'How do you know her?'

'Who – Barb?'

Barb... I had her name.

'My brother went to high school with her sister's fiancé, Kenneth. I met Barb at the party on New Year's – she's a freshman at Wellesley. She's something else, huh? Too much like hard work, though.'

Too much like hard work? Jesus Christ... Didn't he know only the best things in life came with hard work? And a dime like that wouldn't be worth half as much if she wasn't worth trying for.

But at least I know Paul isn't interested in pursuing anything with her.

With Barb.

'She wouldn't be hard work to me,' I'd told Paul.

'Then good luck, my friend. I think you'll need it.'

I gave it an hour to give her time to cool off before I went looking for her. Paul must have really bothered her because I had to walk to the farthest away carriage before I found her with her nose in a book. I decided not to overthink things, as it never seemed to do well for me. I'd just dive right in. She was reading Homer's The Iliad, she must be fan of the classics.

It was so easy to fall into teasing banter with her. She wore a hard suit of armor and seemed afraid of no one. I saw her buttons and how to push them – it was too tempting to resist. I pushed my luck further than I would ever have dared, but I somehow knew I could get away with it.

She's feisty. Fiery. Not only that, the girl is smart... Yet another thing to add to her list of attributes. I could have stayed there all day, needling her and drawing out prickly reactions, but even I knew when to quit.

I didn't give Paul any straight answers to all the questions he fired at me, and instead I slouched in my seat and pretended to doze for the rest of the journey, unable to keep my amused smile at bay.

March 16th, 1940

I wish I could say after our encounter on the train, I gave up any ideas I may labor over the girl. I wish I could say that once returned to normal surroundings, I returned to my normal self. I wish I could say I let all the appropriate things distract me. I wish any of those were true.

If anything, I've become more obsessed. I detest that word. But I have no other word for how I feel. I think about her at some point every day. I wonder what she's doing – is she happy, or is that frown across her face again? Had she met anyone? And the thought I only let drift in among the others when I'm feeling especially reckless – is she thinking of me? No sooner do I let it in do I cast it out again. Don't be ridiculous, I'd tell myself. The handful of times I've seen her I've made an awful impression. And so much time had now passed that I doubted she would recall my face even if we were to stand in front of each other.

Paul eventually stopped talking about her, he knew there was no point. He knows a few girls at Wellesley and said he could arrange a meeting. I declined his offer. He can't understand why – I'm so overwhelmed by the girl, but I wouldn't try to see her again. I told myself that we were all following a certain path in our lives, and destined to end up in certain places at certain times. Hers and mine were undeniably linked. Our paths have crossed too many times now to write it off as a handful of coincidences. I've put all the faith I have into the hope that they'll one day cross again. This is not a thing to be rushed. I'll let it happen the way it was meant to. Nothing will be forced and everything will happen naturally.

It's been a few months now, and I've done everything I can to put the girl out of my mind. I concentrated as much as possible on other things. I studied a little... Not enough, though, and it'll be a miracle if I pass any of my exams. I went to parties with my friends, I even dated. I had a few affairs but none of the girls entranced me the way I needed them to, to get my mind off of her.

But deep down, I know all I'm doing is simply killing time until I next see her.

September 30th, 1940

That has to have been the laziest summer I've ever had. After spending a week with Paul and his family at Yellow Sands before the infamous wedding, I traveled here and there, dropping in on old friends. Back in Boston for the last few weeks before school started back up, I got a job bartending –

mostly for something to do. It's an easy gig – work till the early hours and sleep till dinnertime.

Paul returned for the fall semester and said he hadn't seen Barb since the wedding. He couldn't remember ever seeing her in their hometown over the summer before, not that he'd had reason to look. There had been rumors, though, he said. Of Barb get in deep with a fellow on the Upper East Side. Who came from a good family with plenty of dough.

I can't focus on that. Besides, it was at complete odds with what I knew of her. She wasn't the type to court a guy for his money. If anything, something else was going on that she likely wouldn't want broadcasted to the world.

It took a while to force Barb out of my head and think of her as little as possible. I caught a glimpse of her true self at the wedding, and I adore what I saw. That fiery personality lit her up from the inside and she's one of the most alive people I've ever met. She'd been distracted at the wedding – something had been going on with her that caused her pain and I ached to know the reason so I could take it away.

If I were to guess, I'd say it had something to do with men and her mother. At first it had been amusing, watching her flit around the room to avoid dance offers. But the ugly scene with her mother had been hard to watch, and it cut me to pieces to see her face pinch with pain.

So I did the only thing I could think of – gave her a new target for her anger – me. Only, it felt different this time. She wasn't as guarded, seemed more willing to be with me, talk with me. That dance with her gave me all the hope I needed that this isn't a lost cause. Barb is like a wild horse. I'd say that most of her life she's come up against people who wanted to bend and break her, but I don't want that. I want to stoke her fires and let her run free…and just hope she lets me run with her.

December 31st, 1940

To say I'd been looking forward to this night would be a severe understatement. I spent the holidays with Paul and his family again, and spent the entire time counting down the days until this day.

Paul and I hit a few bars before going to the party. Maybe he thought I needed some liquid courage, or maybe he was just inspecting the general mood of the revelers. At the dance hall, I didn't seek her out right away. I trusted that she would be there.

In the end, I saw her pretty damn fast. She was dancing to a swing number, being thrown around by some guy. And man, she was good. It didn't even occur to me to be jealous because I couldn't help but smile at the carefree happiness on her face. I could only hope her good mood would remain, and I'd get my chance with her too.

When she took a break from her dancing and sat at a nearby empty table, fanning herself with her hand, I was so relieved I could have fainted. She clearly wasn't at the dance with anyone, so I could let myself hope her dalliance with the guy from the city was over, if it had ever been anything to begin with.

Emboldened by the sight of her – and the sight of her alone – I couldn't help but try the sneak approach and placed a glass of Scotch in front of her. The second I did, I felt the change in her. She froze and didn't move a single muscle. Smiling to myself, I turned on my heel and left. I watched from the safety of my own table as she turned with a determined scowl on her face that was gone the second she realized no one was behind her. Her expression morphed into something else. I dared myself to believe it was disappointment.

She never touched the drink. Barb got up out of her chair and went to mingle. She was behaving friendlier tonight than I would have thought possible. She was nice. To everyone, it seemed. I followed her good example and mingled myself, talking to people I'd never met, a few I recognized from the year before and from the wedding. Lois caught sight of me at one point and waved. She's a friendly little thing.

And...finally...I got my time with her. Standing at the bar, sipping my drink, she didn't see me as she squeezed her small frame between the bodies to reach the bar. The bartender moved to the opposite end and didn't see her try to get his attention. I debated on how to proceed. Gentlemanly ways won out in the end.

'Would you like mine?'

It took her a moment to turn. Maybe she was hoping I would turn out to be someone different.

I smiled and prepared myself for the slew of verbal abuse she would no doubt launch at me any second. Instead she said nothing and turned her back on me and tried in vain to get the bartender's attention.

When I suggested my offer again she didn't even turn around to look at me when she answered. The ice crept into her voice. It seemed one of my many talents is lighting her already short fuse. I gently teased her and sure enough my tactic worked – she spun around so quick I thought she would be mistaken for a tornado. Soon the familiar banter was going back and forth. I needled her the way I always did and hoped it would let us eventually break through the normal pattern we had and move on to something else.

I teased her again, and she seemed to soften and grow more curious about me. I thought I was doing well for once, on my way to something better with her. Or so I thought, until she was asked by huge, muscly guy if I was bothering her. Innocent as a rose, she implied that I was, which numbered my days, as the guy could have doubled as Heracles. But I trusted that she wouldn't intentionally get me beaten up. I pretended to pay no attention to the imbecile – who seemed determined to see me as a pile of bones at his feet – and only talked to Barb. My teasing didn't stop and her friend's words grew harsher, which made Barb's concern for me grow.

But then, like a jackass, I went one too far. The guy's face turned puce and he made a lunge for me. He would have knocked Barb over, had the bar area not been so crowded that there wasn't actually the room for her to fall. I caught her arm before she stumbled too badly, and I didn't release it. Anger surged through me. I wanted to kill the cretin for hurting her.

Fortunately for him, Barb read the situation and figured she would have to remove one of us from the equation, and she picked me. Had I not been so angry with the fool I would have jumped for joy at the tiny victory. She motioned for me to follow her as she forced her way through the throng of people. The second we were free she turned on me, eyes flashing.

Irritation seethed out of her but I could tell it was manageable. I'd faced worse from her and lived to tell the tale. And at last! Most glorious wonder of wonders! She agreed to dance with me. For no other reason than to get me to stop asking her, but she could easily have just walked away from me, rather than agreeing to the act itself. Is she starting to warm to me?

I couldn't believe she was in my arms again, and on New Year's Eve! It took Herculean effort to not pull her in close. My hands itched with desperation to feel her silky hair. Those full and rosy lips puckered in irritation a few times. How I managed not to steal a kiss, I'll never know.

Chapter Thirty-One

Thomas loathed me working. I was the one friend he had at his beck and call and now I had a job that occupied my time between nine a.m. and five p.m. Nevertheless, he seemed pacified with my promise to spend weekends with him and have lots of dinners throughout the course of the week.

I found the work at the law office hard, but it brought with it many advantages. I was so busy I barely had a moment to let my mind wander. And the best thing of all—people treated me like normal. The women involved me in their gossip breaks and talked about me behind my back. The men were all very helpful, and a few asked me out on dates. I never agreed to any of them, but it all just felt so wonderfully normal.

Nobody treated me like a piece of fragile glass. I wasn't breakable in their eyes. I wasn't a distraught, grieving woman.

I was just Barb.

Thomas was so relieved that my first week of work was over and done with he took me away for the weekend to his family's cabin upstate. Evelyn thought it was a marvelous idea. It would do me the world of good to get out of the city, especially since the weather was getting warmer.

Even I had to admit it sounded like a good idea.

* * * *

My mind felt clearer the instant we arrived. There was a gorgeous lake near the cabin, and I was eager to explore. Thomas said he would unpack the food and catch up to me. The lake was impressive—clear and still. An enormous weeping willow grew on the shore, its branches grazing the glassy water.

I'd brought Van's journal and I tucked it into my belt. The tree was too good not to climb. It had been years since I'd climbed a tree, and even as a child, I hadn't been terribly good at it. Anna always scolded me when I tried, saying mother would spank me for tearing my dress and scraping my knees.

Somehow I managed to find my footing and heave myself upward. The top beckoned, and finding a sturdy branch, I got myself comfortable and cracked open the journal. I had only a few entries left. I'd survived everything else. Our first kiss, our wonderful summer together in the city, Thanksgiving...New Year's and his announcement. I didn't know what it would contain. The entry I'd last read was Van leaving for basic training.

May 10th, 1942

I feel sick. That's the only word to describe how I feel right now. I feel physically sick. How could I leave that amazing woman and feel fine? Gut-wrenching agony is consuming me...

What the hell have I done?

Barb was so together when I left, but I know inside she was falling to pieces. I have faith she'll get through this distance unscathed. I, on the other hand, am using all my willpower to stop myself running back to safety in her soft arms. Nothing can touch us when we're together, but apart, I'm scared to death. I always feel like a part of me is missing when Barb and I aren't together, but now, I'm not sure… It feels like I've lost part of my soul.

We're facing the biggest challenge we've dealt with. I just have to keep my sights on the finishing line. It warms me, thinking of our future together. I can't wait for it – I want it now, to grab it with both hands and never let go.

Why did I turn her down? She asked me to marry her, and I denied her the only thing she has ever asked for.

I'm selfish. I'm a selfish bastard for doing this to her. But I can't stay. As much as I long for it, I cannot turn my back on my patriotic duty.

I have one thought that comforts me and one that scares me to death. Ironically, they're one of the same. No matter how scared I am to leave, I know that Barb will wait for me, no matter how long I am absent.

This comforts me, because I know how true we will always be to each other. Her face will be on my mind every day while I'm gone, and I know mine will be in hers. Even when I am in the thick of danger, I will feel warmth in my heart.

All week I've told her that I will return to marry her.

But what if I don't?

If I die out there, Barb will still wait for me. It was never in her nature to let herself become dependent on another person, and now she has. Me. She let her soul intertwine with mine, and will forever be linked. I've changed her so completely, I don't know if she would ever recover from something happening to me.

This scares me more than the thought of dying. The image of Barb as an old woman, never married and never bearing children, isn't an image I ever want to come to pass. She deserves happiness and a life filled with glorious moments. We've only had a few – there are so many more waiting for her.

Such a large part of me never wants her to move on, but I could never be so selfish. Not when it comes to her. Barb's happiness will never come second place. I'd even understand if I return from war to find she's moved on. She would have every right. It is, after all, me who is leaving.

May 11th, 1942

I've started my journey. The ship is packed with soldiers. Some look more scared than I do. Inside, I'm terrified. Not of the enemy, not of war, not even of dying. But of the mounting distance between her heart and mine. Each second that passes, we grow farther apart. I can feel my heart stretching, desperately trying to reach her again. I'm being split in two, and will only become whole again when she is in my arms.

I will not write in this journal again.

The last few pages remaining are for the future, when we're together again. I refuse to fill this journal with thoughts of fear during this unholy time we face. I will not write in it when I'm on foreign soil. I'll keep it with me and read past entries. I'll remember with perfect clarity the first time I saw the face of an angel, and the first time that angel kissed me, and the glorious time we first made love.

She will forever be in my heart, and never far from my dreams. I hold our relationship in my hand, now. I will not let those last pages remain unwritten...

* * * *

I flicked past the last remaining pages. Not a blemish, not an ink stain, not even a dent. Fate hadn't allowed our pages to be finished. This was the end, then. Our story could not have been more clearly finished than if he had written *The End* after his last entry. I skimmed the blank pages until I got to the back cover, and saw something peeking out. Easing it free, a sad smile pulled at my lips as I looked at the picture Evelyn had taken the night of the ball. God, I looked so scared. Van looked like the proudest man alive. I had no idea he even had it.

The edges were worn. I knew Van had looked at this every moment he could. I ran a fingertip over his face. I closed my eyes and remembered exactly how his cheek had felt.

I closed the journal.

There was nothing else to read.

Looking out over the lake, I couldn't help but admire how calm it seemed. I had a sudden urge to shatter its peace, to disturb its smooth surface like my soul had been disturbed. I needed in the water, and I needed it now.

I unbuttoned my dress and used it to wrap up the journal. Standing in just my underwear and slip, I carefully released the dress and journal to the ground. I climbed higher up the trunk, until it curved out over the lake. Inching farther along, I stopped once I felt the trunk begin to bow. Sucking in a steadying breath, the ground all at once seemed dangerously far away.

There was no time for fear. This would be therapeutic. Without another thought, I bent my knees and sprang from the trunk. I sailed through the air, the wind on my face invigorating before I broke the glassy surface of the lake. Rising to the top, I gasped in a breath. I swam on my back, enjoying the weightlessness of my body.

I felt better than I had in a year.

Free.

There was the dull ache, but that would live with me forever. It was more like being released from an obligation. Reading Van's fears had only confirmed what I already knew. I couldn't wait for him — there was nothing to wait for. He said my happiness didn't come second, and I felt the same way. His happiness was all that had ever mattered to me. I wouldn't let him down. Not this last time. For him, I would live my life.

Thomas' raucous laughter reverberated around the trees when he saw me. "Barb! Put some clothes on! Someone will steal you away if you carry on like that!"

He startled me, causing me to lose my concentration and sink under the surface. I choked on a mouthful of water as I laughed at his wild accusation. "Come for a swim!" I shouted across to him.

"Don't be ridiculous, that lake is full of leeches."

"What?" I screeched, frantically looking around for a sign of the little critters.

Thomas laughed again. "Best get out, Barb — they'd love to a feast on you."

I didn't need telling twice.

It was a good thing it was Thomas I was with. As I emerged dripping wet from the lake, my slip was practically translucent. I pulled on my thin dress, soaking it with my wet skin, but at least I wasn't entirely nude any longer.

Evelyn had been right. The weekend was just what I had needed. The weight had almost completely disappeared from my shoulders by the time we returned late Sunday evening. I missed my normal pattern, and vowed I would visit with Mrs. Judson even longer the following week.

I was a long way from having a bounce in my step again, but I was on the right path. Late Sunday night when sleep refused to come, I crept out of bed and padded across the cool wooden floor to my desk. Lighting a cigarette, I pulled open my bottom drawer — my Van drawer. It seemed to beat. Never silent. My very own telltale heart. It contained the journal, all his letters, his scarf, photographs and many other pieces of nostalgic paraphernalia. I would never get rid of the items. They were a part of my history and therefore a part of me. I pulled everything out and put each item carefully into a large hatbox and slid it to the back of my closet.

I knelt in front of the box and looked to the heavens. I blew out a shaky breath. "You did an awful thing, taking him from me," I whispered, closing my eyes. "He was mine, not for anyone to take. But I understand now. I realize you have a plan, even if I can't see what it is. I envy you, you have him there. Take care of him." I wiped my face and released a shaky breath. "You will always have a place in my heart. I'll love you forever, Van. Forever."

Standing up quick enough to make me dizzy, I closed the closet doors with a soft click.

My goodbye had been said.

A scab formed over my heart.

Chapter Thirty-Two

The heat of the summer air slowly cooled to the crisp breath of winter. The warm months saw a great change in me. I became more outgoing and stopped shying away from people. I ventured out on my own, not leaning on Thomas or any other friends. No longer did I resemble a battered dog. I'd recovered, and made it through the dark night.

I'd kept all my resolutions, and promised not to make anymore. *I've done well,* I thought. Evelyn was proud of me, that was evident from her smiles. And though he never said, Jack noticed my improvement. He stopped walking on eggshells and treated me like any other employee.

Anna invited me to spend the holidays with her little family. Too long had I let the distance between us grow. Robert was two and a half years old, and I'd missed so much. I invited Evelyn to come along with me, but she declined. Evelyn and I had always been close, but something new had forged between us. We had both experienced excruciating pain, but somehow lived to tell the tale. We had camaraderie now, and it brought us even closer.

* * * *

I surprised Anna by showing up a day early. Tapping on her door, I almost wished I hadn't when the sound of chaos from inside reached my ears. The front door flew open, and something resembling my sister stood before me. Anna's hair was coming out of her bun and she had some kind of food stuck to her dress. I choked back a laugh. Anna threw her arms around me, out of relief, I think.

Robert pushed past his mother's legs to get to me. "Auntie Barb! Auntie Barb!" He tugged at my dress. "Come see my room!"

I laughed and scooped him up. He still had that wonderful baby smell as I burrowed my face into his neck. Of course, it was now mingled with a muddy undertone, and I spotted the dirty fingerprints on my hem.

A laugh bubbled in my throat and I wrapped an arm around Anna's shoulders as the three of us crossed the threshold. Robert dashed all over, showing me every last object in his bedroom. Over dinner, he insisted I try every piece of food on his plate. I was so full at the end of the meal I had to lie down for a while. That was short lived. Robert burst into my room within seconds and jumped on the bed. Anna scolded him, but I told her it was fine. We had a lot of catching up to do.

Robert informed his mother that I was putting him to bed that night. What a job that was… I had new respect for Anna once the chore was done. First the angelic child had insisted staying in the bath until his fingers wrinkled. Once dried, he decided he didn't like the pajamas set out for him, and demanded the ones with blue stripes — not red. After hunting for a solid twenty minutes, my darling sister told me he didn't *have* any with blue stripes. A great deal of bargaining later, we settled on green, along with the promise I would buy him a set of blue ones the following day. He scolded me when reading the bedtime story, saying I wasn't doing the voices right. Sighing, I promised to practice. I kissed him goodnight and turned out the light.

Anna greeted me with a large Scotch.

"Thank God," I mumbled past a cigarette. "How do you do it, Anna?"

"With the right kind of medication."

I snorted a laugh. Finishing my drink, I stretched out on the couch.

Anna rubbed my arm. "How you holding up?"

After thinking for a moment, I sat up. "Some days are easier than others."

"It'll take a while, Barb," Anna said, her eyes round with sympathy. "It's been, what — over a year?"

"Two, come the spring." I looked into my empty glass and wanted to rub the familiar ache in my heart. "Some days I almost feel normal again. I've lived with a certain level of pain for so long I think I'm numb to it. But if something catches me off guard, then I crumble."

"I think you're doing amazingly well," Anna said, squeezing my arm. "Mom thinks so too."

A frown creased my forehead. "You've talked to Mom about me?"

Anna nodded. "Every week. Evelyn gives her updates, and she always calls me to confirm it."

I'd barely spoken to my mother since I left. A — perhaps cruel — part of me assumed she didn't care. I was out of sight therefore out of her mind.

"Don't get too emotional over it," Anna warned. "She still has her old motives underneath it all."

My shoulders sagged. "She wants to know if I've met someone else?"

"She asks every time."

I groaned. "I swear I will never speak to her again if she dares ask me herself."

Anna laughed. "I think she knows this. Why do you think she hasn't already asked?"

I shrugged.

"So, have you met anyone?"

I glared at her. "No, I haven't."

"It would be all right if you did, Barb."

"I know," I admitted quietly.

Robert was delightful on Christmas Day. His excitement was contagious and we all felt the Christmas spirit. A snowstorm between Christmas and New Year provided him with a winter wonderland of perfection. He kept me outside for hours, building a snow fort. It more resembled a snow hill, but still, the kid had imagination.

* * * *

New Year's Eve, 1944

On New Year's Eve, I insisted that Kenneth take Anna out. They rarely got time to themselves, and I owed Anna a lifetime of thanks for being such a good sister. I promised to take care of Robert and not let him stay up late. I also promised Robert he could toast the New Year with me.

The little darling was asleep by nine p.m.

I struggled to concentrate on my book as I waited for midnight. As it loomed closer, my heart felt heavy. The countdown started on the radio and I stood up in the middle of the living room. As *Auld Lang Syne* started, I raised my glass in a toast before knocking it back in one.

"Happy New Year," I whispered.

Another year gone. How many more would I have to live through?

Chapter Thirty-Three

Everybody struggled to get into work mode after the holidays. Everyone except me. I welcomed the distraction. The other secretaries had accepted me, finally. Once they realized I had a sharp tongue and short patience, it was decided they would rather have me as a friend than an enemy.

They chattered about their holidays, swapping tidbits of gossip around like currency. The main focus of talk was the firm's annual Christmas party. It had been postponed before the holidays, and was being held in a few weeks. It would be a good way of getting to know everyone a little better.

Thomas had missed me greatly and insisted on taking me to dinner the first night I was free.

He seemed oddly confident as he escorted me to dinner at La Chaumiere on 163 East 56th Street. He ordered for me in fluent French and regularly topped off my wine glass. Thomas laid his charm on thick — full of compliments and was so attentive I could hardly believe it.

After dinner we went for a walk down Broadway. I loved the lights of the theaters and they never failed to lighten my mood. To me, they represented another world. A world where anything was possible.

"So, any explanations?" I asked as I linked our arms.

Thomas raised his eyebrow. "For what?"

"The way you're behaving. You're being very strange."

Thomas smirked. "I had something I wanted to ask you."

"Oh?"

"An idea occurred to me, and after much thought, I think it would be a perfect solution."

"To what?"

"Our futures."

"*Our* futures?"

"Yes. I want to know if you'll marry me."

I gasped. "You can't be serious!"

"Perfectly." Thomas grinned. "My parents are applying more pressure for me to find a wife, and we're great friends. What more could we want?"

I frowned. "Love?"

Thomas looked down. "Didn't do you any favors, did it?"

"That's cruel, Thomas." I flinched as though he'd struck me and stalked away from him.

"Wait." Thomas quickened his pace. "I didn't mean to upset you, I just—I know what Van meant to you. Do you think you'll ever find that again?"

"Never." Anything else would just be second best.

"Exactly my point. Barb," Thomas said, scanning my face with desperate eyes. "I can give you anything you want— You could go to graduate school, anything. We'd both be entering this with our eyes open. No one would get hurt. I wouldn't expect anything from you."

I scoffed. "I can't believe you are even suggesting this."

"Just think about it, okay? If you decide no, then fine. If yes — great. It's up to you."

With a sharp nod, I turned to hail a cab. I had to get home, had to try to untangle the knot of thoughts in my head. Thomas let me go. Didn't try to sway me.

He did have a point. After Van, any other man would be second best. I didn't expect to find that kind of love again in this lifetime. I wasn't entirely sure I wanted to. He had been the best, no one could ever compare with that.

Thomas' proposition played on my mind for a few days. I consulted Evelyn on the matter. She refused to give her opinion one way or the other, which only confirmed my suspicion that she was for the agreement.

For every argument I thought of, there was also a rebuttal. I avoided Thomas and all his phone calls over the course of the week. I refused to see him while I was still deciding. Thomas had a bad habit of being able to twist my arm on most things, but I wouldn't let him influence this decision.

It was the wedding vows themselves that made my mind up for me. I recalled Anna and Kenneth saying theirs. They had truly meant them. I would be lying before God if I married Thomas. I didn't love him, and I never would. And what would happen if either of us met someone? Were we to have affairs?

No, I couldn't do it.

Thomas took the news better than I'd expected. But his question still weighed heavy on my mind as I worked. It forced me to ask myself questions I didn't have any answers for. What would the future hold for me? I'd been so sure Van would be the one I'd marry, but that was no longer an option. Would I meet someone else? How would it be possible for me to love another? The questions reeled around so much my head spun.

I made a lot of mistakes at work. My letters were returned to me covered in red scrawls from corrections. A few of the other secretaries giggled at this, peering over their typewriters to get a better glimpse of my bleeding letters.

Refraining from lashing out at them, I rose from my desk and hurried into the staff lounge for a coffee and much needed cigarette. While I waited for my coffee to warm, I leaned my head against the cabinet in front of me and blew out a deep breath.

"Bad day?"

I nearly jumped out my skin. Cursing myself for looking so stupid, I turned around. It was Reed Walker, one of the firm's junior partners. He stood in the lounge doorway, holding an empty coffee mug.

"No," I mumbled, my cheeks blushing scarlet.

Reed raised an eyebrow, but questioned me no further. I sank into one of the leather armchairs with my coffee and sucked hard on my cigarette.

"You've been here a few months now, right?" he asked as he poured himself a coffee.

I nodded.

"How are you enjoying it?" Reed leaned against the cabinets as he sipped his drink.

I shrugged.

"Talkative, aren't you?"

"What would you like me to say?" I looked up to find him staring with intensity in his eyes. Shaking my head slightly, I mustered a weak smile. "I'm sorry. I guess I'm having a bad day."

"We've all been there," Reed said, pushing off the counter and heading for the door. "Take it easy."

My concentration didn't get better throughout the course of the day. Sheila, the office manager, eventually sent me to the archive room in the basement where I was to locate some dead files. I spent hours in the cold, damp basement.

It was a mindless job, searching for dead files and making piles of them, but it kept my hands busy and left my brain to wander freely. I coughed and sneezed often, disturbing ancient dust. After an hour or so, I craved clean clothes and a shower. I was itchy and I had an awful headache thanks to the poor lighting. I sat on a cardboard box and lit a cigarette.

"Hello? Anyone down here?" a voice called in the distance.

"Yeah, in here," I replied, halfheartedly hoping whoever it was would miss me. The basement was split into grid lockers for the different businesses in the building. Maybe it would be someone from one of those.

Above the row of filing cabinets, I saw a mop of dirty blond hair approaching. Turning a corner, Reed and his warm smile came into view. "What are you doing down there?" he asked, looking at me with a puzzled expression.

I smiled from my spot on the half-caved-in box. "Pondering the arson charges if I drop my cigarette among all this paper."

Reed laughed. "If you drop it, I doubt you'll be around to worry about the charges."

"Ah. Oh well, one less thing to worry about."

"Jack sent me down to check on you," Reed said, resting his elbow on a filing cabinet. "People have a habit of getting locked in down here in the dark."

"Seriously?" I asked, my eyebrows shooting up.

Reed nodded.

"So why the hell did they send me down here?"

"Because Sheila doesn't want to chip a nail, I expect."

I laughed. What a witch. "Sounds about right."

"Want some help?"

"Aren't you busy?" I asked him.

He considered the question. "A little, nothing that can't wait."

I smiled, a touch more genuine. I doubted his workload was anything but *little*. "That's okay. Thanks for the offer though, that was sweet."

Reed chuckled and ducked his head. "No problem." He turned to leave, but twisted around at the last minute. "Oh, and if the building suddenly goes up in smoke, I saw nothing."

I laughed.

What a nice guy.

* * * *

Evelyn helped me find a beautiful new dress for the office party. Shopping with her had been a bittersweet experience — an echo of a time that now felt so long ago. I was a different girl — a different woman than I had been back then, when I'd been so excited to go to the ball with Van.

But true to her nature, Evelyn kept me from being swallowed by a tidal wave of grief just by being her. We made a day of it, and had lunch at the Plaza. Evelyn splurged and added more than a few new dresses to both of our closets. The one for the party was the most special. It was corseted with a straight skirt pooling around my feet. The deep blue velvet felt incredibly soft as I stroked it absentmindedly as I walked into the ballroom of the hotel Ansonia. I didn't have many work friends, not close ones anyway. Sheila still hadn't forgiven my mental lapse in concentration, and avoided me like the plague. She huddled in a corner with a few of her sheep, and snuck glances at me from under her heavy mascara-laden lashes.

Her behavior was laughable, and my lack of response only further irritated the woman. I dotted myself around everyone else, not staying longer than a half hour in their company. I was asked to dance regularly and agreed each time.

"What did you do to anger the dragon lady?" Reed asked as he appeared at my elbow.

"Oh," I said softly, surprised at his sharp appearance. "You noticed that, huh?"

Reed chuckled. "I think everyone has. There's a pool going for how long it takes for you to quit."

I snorted my derision. "She couldn't make me quit."

"She's a very highly strung and volatile person."

"She's a pussycat." I rolled my eyes.

"You mean she really doesn't frighten you?"

I laughed. "Not at all. Why, are you scared of her?"

"Terrified," he said with such a straight face that I knew he was deadly serious. "They're like sheep, aren't they?" Reed asked, nodding toward Sheila and her flock. "All too afraid to stand up and think for themselves She holds so much power over them."

"A person only has power over you if you let them."

"Talking from experience?"

I shrugged.

"Feel like a dance?"

"Why not?"

Reed led me out onto the crowded dance floor. As I placed my hand on his shoulder, I couldn't help but compare him to Van. Reed was a full head taller, and far broader. I felt like a little girl as I danced with Reed, but he didn't loom over me like a menace. He was a gentle giant. We were quiet for a few minutes, both unsure on what to say.

"Have you always lived in the city?" Reed asked with an awkward smile.

I shook my head. "No, my aunt lives here. After I graduated, I decided to stay with her. And you?"

"Yeah, born and raised. I don't think I could ever leave."

"How sad." I laughed. "The real world isn't all that scary, you know."

Reed grinned. "I know. But everything I need is right here. I have no need to leave." His smile slipped, his face turning serious. "I— If I ask you something, would you mind?"

For such an attractive and physically dominating man, Reed certainly was unsure of himself. It made me check my barbed tongue. "It would depend what it was, I think."

"Well, if I were to ask you to go somewhere at a certain time…with me, would you?"

My brow creased in confusion. "Are you asking me on a date?"

"No, not a date," Reed said in a rush. "Just a meeting. I would pick you up and we could partake in some social activity and I would then drop you off."

I laughed at his awkwardness. "But not a date?"

Reed smiled. "A meeting."

"And what would we do on this meeting?" I asked.

"Have you ever been to the drive-in?"

"No."

"Then we'd go to the drive-in."

"All right. As long as we're clear it isn't a date." I narrowed my eyes at him, as though daring him to contradict me.

He smiled, realizing I was only teasing. "Crystal clear. Are you free tomorrow?"

"No," I said. "I'm busy on Sundays."

Reed's face was awash with disappointment and he waited for an explanation, but I couldn't give him one. I didn't know him well enough, and what would I say? On Sundays I attend church to try to heal my broken heart then I visit my dead lover's mother, even though most of the time she has no idea who I am?

No, I couldn't.

After a moment he nodded and my stomach fell as I wondered if I'd hurt his feelings. I stared at the ground, waiting for the dance to be over.

Reed dropped his arms as I backed out of them, mumbling about the powder room. Standing over the washbasin with my hands clasping the sides, I willed my heart to stop racing. I knew what provoked the response. Reed was asking me on a date with him, and there was only one reason I could think of to decline.

It wasn't a viable excuse.

I didn't stay late at the party. Evelyn was still awake when I got back, only just after midnight.

"You're early. I wasn't expecting you for hours."

"I was tired. It wasn't very exciting." I flopped onto the couch next to her.

"Are you all right? You seem a little down," Evelyn asked as she stroked my hair.

"Not really." I frowned. "I think I almost agreed to go on a date."

Evelyn smiled softly. "You're allowed to date. You aren't breaking any rules."

"I know," I said quietly. "It'll just make everything feel so final, that's all."

"It has to happen one day, Barb."

I nodded. "I think I'm going to go to bed."

"You know where I am if you want to talk."

* * * *

I went early to see Mrs. Judson. Van played heavily on my mind. I saw him across the street as I got into a cab, only to disappear behind a passing stranger. Shaking my head, I got into the cab, trying to rid my mind of ghosts from my past.

As always, Mrs. Judson sat in her chair by the window looking out onto the lake. I placed a hand gently onto her shoulder so as not to startle her. She looked up at me and broke out into a grin. Mrs. Judson stood up and hugged me tightly. "Oh, how lovely it is to see you, Barb!"

It took me a moment to gather my bearings. She had never recalled me instantly before. My breath caught in my throat as I returned her embrace. "You too."

"Is Van with you?"

My heart pinched as it always did when she mentioned him. I hated lying to her. "No, it's just me."

She lifted her eyebrows in surprise. "You came all this way to see me on your own? You didn't have to do that," she said softly, sinking back into her chair.

"I know, I wanted to."

Mrs. Judson grasped my hand. "You are a sweet girl."

I smiled. I loved to be in her company when she was this lucid, but it also brought with it a stab of pain. I wished Van could have seen her like this more often. Mrs. Judson requested tea and cakes for us. She asked all about school and my parents. When I told her I'd graduated and now worked for the same law firm Van had done his internship at, she was over the moon for me.

It was strange, sometimes when I visited she remembered me as Barb — the girl who visits for no apparent reason. Other times I'm just a stranger, but this was the first time she had associated me as Van's girlfriend and recalled me perfectly.

She was what I wanted my own mother to be. Kind, caring, attentive and considerate. I longed to curl up on her lap and have her stroke my hair and tell me sweet lies that everything would be all right. More than anything, she was the only person on the planet capable of knowing how deep his loss had cut me.

* * * *

I threw myself into work come Monday morning. It took every ounce of strength I owned to concentrate on the task at hand, but it paid off. Not one letter came back with corrections. I think this annoyed Sheila even more, as she no longer had a fallible excuse to punish me.

As I tidied my desk at the end of the day, I felt a sense of achievement that I was getting myself back on track.

"Hi."

Glancing up, I saw Reed's tall frame standing over my desk. "Hi."

"How was your day?" he asked, shifting his weight.

"Fine. Yours?"

"Good, good."

I nodded, not really sure where the conversation was headed.

"Are you just leaving?"

"Yeah," I said, standing.

"Would you like to get a drink?"

"Now?"

"Yes, if you would like."

And because I couldn't think of a good reason not to, I said, "Sure."

Reed and I walked in silence to a small bar around the corner. It was busy with office types, unwinding from a long day. I recognized a few faces from my own office, and smiled a few hellos.

As Reed motioned to the bar, I pointed to an empty table by the window. We laughed in understanding and I pushed my way through the crowd. I flopped into my seat and shrugged out of my heavy jacket. Glancing out of the window, I saw Van watching me from across the street. My heart skipped a beat and I hurriedly lit a cigarette, trying not to think too much. Reed returned after a few minutes, placing a wine glass under my nose.

"I'm sorry, I forgot to ask." He blushed.

"This is fine, thank you." I really wasn't fond on wine, but I didn't want to hurt his feelings. "So did you enjoy the party?" I asked, straining to jumpstart the conversation.

"Yes, did you?"

"Yes."

I took a gulp of wine, more from lack of anything else to do.

"Sheila seems to have backed off."

I smiled. "Yeah."

"I can't believe that woman doesn't scare you."

"You've never met my mother."

"I don't want to either, now."

"Wise choice."

The conversation slipped into silence again. I was trying my best to make an effort, but it felt so strained. I lit another cigarette, anything for a distraction.

"So have you thought any more about the drive-in?"

"Um, not really. You didn't suggest a different time to go."

"Oh. I wasn't sure if you were just being polite, saying you were busy on Sundays," Reed said, flustered.

"No, it was the truth."

Reed's face noticeably brightened. "Well, in that case, how does Saturday night sound?"

I smiled. "Good." I was surprised to find I meant it.

We didn't stay late at the bar, what with work for us both in the morning. Reed walked me the short distance home, managing to keep up friendly chatter. He tipped his hat to me as we said good evening at my building. It didn't feel awkward or pressured in any way.

Throughout the week, Reed appeared more frequently at my desk. Sometimes he brought me a coffee, other times he asked if I'd like to have a cigarette with him in the lounge. His confidence with me grew with each passing day, slowly letting himself act more natural. Reed was such a kind man, it was difficult not to be at ease with him.

The other girls started their gossiping about me once again. I didn't pay any attention and let their snide comments float over my head. Sheila, especially, loved the opportunity to talk about me. Their behavior amused me, and was interesting to watch them gather around her desk and whisper past their hands. I imagined it would be similar to watching the behavior of monkeys in the wild.

Chapter Thirty-Four

I wasn't sure what one wore to the drive-in. It was only mid-January, and the weather was bitter cold. Opting for high-waisted black pants and a green blouse, I hoped in the car I would be impenetrable from the icy winter air.

Evelyn was completely charmed by Reed. She knew his mother, naturally. He promised to arrange a brunch date sometime in the near future, much to Evelyn's glee. Wishing us a good time, she all but pushed us out of the door.

Reed kept up a stream of chatter as we drove to the drive-in theater in New Jersey. Once parked, Reed left to buy us soda and snacks for the movie. I flipped open my compact mirror to check my hair, sure I could feel it coming away. Tilting it around, I saw Van standing behind the car. I squeezed my eyes shut, and when I opened them again, he was gone.

The driver door swung open and I jumped out of my skin. "Whoa, you all right there?" Reed asked, handing me my soda.

I nodded, trying to swallow my stomach that had leaped into my throat. I gulped down a few mouthfuls of my drink, attempting to slow my racing heart.

"I hope you enjoy the movie," Reed said, scooching along the seat toward me.

My smile felt forced. I had no idea what movie we were seeing. I didn't follow the movies very often, only if Thomas desperately wanted to see one. I found the war updates at the beginning unsettling, and often had to leave.

The credits soon rolled up and Reed rolled down his window so we could hear the speaker. He turned to face me, and moved his arm around the back of the seat, letting his hand rest on my shoulder. I froze. No man had ever touched me in such an intimate gesture...no one but Van.

I cursed myself. I couldn't — wouldn't — think of him. Not his name, or his smile, or his beautiful penetrating eyes and strong, muscular arms...no, not one thought of him. It wasn't fair to Reed.

Since You Went Away

The name of the movie flashed up on screen. Frowning, I wondered why it caused my stomach to summersault. The name was familiar, had someone talked about it? The movie burst to life, starting the story.

It was a war movie.

My gut clenched. Vomit rose in my throat. I closed my eyes, fighting for control. The movie drew on. I fought a losing battle.

"Barb? You've gone really pale..." Reed's voice sounded a hundred miles away.

"I'm not feeling very well," I whispered. "I'm sorry, I need a walk. I'll be back soon." After shoving open the car door, I ran between the rows of cars, letting the movie fade behind me. My blood roared in my ears as I leaned against a railing, struggling to catch my breath.

What a fool I was. I'd been caught so off guard I didn't have a chance to prepare myself. Seeing a soldier and his wife lit up on screen made me physically nauseous. It wasn't Reed's fault—he had no idea.

Had I made an enormous mistake? Maybe I wasn't ready. I'd been seeing Van an awful lot more recently. Maybe it was just guilt.

A car rolled to a stop alongside me. Reed jumped out, rushing to my side. "Are you all right? I got worried, you've been gone forever."

"Have I?" I thought it had only been a moment.

"Do you want me to take you home?" Reed asked, his warm hand on my shoulder grounding me to the present, pulling me out of the past.

I nodded.

As the distance between the drive-in and my overworked mind increased, I felt myself returning to normal. "I'm sorry, Reed," I said quietly. He had to think I was a total idiot.

"No, don't be. You can't help it if you're sick."

"I'm feeling much better now," I said, and found myself meaning it. I'd ruined the movie for him, but I could try to make it up to him. "Would you like to do something else?"

Reed smiled. "Sure."

"Dinner?"

"Perfect."

He took me to Café Loyal, not too far from Evelyn's building. After a few drinks, I relaxed, and forced all memories of earlier out of my head.

Reed was a charming date. He told me all about growing up in the city. He'd had such a different childhood from me. Where he had been studious and disciplined, I had been rebellious and sought out adventures. We even looked complete opposites. With my milky skin and dark hair, Reed was olive-toned with well-groomed dirty blond hair. I was outspoken, and he was polite.

Reed helped me into my coat, brushing my hair with his hand. I waited for the shiver to snake its way down my spine, the way it always had with Van. But it never came. It was like trying to feel sensation in a lost limb, expecting but never materializing.

I wouldn't compare, I wouldn't.

I insisted on walking off my meal, as it was only a few blocks to the apartment. The night had a chill, but it was refreshing. Reed escorted me up to the apartment, ever the perfect gentleman. "Thank you, for dinner," I said. "I'm sorry again, about the movie."

Reed smiled bashfully. "That's all right. And, you're welcome."

"So, I'll see you Monday?"

"Right, Monday," Reed said, nodding.

"Okay, um, goodnight then."

"Goodnight." Reed dipped his head to kiss my cheek. I moved my head to kiss his. Our simultaneous moves countered each other, and instead of planting a kiss on the cheek, it landed directly on our lips.

Reed jumped back. "Oh! I'm sorry, I didn't mean—"

I wasn't listening. The kiss awoke the beast that lay long forgotten in the pit of my stomach. Roaring to life, the beast was ravenous. My lips tingled in a beautifully familiar way. A thousand memories streaked past, every single one of them Van.

Touching my mouth, I looked up. Van gave me his knee-quivering, lopsided smile. I was dimly aware of a voice—distant and unfamiliar. Van stood silently before me, unchanged by the hands of time.

I touched his cheek. So soft and perfect and achingly familiar...

Without a further thought, I melted into his body. It was the same but different. He was my Van, but there was something missing. Smashing my lips against his, I struggled to recall the missing ingredient. Frantically I tried to push everything from my mind, to simply enjoy the moment. I'd dreamed about this for years now. Dreamed about kissing this remarkable man one last time. To feel his lips, his arms, to swim in his eyes, to breathe all of him in...

Reality hit me like a freight train.

It wasn't Van. It never could be. This was a poor imitation of what I longed for.

Wrenching myself free, I looked up at Reed's flushed face. I mumbled my goodbye and threw myself into the apartment and shut the door firmly behind me.

What have I done?

My actions were inexcusable. All the careful padding I'd wrapped around my heart unraveled. I'd locked all my desires for Van away, only to invite them back recklessly. And what about Reed? Poor, sweet Reed. He was such a good man. He didn't deserve someone like me. He deserved better.

The more I thought about the kiss, the more disgusted I felt. I was a shameful disgrace. Clamping a hand to my mouth, bile rose in my throat. I ran to the bathroom and locked myself in. My stomach emptied itself until there was nothing left but sickening guilt. I pressed my forehead against the cool wall beside me. I had hit a new low.

Chapter Thirty-Five

I tossed and turned all night. Sleep wouldn't take me. In a way I was glad. Sleep was sure to bring dreams. The following morning I told Evelyn I was ill. She didn't believe my phony excuse, she knew it went deeper than that.

I couldn't get out of bed. I lay there in my misery with the sheets pulled up over my head, shielding my traitorous face from the world. Reed called a few times but I couldn't speak to him.

My disgust with myself only dug deeper. I belonged in the ninth circle of hell, along with all the other traitors. How could I have betrayed Van? I'd thrown myself into the arms of another man. Traitorous letch. My guilt consumed me. I'd let everyone down.

By my second day of wallowing in self-pity, I clung to the desperate notion that all was not lost. I'd known the first time I kissed another man would be difficult. I didn't realize just how difficult it would be. I hadn't expected this much guilt. I would just force myself to get back up and move on. After all, it was something I was a pro at now.

My door creaked as I pulled it open, relishing the fresh air that teased my face. Evelyn came running at the noise. "Sweetie, how are you feeling? You look awful. Will you try and eat something?"

I shook my head and padded across the cool floorboards to the bathroom.

"I called the office for you. I told them you were sick," she called to my retreating form.

Closing the bathroom door behind me, I shut out Evelyn — and the world. I stood in front of the sink and stared at the mirror above. The reflection staring back at me was almost unrecognizable. My eyes were sunken deep into their sockets, and my skin was sallow. As I peeled off my nightgown to step into the shower, I noticed how prominent my ribs were. Stepping back to look at my body fully in the mirror, my weight loss was apparent.

My build had always been curvy but slender — now I looked fragile and ill. My hipbones jutted out and the sharp lines of my collarbone stuck out. It was the wakeup call I needed. I sat down in the bathtub, letting the water from the shower cascade over my head. Van would be so unhappy if he could see me. He never wanted this for me. I'd been feeling guilty for all the wrong reasons.

All the warning signs had been around me. I'd been seeing Van more and more. This had to be my subconscious telling me I wasn't ready to move forward, but the last thing I could do was move backward. I just had to take things slowly, that was all.

One date at a time.

I'd said goodbye to Van, I'd felt ready to do it. But my fantasy of kissing him two nights before had opened up the locked doors.

No one asked about my absence at work. Jack sighed when he caught sight of my skinny frame, but said nothing. Sheila and her flock continued their gossiping, thankful for the new material.

Reed found me in the lounge, smoking myself into a frenzy. "Oh, hello," he said. "I didn't realize you were back."

I smiled and knew it looked nervous. I had dreaded seeing him. "Hi."

Reed took the armchair beside mine. "I wanted to apologize. I felt like maybe you were avoiding me, that's why you didn't come to work."

"No, I was sick. Really." There was no lie in my words. Only it was self-inflicted illness that had been the cause.

Reed nodded. "I was worried I came on too strong. It was very uncharacteristic of me."

My shoulders slumped. Of course Reed had blamed himself. It was another thing for me to feel guilty about. "You have nothing to apologize for, Reed. You didn't do anything wrong."

"Okay," he said, smiling as if he didn't believe me. "So, are you feeling better?"

I paused, mulling it over. "I'm getting there."

He leaned an inch closer. "Would a second date be out of the question?"

"No."

Reed grinned. "Good. I promise I won't take you back to the drive-in."

I laughed. "Okay."

"I have tickets to the ballet this weekend, would you like to go?"

One date... One day at a time. "I'd love to."

* * * *

Reed moved our relationship along at a glacial pace. I agreed to a date once a week, never more and never less. It got easier as time wore on, but my guilt never receded. Reed took me on wonderful dates. To the ballet, opera, dances on cruise ships. Slowly, I was able to let myself have fun. As the winter months fell behind us, the spring brought a new lightness. I began to feel like my old carefree self again. I never told Reed where I went on Sundays. I didn't think he would understand.

Van no longer dominated my thoughts. Gradually, days would pass with no painful flashbacks or memories of him. I stopped seeing him as frequently and it slowly slipped to nothing.

Reed was incredibly patient with me. It took a long time for me to relax enough just to hold his hand. And as April gave way to May, I let him kiss me for the first time since the night of the drive-in fiasco.

The weather was warmer, no need for a heavy coat. Reed and I had finished a delicious lunch at the Tavern, and were enjoying a stroll through the park. I slipped my hand into the crook of his elbow and rested my head against his shoulder as we walked.

"Anything wrong?" he asked.

"No." He would never know how much truth there was in that simple word. I leaned farther into him, relishing the closeness. It had taken a long time for me to reach that point with Reed. He was such a charming and gentle man, but I always held back.

Reed and I walked slowly home to Evelyn's. His face was flushed as we rode the elevator. I didn't enquire why. Reed was a sensitive man, and I was ever aware of his feelings.

The norm for our goodbyes was Reed would kiss my cheek and dip his hat before retreating back into the elevator. Today felt different.

"Reed, are you okay?" I asked, concerned over his health. He appeared quite queasy.

Reed nodded.

I stepped forward and placed a hand on his cheek, shocked at the heat radiating from it. "Are you sure?"

Reed took the hand upon his cheek and gave it a little squeeze. He interlocked our fingers, his eyes burning into mine. Now I understood. I'd wondered when the day would come, when he would finally want more from me.

I was ready. It wasn't like last time.

My lips twitched into an uncertain smile and I closed the space between us. I placed a hand on Reed's breast, his heart thumping unevenly beneath my fingertips. I had to stand on my tiptoes to reach his mouth. I planted a tiny kiss on his lips. Reed wrapped his arms around me, securing me against his muscular frame. I didn't object. Instead, I gave in to his kiss, allowing my senses to be fogged.

I wore a smile on my lips when I slipped between the cool sheets that night. I let Reed's happy and goofy smile flood my thoughts, trying to ignore the realization that he cared for me far more than I did for him. He made me happy. The rest would follow in its own time.

Chapter Thirty Six

There was a familiar gleam in Reed's eyes after our first proper kiss. I could feel his eyes on me almost throughout the workday. His concentration would lapse, should I walk past him in the office. The other girls noticed it, too, and never failed to whisper.

Sheila didn't like the attention I received. I was often sent to the basement for some reason or other. I'd finished sorting the dead files, and had hid a book and a pack of cigarettes down there, basking in the knowledge she was actually getting me out of working.

Reed checked on me a lot and brought coffee and assortments of snacks. He arrived empty-handed one dusty afternoon. "How is Ms. Austen today?" he asked, nodding toward my battered copy of *Pride and Prejudice.*

"Very well," I said, placing the book on the decrepit desk I was sitting at. Standing to greet him, I rose onto my tiptoes to press a soft kiss to his full mouth. Reed's lips curled into a smile before he parted my lips to kiss me fully. My body responded to him and I snaked my arms around his neck.

Reed lifted me. He placed me on the desk, his arms not once releasing my body. I parted my legs slightly, to allow him closer. Warmth flooded my blood, excitement overpowering my senses.

"God, I love this basement," Reed mumbled against my lips.

I giggled. "It has its charms."

Reed pulled his face away, reaching out to stroke my cheek. "Take tomorrow off."

"Why?"

"Humor me," he said with a grin. "I have a surprise for you."

"What kind of surprise?"

"You'll see."

* * * *

The weather was warmer as June crept in, the chill that could haunt spring finally gone. So when I discovered my surprise was a baseball game to see the Yankees, I didn't mind sitting outside watching. I'd never been to one before, and he'd gotten good seats. Reed bought me a hot dog and cheap beer and tried to teach me about the game, explaining what all the players did. I didn't understand, and after three beers I knew it wasn't likely I ever would.

The Yankees played the Boston Red Sox, and that was all I knew. The atmosphere was alive, the whole stadium pumped with excitement. I'd never been to anything like that before, and it was certainly an experience.

Reed insisted on driving me home, as I was drunk off my ass on cheap beer. I'd wanted to walk, but he would hear none of it. He opened my door for me and helped me out of the car. Reed swung an arm around my waist to assist in my walking, as it seemed I was having a little difficulty with coordination. I giggled like a schoolgirl and leaned against him, making use of his support.

He unlocked the front door and swung it open. Feeling brave and uninhibited from my beer haze, I pressed my body against his and gave him a clumsy kiss. Laughing my thanks for a lovely date, I stumbled into the apartment.

The small amount of sense I had left told me it would be wise to take a nap before Evelyn got home. She didn't give a hoot about my antics, but I doubted she wanted an intoxicated niece for company over dinner.

The shrill ringing of the telephone kept interrupting my nap. With my head pounding, I pulled it out of the socket, before disappearing back to bed for the remainder of the night.

* * * *

Most of Saturday was spent in the same place. I'd never had a beer hangover before, and I never wanted one again. Evelyn left the apartment midafternoon, and the doorbell rang sometime after. I glanced at the clock on my way to the front door, surprised to see it read five o'clock. A hot shower had worked wonders on my hangover, and barely a trace of it remained now I was clean and in fresh clothes.

Reed clutched his hat, grinning widely as I opened the door.

"Oh," I said, surprised to see him. "Hello."

"Hi," he said. "I wanted to make sure you were all right. Have you recovered yet?"

Groaning, I leaned against the doorjamb. "Just. That was the worst hangover of my life."

He laughed. "I figured. You should get out. Some fresh air will work wonders." Reed's face lit up. "How about a drive?"

I didn't have to think as a smile broke out across my lips. "Sounds perfect." Grabbing my purse, I didn't bother leaving a note for Evelyn. She was used to my erratic comings and goings.

Not too long after, we were in the blissfully quiet countryside with fresh, fresh air. The rolling green hills and fields put me into a peaceful mindset. I leaned my head on Reed's shoulder and smiled to myself as his fingers traced little patterns on my arm.

He pulled off the road and we traveled up an uneven dirt track. Slowing to a stop, Reed jumped out of the car and picked up a blanket from the back seat. He linked his fingers with mine as he guided me down a small hill toward a birch tree.

Despite it being early evening, the rays from the sun still warmed my skin. Reed laid the blanket on the cushiony grass. I stepped out of my shoes and sat beside Reed. He leaned his back against the thick tree trunk and pulled me against his chest.

I closed my eyes and could have cheerfully fallen asleep. Reed sighed and my eyes fluttered open again. "Something wrong?"

He tightened his hold on me. "Not a thing. I was just thinking how right this feels. I feel like I'm right where I'm supposed to be when I'm with you."

I was aware of every breath, every muscle, every heartbeat. Reed was waiting for me to reciprocate his feelings. I couldn't find the words.

Reed never faltered, not even when it was clear I wasn't going to reply. "There's a concert in the park tomorrow. Are you sure your Sunday commitments can't be put off?"

My body tensed. Not once had Reed asked me to miss my Sunday routine. "No," I said quietly. "I'm sorry."

Reed let out a quick laugh that held no humor. "That's all right. I didn't expect a yes."

I poked him in the ribs, trying to lighten the mood. "So why ask?"

Reed sighed again. "A man can hope…"

A bubble of laughter rose up in my throat. "What is it with you men who find me so riveting?"

His pause was deafeningly loud while I waited for a response to my blunder. "You shouldn't be surprised people find you interesting. You're one of the most complex creatures I have ever met, Barb."

To anyone else his tone wouldn't have changed. But I heard all too clearly the new edge. "How did you find this place?" I asked, hoping the turn in conversation wasn't too apparent.

Reed shrugged. "I like to drive around, explore a little. What with you normally only agreeing to one date a week and occupied every Sunday, I have a fair amount of free time on my hands."

"I like it here. It's beautiful." I avoided his slight complaint. The minutes ticked by in tense silence. Cringing, I scolded myself for overthinking everything he said.

"What do you want to do in the long term, Barb?" Reed asked, shattering the quiet.

I frowned. "What do you mean?"

"Well," Reed said, "do you want to be a secretary for the rest of your life?"

"There are a million things I want to do," I said, feeling stung by the sharpness of his words. "I want to see the world, I want to write, I want to learn more, I — I want to do a lot of things."

"So why aren't you?"

I shrugged, wishing he would drop it. "Like you said, the rest of my life. It doesn't all have to happen right now."

He took a moment to respond. "I suppose. If I had something besides law I was passionate about, I would pursue it endlessly."

"So you want to be a lawyer for the rest of your life?" I asked, grinning.

Reed laughed. "I don't have any notion for a career change yet anyway."

"And what else do you want to do?"

"I'm already doing it."

Chapter Thirty Seven

Mrs. Judson sat at her usual seat by the window. She smiled vacantly at me as I lowered myself into the chair opposite her. My heart sank as I knew she wasn't lucid.

"Are you visiting someone?" she asked.

I smiled. "Yes. I thought I'd enjoy the view."

Mrs. Judson's smile widened. "Yes, it is a lovely lake, isn't it?"

I nodded.

"My son came to see me today."

"How lovely."

"He's a sweet boy to come see me."

"Sounds like you have a very charming son," I said, forcing a smile even though a hard lump lodged in my throat. We'd had the same conversation countless times. The doctor had told me she slipped into different memories of her past and didn't realize how far back they were.

"Oh, he is. I have a feeling he would like you."

"Mrs. Judson, it's time for dinner." A nurse placed her hand on Mrs. Judson's shoulder.

I glanced at the clock and saw it read six p.m. I must have left later than I thought. It was a struggle to get myself together today. Reed's words from the evening before played in my subconscious.

"Bye, dear," Mrs. Judson said, patting my hand as she rose from her chair.

"It was lovely talking with you."

I wished I'd had longer with her. I always missed her when I had to leave. Sighing, I stood up and paused in front of the mirror above the fireplace before leaving. I shuddered at how ashen my face looked, despite the thick layer of makeup caked upon it.

Movement behind me caused my eyes to flicker toward it. Van stood a little ways behind, watching me with a curious, almost cautious look. Squeezing my eyes shut, I took a deep breath—in and out. Opening them he still lingered.

I tried again.

He was still there…that had never happened before. My panic started to mount. I squeezed my eyelids together as tightly as they could. "Go away," I mumbled through clenched teeth.

A tear slid down my cheek and I prized my eyes open.

He was gone. My legs felt like jelly as I walked out front. *I must be going crazy.*

* * * *

My appetite had disappeared in time for dinner. I still felt shaken up. Evelyn told me Lois had called for me several times. I think she was annoyed at me for unplugging the phone, as she didn't notice until late in the afternoon. Lois could wait until tomorrow. I didn't feel like speaking to anyone.

My sleep was unsettled that night. Van's face flashed before me countless times, allowing me no rest. My mood was cloudy come the morning, and the hot water from the shower didn't lift it. Sheila caught my bad mood and further increased it by sending me down to the basement again.

Reed came down at lunch to take me out for a much-needed drink. I smoked away my bad mood and felt better for it. "Are you working in the basement this afternoon?" Reed asked as we took the elevator back up to the office.

"Yeah, I'm going to make a coffee and then go back down."

We went in different directions as the elevator opened onto our floor. I headed for my desk and rummaged around in my drawer for a fresh pack of cigarettes. Standing up, I glimpsed a familiar frame in Jack's office. I ducked back down quickly. *What the hell is he doing here?*

Averting my eyes as quickly as possible, I snuck to the side of the room — probably looking as inconspicuous as an elephant — and disappeared down the hall into the lounge.

"Avoiding someone?" Reed's voice in my ear made me jump as I peeked out of the door, trying to see if Mr. Judson was still in Jack's office.

"Oh!" I laughed. "Maybe."

Reed grinned. "Anyone I know?" He leaned out of the door to see who it was. "You know him?" An icy tone took over his normal pleasant voice.

"No, not really."

Reed searched my face. "He's a good friend of Jack's, I hear."

"I wouldn't know," I said, shooting him a distracted smile. "I should get back to the basement before Sheila has a cow." I kept my back to Jack's office as I snuck toward the elevator. I breathed a sigh of relief as the doors slid shut, and felt foolish. I don't know why I felt the need to avoid him. Mr. Judson probably wanted to see me as much as I wanted to see him.

Time crept away from me, and it was almost six before I escaped the cold clutches of the basement. Most of the secretaries had already left, and only a few desk lamps shone from various offices. Reed had left a note on my desk asking me to have dinner with him, he would pick me up at eight. I left work considerably happier than I had entered.

"Barb?" Evelyn called as closed the door behind me.

"Yeah? I can't talk, I'm going out to dinner and need to be hosed down!" I laughed. I ran into my bathroom and scrubbed the dust and grime of the basement off me. I dressed in a pale blue wraparound dress with matching shoes. For once, I wasn't running late. My makeup and hair were both finished exactly one minute before eight p.m.

I was checking my makeup a final time in the hall mirror when Evelyn stood next to me. "Barb, I need to talk to you."

"Okay," I said.

"No, properly," she said with a frown. "When will you be home?"

It wasn't like Evelyn to question my comings and goings. "I'm not sure." I laughed. "Van's father was at the office today, so I'll probably be drinking to forget all about it."

Evelyn's frown deepened. "Van's father was?"

A quiet tap on the door saved me from answering. I kissed her on the cheek. "We can talk when I get home, okay?" I threw open the front door. "Hi." I greeted

Reed. I gave Evelyn a small wave as I shut the door behind me.

"You're certainly eager to get out," Reed commented as we waiting for the elevator.

"I'm eager for a drink." I laughed.

Reed took me to Savarin in the Waldorf-Astoria. I felt incredibly self-conscious dining among the other patrons — it was hardly the sort of place I was used to. Reed seemed oblivious to everyone else and only focused on me, easing some of my discomfort.

"So," I said with a smile as I reached for my water glass. I was stuffed full from the lobster and couldn't even contemplate the dessert tray. "Any reason for tonight?"

Reed smiled. "What do you mean?"

I gestured around the room with my hand. "I mean, why did you bring me down here? I would have been just as happy with dinner at the Chinese restaurant down the street for forty cents."

"I suppose I just felt like being extravagant," he said, reaching across the table to take my hand. "Would you like anything else?"

"No, thank you."

"Shall we then?" Reed stood and helped me too my feet. I slipped my hand into the crook of his arm as we walked back to Evelyn's, taking a detour through the park. "I have to say, I'm surprised you agreed to dinner tonight. You've always been so strict about your one-date-a-week rule."

"Maybe this was it. Who said you were getting another one this week?" I asked, nudging him with my elbow.

Reed grinned. "Ah, but you know we have tickets to the ballet this Saturday." He paused in front of the Bethesda Fountain and I took a moment to admire its beauty. "I must admit, I had an ulterior motive for taking you out tonight."

"Oh? What was it?"

Reed turned to face me and grasped both my hands. "I'm hopelessly in love with you, Barb. I have been for a long time."

His sudden urgency startled me. My heart thumped and my blood rushed behind my ears. I could barely form a coherent thought.

"You're all I can think about. You're the first thing on my mind when I wake in the morning, and your face is the last thing I see at night," Reed continued.

My voice stuck in my throat. I cleared it, and tried again. "Reed, I don't know what to say."

I gasped as Reed crouched down on one knee, still clasping both my hands. "Barbara Howell, will you do me the divine honor of becoming my wife?"

I'm going to be sick. Blood rushed to my head. I had no idea how I didn't faint. I shook with nervous energy. His question played on a loop in my mind and I had no clue as to how much time passed.

Reed laughed quietly, a nervous sound. "I wanted to ask you to marry me tonight. I've had it planned for a while. But you seemed different today. Something has been playing on your mind and I wasn't sure you were ready for me to ask."

'I'm going to ask you to marry me, Barb. One day, I will ask you to marry me. But today is not that day. When the day does come, it will be when you are one hundred percent ready for me to ask.'

I heard a different man's voice. One who knew me, inside and out. One who knew me well enough to realize exactly when I would be ready.

The lights from the fountain cast an ominous glow on Reed's face. I ached to take the pain away that I knew I was causing him, but I didn't know how.

Slowly, Reed stood up. "I'm in love with you, and I think I know that you aren't. I just keep hoping that one day you will."

I opened my mouth to speak but no words would come out.

"You know how I feel. I want you to think about it, take your time in making a decision." Reed placed a hand on the small of my back, guiding me forward. As was his habit, Reed escorted me all the way to my door, never breaking his silence.

Tears stung my eyes as he leaned to kiss my cheek briefly. The hurt hadn't left his eyes and I hated that I had the power to take it away…but couldn't. "I'll see you tomorrow," I whispered.

I crept inside the apartment. After Reed's ambush proposal, I wasn't up to talking to Evelyn about whatever was on her mind. Once in the safety of my room, I curled up on my bed and wondered how I'd gotten it so wrong with Reed.

Chapter Thirty Eight

The weekend rolled around slowly. Work passed with no excitement and Evelyn and I seemed to keep missing each other. Reed never mentioned our discussion, and acted as he always had. I attended the ballet with him on Saturday with fear in my heart. The dread that I felt whenever I thought of his proposal should have been a clear indication that I wouldn't say yes. But I kept imagining myself accepting. Reed would be an attentive husband, and I would struggle to do better. But no matter all the things he had and could offer me, he would always be second best. Even I wasn't selfish enough to subject him to that kind of treatment.

I declined his offer to go for drinks after the ballet. I wanted to run home to bed and rest my weary head. I longed for Sunday to roll around.

Father Morgan understood my feelings. He had become a valuable confidant, one I kept close to my heart. He always listened without judgment, and instead of offering his own advice, simply nudged me along the path I knew myself I would take.

Gray clouds gathered thick and fast above the care home, making the skies threatening and uninviting. I stepped out of the cab and wrapped my arms around my body in a dim attempt to fight off the sudden chill in the air.

"Hello, Ms. Howell," the receptionist greeted me, handing me my visitor's badge. "How nice that Mrs. Judson has another visitor."

I paused as I pinned on the badge. "Has someone else been to see her?"

She nodded. "I think he's still there."

Damn. Mr. Judson and I never bumped into each other anymore. I thought he'd figured out my pattern and was avoiding me.

Maybe it wouldn't even be him.

I smiled my thanks and walked into the lounge. The dry summer air made me parched, so I got myself an iced tea and sipped it as I made my way to Mrs. Judson. She came into view — by the window, as usual.

Van sat opposite her.

As I made to close my eyes to make him disappear, Mrs. Judson raised her hand and touched his cheek.

A million thoughts raced through my mind. The first was that Mrs. Judson was dead and I was staring at a pair ghosts. I quickly cast that out, because not only was it ridiculous, but the receptionist had told me she had another visitor, so she couldn't possibly be —

My heart skipped a beat.

Another visitor…

The glass slipped out of my hand and smashed at my feet, soaking my shoes and splashing my stockings.

Both Judsons turned to look at me. Van stood up quickly, but didn't move toward me. The blood drained from my face. I struggled to keep my eyes focused…

Darkness encroached my vision... Words drifted past my ears but I couldn't understand them.

The blackness began to fade and colors invaded my sight. Shapes reformed, and I found myself looking at the chandelier hanging from the ceiling. I was on the ground. *Why am I on the ground?* I sat up and my head spun with the sudden motion.

"Whoa, whoa, not so fast."

That voice...

I couldn't allow myself to believe what I heard. His voice was so silky, so close to my ear. So real I thought I could feel his warm breath teasing my hair.

With a whimper, I grasped at my head to try to stop the spinning. A hand brushed a lock of hair from my face.

"Are you all right, Barb dear?" Mrs. Judson's sweet voice asked.

I turned to look at her, her face a mask of concern. She held out her hand to help me to my feet. Raising my hand to accept her help, I became conscious of a pair of arms wrapped around me. Nothing made sense. Everything was confusing. Together with Mrs. Judson's help and the poor unfortunate who'd had to catch me, I made it onto my feet. "I'm fine," I said, wishing it were true. "I thought...I thought saw — never mind, I'm sorry."

"You fainted, you should eat something," Mrs. Judson said. "You're far too skinny, no wonder you fainted. Tell her, Van."

I wrenched away from the person who still grasped my elbow. Whipping around, my head spun all over again. I wasn't imaging it this time — he was really here.

I darted my eyes between them like a frightened animal as I backed away from them both. As my panic rose, I turned on my heel and ran from the room, all the way outside where the cool air made my skin goosebump. I sucked in deep breaths, trying to still my racing heart.

The sound of gravel crunching under foot grew closer. I turned and was face to face with my past.

This was no figment of my imagination.

This Van was different. His eyes were aged, tired and excruciatingly sad. He was much more frail than he had been, more slight in build.

I wasn't even aware I was crying until I heard my breath hitch.

Van opened his mouth to speak and closed it again. He reached out for me, tentative, like I really was a wild animal.

"No," I snapped, stepping out of reach. "You're really back, aren't you?"

"Yes—"

"When?"

"March."

It was like taking a baseball bat to the gut. The breath was knocked out of me and I held my middle to try to keep myself together. "Three months," I whispered. "You were never going to tell me, were you?"

"I was," Van said, his voice croaky. "I thought you didn't want to see me."

How on earth could he possibly imagine that? In what universe would I not want to see him? He was my world... He was a part of me.

"You saw me, you told me to go away," Van said, as though the admission physically hurt him.

My heart broke as I recalled seeing Van in the mirror last Sunday. It had taken three attempts to make him disappear...

"You saw me—" Van repeated.

Whatever loose grip I held on my sanity snapped. "I've seen you every goddamn day since you died!" I screamed. "I saw you everywhere!"

"Barb—"

This couldn't be happening. Not now. Not after everything I'd gone through all these years... Everything I'd put my family through. After I had somehow pieced myself back together, however disjointedly. "No... I said goodbye, Van. You died, you left me."

His face twisted in pain. "I'm sorry."

A sob hiccupped in my throat. "You left me," I repeated.

"I'm back, I'm here." Van took a quick step forward and grabbed my hand.

An electric current shot up my arm, igniting every cell in my body. I jumped and Van released my hand. I stretched out to touch him, my fingertips landing softly on his breast. How solid he felt. So real. I took a step closer, and another until we fell into each other. I pawed at him, tugging him closer and pinning myself to him. His scent clouded my senses. That beautiful scent of his, that was what had been missing the night I first kissed Reed—the missing ingredient to the delusion I hadn't been able to put my finger on until now.

I burrowed my face in his neck, my lips automatically seeking his skin. I kissed his throat and didn't stop—I kissed every inch of his face I could get to before his mouth captured mine and stole my breath. I wanted our bodies to forge together...I couldn't get close enough to him.

The kiss was salty from both our tears. As the kiss slowed, I didn't pull my lips away. Van stroked my face as I grasped handfuls of his hair.

"You son of a bitch," I whispered into his mouth.

Van pulled me away from the care home, leading me down the street. We arrived at an old Victorian house with a bed and breakfast sign hanging by the front gate. Van pushed it open and rushed me into the house and up the stairs. With the door firmly locked, Van swept me off my feet and carried me to his bed.

* * * *

It was dark outside when I woke up. A smile curled my lips as I remembered falling asleep in the arms of perfection. I reached over to find him, but he wasn't there. A fleeting moment of panic had my heart racing — had I imagined it all?

Pushing myself onto my elbow, I scanned the darkened room for him. The white of his undershirt shone in the moonlight from his seat at the window. "Van?"

He moved at the sound of my voice. His shirt lay at the foot of the bed where it had been tossed. I pulled it around my shoulders as I got out of bed and sat on his lap. Van wrapped his arms around me, tighter than he usually would have, as though he was as scared as I was that any moment this could be ripped away from us.

"What's wrong?" I whispered, twisting my head to press my face into the crook of his neck.

"Nothing," Van said, his voice low and gravelly. "I have a hard time sleeping sometimes."

"What happened, Van?"

"Shh, there's plenty of time for talking later," he whispered. He kissed my forehead, closing the subject.

When I woke in the morning, Van's eyes were locked with mine when they fluttered open. I dimly recalled Van carrying me back to bed and falling asleep with him stroking my hair and planting soft kisses across my brow.

He called a cab to take us into the city. Evelyn would be worried. It wasn't a question of whether Van would come with me or not — neither of us had the option of separation.

Van remained quiet in the cab, but watched me with an attentive frown. He was still silent in the elevator and as I unlocked the door. Evelyn sat in the dining room, sipping a cup of coffee. Her face was pale with dark circles under her eyes.

I rushed into the room, feeling awful for not having thought of her. "Evie, I'm sorry. I didn't think to call — "

She looked past me to Van and held her hand up to stop me. "I understand. No need for apologies." Evelyn rose from her chair and crossed the room to us. She wrapped her arms around Van's shoulders and held on to him for a long moment. Van was hesitant as he returned her embrace. Pulling back, Evelyn touched her palm to Van's cheek. She gave me a small smile and left the room.

I slipped my hand into Van's and motioned for him to follow me. I closed my bedroom door with a soft click. Van had never been in my bedroom before, but rules were the last thing on anyone's mind.

We both dreaded the conversation that was to come, but it was unavoidable. Van loitered in the center of the room, his eyes roaming without really seeing. I slid to the middle of my bed and drew my knees up, resting my chin on them. Van remained silent, time ticking endlessly slow. I lit a cigarette in the attempt to distract myself. At my action, Van faced me. I offered him one, a pensive smile pulling at his lips.

"It's still a novelty," Van said, taking the cigarette. "Having one whenever I want."

I looked down and picked at an invisible thread on the quilt. "What happened Van? They told us you were dead."

It was another long moment before he spoke. "We were attacked one night. Almost the entire unit was killed by the Japs. Those of us that survived were captured, myself included." Van sat on the edge of the bed, his back facing me.

"But how could our army make that big a mistake? How could they think you were dead?" I asked, swallowing the lump in my throat.

"War isn't neat and tidy. It's loud and messy and dark — especially out there. Jesus, if you could have seen what they did —" Van's voice cracked. "Things get mixed up, people get lost. I suppose, they just lost me."

"That isn't good enough!" I shouted, my voice breaking. My God...the lives that mistake had ruined. If they'd made the mistake with Van, how many others had fallen victim to the same cruel twist of fate?

"There was an obscene amount of soldiers in the camps. Not just Americans. Brits and Norwegians alike. The Japs were cruel, inhumane. Disease was rife among the prisoners — the death toll was higher than the survival rate. They...the Japs issued a warrant to slaughter us all. They knew the Yanks were gaining momentum, I think. They shot the prisoners, lined them up in ditches and opened fire." Van started shaking. "Some of us got out, made it away from the camp. The Japs followed us — slitting the throat of anything they saw moving..."

Terror griped my heart, not just from painfully visualizing the horror Van had witnessed, but the horror in his tone.

Van's voice shook as he continued his agonizing story, "Not many of us made it out... We found Filipino guerrillas, they helped us. I don't really remember much after that. I can remember being carried onto the boat to bring us home, but very little of the actual voyage.

"I was taken to a veterans' hospital in Washington. It was a long time before I could make any sense, the malaria drove me into a state of madness. I left there and came straight to see you and my mother."

And I sent him away. "I'm sorry…" I whispered, trying in vain to stop my tears.

Van turned, was in front of me in heartbeat. He cradled my face in his hands. "Don't, I never meant… I didn't mean to leave you…" he said in a thick voice.

He looked exhausted and so, so sad. I pulled him toward me. Van lay with his head in my lap, grabbing fistfuls of my dress. He soaked it within moments, his tears coming thick and fast. I stroked his hair and crooned. My heart broke for him, wishing I could take his horror away and heal him.

It was a long time before he fell quiet and slipped into a restful sleep. I didn't move. I let him sleep there with his head burrowed in my lap, still desperately clutching me. Cigarette after cigarette I smoked, unable to stop the awful images flashing in my head.

He said he had been taken to a veterans' hospital in Washington. Lois had called me repeatedly over the course of the last week, and I'd missed them all. Was that why she had been calling?

It was late in the day when Van stirred. He didn't move right away, simply held me a while longer. When he rolled onto his back and stared up at me, I stroked his brow and wondered what to expect.

Van caught my hand and held it over his heart. A long moment passed — neither of us speaking. I hadn't seen his face for three years, yet I remembered every line, every plane. His eyes were just as piercing and could still look into the innermost secrets of my soul. But now they were also haunted. Something that only came from seeing true evils in the world and living to tell the tale.

He stared at me, eyes with a burning intensity, as if trying to make up for the lost years. I felt as if I were dreaming. A weightless sensation had taken over my mind, making everything seem so unbelievable.

Above all else, I felt awful, gut-churning guilt. How could I have given up hope for him? I must have known he wasn't truly gone—I'd struggled so badly in accepting his death. But as difficult as all my emotions were to deal with, I couldn't even comprehend his.

Van lifted himself up off the bed. He lit a cigarette and leaned his forearm against the wall. He hung his head. "I want you to know that I understand."

"Understand what?" I asked with a frown.

Van turned and shifted his pained eyes to mine. "You moved on. You thought I was dead. I know you had to, I even wanted you to."

I rose from the bed, but Van held out his hand to keep me at a distance. "I know last night was a slip. I don't hold you to anything, Barb. I want you to be happy. You deserve to be happy with him." He lifted one shoulder in a halfhearted shrug. "I made Jack tell me. He said the guy is good for you. Helped you get back on your feet."

Reed... "I can't hurt him," I whispered. Reed had been so kind to me, and once again I knew he deserved better.

"I don't expect you to," Van said, his voice laced with emotion. "I'll never forget you, Barb. Your face brought me back from the dark."

A tear slid down my cheek, threatening to open the gates for a flood of them. "Van—"

"Please don't." He tried to smile. "It'll just make it harder. I don't blame you for anything, okay? You don't owe me anything."

"Stop it!" I shouted. "Stop saying those things!"

Van's face twisted. "Barb, don't. I'm trying to make this easier for you. You love him—"

I groaned my frustration—he wasn't listening to me. "I don't. I don't love him. I never did. How could I? When I've only ever been in love with you, it's only ever been you." I took a step closer. He eyed me with suspicion and fear, as though he didn't trust my words. "I saw your face every single day. You were always with me," I whispered. Our bodies met and his breath was shaky on my cheek. "The hardest thing I've ever had to do in my life was say goodbye to you." With the tiniest amount of pressure, I traced his lips with the tips of my fingers. "I can't do that again. I won't."

Van fell against me, almost knocking me to the floor. His arms snaked around my back, pinning me to his chest. We held each other for the longest time. His body felt different. It was bonier, harder, yet somehow still the same.

He was here.

I was finally home.

* * * *

Van and I joined Evelyn for dinner. She prepared a lavish feast for us—succulent steaks with mouthwatering vegetables and delicious gravy. Van smoked like a chimney and drank Scotch like it was water. As I helped Evelyn clear the dishes away, she subtly told me she had no problem with Van *visiting* overnight for as long as he wanted. God bless that woman.

I emerged from my bathroom in my silk nightgown, rubbing lotion into my hands. Van was propped up in bed reading a book with one arm tucked behind his head. He looked peaceful in the dim light of the bedside lamp that cast a soft glow over the room.

Van turned and flashed me a smile. He pulled back the sheets for me to get in, and I realized I'd been staring, trying to soak up every inch of him with greedy eyes. A long pink scar ran along his side, grabbing my attention. That wound...that wound had almost truly taken him from me.

I would thank God every day for the rest of my life that he passed him over.

Uprooting myself from the spot, I climbed into bed and wriggled close to him. Van tossed the book aside and wrapped his arms around me. He kissed the top of my head and turned out the light.

I could breathe again.

Chapter Thirty Nine

The last thing in the world I wanted to do was go to work. Van and I had only just been reunited and I had to tear myself away from him. But I had obligations and commitments to take care of. I talked it over with Evelyn and decided to quit my job. She didn't need the money, and had been saving what I'd given her, and planned to give it to me when it looked like I was branching out on my own. My heart swelled with love for the woman.

There was no reason for Van and me to be in New York anymore. We talked of traveling together, seeing old friends and making new memories. There was his mother, of course, but she would have been the first to encourage us to go. He was re-enrolled at Harvard for the fall semester, but that still gave us three months.

Sheila flashed me a cold smile as I exited the elevator. Grinning at her, I marched straight past and knocked on Jack's office door. He saw me through the glass panel and motioned for me to enter.

Jack stood up from his chair behind his desk. "I was worried yesterday when no one heard from you."

I cringed. If I weren't about to quit, I was sure I'd be getting fired. "I'm sorry, Jack, everything kind of fell out of my head yesterday."

He smiled. "I have a good idea why."

"He's back," I said on a breath. It didn't feel real saying it. I'd lost count how many times I'd had to pinch myself in the last day.

Jack chuckled and he looked younger, more at ease, than I'd seen in the entire time I'd worked at his firm. "I have a fair guess why you came to see me this morning."

I released a breath. This could go one of two ways — he could be understanding and wish me all the best...or angry that I was leaving after he'd given me a chance. "I came to hand in my notice."

"No notice required," Jack said, walking around his desk to stand in front of me. "You've been a pleasure to have around, Barb. A damn hard worker and good asset. But you were never cut out for this life, and I couldn't be happier you're leaving it." He opened his arms and I stepped into his embrace. "You two stop in from time to time, you hear?"

I nodded, wiping under my eyes and trying to preserve my makeup.

Jack smiled again and waved his hand toward the door. "Get out of here. I'm sure you have better things to be doing."

"Thank you, Jack. For everything." I turned on my heel and left his office. But before I left the building, there was someone else I had to see. Reed stood across the room, his eyes pinned on me. I crossed the distance, not caring about the dozens of ears leaning toward us. "Get a drink with me?"

Reed nodded and followed me to the elevator.

"I'm so sorry, Reed. I know I've been acting strange lately. A lot has been happening and — " I gushed the moment we sat in the back of a deserted bar.

He held a hand up to stop me and forced a smile. "No need to apologize. You made your feelings perfectly clear. Or lack of feelings."

My heart sank at his cold tone. "Reed, the last thing I wanted to do was hurt you. If I'd been honest with you, maybe you would have understood me a little better. I should have told you about — "

"Barb, I know. Save yourself the apology. I don't deserve it." Reed sighed. "I knew all about you and Van. I remembered the two of you at the ball four years ago, and I recalled Jack talking about the pair of you. I knew he enlisted and I knew he died. And I still pursued you."

I gasped. "All this time, you knew?"

He nodded, his eyes a mixture of sorrow and shame. "My intentions were never dishonorable. I only refrained from telling you because you didn't tell me. I thought you were trying to leave your baggage behind, instead of carting it into your new relationship."

"I didn't want any pity. And I didn't want you to feel second best," I said, reaching across the table to squeeze his hand. All I could hope for was that Reed one day forgave me. And I couldn't believe that I was his great love… There had to be something better out there for him.

"I always was, though," Reed said, trying to smile but failing miserably. "I knew that, and I accepted it." He blew out a breath and gave me a cautious look. "When I saw Van talking with Jack last week, it spurred me into motion. I confessed my love for you and hoped it would make you do the same. When you didn't, I knew

I would never be the one to capture your heart. It had already been done."

Everyone had known it was him. Everyone but me...
"I really am sorry, Reed."

He shook his head. "Don't be. We were never meant to be."

"You mean a lot to me," I said, pouring everything into the words so he knew how truthful I was being. "You helped me through a really dark time in my life. I will always owe you for that. But I was never the girl for you. You deserve someone much more passionate than me, someone who can return your love."

He smiled wistfully. "I appreciate your honesty with me, Barb."

"I'm only sorry I wasn't honest sooner."

Reed stood up and placed a hand on my shoulder. "Go be happy, Barb. If anyone deserves it, it's you."

I threw myself at him in a fierce hug. "You're such a kind man, Reed. You'll make some woman very happy."

* * * *

Van sat in the lounge with Evelyn when I arrived home. Evelyn rose from her seat and walked to my side. Raising a hand to touch my cheek, she said, "You have another guest."

It was then I saw there was another person in the room. Lois jumped to her feet and rushed across the room to throw her arms around my neck. I closed my eyes as we squeezed each other. It wasn't until now that I realized how much I'd missed her.

"Will you take a walk with me? A quick one, I promise," Lois said, sensing my hesitation to leave Van once again.

I cut a glance to Van. He smiled and gave a little nod. It was the last thing in the world I wanted to do—I'd already been gone longer than I anticipated that afternoon. But I couldn't shrug Lois off, either.

You have forever... You have forever.

Repeating my new mantra over and over in my head, I gave Lois a wide smile. We linked arms as we left the apartment. "I'm sorry I didn't return any of your phone calls. I was really busy, and then a little preoccupied," I said when we were out on the street.

Lois kissed my cheek. "You're forgiven," she said softly. "My main reason for coming was to make sure you were okay."

"I'm fine," I said with a confused frown. I had Van back—how could I not be okay?

"It must have been hard finding out that he was alive all this time."

Pain sliced across my chest. Now I knew what she meant. I still hadn't recovered from the shock, or the anger, that someone had caused us this agony when it wasn't even true. But most of all, I was just so, so thankful that he was here. That he was back. "Of course it was hard—it *is* hard. I haven't really had time to process my own thoughts. I just keep thinking of him, wondering how on earth he's coping with all he has been through."

Lois nodded in understanding.

"How bad was it, Lois?"

She blew out a breath. "I didn't know it was him until that first day I called you, I swear. I worked in a different wing of the hospital, and it was only when I overheard some other nurses talking about some crazy guy who was hell-bent on getting to Wellesley that I dared let myself think it could be him. A lot of patients we had went a little nuts and Van was no exception. His body was rife with disease when he first got back and was on the brink of starvation. It took a lot to heal him. But among all the things he said throughout his delirium, Wellesley was always the most prominent.

"I suppose they didn't realize it wasn't crazy ramblings, that he was actually serious about getting to Wellesley. When I heard what they said, I knew it was a long shot, but I had to see for myself. He saw me the second I entered the room, and grabbed my hand, begging me to let him out so he could find you. He was discharged the next day."

"How could they think he was crazy?" I asked.

Lois smiled wistfully. "Sweetie, he was for a while. Once the malaria haze shifted, he repeated a lot of the same stuff."

A shiver crept up my spine. "I'll never forgive myself for losing hope."

"It wasn't your fault, Barb," Lois said, stroking my arm. "It's a miracle he's here. Even when he got back, I found out it was touch and go for a long time. He'd gotten a pretty severe flesh wound out there. Even under normal circumstances, it would have been serious. It got infected, and it spread throughout his body."

"Flesh wound? How?" My eyes narrowed, thinking of the shiny pink scar.

"He was shot, grazed along the side of his stomach."

It really is a miracle he's here.

Lois let out a laugh after a quiet moment. "You have no idea how frustrating it was not to be able to talk to you, to tell you he was all right."

"I don't think I would have believed you," I admitted.

"What are you two going to do now?"

I shrugged. "We talked a little of traveling, seeing old friends." I nudged her with my elbow.

Lois laughed. "Oh, you must come see me in Washington!"

"We will, I promise." I grinned. "Right now, I think I just keep expecting to wake up, and find this was all some cruel dream."

"It isn't," Lois said softly. "This is no dream. You're wide awake, Barb, and everything is as it should be."

* * * *

Van wasn't in the apartment when I got back. Evelyn told me he'd gone back upstate to collect his things. He would be back before supper. Lois had gone back to her hotel, as she was leaving to go back to Washington the very next day. I was left with a gaping hole of unfilled time, unsure of what to do with myself.

I retreated to the safe confines of my room to hide my nose in a book. I could barely concentrate on the words. My head spun with everything that had happened these last few days. And now that I was alone with my thoughts, I couldn't help but worry.

Even with Van back, and knowing it was for good, our future was still as blank as it had been before Sunday. I had no idea where his head was, what he wanted or even expected. I knew how I felt, and knew that my life would not be anything if it didn't have him in it. But I had to understand that he wasn't the same Van who had left all those years ago. He was a new Van, a harder and colder version of my sweet love. His essence still remained the same, but there was a deep routed trauma that I doubted would ever shift.

What if this new Van didn't want me?

I stirred at a featherlight touch on my cheek. The room was dull when I shook off the last remnants of sleep. My book lay open on my chest, the pages crumpled. I yawned widely and clamped a hand over my mouth. A lazy smile spread across my face. "Hi."

Van's lips twitched. "Hi."

"You're back."

"Yup."

"Good."

Van lay down and pulled me toward him so I lay across his chest. No words needed to pass between us. I was exactly where I was supposed to be. Any doubts I'd had were gone.

* * * *

Van and I spent the rest of the week at Evelyn's. Neither of us were up to traveling yet, and were even less willing to share the other so fast. I woke with a start most nights. Every time I reached out for him, his space was always empty.

Van had difficulty sleeping. He joked and said it was because he wasn't used to a comfortable bed anymore. But I knew it went deeper than that. I would find him sitting at the foot of the bed, staring at nothing. Sometimes the red glow from a cigarette marked his spot, other times I had to feel around in the dark for him. At my waking, he would returned to bed with me.

Some nights we woke each other by crying out. I had terrible nightmares that he never came back at all. Van was haunted by images of the war. His cry was always more fearful than mine.

Our first week together taught us there was so much we had to learn about each other. Both of us had been changed, our cores rocked beyond recognition. I hadn't realized I was any different, but one bad night brought an unpleasant conversation, which revealed a few home truths.

"You used to sleep with me all night. I feel like I don't know you."

"We're different people now. It's only to be expected." Van soothed as he calmed me down after I'd woke in a cold sweat.

"But we shouldn't be!" I cried. "We promised everything would be the same. Before you went away, we swore we would pick up right where we left off."

Van pressed his forehead to mine. "Barb, neither of us anticipated what happened. We weren't prepared for it. We were children back then. I'm different, now. But so are you."

I sat upright. "*Me*? I haven't changed."

Van took my hand. "You have. You thought I wasn't coming back to you. The pain you went through, it changed you."

"In what way?" I asked, frowning.

"You've lost a bit of your fire, your natural spark." He smiled wistfully. "It's like you resigned yourself to lose and now there is no fight left in you."

I drew my knees up and hugged them.

"It's just going to take a little time to get to know each other again, that's all."

"What if you don't like me anymore?" I whispered.

Van wrapped his strong arms around my small shoulders. "No matter who you've become, Barb, I'll always love you."

I twisted around in his arms, leaning on his chest. "Promise?"

"Forever."

Chapter Forty

Anna's house was our first port of call. She flung open the front door and ran down the front walk the second we were out of the cab. She threw her arms around me before moving on to envelop Van in a fierce embrace. Her eyes were rimmed red when she let him go. Anna frowned, as though trying to say something, but she didn't know how. Instead, she took both our hands and pulled us toward the house.

Anna called up the stairs to Robert. The sound of a herd of baby elephants stampeding emerged from his bedroom as he bounded down to meet us. Robert skidded to a stop in front of Van, who raised an eyebrow at the small boy. "Are you a soldier?" Robert asked in awe.

Van laughed. "I was."

"Wow."

I looked at Anna, who shrugged. She'd obviously told Robert about Van. Robert tore his eyes away from Van, and his excitement mounted once again as he climbed up me. I lifted him the rest of the way and hugged him tightly. "How are you, little one?"

"I'm not little!" he exclaimed with an ear-piercing shriek.

I laughed. "All right. How are you, big one?"

Robert giggled into my neck. "Fine. Want to see my room?"

"Again?" I asked, groaning like it was the hardest chore anyone had ever set me.

"Uh-huh." He jumped from my arms and streaked up the stairs. Robert showed me everything he had at Christmas, and a few new items. Once he was satisfied I was appropriately impressed with said items, he let me go back downstairs.

Anna and Kenneth had made us a lovely meal of pot roast and Robert had thankfully passed through his *You taste everything, Barb* phase. He did, however, request that I put him to bed again. Once clarified with Anna on what kind of pajamas he had, I shooed him into the bathtub.

"Auntie Barb, can I ask you a question?" Robert asked as I tucked him in.

"Of course, sweetie, anything."

"Is Van your husband?"

I laughed quietly. "Why do you ask?"

"Because he holds your hand, like Daddy does with Mommy."

"Oh," I said softly. "Well, no, he isn't my husband."

"Do you want him to be?"

"Very much."

"He scares me."

I suppressed a laugh. "Why?"

"He's a soldier."

"He *was* a soldier. Not anymore."

"I think he's still scary."

"There is nothing to be scared of," I assured him. Glancing over my shoulder as if I was checking no one else was listening, I leaned closer to Robert and dropped my voice. "In fact, do you want to know a secret?"

His little eyes lit up, and he nodded.

"The best thing about soldiers?" I paused for dramatic effect. "They know how to make the *best* forts."

"Really?" Robert asked, sitting up in bed. Maybe I should have told him in the morning. He looked as though he would demand Van prove it there and then.

I nodded. "I bet if you ask Van real nice tomorrow, he'd build one with you."

"He would?"

"Only if you ask nice. And stop being scared of him." I tapped his button nose.

"Okay."

"Okay." I smiled and bent to kiss his forehead. "Sleep now."

Robert yawned and I crept from his room.

* * * *

Van had a friend for life after he built Robert his fort. He constructed it in the den, draping a sheet over the back of the couch and concealing the entrances with pillows. Robert played in it all day, and insisted on eating his lunch in it.

Robert fell in love with Van. He looked up to him with awe and wonderment in his young eyes after Van had built him his fort. Van, on the other hand, almost kept a distance between them and shied away from Robert's touch.

Van also seemed uncomfortable around Kenneth and Anna. Anyone else might put it down to Van feeling awkward because he hadn't seen them for years. But I started to think it was because he hadn't seen much loving human interaction in so long, and found it difficult to watch, as if he were intruding on a special moment not meant for his eyes.

I wondered if it was because he knew I spent each day expecting a proposal. He'd promised he would before he left. Had said it was the first thing he'd do when he got back. Maybe now it was him who wasn't ready.

Robert howled when we left two weeks later. We ventured to Washington, to visit Lois as promised. She was busy for the most part, so Van and I took the opportunity to sightsee around our nation's capital.

On her evenings off, Lois showed us around her haunts. She was forever being called on, waved to, hugged. But that was our Lois—she could make a lifelong friend in an empty room. She did, however, show a sign of change in her carefree personality. We all sat in a booth in one of Lois' favorite bars, and Van kissed the top of my head as he left to get drinks. She caught the intimate gesture and a hint of longing flashed on her pretty features. As quickly as it appeared, she wiped it from view, and dashed into her stream of excited chatter once again.

After Washington, Van and I took a trip to Yellow Sands, to make a few new memories. Each evening was spent dancing. I laid my head on Van's shoulder, blocking out everything except the two of us. The days saw us acting like children again. We took bike rides around the town, exploring nooks and crannies. We swam in the sea and sunbathed on the beach.

We didn't play tennis.

We stayed for three glorious weeks. I enjoyed every second of it and was melancholic on our last night. Van and I danced, pressed close like always, swaying in time to the music.

"You're quiet tonight," Van murmured in my ear.

"Am I? I don't mean to be."

"What's on your mind?"

I sighed and stroked the hair at his nape. "I was just thinking how I don't want this to end. You'll be starting school soon. I'll get a job somewhere."

"And this is a problem?" Van asked, letting out a chuckle.

My heart skipped a beat. Wasn't he upset? "To me it is. I feel like I've only just got you back, and now you're disappearing again."

"Hey," Van whispered, pulling back so he could see me. "I'm not going anywhere."

"But you are," I said with a frown. "It'll be like before — only seeing you at weekends."

Van's eyes searched mine. "Is that what you want?"

"No, not at all." I looked down. "Since you got back, I've had you with me every night. I don't think I could handle not having you sleep beside me anymore."

"Barb, like I said, I'm not going anywhere." He lifted my chin. "I'm not prepared to live without you. You said you don't think you could handle it? I *know* I couldn't. I need to be with you every single day for the rest of my life. It's as simple as that."

"Really?" I whispered. "Why didn't you say anything?"

Van shrugged. "I didn't think you would want to get a house with me. You said once you wouldn't bring that kind of shame to your family. I suppose, I thought you wouldn't want to live in sin with me."

"I would live in hell itself, if it meant I was with you."

Van smirked. "Careful, we may end up like Francesca and Paulo."

I smiled. "Like I said, hell itself."

* * * *

After Yellow Sands, we went back to stay with Evelyn for one final week before going to Boston to find accommodation.

Evelyn had missed us in our absence. She spoiled us rotten while we were there, and slipped Van a handsome check to help us get started in Boston. I'd miss Evelyn dearly, our connection ran deep now, and would never be broken. We both promised to stay in touch more often than we had in the past, and were welcome anytime in each other's homes.

Our farewells were tearful. Evelyn waved her hanky at us, the tears ruining her perfectly made-up face. Thomas had come also, and hugged me fiercely before I got on the train. I was pleased he came. I hadn't seen him much, with everything that had happened.

Butterflies fluttered with uncontained excitement as the train rolled out of the station. I bounced in my seat, not able to sit still for more than a few seconds. Van held my hands, and tried to hide his amusement.

It was midafternoon when Boston greeted us. I hadn't been back since the day I'd broken the window. I was eager to get started on the search for our new home, and Van allowed me to rush us out of the hotel once our bags had been left in the room.

Van knew his way around Boston far better than I did, and knew the right kind of area to begin our search. We trawled around the Harvard Square area for hours, trying to find the building that felt right for us. As I stood on the corner of Main and Pleasant, a large redbrick apartment building loomed over me. I turned farther onto Pleasant Street and looked up at it from a different angle. I loved the jutting bay windows and could visualize myself in the top window, reading in the sunlight or watching for Van.

I tugged on Van's arm, damn near hauling him into the building. We talked the manager into showing us around a recently vacated apartment on the top floor. I fell in love with it the second the door opened. The flooring was the shiniest mahogany wood. A beautiful ivory fireplace dominated the lounge. I walked across the room to peer out of the window. Kneeling on the cushioned window seat, I pressed my hands to the cool glass and looked down to the street below.

This was the window I'd pictured myself in, and now that I was there I knew I had to have it. Van winked at me, and slipped his hand into mine as we followed the manager around the rest of the apartment.

"Good starter home," the manager said as he locked the door. "You kids just starting out?"

"More like starting over." Van smiled, squeezing my hand.

I stood on the front stoop as Van talked with the manager. My fingers fumbled with my lighter as I lit a cigarette. It seemed like an age before Van emerged from the building, his face unreadable. He smiled at me and walked on.

I raced after him. "Well? What happened?"

"With what?" Van asked with an innocent smile.

Oh, the – I groaned. "You know what!"

"Oh, you mean the apartment?"

"Yes!" I cried. "What else?"

Van said nothing.

"Van?"

"Yes?"

"The apartment?"

"Oh, right." Van grinned. "When do you want to move in?"

There was a moment or two where the words sank in. Once they had, I shrieked and launched myself on him. Van lifted me off my feet, almost crushing my bones in his tight embrace. "Tomorrow! Now! Yesterday!" I laughed.

Van sighed into my neck. "I had a feeling you might say that." He fished in his pocket and dangled a set of keys in front of my nose.

Another squeal escaped and I kissed him in a way that should really be reserved for private.

* * * *

The previous owner of the apartment had died, and his family was leasing it out via the building manager. They'd taken all the furnishings, but Van had assured the manager we could bring our own things. Van had received a lump sum from the army and together with savings he already had and the check from Evelyn, we didn't have to worry about affording furniture.

The next three weeks were spent scouring furniture stores and yard sales. It took a little time, but was worth it in the end. At the beginning of the fourth week, all that was needed in the apartment was us. The dishes and crockery were in the kitchen cupboards and the refrigerator was fully stocked. The bed had been delivered and had been made up with fresh linen. We'd bought a thick cream rug for the center of the lounge and a mahogany coffee table. Our couch was also cream, and luxuriously comfortable. A tiny two-seater table lived in the kitchen where I looked forward to spending the mornings drinking coffee and reading the papers with Van.

An enormous built-in bookcase ran the length of one wall in the lounge, and I itched to fill it. Evelyn sent the rest of my things, and as I unpacked my life, it was hard not to notice how sparse Van's possessions were.

"Van?"

"Hmm?" he asked, not lifting his eyes from the book he read while lounging on the couch.

"What happened to all your things before you left?"

"I gave everything to Goodwill," he said, turning the page. "I didn't have anywhere to store it all and it was only clothes and books." Van looked up and flashed me a wink. "You have all my favorites anyway."

Still flustered that he'd given his life away, I stood up and shoved my hands on my hips. "Well, you'll need some new things for going back to school."

Van's lips twitched. "Yes, Mom."

We slept in the apartment for the first time that night.

Not that a great amount of sleeping happened...

When eventually our appetites were sated, Van gave in to sleep first. I lay in our warm bed, just watching him. A tiny frown pinched between his eyebrows — the sign that even in sleep he wasn't truly at ease.

This was where I was meant to be. I'd finally found my way home.

Chapter Forty-One

The week before Van started again as a freshman at Harvard Law, our country rejoiced. Like the day Pearl had been hit, people ran from house to house, shouting for others to turn on their radio. One of our neighbors banged on our door. Van swung it open to see the lad thump with his fist on the other doors.

"What are you doing?" Van asked.

"Turn on your radio!"

My stomach dropped. Fear grasped at my heart, terrified of what the radio would tell us. I still didn't follow the war closely, bad as that sounds. It reminded me too much of the pain I'd felt. It brought back too many unwelcome reminders, and my heart always broke as I thought of other women whose men were still abroad.

Van clicked the radio on. President Harry S. Truman's voice filled the room, and brought with it the news we longed to hear.

The war was over.

My eyes welled up and spilled over, dripping down my face and onto my dress. Van and I fell into each other, holding the other up. It was over. We were free from danger. The world celebrated that day, but we also mourned. Our losses had been great, but our victory had been greater. Never again would we be crippled. Never again would we be a target for our enemies. America had grown strong, and we would do everything in our power to remain that way forever.

We could have gone down to the bar on the corner, whose patrons celebrated loud enough for us to hear all the way up in our apartment. Instead, we chose to be unsociable. We stayed in our home all evening, drinking highballs and dancing around the coffee table. The cloud had been chased away, and my sun was finally shining high in the sky again.

I wished President Roosevelt could have been alive to see this day. He had been taken into God's divine paradise on April 12th after suffering a cerebral hemorrhage. The *New York Times* had said, '*Men will thank God on their knees a hundred years from now that Franklin D. Roosevelt was in the White House...*'

The world seemed able to breathe again, every person letting out the four-year-long breath we'd all been holding. When I woke in the night, groggy from my highball haze, I found Van sleeping soundly next to me, his forehead smooth and unblemished — a first since he had returned.

* * * *

My days were long and tiresome when Van started his classes. He told me I didn't have to get a job if I didn't want to. I'd been toying with the idea of going to grad school next fall, but the thought of my days being that boring for an entire year was just depressing.

While reading the newspaper over coffee and a cigarette one morning, a job advertisement caught my eye. Newman Prep was looking for elementary teachers. As with most jobs, the war had diminished the supply of teachers. Once Van had left for his morning lecture, I called the principal and set up a meeting.

Mr. Warren, at first glance, seemed severe. He peered down at me under heavyset eyebrows, but he softened once he got talking. I guessed the façade was for the benefit of the pupils. He was impressed with my level of study at Wellesley, and said that it didn't really matter I hadn't had any teaching experience before. At this time, no one could afford to be picky. The teaching spot was for the third grade, and Mr. Warren asked if I'd be interested in meeting the class. I jumped at the chance. They were a great group of kids and I warmed to them in an instant.

I asked Mr. Warren if I could sit in with the class for the rest of the day, and watched how the substitute teacher handled things. It seemed challenging and I had no idea how on earth I would ever pull it off. But by the end of the day, I found myself eager to try the challenge.

Mr. Warren and I talked it over, and he assured me the lesson plans were very structured and had been prepared for that semester in advance already, so all I needed to do was follow it. The other teachers were very friendly and would be able to help me with anything if I needed it.

I started the next week.

That night I cooked Van a steak dinner and poured a generous amount of Scotch into a glass for him. He raised an eyebrow as he came home and caught me lighting candles.

I crossed the room to meet him and captured him in a passionate kiss before he could utter a word.

"Is this how we say hello now? I like it," Van mumbled against my lips.

I broke away and pulled him toward the couch. I pushed him down and sat on his lap. "Guess what."

"What?" Van asked, pulling me closer to kiss my neck.

"I got a job today."

"Oh?" he said, and I doubted he was even following the conversation.

"Don't you want to know where?" I asked.

"Not right now," Van whispered, unbuttoning my dress. I slapped his hand away and he laughed. "Sorry. Right, job. What kind of job?" Van asked, a visible sign of concentration on his face.

"Teaching. At Newman Prep."

"Really?" Van's eyebrows lifted. "Barb, that's great. Really. When do you start?"

"Monday."

"I think I'd better take you out to celebrate."

"I already took care of that."

Van twisted around and saw the table set in the kitchen. "Is dinner ready right now?"

I nodded. "It's keeping warm in the oven. I just need to dish it up."

"Will it keep?"

"Yes, why?"

Van stood up, lifting me in his arms. I giggled as he pushed open the bedroom door and kicked it shut behind us. "Because we have celebrating to do. And it may take a while."

* * * *

It felt as though the roles were reversed as I walked up the steps toward the school. I recalled again the fear I'd felt on my first day at Wellesley, but that fear was nothing compared to now. I pushed open the staff room door and the occupants fell silent. My smile wobbled, showing my nerves.

Mr. Warren crossed the room to stand by my side. "Everyone, this is Barbara Howell, our new third grade teacher. Be nice."

The ages of the other teachers ranged considerably. Some women looked positively archaic, a few of the men, like Mr. Warren, seemed to be my father's age. A couple didn't seem much older than I. Mr. Warren patted my shoulder and vacated the room, leaving me to face the pack alone.

"Hi, I'm Clara Roberts." A vivacious redhead stepped in front of me. Her eyes were fierce as she assessed me, and I was instantly terrified. I had a feeling this was not a woman whose bad side you wanted to be on.

"Hi," I squeaked.

Clara hitched her thumb to the crowd of teachers. "Don't let these jerks scare you, probably just jealous 'cause half of them are dead from the neck down."

I stifled a laugh, shocked she didn't even attempt to lower her voice.

She moved to the row of cubbies. "You can use this pigeonhole, and just keep your things with you in the classroom closet. Do you know where it is?"

I nodded.

"Come on, I'll come with you to help set up." Clara turned on her heel, not looking back to see if I followed. I did. "They each have their own set desk, their things are inside." She looked me up and down. "Though, I'm sure you remember — couldn't have been all that long ago for you."

I stared at her, the insult taking a long second to sink in. "I'm twenty-five."

Clara did a double take. "Remind me to borrow your night cream."

Ha. I smiled.

Clara showed me where all the supplies were, and the roster and seating plan for the class. I scribbled my name on the chalkboard, noticing my hand shake as I did.

"All set?" Clara asked.

I nodded.

"Good. My classroom is across the hall, yell if you need anything." Clara swung the door open. "Oh, and try to brave it up. They can smell fear, you know." She winked and slammed the door shut, causing the glass to wobble in the frame.

I sat behind my desk, looking out over the rows of empty little ones in front of me. The bell rang through the corridors, marking the beginning of the day. The once vacant hallways teemed with children.

Letting out a long breath, I steeled myself and rose from my seat to open the classroom door. A steady stream of children filled in. They took their seats, and the last few stragglers came in, panting from the run.

"Can everyone take their seats please," I called, surprised my voice was level. The command had been received, yet one or two still pushed their luck and slinked toward their empty desks as if they had all the time in the world. "Now," I said, in a firmer voice. That seemed to do the trick, and a room full of students looked up at me with expectant eyes.

"Good morning, everyone," I said, with a smile. "My name is Ms. Howell. At the beginning of every day I'd like you to find your seats immediately, no loitering." I looked pointedly at the guilty party. They had the decency to look ashamed. "We'll do roll call every morning, all right? Now today, since we're getting to know each other, when I call your name, I'd like you to stand up and say a bit about yourself."

The children looked terrified.

I stood a little taller.

As I rattled off names, each child stood in turn and mumbled a few incoherent words. After a few had done this, the others slowly got more confident, and weren't as shy. By the time the last child had spoken, they all looked thoroughly relaxed.

We did math for the rest of the morning, and reading and art after lunch. When the bell rang to mark the end of the day, I thought I would drop dead on my feet. As enjoyable as it had been, it was definitely tiring.

I checked my cubbyhole before leaving, and saw the staff room deserted. I guessed not many of them stuck around longer than they had to.

My first week flew in, and the second and the third. By the end of the fourth, I felt as if I knew what I was doing. My students had warmed to me, and I was lucky to have such a well-behaved class. The majority of them seemed keen to learn, and always pestered me for further information.

Van said he loved the change in me. I had a purpose now, and it showed. We settled into a quiet routine, and it could not have been any more perfect.

Chapter Forty-Two

"I have a surprise for you," Van said, coming up behind me and kissing my shoulder.

I grinned and twisted around from my seat at the kitchen table to peer up at him. "Oh?"

He nodded. "We're going out tonight."

My heart lifted. "Where? Do I need to dress up?"

"No, you look beautiful anyway." Van winked. "But don't let that stop you."

I opted for my black wraparound dress, which I knew he loved. I was excited as we got into the car, with no idea where the destination was. Only minutes into the journey, I recognized the route. Forty minutes later, my suspicions confirmed, Van drove us along the familiar streets of Wellesley. He slowed to a stop outside the Lakeside. Grinning, Van hopped out of the car and ran around to open my door. He took my hand to help me out, and gave it a quick squeeze.

Van fidgeted during the meal. Once I even saw his hand shake as he raised his glass to his mouth. "Feel like a drink somewhere?" he asked once our plates were gone and glasses drained.

"I can only think of one bar around here," I said with a wide grin.

The Dragon had changed none. Joe was no longer there, having long since left for bigger and better things, I hoped. The walls were the same putrid green, the floor still littered with broken peanut shells. A crowd of college kids took over the pool area. Van guided me to a stool in front of the bar, and ordered us a couple of highballs.

"Any particular reason for all this?" I asked, arching an eyebrow.

"Thought you might appreciate a trip down memory lane." Van smiled.

It seemed a million years ago that I used to frequent this bar. I could almost hear Lois' pealing laughter coming from one of the booths. We'd all had so many good times in the bar, ones I cherished dearly.

"Feel like taking a walk?" Van asked as I sipped the last of my drink.

While it was nice being somewhere so familiar, doing anything with Van — be it just a walk — was always the sweeter option. I nodded, my heart giving a little jolt as Van slipped his hand into mine.

It was colder again. I wrapped my coat tighter around me. My breath steamed the air, creating a mist as I spoke. "It seems like so long ago, doesn't it?"

Van caught my meaning. "It was. We aren't the same college kids anymore."

I leaned into him. "I think we're something better."

"Do you remember the first time I walked you home?"

"I remember everything," I said quietly.

"This town holds some good memories, doesn't it?"

"Some? Try a lot." I grinned. My smile drooped a little. "A few bad ones too."

Van paused, placing a hand on my arm. "I'll spend the rest of my life making it up to you, Barb. I wish there was a way to release you from the memory of that pain."

Shaking my head, I stepped into his body and rested my hand on his chest. "There's no need. All it's done is make me appreciate you all the more. Take nothing for granted, and enjoy everything."

He dropped his gaze to the sidewalk. "I heard you talking to Robert that first night at Anna's. When he asked you if I was your husband."

I blinked at the sudden turn in conversation. "Yes, he did. He also said he was scared of you."

Van frowned. "Do you remember your answer? Do you still mean it?"

"Do I still want to marry you?" My eyes widened. "Of course. I think about it every day. You... Before you left, you said the first thing you were doing when you got back was proposing. But you never did."

"I couldn't," Van said, his voice thick with emotion. "So much had happened. I had to be sure it was what you still wanted. I needed to wait, until we knew each other again." He let out a laugh. "I had to bite my tongue every day from not blurting out the question."

My heart began to pick up speed, a lump forming in my throat.

Van sighed shakily. "Remember that first time I walked you? I gave you something that night."

"Your scarf." I smiled. "I still have it."

"How would you like to wear something else of mine for a while?" He knelt down in the street, his knee in a puddle, and opened a black velvet jewelry box, revealing a sparkling diamond. Delicate and extraordinary, it was quite possibly the most beautiful thing I'd ever seen. The ring's center diamond was embedded in a platinum setting, flanked by rose-cut diamonds in an aerial wing arrangement.

My tears were cold against my cheek. Words could not describe the emotions that flooded through me. I laughed through my tears, nodding furiously.

"Is that a yes?" Van asked, his voice thick.

I laughed again and bent into his arms. I kissed every inch of his face, almost toppling him over. In a fluid movement, Van lifted us from the ground and held me to him. He spun me around, a laugh escaping him. He set me on my feet, and his hand was shaking as he slid the beautiful ring onto my finger. A perfect fit. It would stay there for the rest of my days.

* * * *

I couldn't stop staring at my ring. I pressed against Van's chest during the drive home, and kept holding my hand out in front of me and wiggling my fingers. Van kissed my head, telling me with his kisses how happy he was.

The second our front door locked, I jumped into his arms, kissing him with everything I had. We made love all night long until the sun beamed through the thin drapes, lighting the room. Exhausted and ravenous, we lay among the crumpled sheets.

"Are you happy?" Van asked, tracing lines up and down my stomach.

"Gloriously, desperately, unbelievably happy." I grinned.

Van kissed my belly button. "How do you feel about leaving all the details to me?"

"You mean the wedding?" I laughed. "I had no idea you were such a woman, Mr. Judson."

Van rolled his eyes. "I just have a few ideas that I'd like to be a surprise, that's all."

Laughing, I ran my fingers through his soft hair. "Whatever you want, my love." And if it meant I didn't have to argue with my mother on details, all the better.

He flashed me a lopsided smiled before capturing my mouth in another breathtaking kiss.

* * * *

I dropped the phone in fright as my mother screamed. I picked it up, and said, "Mom — are you there?"

Silence.

Just as I began to think I'd given my dear old mother a heart attack, my father came on the phone. "Barb? What the hell did you say to your mother? She's sat on the floor crying her eyes out."

"Van and I are getting married."

More silence.

Sighing, I lit a cigarette. This could take a while.

* * * *

Van remained elusive about everything wedding related. All he told me to do was find a dress. I knew he was in cahoots with Lois and my mother, as there was plenty of hushed phone calls and abrupt conversation changes should I walk into the room.

The Monday after Van proposed, Clara caught sight of my engagement ring. She cooed over it so loudly a small crowd gathered to see what the fuss was about. The following day, one of the older teachers brought in a cake for us all to share.

Lois came to visit a few days after I called her. The second she saw me, she ran across the train station. Dropping her suitcase at her feet, Lois threw her arms around me. There were tears in her eyes as she pulled away from me. She demanded we go dress shopping right away.

I showed her my apartment first, and she loved it. There was only one downfall she said with hand on hip, she wanted to know why we hadn't considered her when taking the apartment, as she didn't have her own room.

Lois was the perfect person to shop for wedding dresses with. She was brutally honest in her opinions, and found some good selections. But every one I tried on just didn't feel right. Lois' patience began to wear thin as I declined what had to be the thirtieth dress of the day.

We walked the streets for hours, searching the racks of every bridal dress store. We stumbled upon a tiny one, down some back street, completely by accident. A bell chimed as we opened the door, and the musky smell of vintage fabric wafted under our noses. Most of the dresses were hideous, not even worth trying on. But one stood out from all the others.

Like with the apartment, and even with Van himself, something felt right when I looked at the dress. Lois smiled as I met her eyes, and spoke in a rushed voice to try it on. My heart thudded in my chest as I looked at myself in the full-length mirror.

Lois' eyes filled with tears for the second time that day. "Barb..." she choked.

It had a sweetheart neckline that flattered my feminine shoulders. And the fitted bodice with built-in bone corset was decorated with floral appliqués and small pearls. The bustline was encircled by horizontal pleating and also the short sleeves. It ended in a point at the center of the front and back of the gown. The full skirt gathered into the bodice and lace decorated the hemline. I'd found my wedding dress.

* * * *

"Do we *have* to go?" I yawned as Van locked the apartment door.

"Yes," he sighed, lifting the suitcases and leading the way downstairs.

"Why?" I pressed.

"Because it's Christmas and they're your parents," Van said, agitated by my persistent questioning.

"But we'd have a much better time if we stayed here." I pouted. "Just imagine — it could be like Thanksgiving, all those years ago."

Van gave me a pained expression but quickly removed it. "Look on the bright side, Anna and Robert will be there. It isn't like you're facing your mother on your own."

I brightened at this. "I guess you're right."

Van and I were catching the early train, since we left a day later than intended. My attempts at persuasion had worked a little better the day before. I dozed for most of the journey to New York. As we boarded our connection train, I wished we were visiting with Evelyn instead.

My mother pulled us into stiff hugs when we met her at the station. Dad winked at me, and patted Van on the back. Mother informed us Kenneth, Anna and Robert had already arrived, and were also staying at their house. My parents only had a three-bedroom house... I arched an eyebrow at my father, who shook his head.

The house erupted into excitement when we arrived. Anna and I hugged tearfully as always, Kenneth and Van slopped off to a corner to escape the theatrics, and Robert danced about, trying to get among some of the excitement.

"Where is everyone sleeping?" I whispered to Anna in the kitchen, out of earshot.

She looked amused. "Kenneth, Robert and I are having my room. Mom put an old cot down for Robert to sleep on. And you and Van are to have your bedroom."

I clasped a hand over my mouth to stop my laughter. "*Really*? I would never have thought Mother would allow that."

Anna rolled her eyes. "You two are engaged. And you've been living together for long enough now. I don't think she sees the point in keeping you separated."

I giggled. *Wow.*

* * * *

Christmas passed with new excitement that year. The past few had been so dull and laced with depression, it was a pleasant change to invite in the merriment. It was all made more special since Robert was at the perfect age for it. He knew all about Christmas and how it was cause for great excitement. We all spoiled him rotten and loved every second of it.

Anna and I helped Mom cook Christmas lunch, and for once, not an argument passed between us. I looked forward to New Year's. For three years I'd loved the parties, then they developed a dark edge to them. The last New Year's party I attended, Van had told me he was enlisting. I planned to spend every second of this coming party with him, and dance with him as often as my shoes would permit. I vowed to bring in the New Year with love in my heart, and safe in the knowledge that nothing stood in the way of Van and I any longer.

The house was in a state of frenzy when I woke on December 31st. Van's side of the bed was empty and I could hear a ruckus downstairs. Swinging my legs out of bed, I pulled on my robe and padded down stairs. Activity ceased when I entered the kitchen. Mom poured me a cup of coffee and placed a plate of pancakes under my nose. Everyone avoided my eye.

Glancing around, I couldn't see Van. My stomach dipped. "Where's Van?"

My father didn't look up from his newspaper. "He went for a run with Kenneth."

"I'm going to church later," Anna said, drawing my attention to her. "Do you want to come?"

I thought back to Trinity Church and Father Morgan. I owed a great deal of gratitude to him, and to the church. They'd helped me through a very dark time in my life. "Absolutely."

Anna smiled. "We'll leave in an hour."

* * * *

Anna and I walked arm in arm toward the little church in town. She pushed open the double oak doors and looked at me over her shoulder with a wide smile. I chuckled in confusion at her expression, but it died in my throat when she Anna stepped to the side and I saw the church beyond her.

Beautiful white flowers adorned the end of each pew, trails of white ribbon bows cascading to the floor. "Isn't there a service on this morning?" I asked, looking at my sister in confusion.

"That's later," Anna said, walking to the rear of the church. "Come this way." She pulled open the doors and walked down a narrow hallway.

"Anna? I don't think you're allowed in here," I called as I followed after her.

She turned to grin at me, before opening another small door. "That dress doesn't suit you," Anna said facing me, with her hands on hips.

I looked down. "What's wrong with it?"

She frowned. "Nothing, not really. I just think this one would suit you better today." Anna folded back a screen and my wedding dress hung on a rail.

"I don't understand." *What?* Van hadn't ever told me a date — I'd just assumed he hadn't set one yet.

"You're getting married today." Anna's eyes welled up. "Van has been planning for months. Me, Mom, Lois, we were all in on it. We've been helping him plan this. For you, for today."

A single tear slid down my cheek. "Today?"

"Soon," Anna said with a nod. "Well, no time for crying now. We need to get ready."

I threw my arms around Anna's bony shoulders. "Thank you, Anna."

"What? No thanks for me?"

Spinning around, Lois stood grinning. I pulled her into the hug, too, the three of us laughing and crying like three strange, normal women.

When our tears stopped, Anna and Lois set to work styling my hair and doing my makeup. They lifted the dress over my head and Lois tightened the corset within an inch of my life.

Breathing wasn't an option today, apparently.

Lois had told Van where my dress was, and had sent the woman a check to make sure it would be ready on time, and to send it to my mother to keep. Lois and

Anna found their own bridesmaids dresses, beautiful champagne-colored straight dresses. No puffiness in sight. Sighing with relief, I guessed my mother hadn't been given much control.

Lois lit me a cigarette, as I found pacing too difficult in my dress to calm my nerves. A gentle tap at the door broke my train of nervous thought. Anna opened it wide to let in my mother. Lois and Anna shared a look and disappeared out through the door.

"You shouldn't smoke in your dress," she said with a stern frown.

I rolled my eyes. "Not today, Mom, please."

Mom sighed. "Sorry." She touched my cheek. "You look so beautiful."

"Why? Because I'm in a wedding dress?" The words were out before I even realized I'd said them.

Mom looked down. Regret invaded my mother's eyes as she raised them to meet mine. "I've only ever wanted the best for you, Barbara. I may not have projected my views very subtly in the past, and for that I apologize." She sighed. "You were always so much better than all of us."

"I—"

She raised a hand to hush me. "You were—*are*—better than us. I knew it, and it frightened me. You have always been so fiercely independent, so strong and brave. I admired you. Anna was the sweet one, but you— You were different. We knew Anna would have no trouble finding love and be content with it. But I was so scared that you would never find anyone." Mother laughed quietly. "I know, I know, having a husband doesn't necessarily make you happy. But life sure can be lonely without one. I only ever wanted you to have *everything* life has to offer.

"I am so proud of you today, Barb. And I'm so sorry I pushed you for all those years. If I had just let you be, who knows, maybe you would have had this sooner."

I squeezed her hand, trying to force away the tears. "If you had, I wouldn't be here today. Because of my stubbornness, I refused to give any man a second look, until Van. If you'd never forced any opinions on me, I may have married the first bum who proposed." I laughed. "So, thank you. *You* are the reason I'm here, and for who I am."

My mother cupped my face and kissed my cheek. I clutched her wrists, leaning into her "He's a lucky man, Barb. I know you will take good care of him."

"Thanks, Mom."

She smiled. "Come on, I think there is someone waiting for you." Mom took my hand as we walked out of the room. My father waited for me in the hallway, pacing back and forth while wringing his hands.

Mom squeezed my hand before entering the church.

Dad stared at me for a long, hard moment before blowing out a breath. "There are certain things a father is supposed to say to his daughter before she walks down the aisle. But I can't think of any."

I laughed, but stopped when I saw the emotion mounting in his eyes and hugged him instead. "Love you, Dad."

He choked out a few undeterminable words.

A few moments later, the wedding march started. It was time.

Anna walked down first, followed by Lois. Robert walked painfully slowly, his little pink tongue poking out of the side of his mouth as he concentrated. He carried a pillow, which I knew would carry the rings. Finally, it was time for me and Dad.

I thought I was going to faint, throw up, everything. I had no idea how my legs held me up as I couldn't even feel them. My stomach rolled in summersaults. Every piece of intelligence I held in my brain somehow escaped out of my ear. How would I be able to repeat the vows? I doubted I could say anything intelligible.

Only a second had passed. Robert was one-third of the way down the aisle, and it was time for me to start walking. As I lifted my foot to take that first step, my fingers dug in tightly to my father's arm, whose name I had now forgotten. I raised my eyes, locking them with Van's. In that instant, all my fear dissolved.

There was nothing to be afraid of — it was me and Van. What was scary about that? I floated toward him, everyone else falling from my sight. There was only him. I was dimly aware of my father kissing my cheek before placing my hand in Van's, which trembled.

Apparently the sight of me hadn't cured Van of his fears. I grinned at him, which seemed to ease his discomfort a touch.

Our eyes never left the others, not once. Our vows were recited perfectly, not one word stumbled over. Time stood still as Van kissed me, our first kiss of many as husband and wife. I thought I'd burst as pure contended happiness coursed through my veins.

The room exploded into applause, but I couldn't pick out a single face. I bit my lip as I touched my forehead against Van's. Van held my hand tightly as we walked out of the church to stand on the front steps for pictures.

It was a lot of fun, though we tended to get lost in each other's eyes and had to be prompted to turn and smile at the camera. Lois, Anna and I had our picture taken together, and lots of group ones.

Van and I stood for one final picture. Something cold touched my cheek. And my hand. I looked up, and tiny snowflakes kissed my face. Laughing, I threw my hands up and twirled around. Grinning, Van caught me and spun me. I clung to him, and kissed my gorgeous husband.

* * * *

New Year's Eve, 1945

A few of us went for an intimate lunch at a nearby restaurant. Mother had baked our wedding cake herself, big enough for everyone to have a slice. Robert grew fussy and whined that his suit itched. Anna and Kenneth took him back home to get changed. Lois and Evelyn winked at each other, before disappearing. Mom and Dad made their excuses to leave soon after, and it was just my husband and me.

We caught a cab to the bed and breakfast Van had booked for us. He helped me out of my dress, and I could finally take a deep breath. "Better?" He shrugged out of his jacket.

I nodded and reached for Van's tie to pull him toward me. An amused smile twitched his lips. "Isn't there another tradition we should be doing?" I asked, raising an eyebrow.

Van lifted me up with ease and kissed me hard on the mouth. I wrapped my legs around him as he carried me to the bed.

* * * *

Van held me for the longest time. I stroked his face as his fingers traced delicate lines up and down my thigh. It was bizarre to think that six years had passed since our first encounter at the New Year's party. Six long years that had seen so much change. It didn't matter how long the journey had been, or how painful. We were exactly where we needed to be.

As the darkness crept in from the fading day, I vowed I would spend every day showing my love for Van. He would know exactly how he made me feel, and how extraordinary everything seemed with him by my side.

Van took my hand and kissed it. "We should get up."

I wriggled closer to him. "No."

Van sighed. "Barb…"

"Let's stay here. It's cold outside."

"Maybe, but we have a party to get to."

"We do?" I asked, confused.

He nodded and leaped from the bed. "You can't skip out on your own wedding reception." He opened a case and pulled out a beautiful cream dress. I reached out to touch the cool silk fabric. Van winked at me before disappearing into the bathroom.

We got dressed and Van called us a cab to take us to the reception. Van hadn't arranged a traditional reception—he knew I'd hate the fuss. Instead, we were all going to the same New Year's party we always had. Mother had invited more people, and the bar and band knew we were coming, and promised to accommodate us all.

We were inundated with hugs, well-wishes and drinks. Faces I didn't recognize congratulated me. The evening felt surreal. Van and I danced often, and he always looked disappointed should anyone else cut in.

Thomas had escorted Evelyn to our wedding, and another few Manhattanites were also present. Jack Tate and his wife Camilla came, much to our delight. They also brought another guest with them. Reed stood at the bar, holding his drink like a life raft. I could feel his awkwardness radiating off him in waves. I left Van with Jack and Camilla, and cautiously approached Reed.

Reed's face warmed when he saw me coming. He allowed me hug him, not letting it last too long.

"I have to say, I'm surprised to see you," I said, taking a step back to give him his space.

Reed's face flushed. "Jack asked if I wanted to come. I wanted to congratulate you."

His kindness knew no bounds. Once again, I regretted the hurt I'd caused him. "You didn't have to, Reed."

"I know." He smiled, but it didn't quite meet his eyes. "I suppose...I wanted to make sure you were happy. You are happy, aren't you?"

I smiled softly. "Very."

"I'm pleased. Really, I am."

I searched his eyes and found them almost truthful.

"Can I get you a drink?" Reed asked, already motioning for the bartender. "White wine, please."

Reed handed me the glass and I took a tiny sip.

There was a pause, an awkward break in the conversation. "How's the office?" I asked weakly.

A grin spread across Reed's handsome face—seeming happy with the small talk. "Oh you know, gossip and crime. The usual."

I grinned with him and felt an arm around my waist. Van kissed my cheek. "Damn, it's hot in here."

"It is." I agreed, leaning into him.

"Hi there," Van said, smiling at Reed and extending his hand. "I'm Van."

Reed shook it. "Reed Walker."

Van nodded in recognition. "Jack's told me a lot about you. Sounds like you have a promising career ahead of you." Van glanced at the wine glass in my hand and laughed. He asked the bartender for two glasses of neat Scotch. "Where did you get that? You hate wine." Van swapped the wine glass for a Scotch tumbler.

I blushed.

"You hate wine?" Reed asked, his eyes intent on my face.

Van smirked and gave me an amused look. "Nah, not really. It just makes her sick."

Camilla approached us and dragged Van off in the direction of the dance floor. He kissed my cheek and laughed as he was kidnapped.

"Is that true? It makes you sick?" Reed asked.

My blush burned my cheeks. "Only if I have too much."

"I never knew you at all, did I?"

I placed my hand over his on the bar. "In a way, no, you didn't. The Barb you knew, she wasn't real. It was like I'd been shut down, and my shadow was all that remained. I only let you see my shadow."

Reed paused a moment before smirking. "I'm glad. If that was just a shadow, I don't think I'm man enough to handle the whole thing."

Huffing, I swatted him on the arm and a weight lifted from my shoulders. "How come you aren't dancing?" I asked, eager to change the subject.

Reed shrugged. "No one has asked me."

I laughed. "I only know one woman here who would ask a man to dance." A flash of genius struck my mind and I knew how I could make everything up to Reed. He deserved someone, and would be a good man for any woman. But he was a very subtle man, and needed his partner to be passionate. I could think of one person. "How would you like to meet a friend of mine?"

I led him to a faraway table, where Lois hovered, smoking a cigarette and shifting her hips in time to the music. "Lois, I'd like you to meet my friend, Reed." I turned to Reed, who looked flabbergasted in the face of my beautiful friend. "Reed, this is my darling friend, Lois."

I flitted a glance between their faces. Reed wore a goofy smile, holding out his hand to shake Lois'. And Lois, looked, well, different. A scarlet blush stained her creamy cheeks. She let out a nervous laugh.

I nudged Reed with my elbow.

"Would you care to dance?" Reed asked.

Lois nodded, and Reed pressed a hand to her lower back, guiding her toward the dance floor.

A pair of arms snaked around my middle. Van rested his chin on my shoulder. "What are you up to?"

"Making amends," I said.

"Feel like a dance?"

I turned around in his arms. "I don't know, what would my husband say?"

Van arched an eyebrow. "I think he shouldn't have been stupid enough to leave his beautiful wife unattended."

"So do I. It had better not happen again." Ever. Ever, ever.

Van's breath was hot on my lips as he leaned closer. "Definitely not."

"Good," I mumbled against his lips.

Van chuckled. "Come on, woman. We're going to miss it, if you keep this up."

"Miss what?"

"Midnight." Van clutched my hand as he led me through the throng of people. Finding a good spot on the dance floor, he pulled me into his body.

I laid my head on Van's shoulder, peering out at the crowd of familiar faces. Thomas spun Evelyn around the dance floor with ease and she tipped her head back to laugh at his antics. Reed and Lois wore soft, intimate smiles as they moved slowly to the music. Paul, who had remained Van's best friend throughout all these years, and made it home safely from Europe, chased a poor waitress, who didn't look all that upset at having a handsome man follow her around. Anna and Kenneth danced with Robert, a happy little trio.

At Anna's wedding, Van had told me something that had never really occurred to me before this moment. Looking at my friends, at my beloved family, I realized Van's words had come true.

I had found my people.

I wrapped my arm around Van's shoulders and burrowed my face in his neck. Taking a deep gulp of pure Van, he drowned my senses in his intoxicating scent.

"You know, they say how you spend New Year's Eve is how you will spend the rest of the year," Van whispered.

The band started their countdown.

I pressed my cheek against his. "Then kiss me quick, and it will be a very pleasurable year."

Van's hands framed my face as the room exploded. His eyes pierced my soul, which was forever entwined with his.

"I'll love you forever, Mrs. Judson."

I closed my eyes and smiled. "Say that again."

He touched his lips to my ear. "I'll love you forever, Mrs. Judson."

A delicious shivered snaked up my spine. My lips found his and I couldn't stop kissing my husband... My beautiful husband. As though it were the first time, every cell in my body ignited and roared to life.

I would remember that moment forever.

Chapter Forty-Three

I felt a little sad leaving my family. Mom and I had wrapped a bandage around our broken relationship, and given enough time, it would begin to heal. Anna and I cried as we always did, and Robert was upset that he couldn't come with us. Evelyn stayed behind for a while, reacquainting herself with the town she'd grown up in.

We waved from the window on the train, smiling at the small gathering of friends and family. We'd see them soon enough.

Van lifted his arm for me to rest my head on his chest. I could hear every heartbeat, and lost myself to its rhythm. What a year it had been. On reflection, it was one of the best years I'd ever experienced. The war had ended, Van had returned to me, and we had made our vows before God to love and respect each other until the end of time.

* * * *

Van lifted me over the threshold of our apartment and dipped his head to kiss me as he carried me to our bedroom. He placed me on the bed, the familiar hunger flashing in his eyes.

Resting a hand on his chest to keep him at bay, I whispered, "Wait." I wriggled out of his embrace and opened my closet. Pulling out the floral-print hatbox, I put it on the bed next to Van.

He arched an eyebrow at me.

"I've been trying to find the right time to return something of yours. I suppose…now is a good time. Call it a wedding gift." I lifted the lid from the box.

Van's eyes darted over each familiar item. He picked up his scarf and thumbed through his letters. At last, his eyes fell on the most beloved item of all. His journal had remained untouched since the night I'd laid it to rest in the hatbox tomb. Van rubbed the faded brown leather cover with his thumb. His attention snapped back to me and searched my face for answers. "I thought it was lost," Van said in a thick voice.

I shook my head. "Just sent home. You said the last pages were for our future. We're in it, Van. That journal deserves to be finished."

Van stroked my cheek, a half smile on his lips. He rose from the bed, casting everything but the journal aside. With it still clutched in his hand, he bent to press his lips against my forehead. Van left the room and I heard the front door open and close.

It was almost dark when he returned, but I never worried. The journal was important to Van, and I knew it would be a difficult thing to deal with. With the thought it had been lost forever, Van had given up hope of ever seeing the journal again.

I knew he would have poured over the old pages, reminiscing of the early days. I also knew how difficult it would be for him, faced with the realization that everything had worked out for us. Despite the horrific obstacles flung between us, we'd made it. The race was finished. We'd won.

It was never discussed. I didn't see where the journal was placed when he came home. Van kissed the top of my head and lay with his head in my lap as I read our favorite book for the hundredth time. I never asked about that afternoon or what he wrote.

I didn't need to.

I was too busy enjoying our future to read about it.

Epilogue

June 17th, 1959

Today is my daughter's sixth birthday. She's dancing around the living room in the pink party dress Lois gave her earlier when she, Reed and their brood came to visit. Barb is tinkering away in the kitchen, putting the finishing touches on the birthday cake she made for our daughter.

Everything is the same, yet something is different. A shift in the atmosphere, oblivious to everyone but me... So why the sudden change? Why have I picked up this dusty old journal after more than seventeen years? I'm not entirely sure. Little Evie had ran into my study, sobbing her heart out. She clambered onto my lap and burrowed her tiny face into my neck. The boys popped their heads in, seeking out their sister, whom they mercilessly loved to tease. Harry called her a tattle and a crybaby. As I opened my mouth to scold him, Evie's head snapped around to face her older brother and warned him to leave her alone in a tone – not even me, a grown man – would mess with.

Her eyes had flashed with an odd familiarity. It took me a time to place the look. Barb heard the commotion and came to investigate. She swatted the boys with her dishtowel and scooped her beloved aunt's namesake into her arms.

It was seeing their faces together that made the pieces slot into place. The look Evie had shot her brother was one I'd been on the receiving end of more than a fair share by her mother. I chuckled to myself and the girls left me to my thoughts.

Evie has her mother's fighting spirit and prickly nature. At six years old, she didn't back down to anyone, and I sincerely hope she makes whoever falls for her beautiful face work his ass off for it, as I did, so many, many years ago...

Seventeen years have passed since my last entry. Do I regret neglecting it? Not in the least. Evie's look reminded me so much of the young, tenacious Barb. The strange and perverse woman who captured my soul from that very first sighting...

When Barb returned my journal after thinking it was lost forever, I almost wanted it to be. I remember leaving our first apartment and going to Boston Common to think. I knew that Barb expected me to write, but not a drop of ink was spilled that day.

I'm not sure how to put into words how I felt as I looked over the forgotten pages of my journal that crisp January day. This journal was meant to represent the pure and unblemished love I felt for Barb. I originally started it, hoping by writing down some of the insane and obsessive thoughts I could somehow make sense of the intense range of emotions I felt toward the woman I didn't even know.

As our acquaintance progressed to friendship and then at last to love, the journal served as a reminder of everything that I felt when I was with her, my glorious Barb... I didn't want time to rob me of my memories of her. How she felt, tasted, made my heart pound so hard I'm not sure how it didn't explode from my chest.

I never wanted her to read those thoughts — not then at least. As I wrote the details of Thanksgiving in '41, that beautiful holiday will always remain my most treasured *memory, I wrote it with a goofy, childish grin on my face. I'd imagined myself presenting Barb with this journal on our wedding night. It would represent the love I felt for her, and allow her to see just how amazing she was to me, and how I'll never understand why it was me she chose to spend her life with.*

No... It breaks my heart, even now, to think about Barb reading this godforsaken journal in the circumstances that she did. It was meant to be a thing of happiness, but it was tainted with heartache.

As I sat in Boston Common with strangers passing me by, I reread the entire journal. It reeked of cigarettes and perfume. A faint aroma of Scotch lingered and I'd guessed she'd spilled some while reading it, no doubt numbing herself to the pain. Some of my words were indistinguishable. Her teardrops were fat and a few pages couldn't be read at all, so heavy her tears must have fallen.

She'd never reread this – she would have told me of the damage she caused. It had brought her unnecessary agony, and for that reason, I came to hate this journal.

Barb had wanted me to fill in the missing pages, as I'd said I would. But I couldn't do it that day. Not because I didn't think we had a future, but because I didn't want to tarnish said future by putting it between the covers of this source of pain.

Why now? I imagine Barb giving me her trademark scowl, were she to find out it had taken me so long to press my pen against these pages. She would roll her eyes and walk away from me, no doubt muttering something that, despite the words, would make me smile.

I find myself wondering why I'm even bothering with this entry at all, given how much distaste I have for the journal. I think it needs finishing though, and I cannot leave the pages unwritten. But how does one put into words what I feel every day?

The bulk of this journal was written by a boy. A naïve boy whose views on the world were romantic and pure. I'd had no trouble writing about Barb, or my feelings, back then. But the intensity of my love for her has grown so much over these years, I honestly cannot think of words strong enough to do those feelings justice.

How do I portray accurately that everything I saw after returning from war was wrapped in darkness? How can I say how afraid I was of every little thing? It was like someone had adjusted the settings of my eyes, and everything was darker with a cruel edge to it. Everything except her. My whole life was dark, but she was my sun — bright and warm. I wore blinders, and she was all I saw.

Gradually, as the years passed and our family grew, my blinders widened, and more things were light. But Barb will always be the brightest of them all.

I look at the woman she has become and I am so proud of her. She's the strongest person I know, and I can think of no one I'd rather spend my life with. My Barb... My sweet and loving, tenacious and headstrong wife... Mine...

About the Author

Pamela has adored books since she can remember. There was no greater pleasure than discovering a new world to venture into, a new character to fall in love with…until she created her own and realized there was something even more magical.

When she isn't locked away at her computer, or scribbling in a notebook, Pamela can be found as her alter ego—namely wife to Matthew and mother to Todd. They also share their home with a bonkers cat and two greedy goldfish.

Pamela L. Todd loves to hear from readers. You can find her contact information, website and author biography at http://www.totallybound.com.

Home of Erotic Romance